INTO
THE
GLOOM

SAGA OF THE
SINGING SWORD BRIGADE
BOOK TWO

INTO
THE
GLOOM

J.M. MACLEOD

AMBASSADOR INTERNATIONAL
GREENVILLE, SOUTH CAROLINA & BELFAST, NORTHERN IRELAND
www.ambassador-international.com

Into the Gloom

Saga of the Singing Sword Brigade, Book Two

© 2019 by J.M. MacLeod

All rights reserved

ISBN: 978-1-62020-977-6
eISBN: 978-1-62020-991-2

This is a work of fiction. Names, characters, and incidents are all products of the author's imagination or are used for fictional purposes. Any resemblance to actual events or persons, living or dead, is entirely coincidental. Any mentioned brand names, places, and trademarks remain the property of their respective owners, bear no association with the author or the publisher, and are used for fictional purposes only.

Cover Design & Typesetting by Hannah Nichols
Ebook Conversion by Anna Riebe Raats
Edited by Daphne Self

AMBASSADOR INTERNATIONAL
Emerald House
411 University Ridge, Suite B14
Greenville, SC 29601, USA
www.ambassador-international.com

AMBASSADOR BOOKS
The Mount
2 Woodstock Link
Belfast, BT6 8DD, Northern Ireland, UK
www.ambassadormedia.co.uk

The colophon is a trademark of Ambassador, a Christian publishing company.

Gird thy sword upon thy thigh,
O most Mighty,
With thy glory and thy majesty . . .
Ride prosperously because of truth,
And meekness and righteousness.

David ben Jesse

CHAPTER ONE

ANGRY VOICES FROM OUTSIDE WOKE Jeda. Her bare feet skimmed lightly over the cold, stone floor to the window where she pulled back the curtain. Through the lingering dawn mists, she recognized the men in the courtyard below. Blatch and Orvy, her father's thug-bodyguards, shoved Artka, her fraternal twin, down the stairway. He was being evicted from the house. Grieved, but not surprised their father had sunk so low as to disown his only son, Jeda feared for Artka's safety. Those men were often violent without cause.

Artka whirled around catching Blatch unaware, pulling him off balance.

Jeda gasped and pressed her fingertips to her lips.

Artka seized a stick—his training sword?—and struck Blatch on the neck. The thug slumped to the pavement. Artka then turned on Orvy who fumbled in his belt for a knife. Artka's blow was quick as a falcon's strike. Orvy's elbow bent unnaturally backward and the brute teetered, spun, and toppled over. Artka stood triumphantly over Blatch who groggily stared up at him. Artka shook his fist at the fallen ruffian, then turned toward the house and shouted loud enough for Jeda to hear, "I'll return! Count on that!"

Jeda stepped back. A tear seeped from the corner of her eye as Artka went through the gate and down the road. She was alone now; Artka was banished. Not alone without people, but alone with none to understand or commiserate. Her mother was contemptuous of her, her father ignored her, and the saucy, younger twins, Velnu and Cornil, made life miserable every chance they had.

Life was only tolerable because she nursed a perpetual hope for the times Artka might unexpectedly show up and for a brief moment life would again have meaning. But now Artka was headed to war against Ecclessa. When he returned he wouldn't be the same. War changed men. Tears splattered on a flagstone as mists engulfed her departing brother. No one understood her like Artka.

When Artka had run off to join the feral boys in the hills surrounding Cosmopolis, he often returned to the family from time to time and enthralled her with his daring exploits. She'd tell him of her doings, mundane as they were by comparison. But Artka paid rapt attention as if her babblings were the most interesting conversation in all Carnalia. Life without Artka was unthinkable.

"What are you staring at?" Lord Kway snarled from the bedroom doorway.

Jeda hadn't heard her father enter. She turned away from the growing light of the window. Her father, Lord Kekinor Kway, department head of the Bureau of Re-Education, filled the doorway with his broad shoulders. His eye sockets appeared in the subdued light like eyeholes in a skull. As a father, he'd never been close to either Jeda or Artka, or even Velnu and Cornil. As promotions came and he gained more prominence in the empire, his uncaring attitude grew into resentment. Now, glowering from the doorway Jeda palpably felt his resentment, even hostility.

"Watching the dawn, Father," she hoped her tear-tracks weren't visible.

Her father stared a long moment before replying, "He won't be back."

Jeda bit her lip; tears brimmed afresh.

"You're leaving, too, this morning. Gather your things together, all you can carry in one satchel. Blatch will take you after breakfast." He turned to go.

"I . . . I'm going? But where?"

"You'll find out in due time. Now, best see to your packing." His footsteps faded down the hallway, but his cruel words still seemed to echo off the bedroom walls.

Jeda sat on the window seat, face in hands; weeping for Artka, for herself, for the very despair and unfairness of life. "Is there nothing good? Wicked kings and harsh emperors . . . Is there no place the powerful don't manipulate weak and unimportant people?"

Out of the corner of her eye she saw a twinkling column of light near the window, but when she turned to look nothing was there; just the sash, glass panes, and the gray mist.

"Whatever is the matter, Jeda?" Cornil stood in the spot just vacated by their father. Velnu peered over her twin's shoulder holding a candle aloft, a luxury Jeda wasn't permitted. "Your blubbering woke us. What's going on?"

Jeda glared at the younger twins, but her anger passed. "I have to leave."

"Poor dear," Velnu pushed past her chubby sister and sashayed into the room. "Come to think of it, Mother did say something about trotting you off somewhere, but we didn't pay much attention, did we?"

"No," Cornil followed her likewise portly twin. "You know how she always threatens something, but then never does. We didn't think she really meant it."

The pair went straight to Jeda's closet and rummaged through her clothes. "Are you, ah, going to need all these?" Velnu held up a sleeve of a gown among the dresses hanging inside.

Jeda's face flamed, and she wanted to rage at them. They always had whatever they wanted when they wanted it, while she had to make do or go without. She took a deep breath and disguised her feelings. Even now when it no longer mattered, she meekly said, "I'll be leaving most of them."

"Ooh! I've always adored this velvet, wine-red gown. You won't need this, will you?" Cornil rubbed a sleeve of the garment in question.

It was Jeda's favorite. The only fancy, special garment she owned. Mother had obtained it for Jeda, as the eldest and soon-to be-marriage-able daughter, to wear on important evenings when governmental dignitaries visited the manor. "It's necessary for those who can help your father climb to higher positions, to know that he's a family man," her mother explained upon the unexpected presentation of the dress to her.

"Yes!" Jeda said defiantly to Cornil. "I'll certainly need that, you little vultures. You'd only split the seams trying to get it to fit your bloated bodies! Now, get out of my room. When I'm gone you can squabble over what's left, but right now this is still my room and those are still my things." It felt good to vent her anger at the brats. She'd kept those feelings inside for so long.

"Well! I never . . . " Cornil dropped the sleeve.

"Mother was right, you're too vulgar and common to associate with refined people like us. I'm glad you're going," Velnu said with a toss of her curls.

"Well, I'm glad, too." Jeda raised her fist. "At least I won't have to put up with you spoiled imps anymore."

The twins took to their heels, and the candle with them. Their pitiful wails rang back from the hallway, "Mother."

Jeda sat on her bed regretting being so sharp, though they deserved it. Down the hall their whining jabber was heard followed by a maternal *hmmph*, and she knew their one-sided account distorted the facts. Consequences would follow. It didn't matter. She was being disowned, it seemed, what more could they do?

Shuffling footsteps drew near; Jeda cringed.

"How dare you threaten your sisters?" Dame Adana Kway sallied through the portal with anger flashing from her eyes.

Excuses were useless.

Dame Kway wagged a finger under Jeda's nose. "Don't you know you don't own anything but what your father and I have given you? Just who do you think you are? And after your sisters came to comfort you! Worthless wench! How I ever gave birth to such an ingrate, I'll never know. I'll tell you what things you may take. Besides," her voice evened out, "where you're going, you won't need anything fancy."

"Where am I going?"

"Your father didn't tell you? Then it'll be all the more a surprise. But I'll say this, you certainly deserve it. Now get dressed. I'll send Gwinnid to help you pack. When you're dressed, report to the kitchen for a servant's breakfast. You may as well get used to it." With a swish of her nightgown, the rotund woman swept out as swiftly as she'd entered.

Jeda stared at her closet, resting her eyes on the wine-red, velvet gown. With a defiant toss of her head she seized the garment. "At least I'll leave in style and keep the brats from getting everything they want."

She donned the luxurious dress, putting her long, silky-blonde hair up, as if she were preparing to attend a banquet, then applied make-up, added some trinkets of jewelry, and stood back to observe herself in the mirror. Even to her own eyes she looked attractive. Though beautiful of face and form, she'd borne the brunt of her sibling's insults so long, no amount of compliments, even from Artka, would convince her she was pretty. Yet this morning, as she studied herself, she dared hope that her accoutrements made up for her personal lack, and that those to whom she was being taken might find her appealing.

Gwinnid, her mother's personal maid, bustled into the room carrying a dusty hand-satchel. "Oh my, Miss Jeda, but don't you look nice," she encouraged. "Hardly what I'd wear for traveling, but then, I'm not the one going, am I?"

"Do you know where they're sending me?"

Gwinnid turned away.

Grasping the maid's arm Jeda turned her around and persisted, "You do know, don't you? Look at me, you do know!"

"Please, Miss Jeda, I don't want any trouble. I was ordered to say nothing. If you force me, they'll find out, and . . . and I'll be punished."

Disobedient servants were often punished harshly, and Gwinnid wouldn't be spared for her age. "I'm sorry, Gwinnid. I guess I have to face whatever lies ahead on my own."

"I don't expect it will be all that bad, Miss Jeda. At least, from what I hear." Jeda noted that Gwinnid packed the hand-satchel with unglamorous, durable garments from the bureau and closet.

"It's a work house, isn't it?"

"Not exactly. You'll see soon enough. Please don't ask me more."

"If you can't tell me where I'm going, will you do something else for me?"

"Well, what is it?"

"It concerns Artka."

"Master Artka? But he's gone. Left a little bit ago, he did. The mister says we'll not likely see either of you again." Gwinnid sniffed and dabbed a pudgy finger to her eye.

Jeda was surprised that Gwinnid might actually care; it was some comfort that someone felt bad at this turn of events. "Gwinnid, I'll miss you."

"And I, you. Now, what about Master Artka?"

"If he comes back, will you tell him where I've gone?"

"It's not right what they're doing to the two of you, Miss Jeda. Aye, I'll tell Master Artka where they've sent you, that is, if I ever see him again."

"He'll be back, and when he comes, tell him where to find me. Will you promise me that, as a parting gift?"

"I promise. I'll tell him everything I know—if I see him again." The determination in Gwinnid's eyes comforted Jeda.

"And this, Gwinnid, is my parting gift to you." Jeda removed a string of pearls from her neck and held them out. "When I was six and the only daughter my mother thought she'd ever have, she gave these to me. Since Velnu and Cornil were born, however, she's given all the pretty things to them. But I want you to have this."

"Miss Jeda, I couldn't. Something as grand as this is way above my station. I could never—"

"Please take it. They're not all that valuable. Besides, they'll only remind me of this dreadful day. Please Gwinnid, sell them if you want, or stow them away, but, please, accept them."

"All right, Miss Jeda, I accept. Just to remind me of you and how kind you always were." Tears glistened afresh in the maid's eyes as she applied her weight to force the hand-satchel shut and tie its leather thongs. "Oh, Miss Jeda, I wish I, I wish you'd let—"

Jeda embraced the old housemaid. Gwinnid hugged her back for a moment then pulled away, straightened her apron, and said, "I'd better fetch my husband, Smid, to carry this. I've loaded it too full." With that, she was gone.

Jeda washed her face from the nightstand basin, finished tucking her hair up and took one last look around the room. Then, determined to reveal no fear, marched head held high down the hall. At the bottom of the stairs she caught herself about to take the door to the family quarters. This morning she'd been ordered to take her meal with the servants. She passed through the door on the left.

Good smells and a cheery warmth greeted her entry to the kitchen. It had been a long while since she'd visited here. No one was around; everyone was off attending duties, or were they simply avoiding the unpleasantness of her disgrace?

"It doesn't matter," she told herself, but it would've been nice to see a couple of the servants one last time, especially the older servants she used to play around. Tears blurred her vision again.

On the trestle table was a pastry beside an empty cup and a samovar half-full. She poured a cup of tea, added a spoonful of honey, and sat. The first sip of tea awakened her appetite. She divided the pastry with a knife, took delicate, lady-like bites using her fork and took another sip of tea. Her eyes wandered about the room as she ate, examining ladles, spoons, pots, and pans hanging from rafters. More utensils dangled from posts, brooms and mops leaned into a corner. Wait, what was that behind the corn brooms? A soft, bluish light caught her eye. She left her pastry and tea and went to investigate. She passed the brick oven and felt a wave of heat from its glowing coals on her way to the broom corner.

On closer inspection she discovered a metallic object glowing of its own accord! A gasp escaped her lips as she pushed aside the brooms. A sword leaned into the corner, point downward, not a black Carnalian sword like she'd seen on Carnalian soldiers and sharifs, nor was it a wooden training sword like Artka's. This sword was unlike any she'd ever seen. It was dull gray most of its nearly four-foot, double-edged blade except for five inches from the point which glowed with a blue light. Curious writing was etched along the fuller of the blade. The haft was artfully wrought into two diverse birds. One side presented a bird of prey, the other a dove. They were forged back to back, their outstretched wings merging as the hilt guard and their fanned-out tail feathers forming the pommel.

She moved more brooms and mops out of the way. The sword didn't look sharp, at least in the larger, gray area. She extended her hand toward the handle, but then hesitated, her fingers poised just inches from the handle. Then casting caution to the wind, Jeda grasped the haft. With a static crackle the blue glow receded to the tip and was extinguished altogether. Jeda jerked upright, stepped back, and dropped the sword. Brooms and mops toppled pell-mell as Jeda reeled backward into a stack of pots that clattered across the stone floor.

The kitchen door burst open. Smid, Gwinnid's husband, entered and stared with narrowed eyes at her.

Gwinnid breathlessly bustled up behind him. "What? What's all the racket?"

"She's found our 'Child of the Stars'."

"Oh? Oh, dear!"

Both servants entered the room and shut and barred the door.

"I . . . I'm sorry I made such a mess," Jeda said. "I'll pick it up—"

"What were you looking for, Miss Jeda?" Smid's face was so stern that Jeda trembled.

"I . . . I was curious about the blue light." Should she admit to touching the sword?

Gwinnid crossed the kitchen to the other entrance and wordlessly closed the door and dropped the latch bar in place before returning to Smid's side.

"Come sit down, Miss Jeda," Smid indicated a long bench.

Jeda had never seen the house servants so authoritative. They'd always seemed rather timid and not very bright. Was it possible she'd never known them at all? Keeping her eyes on them, she complied.

"I see no blue light," Smid said, standing over her, boring his clear, sparkling eyes into hers.

"B-but there was a blue light. Over in that corner."

"Don't be so hard on her, dear. See how frightened she is?" Gwinnid nestled on the bench beside her. "She'll not report us—will you dear?"

Smid grunted and picked the sword up off the floor. The blue light reappeared to its original five inches.

"H-How did you make the light come back?" Jeda stared wide-eyed, her own troubles temporarily forgotten.

Smid smiled and sat across the trestle-table from the women. "It's not what I did, but rather, what I have."

Gwinnid nodded with a smile.

"But the glow disappeared when I touched it."

"Because of what you don't have." Gwinnid extended her hand. "Let me have it, Smid."

The elderly servant handed the sword to his wife. As soon as she touched the hilt the bluish glow receded two inches. "I'm afraid I haven't had the time Smid has had to work on it; he's sharpened more of it than I."

"You mean you haven't made time, dear. The day has the same number of hours for both of us."

"Where did you—? What are you—? Why—? Such a mighty weapon," Jeda said, "ought to be in the hands of young warriors, not—"

"Old house servants?" Smid said. "Well, this was a gift to me, when I was a great deal younger, from a great prince after I lost a duel to him." Smid had a faraway look in his eyes.

"Do we have time?" Gwinnid anxiously checked the barred doors.

"I think so. The other servants are about their chores, and it'll be a while before the carriage is due, and, well, I think Alfomega has arranged this. We must take advantage of every opportunity."

"I suppose you're right. Only, do hurry." Then to Jeda, "He gets carried away when he tells this story."

CHAPTER TWO

"I MARCHED WITH THE EMPEROR'S army down in the Forbidden Mountains," Smid said, "hating every minute of it. We'd just swooped down on an isolated Ecclessite outpost, slaughtering every man, woman, and child. It bothered me, of course, but—I had orders, or so I persuaded myself.

"Afterward as we camped, and recruits showed off their newly-acquired steel swords and sported red plumes in their helms and bragged about their victims, enemy trumpets suddenly blared from every side.

"Three kingsmen brigades had secretly surrounded us. Sharpointers attacked first, howling, 'Lives for the king,' as they charged."

"Oh dear!" Jeda put a hand to her lips.

"Now see what you've done." Gwinnid chided. "You've frightened the poor girl with your tales of war and glory. Just skip all that and get to the part about your 'Child of the Stars'."

"No, no, please," Jeda said, "I'd like to hear it all. It's just that . . . I was thinking of Artka facing an attack like that."

"Have no worry then, for the king's armies pose no threat."

"Why are we at war then? Why don't they just leave Carnalians alone and not attack them?" Jeda stared from one to the other and back again.

"Artka has more to fear from his own comrades than any kingsman," Smid said.

"Get back to your story dear, that will explain."

"All right." Smid sighed. "Where was I?"

"The Sharpstabbers were shouting about killing you for their king."

"Eh? Oh, ha ha, no, no. *Sharpointers.*" Smid reached across the table, receiving the sword back from his wife. The blue light sprang two more inches down the blade. "See how the point glows? This is how Sharpointer swords look, that is, if its owners have spent time honing them. Ecclessite military units are identified by how we sharpen our swords."

Jeda's eyes grew round. "That's a, then . . . you're—?"

"Ecclessites? Yes, Miss Jeda, we are members of a kingsmen brigade here in Cosmopolis."

Jeda jumped to her feet, her face felt drained of color.

"Sit, Miss Jeda," Gwinnid ordered, tugging Jeda's gown. "We'll not harm you. Let the mister finish."

"Please, Miss Jeda. You've known us these many years; have we ever harmed you?" Smid added.

"Well," Jeda sat, keeping a wary eye on their sword.

"I escaped into the mountains after that battle and hid out for two days. Thirst and hunger finally drove me back to the lowlands. I discovered that all my commanders were dead—killed by freak accidents, mind you, not Ecclessites. The rest of my platoon had either scattered or surrendered.

"A man came and stood beside a well as I slaked my thirst, informing me of the battle's outcome. He offered me bread, which I ravenously devoured. When I was finished, he stood to full height and said, 'You're the last trainee I need to complete a brigade. Are you ready?'

"I looked up, protesting, 'I'm no recruit! I've earned my steel and plume. I'll join your brigade, if you like, since my own is disbanded, but I'll not need training.'

"He smiled, 'We'll see.' I followed as he headed out toward the Flaming Sword River. I remarked that we were getting awfully close to enemy positions, but he assured me that only friendly brigades remained nearby.

"We walked then in silence, yet all that time I felt as though I was telling him details of my life . . . that I hated serving the emperor. Finally, at a bend in the road, he turned and levelled a fully glowing sword at my chest. It wasn't until then that I recognized he was King Elyon's son. He challenged me to a duel. I declined. 'How can I fight you?' I said. 'I can't resist your power.'

"'You've been resisting me all your life,' he said, then added, 'and now you drank from the well of my veins, and ate of my flesh, and were revived. Will you waste what I've done for you, or become wholly mine?'"

"I fell to my knees begging for mercy. He assured me that mercy was his intention, and then drew his sword and pierced my heart. I swooned. In that moment I realized that my whole life had been crime after selfish crime against him. His blade piercing through to my heart exposed me for what I was—wicked through and through. In one awful moment I knew that serving the emperor and serving myself were the same thing— crimes against the king, punishable by death. My conscience was in torment; I saw my filthy self as the Prince of Ecclessa saw me. I wanted to crawl in a hole.

"'I am Alfomega. You have ended, and I am beginning,' he said. Looking about I saw that we were no longer on the road, but up high on a towering rock overlooking a torrential river. His fingers were in my chest, healing the sword wound he'd caused. I knew that all my crimes against him were forgiven. I felt joy surging as wild and untamed as the river beside us. I hadn't even realized the bondage I'd been in, much like you, Miss Jeda."

"Me?" Jeda started. "What makes you think I'm in bondage?"

"Haven't you ever felt life ought to be better? Haven't you ever thought things should be different?"

"And just how are things?" Jeda asked haughtily.

"I'm sure you know: all Carnalia is governed by harsh policies of the powerful; the poor and weak are victimized by the strong; the few maintain an iron-fisted grip on humanity with lies, deceptions, and cruelty masquerading as laws of the state. Does this system seem right?"

"No, of course not."

"But you, yourself, are part of it, aren't you?" Smid stared unblinkingly into her eyes.

Jeda recalled times when she'd bent the truth or manipulated others to her own selfish ends. But now she was the victim. *Yet,* she rationalized to herself, *I'm not greedy or nasty like Cornil and Velnu. They deserve what's happening to me more than I.* But aloud she responded, "I suppose."

"You don't have to be either victim or victimizer," Gwinnid smiled warmly. "You can surrender to Alfomega like the mister did, and like I did."

"What are you talking about? Your Alfomega wouldn't dare show his Ecclessite face here in Cosmopolis, so how could I surrender to him, even if I wanted to?"

"If you want him, he'll meet you wherever you are," Smid laid the sword on the table.

"Wait a minute, I thought you lost that duel to Alfomega, not just gave up without a fight."

"I'd dueled him all my life, just as you are now."

"I'm not fighting anyone."

"Well then, if you're not fighting, yield to him. Let me pierce your heart with this 'Child of the Stars'." Smid picked up and leveled the sword tip at her chest.

Jeda jumped up, nearly knocking Gwinnid off the bench, screaming, "Away with you! You're trying to kill me!"

All color drained from Gwinnid's face, but she reacted with surprising agility for a woman of her age and girth. A beefy palm clamped over Jeda's mouth and the other hand slipped around Jeda's waist, holding her firmly.

"Nay lass, don't cry out like that. We'll do nothing unless you allow," Gwinnid whispered. "Now, I'll release you, but you mustn't cry out. If we're found out, it'll be our death."

Jeda searched Gwinnid's eyes and knew she meant it. She nodded, and the maid released her. "Why do you want to stab me?"

"It's necessary," Smid said, "else, you'll never know how loathsome you truly are."

"Now see here, I'm not near as bad as other people I could mention."

"Oh, we know that, dear," Gwinnid comforted, patting her hand and leading Jeda back to her seat. "In fact, the mister and I often commented on how sweet you were, and out of place in this greedy house. Yet, you're not purely good, are you?"

"Nobody's that—"

"Alfomega is." Smid said. "And King Elyon demands that degree of purity in his subjects."

"Now, don't tell me that you and Gwinnid have achieved purity. I know you too well."

"Alfomega has given us his purity."

"What? How can someone give their purity to another?"

"Please, Miss Jeda," Gwinnid said. "Alfomega means so much to us. He's our comfort and hope that all evil will someday be overthrown. He could be your comfort and hope too, especially as uncertain as your future looks right now."

Jeda stared at the glowing sword tip. "I don't know, I have to think about it. What would I have to do?"

"Allow a 'Child of the Stars' to pierce your heart, then seek Alfomega's healing touch," said Smid.

"I'll think about it."

"Then think about this; if there really is a better life, a life of love, kindness and gentleness, isn't that what you'd choose rather than selfish ambition, hatred and cruelty?"

"Of course, who wouldn't?"

"Many. But you must make that decision yourself. We'll not be able to help after you leave, nevertheless, should you decide to serve the king, just say the phrase, 'Words of the word', and a kingsman will soon enough be revealed to help you," said Smid.

"I hear the carriage coming up the alleyway," Gwinnid rose from her seat. Then to Jeda, "Please think about it, child. Don't put it off. You need Alfomega. Remember, casually use the phrase 'Words of the word' when you're ready to let your heart be pierced, and you'll be contacted. We'll be speaking to Alfomega about you."

Jeda felt disoriented on discovering that these people she'd considered doddering, old servants were secretly enemy agents. She also felt uneasy about them talking about her to Alfomega, however they might accomplish that. The last thing she wanted was her name mentioned among Carnalia's enemies. She was about to ask them not to do that when the stomp of boots and a beefy hand rattled the door latch.

Smid hurriedly stashed the sword among the brooms in the corner, covering it completely.

"Here now, what's this?" demanded a gruff voice from outside. "Why be's this here door barred?"

"Coming, coming," said Gwinnid in a singsong reply, bustling to the portal. She turned briefly to make sure the sword was concealed, then lifted the bar, exclaiming in a dumbfounded voice, "Now how do you suppose that happened? Smid, haven't I told you to remove the bar all the way, and not rest it on its perch? It's gone and fallen locking the door again."

The stable hand, tall, dirty, unshaven, hair poking oddly out from under a knit cap, his mouth shaped in a sneer, entered.

"Snetch? What are you doing here?" asked Smid. "You're supposed to be cleaning the stables."

"Humph. Thinks yer kens everybody's business, doncher? Well, his lordship tole me ter escort the lass away."

"I thought Blatch was going to."

"Things be's changed. Blatch be's, er, indisposed. I be's gonna take her. Be's yer ready, Miss?"

Jeda shrank away from Snetch. Whenever she'd gone to the stable in times past he'd be there, leering at her. The older she became, the worse the leering. She loathed being near him. Now he was to take her, alone, to some unknown destination? Jeda shuddered.

Catching her reaction, Snetch grinned wickedly. "I asked, be's yer ready?"

Jeda's knees went weak. "Oh, I can't."

"Yer gots no choice, Missy. Heh-heh. It's jest yer an' me, all alone on the road."

"Oh, didn't they tell you, Snetch?" interrupted Gwinnid. "I'm to accompany the young lady, you know, see her off in place of her mother, and all?"

"Whut?" A fierce expression crossed the stable hand's face.

"Oh, yes, I'm sure Blatch knew all about it," continued the maid as she removed her apron and took hold of Jeda's satchel. "In the hurry of switching drivers, they must have forgotten to tell you. Come along, Miss," she called over her shoulder as she went out the door, tugging Jeda along with her free hand.

"But I was tole—" Snetch argued, but seeing it was useless, shrugged his shoulders. "Pitland! This hain't at all whut I was figurin'."

"Best hurry, Snetch," Smid hinted. "If I know Gwinnid, she'll leave without you. She can handle a team as well as a man, you know."

"Bah!" Snetch slammed the door on his way out.

Gwinnid nestled in beside Jeda, holding the satchel so as to leave Snetch no room. He was forced to shorten the reins and shift over to a footman's perch.

"If'n I'd a knowed yer was comin', yer tin o' lard, I'd a brung the coach 'stead o' the buggy. Now there hain't time ter go back an' rig it."

"Ntch, ntch." Gwinnid winked at Jeda.

"Bah!"

Jeda glanced gratefully at the maid.

In frustration, Snetch cracked the whip sharply, unintentionally striking a horse's flank. Snetch's legs flew over his head as the buggy lurched forward. He grasped at the siderails to right himself, barely clinging to his precarious, albeit, uncomfortable seat.

Jeda's and Gwinnid's hands covered their mouths to keep from laughing as Snetch nearly tottered overboard in his struggle to gain control of the horses. Righting himself, the stableman glowered at his passengers muttering, "Ain't at all whut I was figurin'."

CHAPTER THREE

COSMOPOLIS WAS SITUATED IN A rugged mountain range some two-hundred miles inland from the western coast of the Great Lost Sea. All roads in Carnalia led to this capital where Lurcan, the Emperor reigned from his ebony-stoned fortress.

Mass troop movements lately mustered to the war overwhelmed the burdened highways that were already cluttered with merchant caravans and wayfarers, adding seemingly endless martial columns and making travel an insufferable chore. Grim-faced veterans and eager recruits streamed in from north, south, and west and were all dispatched east, further clogging the turnpikes. This hardship, however, was endured by the population only because they were persuaded such inconveniences were was necessary to defend Carnalia against Ecclessa's incursions. The citizenry was constantly inundated with warnings that even small kingsman outposts and fortresses, once established throughout the empire, would bring about Carnalia's downfall. This war against Ecclessa had gone on for as long as anyone alive could remember.

Ecclessa's oppressive king had launched countless invasions into the empire in an effort to enslave freeborn Carnalians, making them mindless slaves like the Ecclessites who gave abject and immediate obedience to King Elyon's insatiable desire for glory. The empire's Ministry of Re-education made it quite obvious to the peoples of the unified nations of the empire that Ecclessa's drudge citizens were victims of propaganda. Despite the exorbitant cost and inconvenience, the war must go on lest Ecclessa encroach more and more into the empire, eventually subverting and subjugating all humanity to Elyon's harsh rule.

The buggy bearing Jeda, Gwinnid, and Snetch topped a knoll as it approached near Cosmopolis and was forced to a halt. The crossroad ahead was swollen with black-clad warriors in coarse, woven uniforms and leather body armor replete with red-trimmed capes and crimson plumes fluttering from polished ebon helms.

Snetch uttered an oath as he reined in the horse. They were the most recent to join a backlog of travelers jammed back up the hill from the crossroad waiting for the martial parade to take a break and allow regular traffic across the intersection. Snetch maneuvered the buggy out of line and along the berm down toward the front of the queue, ignoring irate comments from those they passed. At the last remaining merchant wagon, two young men brandishing dirks jumped from the rear of the dray to block Snetch's progress.

"Git outta me way, afore I runs yers over." Snetch growled.

"Try it, and see what you get," said an older man standing off to the side as he nocked an arrow and drew his bowstring taut. "You can't just bully your way to the front. We've been waiting over an hour, like most of those you've jumped line on. That's as far as you go."

Snetch narrowly eyed the bowman, then changed his tone. "Oww, its thet I be's on urgent empire business. Doncher see the seal on me carriage? It be's important ter git the lass ter the palace afore noon."

Jeda gasped in Gwinnid's ear, "The emperor's palace?"

Gwinnid chewed her lower lip but said nothing.

The young men stood their ground. Snetch looked nervously from the older man to his sons, then back again. The bowman relaxed and motioned with his arrow; the young men stood aside. "I'm very sorry sir, I didn't know you were on empire business. It won't make much difference though. One of the sergeants told me there's no stop scheduled for at least two more hours."

Jeda watched the soldiers filing by: some were as old as fifty, others as young as eighteen with every age in between. Each kept step with the resonant booming of a cadence drum.

"Artka will be in a battalion like this," she wistfully intoned to Gwinnid, who responded with a dutiful nod.

Snetch dismounted and talked privately with the archer. The men turned and looked directly at Jeda with enigmatic expressions. Snetch continued, animating his words with gestures.

"Gwinnid, am I going to the palace?"

"Well, sort of, Miss Jeda. I do wish you'd have let Smid pierce your heart when we had opportunity. Then, no matter what, he'd always be with you."

"Little help another enemy would be," Jeda said.

"He's not your enemy, child, he's the emperor's enemy."

"Seems like the same thing, but I will think about what you said."

"That's all I ask."

Snetch spied a sergeant coming along the outer file and abruptly broke off his conversation with the bowman to address the sergeant. He fell in beside him, matching the sergeant's pace, pleading his case. The sergeant turned aside and studied the emblem on the carriage, then shrugged and pointed at the sun, as if to say that he was merely a sergeant and didn't have the authority to interrupt the march.

Snetch threw his hat on the ground and hopped up and down, waving his arms, pointing at Jeda, then at the palace off in the distance.

Gwinnid squeezed Jeda's hand. They both knew Snetch could be unpredictable, even violent when crossed.

A mounted captain riding alongside the column spotted the dispute. The officer, flanked by aides, drew up in front of the carriage. He addressed the sergeant who pointed at Jeda, then Snetch. The officer dismounted, gripped Snetch's upper arm in one hand and dragged him over and pinned him to the buggy.

The officer removed his brightly plumed helmet, bowed politely to Jeda and said, "I'm Captain Fitcher. How may I be of service to your ladyship?"

"Ere, I tole yer, she hain't a ladyship no longer. She's bein' took ter—"

"Hush, you Eroton scum. I don't care if you do work for Lord Kekinor Kway, you'll be a better servant when you learn to hold your tongue."

Turning back to Jeda he said, "I appreciate the delicacy of your situation, Miss. Nevertheless, until you arrive at your destination you should be given the respect of your station. I explained to your man here, as has my sergeant, that the parade will break in about two hours. Then you may cross the road."

"Bah! I'll be blamed fer bringin' her late."

"And I hope you're soundly whipped for your indolence," Captain Fitcher snapped. "Now Miss, would you do me the honor of letting me know your name?"

"Well, I—"

"Please, Miss. I mean you no harm."

"Well, I'm Jeda, of the house of Kway."

"Yes, I see that by the emblem here." He tapped the coach door. "Your father is Lord Kway, then?"

"Yes."

"And your mother is Adana?"

"How did you know?"

"I had the pleasure of visiting your home about a year ago during one of the soirees your parents hosted for newly appointed commandants. I remember it well because I was one of the honorees."

"Well, Captain, uh—"

"Fitcher."

"Yes, Captain Fitcher, I'm in no hurry."

"I can understand."

"Has he told you what's to become of me?" Jeda nodded toward Snetch.

"You don't know?"

Jeda shook her head. "No one will tell me."

"Ahh, I see. Well then, let me give you some advice. Unless I miss my guess, yes, you'd certainly have to pass under her scrutiny . . . Tell the woman in charge that Captain Fitcher wishes, emphasize 'wishes', that you be sent to brooms and kitchen. Understand, brooms and kitchen?"

"Ere, thet's not the idee at all. She be's assigned ter the house o' pleas—"

Captain Fitcher's open palm struck Snetch on the mouth, ending his outburst. Two burly bodyguards leapt from their horses and wrenched the stableman's arms behind.

"I warned you to hold your tongue, Eroton. Now you'll lose it." The captain drew a curved knife and held it to Snetch's mouth. "Open up or I'll have an eye instead."

"Oh no, Captain, you mustn't!" Jeda pleaded.

Both the Captain and Snetch looked up in surprise.

"Very well, for your sake, Lady Jeda of Kway, I'll spare the maggot's tongue. But if ever hear that he's harmed you, or even speaks unkindly to you again, he'll pay dearly. Release him."

The soldiers obeyed and Snetch fell onto all fours.

Captain Fitcher remounted, reiterating, "Remember, brooms and kitchen." He then whispered to the two bodyguards, who nodded in reply. Then, with a smart snap of his quirt against his horse's flank he and the rest of his entourage resumed down the road.

The remaining bodyguards regarded Snetch coolly as he got to his feet.

"Thank Alfomega," Gwinnid muttered.

Jeda, eyes wide, whispered, "Is Captain Fitcher one of you, too?"

Gwinnid gave Jeda a puzzled look, then smiled. "Oh, no, of course not."

"Then why did you thank—you know who?"

"He influences even his enemies to do what he wants. But, hush now, it's not safe to speak openly."

Snetch leaned against the carriage, sneering back at the bemused stares he received from people in line. He bared his teeth and growled at children peeping from under a wagon canvas cover making them duck back inside. Then, preferring shade and anonymity to being a laughing stock, Snetch crawled beneath the coach to wait out the procession.

The column paraded by longer than the anticipated two hours, filling the roadside with the noisy cadence of drums and tramping feet and stirring up dust that hovered over the roadway.

Jeda and Gwinnid played word games to pass the time. Snetch kept muttering to himself under the carriage, looking out occasionally to see if the bodyguards had left their post, which they hadn't.

At long last a command echoed down the rank and file and the drums changed their measured *poom, poom, poom* tempo to a rapid roll at the end of which every soldier's feet halted precisely at the same moment. The sudden silence was startling. Many travelers roused, others suddenly lowered their voices. Sergeants disrupted the quiet by barking orders and then huge squares of weary, dust-encrusted soldiers gratefully moved off the road to lounge in the grass and nibble a piece of hard tack or take a sip of water.

"Awright, yers kin git movin'," announced a corporal to the assemblage waiting to cross.

Snetch crawled out from under the buggy and quickly shored up the reins of the grazing horse then climbed aboard his perch still smoldering. He cracked the whip striking the horse's flank making it bolt. Snetch again nearly toppled backward off his perch. He clung desperately to the siderails to stay aboard. Children giggled, and adults hooted openly. Snetch cursed and plied his whip again. Without Snetch in control of the reins the buggy veered right and lurched into a rut, tipping him even more off balance. He grasped the perch in both hands as his feet flew over his head.

Soldiers reclining in the grass guffawed loudly, pointing him out to their companions.

Jeda and Gwinnid had to grasp their seat rails just to stay upright. They knew better than to rebuke Snetch; Captain Fitcher's guards no longer accompanied them.

The buggy rocketed out of the trench and across the intersection well ahead of other travelers and didn't slow until attaining a gentle turn on the down side of a hill far enough distant from Snetch's scene of embarrassment that he no longer heard the catcalls. Bloody welts on his master's horse sobered his rage; he'd need a good excuse to escape a similar lashing. Jeda caught him glancing crossly at Gwinnid who'd likely testify to his foolish behavior. "Now I be's fer it."

Snetch reverted to sullenness.

Jeda was just glad she wasn't being tossed about, not to mention breathing without filtering out dust with a handkerchief. A little sediment had settled on her now less-than-striking, wine-red gown, evoking a sigh. She brushed off her clothing then lifted her eyes to a panorama that reminded her that she wasn't on a lark. Up ahead loomed the towering black walls and parapets of Cosmopolis' castle. Her stomach tightened. Inside that ominous assembly of buildings, gates, and walls lay her unknown future.

Gwinnid took Jeda's hand. "'Words of the word'. Don't forget."

"Eh? Whazzat?" growled Snetch, looking around from his perch with a suspicious leer.

"Yes'm, of course I'll send you word, just as soon as I'm able," Jeda looked Gwinnid full in the face. "Thank you, so much," she mouthed.

Why did this elderly servant woman risk punishment just to show kindness to one who never really appreciated the old maid?

Gwinnid just nodded. "He's done as much, and even more for you."

"Yers be's talkin' crazy," said Snetch.

"Well, if you wouldn't eavesdrop on other people's conversations you might be invited to attend it all." Gwinnid huffed.

"*Humph*! Who wants ter?"

They by-passed dilapidated shacks and run-down cottages on both sides of the road, the outer slums of Cosmopolis, Carnalia's vaunted capital city. High over all loomed the grandiose walls and fortified towers of the emperor's palace from which he reigned with ruthless authority. Jeda was to live right under the very shadow of this ominous presence. She'd be at the mercy of those not known for being merciful. How did she come to this low estate? How long would it take before such a place ground her to powder?

Snetch turned down a side alley and drew the rig to a halt. They were at a back entry of the palace. Immense stone walls loomed some sixty feet over them; making Jeda feel even more insignificant. An obscure service portal protruded into the street offering the only visible doorway along the vast wall. A steeply-pitched, slate roof covered an outset doorway which was no more than three feet wide, barely enough to admit two men abreast, or, if need be, one horse and rider, but not a coach.

Snetch jumped down, draped the reins over the -hook, and rubbing his backside with one hand, pounded his other fist on the door. "Open up, yer 'scummy rum bums."

No longer under threat from Snetch, but keenly aware of the uncertainty inside that doorway, Jeda tentatively placed a foot on the buggy's stirrup.

Gwinnid leaned over, whispering, "And remember what Captain Fitcher said, 'brooms and kitchen'."

"Heshup, old crone. I can't tell if'n they heered me inside." Snetch pounded the doorway again looking disdainfully over his shoulder. Before his fist landed the door opened. Snetch's brawny fist nearly struck the guard opening the door. Not taking kindly to being assaulted the guard shoved Snetch backward. In the doorway stood three more guards, dressed in black leathers, capes, and helmets.

Snetch was knocked to his buttocks. "Sure as Pitland, this hain't one o' me better days," he groaned as the guards, hands on sword hilts and itching for the slightest provocation, straddled over him.

"What's all this hollering and door pounding about?" demanded the lead guard.

Snetch fumbled in his tunic and finally extracted a slip of paper which he handed to the guard. "It be's about the girl, there."

The guard studied the note, looked at Jeda, then Gwinnid, then back at the note. "Says nothing about the old woman. Who's she?"

"I'm the personal attendant of Madame Kway," Gwinnid haughtily defended herself before Snetch had a chance to insult her. "I came along to see the young lady off to her, er, new station."

"See her off?" the guard said. "This is no holiday the young lady's going on. Pretty as she is, I suspect she'll be sent straight to the house of—"

"Brooms and kitchen," Gwinnid flatly announced.

"Eh?"

"That's what Captain Fitcher said," insisted Gwinnid, "brooms and kitchen."

"Fitcher? Are you sure?" He turned his wondering eyes to Snetch.

"I tried ter tell the captain . . . "

"Captain Fitcher knows the young lady personally and will not take it kindly if she's mistreated."

"*Humph*," Snetch sat up and crossed his arms.

"Very well, brooms and kitchen it is then, unless Hod-ya decides otherwise. Come along, Miss." The lead guard took Jeda by the arm and guided her through the door into the murky, inner hallway.

The other guards followed, pulling the ancient, massive door to with an echoing thud followed by the clunk of the latch bar in its stays.

A torch was lifted from a wall sconce and the four proceeded down the tunnel. Though she desperately tried to keep up a brave front even in the darkness, tears fell and left a trail on the cobblestone floor.

For several minutes Jeda was ushered down the passageway inside the great wall. She hadn't realized the wall was hollow and concealed other passages.

The lead guard explained, "All wall entries, except for the main gate, which is presided over by very lifelike carvings of the Ten Dreads, are impregnable, no one goes in or out except by permission. In addition, all entries are connected by these wall passages with myriad false doorways. Only certain doors are actual portals to the inside of the castle; most are dummy portals leading nowhere. Besides being a defensive strategy against invaders, the wall maze discourages servant runaways. You'd never find your way out lass and will either be caught and tortured or starve to death wandering about, so don't even think about escape."

Jeda swallowed a lump in her throat as they passed deeper into the gloomy passages. There were small windows high overhead, but this late in the day very little light found its way in, making smoky torches necessary.

The leader led down the dusky tunnel passing more bogus portals, apses, other tunnel entries and archways, eventually stopping at a nondescript door. He took out a key, inserted it in the lock and shoved the door open. "Alright," he gestured to his peers, "I'll take her to Hod-ya. You two return to the Needle Gate, and no turning off to the wine cellar. I'll be right along."

The guards saluted and retreated, leaving one of the torches with the leader.

"Be advised Miss—uh," he briefly checked the note Snetch had given him, "Miss Jeda, it'll go badly with you if you try to escape. You'll never find your way out of the maze, as you've probably guessed; and, should you ever try, with what's left of you after the guards recapture you, the emperor has, shall we say, entertaining methods of execution. So, be smart, put up with whatever your future holds.

"Oh yes, a word about Mistress Hod-ya kar Psa. She's as mean as a bed of nettles, so don't defy her. Rumor has it that she's half-sister to the White Priestess of Pitland. She takes no guff from anyone except the emperor and his warlords. No one else. She's stronger than a man and twice as cruel, so do as she tells you."

CHAPTER FOUR

MALEVOLENCE SATURATED THE ATMOSPHERE. JEDA couldn't stop trembling under Hod-ya's unrelenting scrutiny. Jet black-hair tied severely back, the ebon-garbed mistress of the emperor's house scrutinized every inch of Jeda from her shoulder-length blonde hair to the leather-soled shoes on her feet. Silent moments dragged by as Hod-ya circled. She finally came to a stop in front of her newest servant.

Jeda timidly raised her eyes to Hod-ya's disdainful stare.

Hod-ya towered over Jeda. The woman was neither pretty nor ugly, plain best fit her, yet, this was no innate plainness, but something Hod-ya wore rather than was. There was something else disturbing about her. What lay beneath that forbidding exterior? Jeda had thought her mother and sisters unbearable, but they paled by comparison. Staring into Hod-ya's gaze was like looking at veiled caverns that were filled with unseen denizens peering back out.

Jeda held Hod-ya's gaze only a few seconds before lowering her eyes. This much Jeda ascertained: a seething cruelty resided in Hod-ya. Jeda steeled herself to do whatever was necessary to stay on Hod-ya's good side, if she had one.

"*Humph!*" said Hod-ya. "Not much spirit, but you'll do." She re-read the note. "Yes, you'll do nicely." Her pointy black-polished fin-gernails touched under Jeda's chin as a wicked grin spread across her lips revealing teeth that had been filed to sharp points. "What do you know about this place, girl?" Hod-ya's tongue flicked in and out.

"Nothing, m'lady. If it please, may I speak?" Jeda's audacity surprised even herself.

Hod-ya's smile froze and her head cocked slightly to one side and her eyes narrowed. "Speak, child. Whatever is on your puny mind?"

"I, I was advised to tell you, that, that I should request brooms and kitchen." Jeda swallowed, fearful of engaging Hod-ya's eyes again, yet unwilling to keep staring at the floor like a chastised child. Her eyes finally rested on Hod-ya's belt buckle.

Hod-ya cradled Jeda's chin between her thumb and fingers, remaining silent.

The oval, three-inch-belt buckle was shaped like a serpentine, malevolent spirit-lord with small ruby-red eyes and backward-curved teeth in its gaping mouth. The rubies seemed to come alive, as if glowing of their own accord. A shiver tingled down Jeda's spine, yet she couldn't look away.

"Psa fascinates you?" Hod-ya's voice was deep, almost a masculine rumble that seemed to rise up from a deep cave, "Would you like to learn more about Psa?"

Jeda took a deep breath and shook her head. Then she inadvertently looked up into Hod-ya's eyes. Hod-ya's pupils had become red spots—not unlike the red rubies on her belt buckle. Jeda went cold; unable to move.

Suddenly Gwinnid's advice resounded in her mind. Silently Jeda cried out, "Alfomega."

No warrior crashed through the door, no sudden apparition appeared to make Hod-ya back off. Instead Jeda's knees buckled under the irresistible pressure coming from Hod-ya's eyes. Was there no rescue?

"Alfomega, if you exist," Jeda silently cried again and swooned.

When Jeda opened her eyes Hod-ya knelt over her, shaking her shoulders, "What were you thinking, child?" The deep, rumbling tone was replaced by Hod-ya's normal harsh, guttural voice demanding, "You dare defy me?"

The red glow had vanished from Hod-ya's eyes and the buckle.

Hod-ya released Jeda, stood upright and stepped back, dropping her rage like an overcoat. "Get on your feet, girl." As Jeda rose Hod-ya put her hand to Jeda's chin once more and scrutinized the dazed girl. Finally, she asked, "And just who advises me to assign you to brooms and kitchen?"

The room stopped spinning and Jeda's senses cleared. "Captain Fitcher," Jeda stiffened her knees and barely managed to whisper.

"Fitcher? Fitcher?" Hod-ya stalked across the room to a latticed window. "So, Fitcher uses his final wish on something so frivolous. Well, I may or may not grant that one." She spun around to face Jeda. "But," an evil gleam sparkled in her eye as she paced back toward Jeda, "if I first assign you there, for a short while, and find you, shall we say, unfit, Psa will have his way at the end, while Fitcher will have misspent his last request. Haaaa-aaaah," her triumphant laugh bounced off the stone walls as she rubbed her bony hands so aggressively that Jeda wondered that her nails didn't pierce the skin.

"To the kitchen it is then, for now, at least." With that, barely glancing again at Jeda Hod-ya strode across the room, flung the door wide, and shouted, "Oath girl!" Then she turned and stood beneath the door lintel demanding, "Look at me, child."

Jeda raised her eyes; the black-garbed woman was barely discernible against the murky gloom of the passageway behind.

"A moment ago, I sensed a pulse of power around you, but it's gone now. You tell me, and tell me true, what do you know of Logon Xychirion?"

"He's an enemy of the empire, I think."

"He means nothing more to you?"

"Not that I can think of."

"And you own no allegiance to him?"

"I don't even know who he is."

Hod-ya's stare burned into Jeda's eyes. "Well, that denial would have broken any commitment you might've made to him. Forget I mentioned it. Anyone discovered in allegiance to him will be put to a slow, painful death. Keep that in mind."

Jeda nodded. Who would dare defy such a woman?

"Furthermore, you're to report anyone you encounter that's suspected of allegiance to him. It will go severely with you if you harbor information about spies or enemy agents. You must immediately report anyone mentioning the name 'Logon Xychirion.' Understand?"

Jeda nodded.

Light footfalls in the hallway distracted Hod-ya; she turned and sneered into the corridor, "Took you long enough."

"Sorry, m'lady," replied a soft, feminine voice. "There's much to do, with the muster and all, everything's in a state of confusion." A petite, auburn-haired girl about Jeda's age, dressed in a simple chemise and floor-length skirt stepped into the doorway and curtsied, carefully avoiding Hod-ya's eyes, Jeda noted.

"When I want explanations, I'll ask. Take this wench to Marga and see that she gets properly attired for her new station."

"Ma'am." Then to Jeda the girl beckoned, "Come."

Jeda followed into the dark hallway, fearfully eyeing Hod-ya as she slipped past. But Hod-ya's focus had shifted to other matters. She muttered under her breath as she paced back across the room, " . . . foul-smelling minions following mindless leaders, out to who knows where, and all because that stupid oaf caught me in an unguarded moment, desired three wishes, did he?"

The girl closed the door shutting out the Black Lady's imposing presence.

Torch in hand, the girl led Jeda down the corridor. "My name's Dancel. What's yours?"

"I'm Jeda. Are we going to the kitchen?"

Dancel stopped and quickly turned her face toward Jeda. "Amazing! It took me months to learn the maze, and that under the oath. How do you know where we're headed?"

"I don't. I haven't the slightest idea where we are. It's just that I find it hard to believe Hod-ya actually sent me to the kitchen."

"What's so hard to believe about that? It's no great honor, you know."

"Well, I think I was going to be assigned somewhere else. But a captain told me to tell Hod-ya to assign me to brooms and kitchen. I didn't think she was going to comply."

Dancel held the torch in front of Jeda's face. "Now, that is amazing. No one tells Hod-ya what to do, except the emperor or his inner council. By the way, never look her in the eyes, especially if they turn red, else you'll become her mindless slave. At least that's what they say. Your captain will find it costly to tell Hod-ya how to run her domain, I'm sure. But, come, we must hurry, nice as this socializing is, there's work to do. Every day for the next ten days, a new regiment is setting forth from the castle. Marga will be glad for the extra help, but not if we linger. Marga is a caution, mind you, but only if you don't do exactly as she says. Much of the time she mutters things she doesn't mean, but every once in a while, she really means it and you'd better obey. She clobbered a girl upside the head with a fry pan last week; knocked her senseless for two days. So, have a care."

"I will. Thanks."

"Here we are then," Dancel stopped by a nondescript door chosen from among dozens of identical doors they'd passed. She took a key ring out of her pocket and selected one and applied it to the lock.

"How can you tell which key fits which door?"

"Don't even ask such things. The wall maze is a closely guarded secret, revealed only to trusted servants, and that only under an oath. If I told you, it would somehow become known, even if you never told anyone; there are spies everywhere. Bats, spiders, and roaches have ears, so they say."

"I didn't know."

"Of course, you didn't. But, be advised, don't ask too many questions." Dancel clicked the bolt and heaved the massive door creaking inward on its aged hinges.

Inside a noisy bustle of women and girls scurried about carrying trays or stirring steaming pots or stacking cooking utensils. Vapors from a row of kettles simmering in fireplaces made for a stuffy atmosphere.

"Dancel! Where the Pitland have you been? Fourteen pans of bread charred black because you weren't here. When this rush is over, I'll take a stick to your miserable hide."

"She doesn't mean that," Dancel whispered over her shoulder. Then to Marga, "Hod-ya needed someone under the oath. She sent us this girl, uh, I'm sorry, what's your name again?"

"Jeda."

"Going to a ball?" Marga asked, picking up a sleeve of Jeda's dust-covered, red, velvet gown.

"No Ma'am, I was—"

"Take her down and see she gets properly attired. Know how to use a broom?" The latter was directed at Jeda.

"Yes'm."

"We'll see. Bring her back when she's changed and has been assigned a cot and had the dorm rules explained. Can you handle that?"

"Ye—"

"And be quick about it. With all these daily musters to prepare for—" Marga rapped the top of a nearby girl's head with a wooden spoon, "watch where you're going, cow. With all these musters to prepare for—oh, Annessa, not that way."

Dancel tugged Jeda by the sleeve and led her through double swinging doors into the sleeping quarters. She took Jeda to a cot then over by the wall of dressers and extracted a plain, off-white, servant's dress two sizes too large.

Dancel giggled, "You look like a chicken wearing a bushel basket. Here, tie this cord around your waist. There, that's better. Now we'd best hurry back lest we also feel the wrath of Marga's spoon."

Jeda swished past rows of beds in Dancel's wake, acutely conscious of the stiff, over-sized dress hanging on her.

In the kitchen someone put a broom her hand and nudged her to the ell where Dancel and others busily kneaded flour, eggs, milk, yeast, and salt into dough. Dancel was too busy to do more than nod at Jeda; apparently no one had covered her duties during her absence and she was behind schedule.

"Jeda is it? Good," a girl ordered. "You clean up spilled flour and dropped eggs or splattered milk before it gets tracked through the rest of the kitchen."

Being late afternoon, everyone's face was flushed from the heat and hurried activity; tempers wore thin. A single window at the narrow end of the kitchen afforded the only relief as occasional breezes wafted in fluttering the curtains. Cross words and angry shoves were exchanged as unintentional jostling occurred among the workers. A cloud of flour dust hung in the air filling the kitchen like a light haze. Perspiration dripped from Jeda's flour-smudged forehead, streaking her face, making her feel as ludicrous as she looked.

"Get over here, you lazy sow, sweep this mess up," snapped a nearby voice.

Jeda lingered another moment in the open window's fresh air where she'd been watching soldiers drill in the courtyard below. Jeda was too distant to recognize if Artka, her brother, was among them. She did, however, recognize Psa's scowling face among the other nine dreads engraved on the backside of the main gateway. The legends about the emperor's gates being guarded by the Chimeree—ten mighty, spirit warlords—was true. They seemed so lifelike . . . their images kept malevolent watch over the courtyard.

A beefy hand slapped Jeda's cheek, sending her staggering and bringing tears to her eyes.

"I told you to sweep this mess up, you lazy sow!" A hefty, red-haired woman glared at Jeda, rearing back to strike again.

Jeda dodged backward and interposed her broom handle to ward off the blow.

The redhead yanked the broom out of Jeda's hand and turned it about. "Are you threatening me? I'll teach you—" The broom handle rose. Jeda cowered, shutting her eyes, bending over so her back would receive the blow instead of her head.

The blow never came.

Peeking up to see why, Jeda saw Dancel, meat cleaver in hand, in a threatening stance between herself and the angry, flour-drenched, redhead.

"Leave her be, Annessa," Dancel gritted her teeth, "or I'll plant this between your eyebrows."

All work stopped.

Steam escaping from clattering pot-lids was the only sound.

The only motion was Marga bulling her way and knocking gawking onlookers aside on her way to the source of the trouble.

Annessa stood warily brandishing the broom handle, ready to strike, trickles of sweat etching pathways through the white powder covering her face. Dancel fiercely held her ground, protecting Jeda.

Marga arrived and promptly grabbed both broom and meat cleaver from their possessors.

"All right, it's over! Back to work, everybody. There's a hungry army ready to break down the doors if not fed on time." Then Marga turned to the combatants, "Now, what's going on here? Annessa?"

"Aaah, I was just trying to get the sow, here, to do her job, when she up and threatens me with her broom handle."

"Dancel?"

"She struck Jeda first and was about to hit her again, so Jeda raised her broom to protect herself. Annessa grabbed the broom away and was about to brain the poor girl, so I dumped a tin of flour on Annessa and grabbed the first thing I could find to defend myself."

Ignoring Jeda, Marga looked to another girl for confirmation of one story or the other. "Flanner?"

"S'jest whut Dancel says."

"She's just saying that cause Dancel has privileges," Annessa growled.

The back of Marga's hand struck Annessa's cheek. "You've caused enough trouble in my kitchen, Annessa. From now on you're assigned to the lower kitchen. Go clean yourself off and report to the dungeon. And you, Jeda, don't cower like that; stand up, girl."

Jeda slowly rose to her feet. Marga examined the handprint on Jeda's cheek.

"You'd best learn to defend yourself, girl, instead of hiding under tables, or you won't survive. Now clean this mess up."

At a glance from Marga, the kitchen staff returned to its hustle and bustle.

Later, at mess, not a few soldiers complained about burnt biscuits.

CHAPTER FIVE

FLICKERING TORCHES SHINING IN FROM the courtyard created dancing shadows on the ceiling. Jeda rolled over and pondered her new life. Cool, refreshing nighttime breezes swept through the dormitory's open windows where kitchen and housekeeping staff slept on rows of cots. Soft snoring indicated that others had put the day's events out of mind and succumbed to sleep's relief. A tear rolled down Jeda's cheek. Just that morning she'd been a privileged young lady of the realm with a name and title; now she'd fallen to being a nameless wench with only the blisters on her hands and the ache of her back to claim as her own. What had she done to deserve this injustice? She'd always considered herself as kind and good, so why did this evil befall her?

Artka had called her naive whenever she expressed the hope that goodness would overcome evil. Artka was right; fate cruelly toyed with people. Jeda sighed. Nothing ever came out right. Artka was off to war against a dangerous foe, and she was reduced to drudgery. Another tear dropped to her pillow.

A rustling of sheets drew Jeda's attention. Propping up on an elbow she scanned the dorm. A slight movement in the shadowy darkness near the doorway caught her eye as someone slipped quietly out of bed. Wasn't that Dancel? The girl furtively stuffed her pillow and clothing under her coverlet, fluffing and adjusting until it appeared a human was still abed. Satisfied her ruse would suffice, the girl crept sound-lessly out the door.

Overcome with curiosity, Jeda, clad only in her coarse nightdress, tiptoed to the doorway. She cautiously opened the door and peered into the kitchen. No one was in the passageway, but light from the kitchen's ovens flashed briefly as the door at the end of the hallway opened and closed. Jeda flitted down the passage to the kitchen entry. She paused. She'd already gone too far; if caught now, punishment would be no less severe than if she were apprehended in the kitchen. That decided, she stepped into the kitchen, gently closing the door behind.

A loud click caused Jeda to jump. It was the door bolt on the maze side of the kitchen door. It had to be Dancel; no one else knew the maze of passages. Jeda could pursue no further. But she was in no hurry to go back to the dorm. These were the first moments she'd had to herself since coming to the castle; she wanted them to linger. Illumination was kept low at night with only a couple of candles burning in sconces producing an atmosphere conducive for reflection.

What was Dancel up to? Running away? Probably not, for she had special privileges. Had she been summoned? Unlikely, if that were the case, she wouldn't have left a dummy in her bed. So, what clandestine purpose was she up to? Rendezvous with a lover? That was most prob-able, though Dancel lacked the glow that girls in love usually emanated. But in these baleful environs wouldn't she try to hide every vestige of happiness? That must be it; Dancel was sneaking off to meet a lover. Jeda smiled, pleased at her own clever deduction. What else but love could persuade Dancel to take such a risk? The next chance she had, Jeda would confront Dancel and make her reveal her secret. Something as wonderful as a romance needed to be shared even in this prison of despair. Besides, Jeda desperately longed for a confidant. If Dancel accepted her friendship and trusted her with her secret, Jeda wouldn't feel so lonely in this awful place.

Retracing her steps back to the dorm Jeda plotted how to get Dancel to reveal her tryst. Of course, she must show Dancel she was trustworthy and wouldn't expose her secret to anyone, even under torture. Being taken into Dancel's confidence would confirm to Jeda that Dancel was her friend. Defending her against Annessa might have been friendship, or it might have been nothing more than pity. But exchanging secrets would be a definite sign of mutual trust. Jeda slipped under her covers wishing with all her heart to become Dancel's closest friend.

~

"Hey, yer ladyship, day's a breakin'."

Flanner's face hovered inches above Jeda's. Jeda glanced around trying to recall where she was. Gray pre-dawn trickled through the windows. Girls rose from their beds taking on ghostly appearances.

"Marga don't cotton ter sleepyheads; yer best git yerself around."

Jeda's feet swung to the floor; only then did her stiff muscles complain. This cot was a far cry from the soft, feather bed she'd had at home. Jeda placed her hands in the small of her back and arched, then bent over putting her hands flat on the floor stretching her legs, slowly unknotting taut muscles. Lumps, hard knobs, and a hollow in the center of the straw-tick mat made deep sleep impossible. As if that weren't enough, just when she'd drifted off to sleep, she heard something furtively scratching inside the ticking, making for more sleeplessness. She rubbed her brow to revive her sleep-starved mind, then sorted through her clothing. She'd slept some, she thought, at least she had dozed, for there was a faint recollection of a dream, a fleeting memory of being warm and secure. All that was gone now, leaving only a sense of foreboding.

"Better hurry," Dancel urged, brushing past.

"Dancel, wait—"

"Can't. I've been sent for. Go with Flanner today, she knows . . . " Dancel wheeled around adding, "In fact, stay close to Flanner all day, Annessa has vowed to get even with you when Marga's not around. But don't worry. I've told a friend who will watch out for you."

"Just a friend?" Jeda said with a wink. So, Dancel had indeed, met her "friend" last night. "Will I get to meet him soon?"

A smile tugged at the corners of Dancel's mouth. "Perhaps," she said. "I've got to run." And run she did, out the doorway and down the hall, her footsteps skimming over the floor till the thud of the door at the far end of the dormitory shut behind her.

Jeda abbreviated her usual morning ritual of grooming for the day; even so, she was the last one to leave the wash basins. She was a working girl now, or lower. There would be no more fussing with lotions and powders to accentuate her features; in fact, there wasn't even a large enough mirror in which to tidy her hair, but only a small hand-held looking glass. She combed her hair out to hang as neatly as possible.

"Lookee here, Jeda, Dancel asked me ter stick close by, see, but yer takin' too long, an' well, we'll both be in it deep wi' Marga, see? So, c'mon, qwitcher fussin' 'bout how yer looks. Hain't nobbut gonna take notice nohow o' a scullery maid."

Jeda trailed the girl toward the kitchen, miffed that no one appreciated the pains she'd taken to hasten her daily preparations. Flanner's frank manner stung.

"Well, it's about time," Marga remarked as the girls entered the bustling kitchen.

"When do we eat?" Jeda whispered to Flanner.

"When every soldier an' prisoner has et his fill."

"When's that?"

"Mid-morning most days. Probly be later today. Usn's gots extra troops comin' in this mornin'."

"Flanner," Marga barked without looking their direction, "you an' whatzername take the B'n'B pot down to the prison kitchen."

"What's a B'n'B pot?" Jeda asked.

"Broth made o' blood an' brains."

"Ugh!"

"I know. It's whut's fed ter prisoners, mostly. Keeps 'em alive if nuthin' else."

At an out of-the-way alcove at the kitchen's other end was a door-less portal and ramp descending to the bowels of the fortress. At the top of the ramp, just under the archway three girls waited beside a pot large enough to bathe in. This pot was precariously balanced on a small, three-wheel cart.

"This here's Jeda," said Flanner by way of introduction. "She come yesterday. That'n wi' the short dark hair be's Daddetta. She don't talk. Her tongue was cut out 'cause she sassed her former owner. An' that'n there be's Rissa," Flanner indicated a tall, red-haired girl. "She don't talk much neither but can if'n she wants."

"I'm Glend," ventured a petite blonde with shoulder length hair. "I've been here four months now, but soon my time will be up. Hod-ya said that next time she goes to the shrine of Psa in Pitland, I can go with her."

"You want to go with her?" Jeda asked.

"Those who go, come back to positions of authority. Besides, anything beats lugging this pot of sludge up and down the ramp twice a day."

"More goes ter Pitland than returns." Flanner picked up a rope connected to the cart.

"Because they go with the wrong attitude. Hod-ya says Psa is pleased with me, not that I believe in any of that hocus-pocus, but if it means I've impressed her, I'm moving in the right direction."

Rissa wrapped a section of rope around her arm. "Glend, it's dangerous to crave power, especially from Hod-ya."

"Dangerous to crave power," Glend mocked. "Well, you stay here and slave your life away if you like, but I'm headed for greater things."

"Flanner!" Marga's bellow rolled across the kitchen, "are you girls having a social tea or are you gonna get that pot below?"

"Right away, ma'am." Flanner jumped into action. "C'mon girls. Jeda, yer grab that rope and git ready ter pull back hard, see, like Glend gots it wrapped around her wrist. Don't let go, an' don't let it pull yer off balance. Daddetta, yer steer."

Daddetta stared at Flanner for a moment as each girl assumed her position then went to the fore of the cart. Jeda was given to understand that the four girls uphill were to restrain the cart from careering down the ramp; the one girl in front, Daddetta, was to steer. Flanner kicked the chocks away from the rear wheels .

Jeda was tugged forward as the cart lurched downhill. The other rope handlers, anticipating the weight, braced themselves by leaning back, nevertheless they skidded forward while Jeda tried to regain her balance. The mute, dark-haired Daddetta looked back over her shoulder with wide eyes . If the seething pot rumbled out of control its bubbling contents would spill and scald her severely. Indeed, some of the broth had sloshed from under the lid during Jeda's lapse, permeating the enclosed tunnel with a putrid stench.

"They eat this stuff?" Jeda gagged.

"Twice a day, an' glad fer it, too," Flanner grunted. "Though I dares say they hain't too anxious ter ken whut be's in it."

"Most are advised to gulp it down without tasting it," Glend added.

"But, but it's so horrible."

"Yer'd eat a rotten snake if'n yer was hungry 'nuff. Besides, this way, they hain't nobbut wasted o' the butchered chickens, pigs, cows an' sheep."

"But it stinks—" Jeda breathed easier having passed the spilled broth.

"Hush now," Rissa gritted her teeth. "The ramp gets steeper up ahead. You'll need all your strength to hold the pot back. It's a long way to the first landing. Jeda, dig your heels in, like this, see? It'll help."

The rope bit into Jeda's hands, numbing her fingers. Her back and legs ached already, and it was about to get worse? Footing on the slick ramp was tricky enough; Jeda feared she wouldn't be able to uphold her responsibility.

Daddetta, who had the most at risk, kept darting worried glances at Jeda. The descent into the ramp's cool tunnel became more demanding. Jeda's fingers swelled; fatigue plagued her arms, shoulders, legs, and back. If only the pot weren't so heavy, or the path so slimy, her fingers slipped, but suddenly renewed strength surged in her muscles. The pain was gone, her breath came easier and her hands, though numb, tightened their grip. She unconsciously adapted a sliding-shuffle that kept her from slipping. Her confidence returned; she was up to the task.

Daddetta flashed a smile and returned full attention to the path ahead.

"Yer broke through the wall," Flanner grunted. "I was beginnin' ter doubt yer'd make it, as frail as yer looks."

"Wall?"

"It's like yer strength be's about all in, when suddenly yer gits strength ter keep a goin'. Happens ter message runners all the time." Flanner took a deep breath. "Usn's was worried about yer though. Didn't think yer'd make it. Daddetta was worried most, I think, eh, Dadd?"

An unintelligible sound emitted from the lead girl.

"There's a landing up ahead," Glend said. "Let's rest a bit before going the rest of the way down."

The weight of the pot lessened; within seconds the painful but welcome throb of blood surged back into Jeda's fingertips.

"Wheels chocked," Rissa said. "The steepest part is over."

"I'm glad of that." Jeda sighed and pressed her hands against the small of her back.

"Uhhh-uhhh," Daddetta grunted, nodding vigorously.

"You have no idea how relieved she is," Rissa loosened the ropes around her wrists for a moment.

"And just what were you humming to yourself when Jeda nearly lost it?" Glend challenged Rissa to her face.

Rissa said, "Nothing much. Just a little ditty I sometimes like to sing when times get rough." Rissa's eyes darted from Flanner to Glend to Jeda and back to Glend.

"Whut?" said Flanner, "Singin' again? Seems a funny time ter be a singin'. Pore Dadd there about ter git parboiled, and there yer a-singin' away?"

"I, uh, hadn't really noticed any singing," Jeda massaged her hands.

"Well, I did," Glend said. "Maybe you'd like to teach us your little 'ditty' for when times get rough."

Rissa's eyes lowered to the floor, then she meekly replied, "All right, if you like. Um, I forget some of the words, but it goes like this:

> My feet came close to stumbling,
> My steps had nearly slipped,
> The arrogant and prideful,
> Seem always to endure,
> I staggered in my mumbling,
> I was not well equipped.
> Then "something-something" my security,
> And the wicked will always fall,
> For "something-something" has made me free,
> I'd been such a fool
> To desire empty cisterns,
> And crave barren wells,
> While freely given to all those,

"Something-something-something" is well.

Rissa's song echoed in the stuffy enclosure. The lyrics, incomplete as they were, somehow stirred Jeda's emotions.

"Dangerous song, thet," Flanner said after a few moments.

"More than dangerous." Glend got face to face with Rissa. "It is treasonous. It sounds like the Ecclessite lies spreading confusion throughout Carnalia. Have you been mingling with Ecclessites lately?"

"How yer talks, Glend. Ain't no 'Clessites nowheres hereabouts, an' yer kens it. They's all too afeered to show their faces in Cosmopolis."

"Just the same, you'd better mind the songs you sing if you don't want to wind up in the Final House, Riss."

"Final House? Jeda asked.

"Yer better off not knowin'. Jest hope ter yer wishin' star thet yer never finds out."

CHAPTER SIX

THE GIRLS DREW NEAR A heavy wooden door set in stone at the bottom of the ramp. Brass hinges reflected the light of Daddetta's torch. In the center of the door a small, eye-level sliding port provided communication between the tunnel and the lower kitchen. The B'n'B pot stopped in front of the door; the girls who'd been restraining its weight slumped in relief.

Rissa rapped on the door then opened the sliding portal, shouting, "We're here!"

"S'bout time," said a flour-smudged face appearing in the hatch. "Who's that?"

"This here's Jeda. She come yesterday."

The click of a bolt from the inside was the cue for Rissa to remove the topmost iron bar on the tunnel side of the door. Three more bolts clicked inside, and Rissa removed three more iron bars on the tunnel side.

Rissa explained, "Maximum security, from both sides."

The handle rattled, and the door groaned inward revealing a spacious room warmed and illuminated by several hearths, making it appear like the fabled Pitland Inferno.

The flour-smudged woman eyed Jeda as the group lugged the pot inside. "Ahh, she'll be the one that got Annessa banished down here, then, won't she?"

The woman was short and plump, but not excessively so. Except for a few defiant wisps, her graying hair was tied back in a bun. At one time this woman had possessed a dignified beauty, but hard times and grime now obscured her once pretty face. "And just what are you gawking at?" the woman challenged.

Jeda blushed, realizing she'd been staring. "I, I—"

"Not much, if'n she be's gawkin' at yer," taunted Flanner. "Har, har, har, thet was a good one," she added, pleased at her witticism.

"Humph," joined Glend, "get her; thinks she's a wit, but she's only half right."

"All right, you two," scolded the woman, "you've had your fun. Now get that pot over here before it grows legs and crawls away."

"This be's Caldon, head o' the lower kitchen staff. She gots no sense o' humor," Flanner taunted with a toss of her head. "Long as yer be's down here, yer does whut she says, but she gots no authority past thet door."

The seething pot was wheeled next to a tabletop filled with empty bowls. Nearby sat a cart with close-built shelves, behind it were three more empty carts.

Removing the pot lid, Caldon ordered, "Get busy," as she handed out wooden ladles.

Jeda nearly gagged as the lid was removed and they started dipping into the effluent as rapidly as they dared without spilling. A ladle per bowl was the portion.

"Jeda, as I take a bowl from the table, you place an empty bowl in its place, understand?" Caldon, didn't bother to look up.

"At least the empty bowls don't stink," Jeda whispered to Rissa. "Do we take the carts down into the prison then?"

"Caldon's staff does that," Rissa placed two bowls in empty spaces. "And if you think this stuff stinks, you should get a whiff of the prison!"

"Yer'd swear they kept tophets below," laughed Flanner, rapidly placing bowl after bowl on the cart's racks without spilling a drop.

"Tophets?" Jeda looked up, mildly surprised. "I'd quite forgotten those old fairy tales."

Flanner eyed Jeda. "Fairy tales! Yer thinks tophets be's jest legend? Lemme set yer straight, Miss Jeda. I seen 'em. Not actually them mind yer, but their foggy shrouds. Afore comin' here I was in a brigade whut was layin' siege ter Ecclessite outposts up north near Lustre." Mindful of Caldon's sharp glance, Flanner resumed working.

"Bet I can guess what your function was," mocked Glend.

Daddetta slapped her thigh in merriment.

"Never yer mind," retorted Flanner. "Fer yer information, I was assistant head cook. Anyways, like I was tellin' Jeda afore I was crudely interrupted, when I was wi' the Bordermen, I seen some tophets. Usn's waited behind at the camp while the men was gone an' lyin' in ambush. All o' a sudden there comes this awful stench, 'nuff ter gag a cockroach, an' we seen fog banks drifting upwind headin' fer the battle. Mebbe half a dozen went by. Scrinch, the head cook, pointed an' says, 'There goes tophets'. It be's the second most scariest thing I ever seen in my life."

Caldon paused shuffling bowls long enough to ask, "So, what was the scariest thing?"

"First time I seen yer!"

Caldon scowled and bent back to her task.

"I knew you were fooling," said Jeda.

"Oh, but I warn't, not 'bout them tophets," insisted Flanner.

"I don't believe it either, Jeda." Glend scowled as some of her ladle missed the bowl and splashed on the table. "She's just trying to frighten us. It's had an effect, too. Your eyes are wide as walnuts!"

Jeda blushed.

Caldon snapped, "Get to work you blabbermouths. Last thing I need is a prison riot. You were late enough gettin' here as it is. Before you know it, my staff'll be back, and these carts won't be ready. In fact, they should've been back by now."

"Who's this for?" Jeda lifted a bowl three times larger than the others.

Flanner rolled her eyes. "Yer've gots ter quit askin' questions, girl. It ain't healthy knowin' too much. All yer needs ter ken is thet a certain prisoner needs a mite more than t'others, and yer best not neglect ter fill it full."

Even with six of them working, filling the bowls took half an hour. They worked at a steady rhythm of clicking on the table and clacking bowls on the carts as row after row were filled. The last cart was finally full just as the sound of rumbling wheels came up from the dark corridor at the other end of the kitchen.

Rissa shoved Jeda behind her without explanation.

A second later Annessa barged into the kitchen pushing a cart of crusty, empty bowls. Perspiration dripped from her clumps of red hair. One of Annessa's eyes was swollen shut and discoloration covered her forehead and cheekbone. Following after Annessa came a large-framed, dark-haired girl pushing her own cart, bearing a swollen, bent nose, and deep, black circles under both eyes. Four more girls each pushing a cart followed.

Caldon folded her arms disdainfully and observed the first two. "Well, well, looks like you two sorted out your differences. Scranna, you seem to have gotten the worst of it."

A petite girl with light brown hair, enthused, "You should have seen it, Caldon. It was glorious. Scranna thinks she's gonna surprise Annessa by grabbing a fistful of hair and yanking real hard like, you know, to pull her off balance and let her know who's boss. But Annessa didn't go down. Instead, she spins around quick an' grabs Scranna 'round the waist, picks her up, and runs her into the wall. I thought her eyes was gonna pop clean out."

Eyebrows raised, Caldon looked to the others for confirmation. The other girls nodded.

"Continue, Plendra." Caldon gave a re-appraising glance at Annessa, who stood hands on hips, smirking at Scranna who leaned wearily against the wall.

The smaller girl went on, "Well, Scranna, she didn't stay stunned for long. Whop! A knee comes up into Annessa's stomach, knocking her to the floor. Then the other knee slams into her eye. The two rolled around kicking, pinching, biting, scratching, and hitting at each other, howling and screaming, oh, it was such fun!"

"Get on with it, we can't stand about all day," Caldon, tried to appear disinterested, yet greedily drank in every gruesome detail.

"Then Annessa breaks free and rolls over to a wall where she finds a length of chain hanging from a clamp. She stands up facing Scranna, hiding the chain. Scranna thinks she has her beat and charges. Smacko! The chain busts her nose and Scranna falls in a heap. It took us twenty minutes to revive her, which, by the way, is why we're late." Plendra folded her arms and smiled, pleased with her rendition of the fight.

"Congratulations, Annessa," said Caldon with a faint nod. "Looks like you're the new crew chief. Now, run these carts down the hole before we have a riot."

"Told you I could take her," Annessa gripped the handles of a loaded cart and headed toward the dark maw. "I'm just waiting to get the trollop that got me sent down here. When I get done with her, there'll be just enough to scrape up and put in the B'n'B pot." With barely another glance at the girls from the upper kitchen, Annessa departed, followed by the others, Scranna last of all.

Jeda, lightheaded, released her breath.

"S'all right now, Jeda," said Flanner. "She be's gone. Besides, she probly don't have much fight left in her after scrappin' wi' Scranna. I seen yer turnin' blue but didn't dare draw Annessa's attention by reachin' out ter hold yer up. I'm mighty glad yer didn't keel over."

Jeda shuddered.

Caldon eyed Jeda for a long moment. "If'n I was you, I'd get out of the kitchen as long as that one's around. But I guess you don't have much say in the matter, do you? At any rate, try to not get lower kitchen duty too much."

"How do I avoid it?"

Flanner broke in. "I s'pose it's partly my fault. The last ones inter the kitchen gits this detail. I knowed we was gonna be late the way yer was a fussin' wi' yer hair an' all but didn't say nuthin'."

"No harm done, I suppose, this time," said Caldon. "Annessa will be toting bowls to prisoner cells till after you return with the evening meal. But, just in case, I'll find something for her to do that'll keep her out of the kitchen when you're here. I can't do this every day, understand? After today you take your chances."

"Thanks," said Jeda.

"Us'ns best be gettin' back." Flanner picked up the potlid.

"I'll say," agreed Glend. "Hod-ya might have sent for me, and we've been wasting time listening to fight stories. By the dreads, after I've gone to Pitland you'll not find me skulking in places like this."

"Dreamer," muttered Caldon. "Don't you know you can't trust Hod-ya. When she latches on to someone, she gets more back than she gives, like a leech. Her blessings bring dearth, and her curses . . . There's evil all about her. Avoid her. If she takes you to Pitland, you can be sure it isn't to benefit you."

"Ah, you're just trying to scare me. You don't want me to escape these foul conditions," Glend leaned her weight against the pot.

Caldon pursed her lips and shook her head then resumed scrubbing bowls.

Jeda followed Flanner into the corridor. The torch was re-lit and handed to Daddetta; the door shut behind them, was locked and barred, and each girl assumed a position to push the empty pot back up the incline.

The return was by no means easy, but not as perilous, nor arduous as the trip down. The girls chitchatted about this and that until Rissa asked Jeda about the circumstances that brought her to the castle. They all listened respectfully as Jeda recounted the previous day's events, how her father had ejected his only son, Artka, out of the house, and then kicked her out as well. She mentioned, but not in detail, the unexpected kindness from Gwinnid and Smid—excluding any mention of the sword or what they'd told her of Alfomega. She described Captain Fitcher and how he'd bridled the uncouth Snetch and offered advice on what to say to Hod-ya.

"And that interview is what brought me to the kitchen."

"Brrr! Thet Hod-ya," Flanner shivered, "turns me blood cold, she does. She may have a woman's form but she's no ordinary woman! I'd wager a month's suppers on thet. She's as much tophet as human, an' she'd as soon kill yer if'n she pleased. An' eat yer, too! Cold as snake's breath, that one."

"Careful, Flanner," said Rissa. "It's said her spies are everywhere."

"Hain't none o' her bugs, bats, or vermin down in this hole," Flanner replied confidently.

"I don't necessarily mean bugs or bats." Rissa cast a sideways glance at Glend.

"I caught that!" Glend snapped. "You needn't bother about me. Nothing any of you say is worth repeating, even if I was one of her spies, which I'm not. I'm not a weasel you know, just because I want to better myself. I'm not the kind that steps on others to advance my own fortunes."

"Hmmph!" said Flanner, pushing the rumbling pot up the long, narrow incline.

CHAPTER SEVEN

JEDA GRADUALLY DRIFTED INTO DEEPER slumber. Suddenly something brushed her lips bringing her wide awake. Reaching out, her fingers encountered a face. A hand immediately clamped on her mouth.

"Shh! It's Dancel," a voice whispered.

Jeda quit struggling.

Dancel removed her hand. "Quick, get up, pull on your dress, carry your shoes, follow me quietly."

"Where are we—"

"Shh! Not now. Be quick."

In the dark Jeda groped at the end of her bed to find her work dress.

Dancel, barely illuminated by the courtyard lights below, wadded clothing beneath Jeda's coverlet.

Casting a quick glance at Dancel's bed, Jeda saw what looked like a sleeping person. Jeda grabbed her shoes. "Ready!"

Dancel slipped soundlessly between the cots of the slumbering dorm into the torch-lit hallway. Wordlessly and in bare feet the pair padded to the kitchen entrance. Once inside the kitchen Dancel leaned against a wall and donned her shoes.

Jeda followed her example, tingling with anticipation; fully aware that, should they be discovered, severe punishment awaited. Dancel might give a plausible excuse for wandering about because she was a trusted servant, but how could Jeda's presence be explained?

Just thinking of Hod-ya's penetrating stare sent a shudder down Jeda's spine.

"Are you chilly?" Dancel's question was barely audible.

Jeda shook her head. "Frightened, excited."

Dancel smiled. "Come, we must talk."

She led across the kitchen to the maze door, fitted a key in the lock, and shoved it open. Dancel pulled Jeda into the inky blackness of the secret passageway. The door clunked shut obliterating all trace of light. The girls nervously clasped hands in the clammy darkness.

After a long pause Dancel said, "We can talk now, quietly."

"Dancel, what's this all about?"

"I have some news for you. None of it very good, I'm afraid."

Jeda's stomach tightened.

"Your brother, Artka, embarked days ago. I met someone who knew him and said he was one of the best fighters in the regiment. So, don't worry about him, he'll be fine."

"I'm relieved to hear even that, thank you. I still fear for his safety, however."

"You should fear more for your own."

"What do you mean? Is Annessa planning some—"

"No, it's not Annessa. It's Hod-ya! She's going to Psa's shrine in Pitland and is taking two girls with her."

"I've heard that. Glend thinks she's one of them." Then the implications hit her. "Oh, no! Not, not—"

"Yes, Jeda. You're the second girl."

Jeda bit her lower lip.

Dancel wrapped an arm around Jeda's shoulders.

Jeda wept quietly for several minutes. Finally, in a strained voice she asked, "Are you sure?"

"There's no doubt. This morning I ushered an officer from Captain Fitcher's battalion in to see Hod-ya."

"I know a Captain Fitcher."

"Yes, obviously you do, for you were the subject of their conversation. Something was said about a granted third wish paid off her debt. He was shown the roster of servants and mumbled your name aloud, 'Jeda, of the house of Kway: kitchen staff.' That satisfied him, for he left off reading the list then and there. Later as I took him back through the maze, I quizzed him about Artka, leading him to believe we were sweethearts. He told me that Artka's unit had marched.

"Hod-ya summoned me back to her quarters right after he left. She was exultant, pacing back and forth and cackling in her hideous way, muttering about how the fools were no match for her. Upon spying me in the doorway she ordered me to notify you and Glend that she was taking you to Pitland within the next couple of days. Then she checked herself and said to notify Glend but say nothing to you."

"But, why?"

"Afraid of your reaction, I think. Anyway, if it ever gets back to her that I've revealed any of this I'll lose my tongue, and probably my eyes."

"Dancel, I'll never betray you as long as I live."

"Then you mustn't try to run away. You must go to Pitland with Hod-ya."

Tears welled again in Jeda's eyes. "Why'd you tell me if you're not helping me escape?"

"I didn't bring you into the maze just to tell you about Artka, nor to help you escape. I brought you here to see if, that is, to decide if you're ready to meet . . . what I mean is—"

Jeda brushed her tears aside. "Oh, I already know your secret." Despite the ill tidings Jeda's spirits rose at the prospect of finding out about her friend's secret love.

"You know? But how?"

"I saw you sneak out the other night. It wasn't hard to guess why. Am I going to meet him tonight?"

"You don't understand, Jeda. I'm deciding whether to take you to a place where you can get prepared for your journey to Pitland."

"Outside? You mean a place outside the castle walls?"

"Yes. But I can't take you unless I have your word not to flee. Otherwise, I'll open the kitchen door and back in you go."

"On my honor, Dancel, I'll not betray you. I give you my word of words!" She hadn't intended to say exactly that, it just came out.

"What'd you say?" Dancel's voice became earnest.

"I said, 'I'll not betray you.'"

"No, after that."

"Uh, I don't know. Something about my solemn word."

"Is that all?"

"I think so, why?"

"For a moment I thought you said the passw—well, I thought maybe you said something else."

Flanner's comment about Dancel being "slightly cusp-touched" came to mind. What did Jeda really know about this girl? True, Dancel defended Jeda from Annessa and helped her get adjusted to her new station in life, but wouldn't any decent person have done the same?

Besides, Dancel was under an oath of loyalty as keeper of the maze keys. Not just anyone was entrusted with that privilege. And what of her sneaking out at night? To do what?

In the time she'd been here Jeda heard hideous tales about mystical rituals done in secret. Was Dancel a participant? Was she perhaps, even now, pretending to be her friend while luring her to torture, or death? Was Dancel betraying her into the hands of tormentors?

Jeda's throat constricted, breathing became difficult, darkness closed in, the ceiling felt mere inches above her head; it felt like the walls were squeezing in just beyond her outstretched fingers. Why didn't Dancel light a candle? Why did she linger near the kitchen entrance if she was on her way to meet someone? What was Dancel doing? Did she have a weapon? Was she even at this very moment planning to strike her? She must find help, but if she screamed or ran, she'd be caught and punished severely. But, if she didn't . . .

Gwinnid's voice rose from the recesses of her mind, *Just say 'words of the word' when you're ready.*

What did it mean? Of what possible use was that phrase in this desperate situation? *Just say, 'words of the word'.*

"Jeda, are you all right? Why, you're trembling."

"Leave me alone! Don't touch me," Jeda backed away.

Dancel withdrew her hand.

Feeling lost, alone and vulnerable, Jeda with great effort, gasped, "Words of the word."

"You did say it," Dancel exclaimed jubilantly. "Alfomega conquers!"

Jeda blinked away her tears. "What?"

"I'm not sure how much to tell you, or how much you can understand, or even believe, but we, you just survived a cusp attack."

"You mistrusted me, too?"

"I sensed what was happening to you. For the time being, accept this explanation: Lurcan, the emperor, has unseen creatures that sometimes afflict people with irrational fears. Those agents are especially effective in the dark. But they're gone now, so have no fear."

"What were they? And why me? Won't they report our presence here?"

"Well, if you can accept it, they were shadows, that's all. Mere absences of light and substance. Their power lies in distorting reality. But they have no influence over those who seek truth. They're drawn to fear and vulnerability like wolves to a newborn lamb.

"They'll not likely report us, though. They've often seen me come and go when I wasn't on empire business, but never reported me. I think they specialize in tormenting with fear, not spying. Now, aside from all that, do you trust me?"

"I, think so. Yes, I do."

"Well, I had my doubts about you, not caused by cusps, mind you, but well-founded doubts. But since you uttered the password, I have no choice but to take the risk."

"Do you mean 'words of the word'?"

"Yes."

"But, what does it mean?"

"It's a phrase kingsmen use to signal each other, or, sometimes, give it to someone they feel will become a kingsman. Alfomega is the 'word', if you will, of what King Elyon is like. Many false notions about the king and his son cause people to fear them. It's believed that the king forces his subjects to perform servile, useless or defiling tasks, and that any deviation from his commands is met with swift and severe retribution. Alfomega, the king's son and heir, became human to teach the truth about King Elyon. His 'words' are his teachings; thus we say, 'words of the word'. Did someone advise you to say that?"

"Yes, I was told to say that aloud if I needed help. What is King Elyon like?"

"He's good, and loving, and understanding, and just, but also merciful. He punishes those who choose to keep their rebellious, evil ways instead of receiving his amnesty," explained Dancel. "We'll talk more of that later. Right now, we must hurry."

"Hurry? Where?"

"I'm meeting someone, remember?"

"Oh, yes. I'd forgotten. Is he a kingsman, too?"

Dancel laughed. "In a way, I guess, you could say that."

"I don't think you're cusp-touched like Flanner says, but I think you might be a bit idealistic, just the same."

"Come." Dancel pulled Jeda down the dark passageway. "So, that's what Flanner thinks of me," she chuckled.

"Please don't tell her I said so."

"Don't worry. I take no offense. In fact, it's what I thought about the person who told me Alfomega's story."

"You're a good person, Dancel, but you must learn that life is hard and cruel. There are no happy endings."

Dancel led on, saying, "Oh, Jeda, that's not true. Alfomega really is good, and makes things come out for the best. I used to think like you; now I know better."

"How can you say that? How is it better for you? You're a slave like everyone else in the empire. King Elyon and Alfomega are far, far away, kept at bay by the emperor's armies. How can you hope in goodness and justice? How can you think Alfomega is so powerful when he can't even overcome the armies of Carnalia much less suddenly appear here when you need him?"

"It's not like that, Jeda. Alfomega could instantly destroy the emperor and the empire in one fell stroke. But he doesn't. He wants to rescue as many Carnalians as possible before visiting judgment on the rebellious. He'll know when no one else is willing to receive his amnesty. On that very day he'll smite the empire with fire and water, leaving a cleansed earth for the rebuilding of a kingdom of goodness and justice."

"You really believe that, don't you?"

Dancel stopped abruptly causing Jeda to bump into her, and although she couldn't see in the dark tunnel, Jeda sensed Dancel's face close to her own. "I believe it with all my heart. What's more, I think you do, too, or at least want to."

"Oh, Dancel, if I only could."

"Jeda, you have no idea what kind of life I had before I met Alfomega. I was—"

"Wait a minute. You met him?"

"I know what you must think, Jeda, but I assure you I'm not crazy. I met him in, well, a way you don't meet other people."

"You're not the first one to tell me this."

"Oh?"

"One of my father's servants claims to have dueled with King Elyon's own son. He told it so convincingly that I almost believed him."

"Come, we must hurry. You'll understand better when we get there. Now, listen carefully. We're coming to a door, once we pass through make no noise till we reach the other side, understand?"

Jeda whispered, "Okay."

Dancel led on through the inky blackness. Minutes later Dancel paused again. "This is it. No noise whatsoever, understand? And you do promise to come back with me, don't you?"

"Despite loathing Hod-ya and fearful of going anywhere with her, I mean it."

"I believe you. It's just that so many other lives are at stake, I have to be sure."

"Whose life is endangered?"

"You'll see soon enough. Silence now."

A door swung open and a soft reddish glow splashed around them. A narrow catwalk crossing high over an enclosed room as large as a ten-acre field stretched before them. Dancel flitted through the portal and out onto the catwalk. Jeda followed, imitating Dancel's tiptoe technique. The spring-balanced door swung silently closed of its own accord.

After the cool, darkness of the tunnel the stuffy heat in the massive manufactory was oppressive, but the soft glow of light was a welcome relief to Jeda's eyes. The catwalk, little more than a foot wide with no handrails, was suspended fifty feet above the floor. Anyone below chancing to look up would espy the girls, yet no one did. Below and on either side of the runway, creating the oppressive heat, were dozens of spark-and fume spewing forges that sent columns of smoke spiraling toward the ceiling.

So, Jeda mused, this was the source of the murky air that shrouded greater Cosmopolis on humid, windless days. Far below workers of all ages were chained to their forges while whip-cracking overseers made sure productivity didn't slacken. Elderly men, women, and even younger children were put to toting baskets of charred wood to feed the forges. Bundles of spears, arrows, shields, and swords were stacked everywhere, waiting to be gathered up and carried to outfitters who applied finishing touches to the weapons, adding fletching and hafts as well as making sheaths and quivers for the armaments.

Jeda was so absorbed in the scene unfolding below that she slowed her pace. Looking up she discovered her guide was nearly at the other end. Jeda almost cried out but caught herself in time.

Dancel, unaware that Jeda lagged so far behind, kept plodding toward the doorway at the far end.

Jeda was tempted to run despite the danger of drawing attention. But she forced herself to remain calm and focus on the catwalk instead of the pitiful scene below. Dancel, having arrived, turned, saw Jeda and started back.

A high-pitched squeak drew Jeda's attention upward. To her horror, a giant, dog-sized bat hung from a rafter directly overhead. Its beady eyes reflected the foundry's red glare. Its nose crinkled searching for her scent and its ears twitched, receiving echoes off her body.

Jeda's hands went numb, her mouth opened to scream but no sound came out.

The bat dropped straight down, spread its wings and glided toward Jeda who could only stand open-mouthed and wide-eyed.

"Eeeeeka—eek!" chirped the leather-winged beast.

A rush of air from its flapping wings whooshed through Jeda's hair and work dress creating a moment of sheer terror. A wing tip flitted inches from her nose and then the flying mammal soared up and out through an exhaust vent into the night.

Dancel's arm circled Jeda's waist guiding her toward the safety of the far end.

"Come Jeda," she whispered, "don't stop. I'm sorry, I should have warned you. They're quite harmless, just frightening the first time you encounter one. I'm so used to them, I forgot to mention them."

The girls reached the catwalk's exit and gently closed the door. Safe on the other side of the door Jeda wanted to scream but Dancel put her finger to Jeda's lips. "Take a deep breath, it'll pass. Screaming will only put us in jeopardy."

Jeda filled her lungs with cool air and slowly exhaled. Then again. And yet a third time and her panic subsided.

"We're nearly outside. Just a little farther." Dancel tugged Jeda along by the hand. "Shh, I must time the patrol." They were stopped at a large wooden door where they waited several moments. Finally, the shuffle of approaching feet was heard outside. Muffled voices and harsh laughter indicated that a sharif patrol was on its rounds.

"There he hung in mid-air, jest his arms an' head stickin' out; the rest o' him inside the foggy bank. He looks at me, callin' me all kinds o' names fer not rushin' ter his aid. An' I says ter him, I says, 'I'd like ter help yer Glag, but I cain't hardly see whereabouts yers at!'"

Uproarious laughter followed from his companions. "Har, har, har," continued the speaker, "Then his eyes near ter bugged out as he says, 'Oh kings, it be's gonna swaller me whole. I'll git yer fer this,' he says, then bonko! Outta sight he goes! Funniest thing I ever seen."

"Ahh ha ha ha ha ha ha ha! All because yers wouldn't bathe regular," chortled another. "Oh, thet's so-oo funny! May all lieutenants suffer similar fates."

"Aye. I drinks ter thet. Moved away from the circle o' the fire cause he couldn't stand our smell. Whut be's even funnier, it warn't usn's he smelt! He caught a whiff o' the tophet an' thot it was us'ns. Up he stands, an' says, 'I hain't sleepin' wi' swine whut won't bathe regular,' an' moves his sleepin' roll away out where he wouldn't smell usn's no more."

"Hey! Lookit there, Sarge. Hain't thet bat out a bit early tonight?"

"Huh, oh yeah, so 'tis. Oh, let me tell yers 'bout the time four lieutenants camped in the Valley o' Shadows, cusp country, but didn't ken where they was. All four o' 'em went stark ravin' mad afore mornin'. I knowed they had oughtter . . . " The sergeant's voice faded except for occasional, loud guffaws at someone's misfortune.

Dancel clicked the door open and they both stepped into a flood of moonlight. It was Jeda's first time outside the castle precincts since she'd come.

"Act like we've been drinking intoxicants, talk loud, and laugh as we go through the streets. That way we'll blend right in," said Dancel. Thus, arms about each other's shoulders, the two reeled through the streets and alleys of Cosmopolis toward Dancel's mysterious destination.

CHAPTER EIGHT

Jeda and Dancel arrived at a nondescript house on a dark, back street. A candle shining from a second-floor window was like a beacon, all else was dark. Dancel rapped on the door after checking up and down the street. Jeda peered over Dancel's shoulder.

A spy hole slid open. A stern man with a scar across his nose and left cheek stared out at them. "What is it?"

"Do you know where the Wards of Ward Street live?" replied Dancel.

"Are you being watched?"

"No."

The spy-hole clicked shut and the door opened. Dancel preceded Jeda inside.

"Who's this?" asked the man with the scar.

Now that she saw more of him Jeda decided he wasn't so stern-looking after all. An unkempt shock of silver and black hair overhung his forehead down to his piercing eyes, but there was softness in his smile.

"She said the phrase." Dancel took a seat at a table where four glasses filled with a red beverage waited. "Sit down, Jeda," she ordered.

From another part of the room a woman joined them. Streaks of white mingled in her honey-blonde hair; lines around her eyes and mouth bespoke a care-worn life, yet her eyes evidenced a deep peace.

"This is Jorna," Dancel introduced. "And that's Flan, her husband. This is Jeda of the house of Kway."

"The house of Kway?" repeated Jorna.

"Well, formerly. It seems I've been disowned." Jeda shrugged, half-embarrassed at admitting it.

"You've come to the right place, then, child."

Jeda immediately disliked the woman's condescending tone.

"Would you be lord Kway's eldest daughter, then?" Flan inquired.

"Yes." Jeda cocked her head to the side. "There's another set of twins, my younger sisters. You know my family?"

"Jorna, this is the girl we were advised to keep an eye out for. Didn't I tell you as soon as we spoke to him about her, I had a strong sense she'd come?"

"Yes, you did, but hush, you're frightening the poor girl. Oh, Sweetie, please don't drink that, it's only for show."

"Show?" Jeda paused with the glass halfway to her lips.

"Haven't you explained our procedure, Dancel?"

"I thought she'd understand better by doing. Besides, there wasn't time. The streets are busy tonight."

A knock came on the door. Flan went over and slid the spy-hole open and gruffly asked, "What is it?"

A voice replied, "I seem to be lost, do the Wards of Ward Street live nearby?"

Flan responded, "Is it clear?"

"Seems to be."

Flan unlatched the door.

Dancel stood and said, "Jeda, it's time we go inside."

"Inside?" Jeda blurted. "I thought this was inside."

"This room is a front; in case any sharifs intrude they'll only find a couple of friends dropping in to visit Flan and Jorna."

Flan ushered three newcomers to the table even as Dancel led Jeda to a wall hanging. She slipped her hand beneath the tapestry and pushed. Dancel lifted the tapestry. A door covered by the tapestry swung away into another room behind. Dancel nudged Jeda into the larger room.

Inviting lantern glow illuminated the room. The tapestry fell back into place and the door panel closed behind them. They meandered among several people who were seated on the floor singing softly. Jeda nervously studied the faces around her.

She gasped and squeezed Dancel's arm upon recognizing the familiar, plump form of Gwinnid leaning against a back wall. Dancel smiled with a knowing look, put her finger to her lips and whispered, "You can visit them later. For now, try to learn the song."

Jeda quickly picked up the melody and hummed along. The song was repeated several times. Jeda gradually learned the lyrics but didn't understand the meaning.

"Deep flows the river, crimson red,
Those bathed in love's purest flow,
Fear not the tophet, cusp nor dread,
No matter where they chance to go.

Shades of dark, their powers fail,
Threats subside, Short their reign,
For rescue comes midst their assail,
The salvage work, the king will gain.

Fulfill the call, rise to your part,
Cleansing comes at his command,

> *Waste not the day, but guard your heart,*
> *Great power supports the king's command."*

Fifty or more people softly sang the triumphant anthem, eyes closed, meditating on the words. Jeda had been warned about such secret, subversive meetings filled with nefarious infiltrators, but these gentle, peaceful people couldn't possibly pose a danger. Nevertheless, this was an illegal meeting, and if they were discovered . . . Yet in such a joyful, peaceful atmosphere they were willing to face that risk. Jeda couldn't help but admire their courage.

Leaning toward Dancel, Jeda asked, "Is your 'friend' here?"

Dancel opened her eyes and looked blankly at Jeda. Then realizing what Jeda meant, answered, "It's not what you think. My friend is the one everyone has gathered to meet. He's here. Don't you feel his presence?"

"I feel only a sense of calm."

"That's evidence of his presence. He always brings a sense of peace."

"But who is he, which one?"

"Jeda, he's Alfomega."

"Where?" Jeda's eyes widened as she looked about the room.

"No, Jeda, you can't see him with your eyes. Sense him with your heart."

"My heart?"

"Never mind. For now, just sing along."

The first song ended and was replaced by a lilting melody:

> *You bring the light into my life,*
> *Yours is the joy, ending all strife,*
> *Desire of the ages, stay close to me,*
> *I'm full of your love, it's setting me free.*

After several more repetitions the singing stopped abruptly. Flan, who'd entered the room sometime during the last song, stood amid the gathering. In his hand was a sword like the one Jeda had seen in the kitchen of her home. This sword, however, had more glow than Smid's.

"Brothers and sisters," Flan turned his head making eye contact with all as he spoke, "suffering will come." He held the sword aloft; a rune shone like a blue coal. "The rune of 'Long-suffering' would speak to us tonight." Others around the room examining their own swords allowed others to look on. Though each individual sword varied in brightness they all had the same rune ablaze.

"We live behind enemy lines; we're so deep in enemy territory that we don't dare build and defend a fortress like our sister brigades near the borders of Carnalia. Though our existence is secret we should seek out any who might be willing to follow Logon. Logon's own will hear him when he calls. Our part, no matter how dangerous, is to reveal him to potential followers. I'm not saying to be foolish, however, for that would accomplish nothing. Be wise, learn to recognize and follow the Advisor's prompting in such matters."

Jeda whispered to Dancel, "That name, Logon, Hod-ya asked me if I knew it."

Dancel put her finger to her lips and returned attention to Flan.

"Some will, no doubt, be called upon to suffer for taking such risks. Be assured that Logon will be with you and give you strength to endure. Remember, he suffered for us that we might have a permanent home in Splendora with him. We likewise, if so called upon, ought to suffer willingly for the privilege of sharing his promises to others. Whatever heartaches we face in this realm don't even compare to the joys we'll share in the next realm. Prepare yourselves to be true-hearted, unflinching soldiers, loyal to king and prince. Your life in Carnalia isn't worth clinging to at the expense of losing Logon Xychirion. You were once deceived and hostile to Ecclessa, as are those still under the evil one's control. Your duty now is to forgive when they reject and mistreat you, just as Logon forgives.

"Never deny knowing him, not even at the cost of your life, for then he must deny knowing you! He cannot be untrue to the pact that brings us to his father. Only as we cling to his name are we under his protection. The worst they can do only affects our physical bodies; our spirits will never be harmed unless we try to salvage our Carnalian lives by renouncing him."

Such concepts were strange to Jeda; she wondered if the people surrounding her really believed such bizarre things. Artka would have considered such beliefs the vain hope of frightened and ignorant people. From what Jeda observed so far, though cautious, these people were far from frightened and ignorant. Much to the contrary, they were courageous to meet clandestinely in the very hub of Carnalia. She liked these people but accepting their belief system was another matter. Nevertheless, rebels meeting so boldly behind enemy lines were worthy of admiration, if nothing else.

Flan paced in a small circle, addressing the crowd, "Any day now the Trumpets of Doom will sound, initializing events that will culminate in the dethroning and imprisonment of Lurcan and his hordes, ending their insurgency against the true lord of all realms, King Elyon. Until then, apply yourselves to your swords, and seek to hear and comprehend the Advisor's leading in all things.

"If there are any here tonight who don't know Logon, perhaps you know a little about him, now would be a good time to allow his sword to pierce your heart. There's no other way to enter Splendora. Allow the sword to enter your heart, confess all your crimes against the king and his son and be forgiven and healed by Logon's touch."

Flan glanced briefly at Jeda.

"Jeda, do you . . . ?" Dancel whispered in a voice so low only Jeda could hear.

"I don't know, not yet." Jeda dropped her gaze to the floor.

"Only Logon can help where you're going," Dancel persisted.

"Oh, Dancel, I know I promised, but do I have to go back?"

"If you fail to come back a search will be made. I'll be discovered. Then everyone in this room will be at risk." Dancel peered unblinkingly into Jeda's eyes.

"But, but, Hod-ya! And the shrine of Psa, in Pitland!"

Dancel held her gaze, saying nothing.

People all around began softly singing.

Three people slipped out to the front room preparing to inconspicuously re-enter the streets of Cosmopolis.

"Very well, I'll go back with you. If you don't feel guilty about me going to Pitland against my will though, I don't understand all this talk about love."

"Whatever happens is in Logon's hands, Jeda."

"That's so easy for you; you believe all this stuff."

"Wouldn't you like to believe it?"

"Not if it's not true."

"And if it is?"

"It's too impossible."

Others continued exiting by twos and threes at timed intervals until only a few remained in the large room.

"Jeda, listen to the yearning of your heart. Deep down, don't you know that what you've heard tonight is how things must be? Don't you sense that evil and cruelty aren't all there is?" Dancel placed a hand on Jeda's shoulder. "That the empire is the abnormality, haven't you ever felt that?"

"At times I did. But, how can I be certain?"

"Logon gives that assurance once you yield to him, don't you see? Your yearning for goodness and truth is Logon calling you to follow him." Dancel brushed away a strand of hair that had fallen over her eyes.

"If I decide to follow him, will he keep me from going to Pitland?"

"I can't promise that. But I can promise that he'll be with you wherever you go."

"That's not much comfort."

"Not now maybe, but when you learn how he does things, you'll understand."

Jeda shook her head. "This doesn't make sense. How can I believe before I understand?"

"If you let him, he'll help you."

"What if I ask, and nothing happens?"

A masculine voice came from behind. "You let him worry about that, Jeda."

Gwinnid and Smid were joining them. Jeda rose and hugged them.

Gwinnid simply asked, "Are you ready?"

Jeda's misgivings faded. Whatever it was that these kind people had, she wanted. She shrugged. "I guess so."

Flan joined them, sword in hand.

"I think she's ready," Gwinnid nodded at Flan.

By this time the room was nearly empty, most of the others having departed under the cover of night.

Flan stood directly before Jeda pointing the glowing tip of his sword at her heart. "Don't worry, this won't hurt."

"Is this really necessary?" Jeda asked.

"It's the only way you'll know how much you need him, Jeda," urged Flan. "It's the only way he's devised. Who are we to change his decree?"

Jeda nodded, took a deep breath and closed her eyes.

There was a slight pressure on her chest as the sword's cool, glowing tip entered. She suddenly realized how selfish she'd been all her life, and cruel, and proud! She'd acted haughty and arrogant and never knew it. She'd thought herself good, tolerant and generous compared to others, but the sword's incision showed her the true meaning of goodness and purity. She'd always considered herself better than others, but now she was ashamed. Most of her goodness had been due to either a lack of opportunity to do wrong or else fear of consequences, but certainly not out of desire to do right. In fact, she often envied those who got away with nasty or unethical things.

Logon Xychirion, the Alfomega, was the righteous standard, and by that comparison, she saw herself utterly corrupt and wicked. Comparisons with others no longer mattered. She now faced her own desperate unworthiness. Past words and deeds flowed unbidden through her mind; she wanted to hide, certain that everyone in the room also knew how horrid she'd been.

"Oh, I can't do this. He'd never want someone as wicked as me," Jeda cried tearfully.

"Courage, Jeda. That's the effect of the sword upon piercing your heart. It must first reveal that you need cleansing. You have only to ask him to forgive, cleanse, and heal you."

Bitter tears of remorse and shame coursed down her cheeks as she pleaded, "Logon, please cleanse me, heal me; don't reject me."

A gust of wind took her by surprise. Opening her eyes, she found herself standing upon a large rock overlooking a rapidly flowing river. Before her stood a man dressed in a gray robe and cowl. She was in awe knowing who he was. She felt a tingle and glanced down as his fingers touched the wound in her chest, the cut made by Flan's sword. He was healing her, leaving a telltale scar that all true Ecclessites bore.

"Jeda, do you know this place?" He stepped beside her and swept with his arm across the horizon.

"No, my liege."

"This is the rock where I bled out. It was here that I won your release from Carnalia. Here I won the right to claim you as my child. I forgive you of all. Release the hate and anger you hold against your parents and sisters. Let me fill you with my love for them."

He knew even that! He knew every little secret, yet, accepted her. She lifted her eyes to his and saw much more than acceptance. He loved her with a love that drove him to suffer the cruelest of deaths. She mattered that much to him. Her understanding of love was transformed in that moment. What she'd thought love to be was merely a wispy shadow.

He smiled.

Joyous elation leapt up within her; she was no longer the same!

"I've placed the Advisor within you as a guide, Jeda. He'll teach you about my father and me, but he'll only reveal as much as you're willing to obey. Obey him, and my presence will abound in you. Disobey him, and my presence, though still with you, will not be sensed and your white dress will become spotted, stained."

Jeda looked down to see what dress he spoke of and was delighted to find a simple yet elegant, woven garment of purest white covering her.

"I spun this fabric and wove it into cloth for you while I lived among men. The sword's runes tell of this. Nothing will stain this garment except your desires that are contrary to my will. When you stain your garment, it can only be cleansed by coming to me and admitting those desires and actions and seeking my power to enable you to forsake them. The Advisor will help you avoid thoughts and actions that stain, and will alert you to danger, but you must heed his warnings lest your heart become hard and his voice grow distant. There is that within you that would still wander from me."

"Why not take it all away now? I want nothing more than to walk with you, m'lord."

"There is much in your heart of which you aren't aware. Understand this, I never force my servants but rather seek their cooperation. It's in the day-to-day twists and turns of life that your heart will be fully disclosed and even then, only as you faithfully toll your Child of the Stars and heed the Advisor. He'll expose desires that endanger your relationship with me. Ignore him, and he'll grieve for you. Continue ignoring him, and my working through you to draw others to myself will be imperiled."

"Oh Logon, I could never—"

"Do not presume to base the rest of your life on what you feel at any particular moment. Right now, you know the exhilaration of truth and justice met with mercy as it lives in me. You're overjoyed to know freedom from Carnalia's evil. You'll not always feel this way. Sorrow and suffering are in the path of those who follow me, for you dwell amongst my enemies.

"You'll meet many who will aid you along the way, but beware; many claim to be of me but are not! The more you sharpen your sword the easier it will be for the Advisor to teach you and show you who is true and who is false."

Jeda fell silent. She wanted to stay in Logon's presence forever, basking in his love and attention.

He smiled gently, as if knowing her thoughts. "You will face severe trials and be tempted to doubt. But I will never despise you. Call on me when all seems lost."

He stepped back, drew a sword from his robe, held it aloft and uttered:

"Words of the Word,
Powers of the Source,
Light in the Dark,
Breaker of the Curse,
Open the eyes,
The mind, heart and soul,
Grow ever brighter,
With each stroke of toll."

Logon lowered the blade, resting its handle firmly on the rock between himself and Jeda. The point of the sword glowed brilliant blue. Logon grasped the brightly shining tip between his thumb and forefinger; every rune on the blade became evident, although not aglow. He continued his canticle:

"Fire of the heart,
Teacher of the song,

Mender of the broken,
Finder of the lost,
Colors of the vow,
Humbler of the wielder,
Exalter of the meek,
Champion of the yielder."

Several runes blazed from tip to haft at each phrase until every rune on both sides glowed almost blinding Jeda to all but the sword and the one holding it.

Logon remained silent several more seconds as the glow faded leaving only the point glowing bright blue. Logon extended a stone file to Jeda. When she took it, he also held the haft of the sword toward her, saying, "Take this sword, Jeda, and sharpen it with this toller. Use no other file upon my blade and use this file upon nothing else."

The rock and river disappeared as soon as Jeda's fingers closed around the sword handle. Gone, too, was Logon. Instead she saw Flan, Smid, Gwinnid, Dancel and Jorna smiling at her.

"Was it a dream?" Jeda searched their faces.

Flan smiled. "What's in your hands, Jeda?"

Jeda looked down and saw the sword and toller. "Was I, did I leave? Did he come here? How—?"

"We have no idea how he does what he does; all we know is that he does it," laughed Smid.

"I had to fight my way through the Valley of Shadows," said Flan, "to find Logon's Rock, the actual location, to have it happen to me. Jorna, my wife, met him in a gathering, like you. But we were both healed of our heart's wound and received new lives. The ways he calls us may differ, but the same thing happens to all that come. Welcome to Elyon's Kingdom."

"It's not likely she'll be able to meet with us again," intruded Dancel. "Tomorrow, or the day after, Hod-ya is taking her to Pitland."

Flan's brow wrinkled, and he thought for a moment. "Then we must ask special mercies for her. Especially since she's more vulnerable to enemy attack now. Join hands with us, Jeda."

Jeda complied. The six formed a small circle in the center of the room. One by one, each spoke to Logon as if he were in their midst, seeking Jeda's safety. Jeda, eyes open, studied them, wondering how they could see him when she couldn't.

Dancel peeked up and saw Jeda's bewildered expression . "We can talk to Logon anywhere and whenever we want. He always hears us, so if we need something, or just want to talk to him, we talk out loud, or sometimes just think our thoughts to him."

"But, how?"

"Through the Advisor he invested in each of us. Logon and the Advisor are inseparable, always in contact with each other and the king."

"Oh."

"Would you like to try talking to him?" Jorna encouraged.

"Oh, I don't think I could."

"You were doing fine just minutes ago."

"I was?" Jeda's fingers went to her lips. "Oh, dear, but then I could see him."

"Just talk to him," urged Gwinnid, "he'll hear you."

"Well, okay. Logon, uh, please protect me from Hod-ya, and Psa. Do I have to go? Can't you keep me from going?"

"Jeda, look, there's a rune glowing on your sword," Dancel pointed.

"May I see?" Flan broke the ring of hands to better examine Jeda's sword. "It seems Logon wants you to go but also to trust that he'll be with you and protect you."

"How do you know that?"

"By two things. First, as you talked to Logon, a sword rune came to my mind. It was a from runesong about journeying safely through grave dangers. Secondly, the rune that started glowing on your sword is the rune *'Crella'*, which tells the story of three young kingsmen captured by the empire and sentenced to death. However, they passed through fire and water unharmed because of their loyalty to the king. *'Crella'* interpreted means 'safe passage'."

Smid added, "When you leave here tonight, you'll likely get beset with many doubts about all this. The doubts will hurt you only if you allow them to remain in your mind."

"Are you saying you know how to make doubts go away?"

Smid smiled warmly and pointed to the sword and toller on her lap. "Some doubts are natural, others aren't. Since you have no reason to doubt Logon's faithfulness, any doubts about him need to be recognized as from your enemy and resisted. That weapon is how you resist such doubts."

"Oh, I see."

"Remember Jeda, Carnalia considers you an enemy now," warned Jorna. "As bad as situations seemed before, they'll get worse, much worse. But you also have access to help far greater than whatever attacks you if you use it."

"Why wouldn't I use it?"

"You'd be surprised. All manner of rational arguments will present themselves to your thinking, things like: 'Logon wouldn't get involved in something so trivial', to 'things have gone too far now, it's too late'. Don't let those cusp attacks paralyze you. Call on Logon and use your sword even if you've let it get dull, use it!"

CHAPTER NINE

THROUGH QUIET STREETS THE TWO girls retraced their steps from the outskirts of the city to the center of the metropolis and the emperor's palace. Their footsteps echoed off cobblestones as they conversed in breathy whispers.

"I have so many questions, Dancel."

"I'm afraid I'm not well versed in answers."

"I just need to know simple things, like, for instance, where's your sword? When do you get to toll it? Why is it I've never seen your Logon dress? How can you keep from telling everyone you meet about this joyous experience? Why didn't—?"

"Whoa, Jeda, one at a time, please."

Both girls laughed.

"I hide my sword behind some loose stones in a seldom-used passageway. I go there as often as I think safe."

"So that's where you went the night I saw you slip out of the dorm?"

"Nighttime is the best time. The people that I run errands for are usually asleep then."

"Don't you get tired during the day?"

"Sometimes, but it's worth it to spend the time with Logon. I used to keep my Child of the Stars hidden in my skirts, like I showed you. But it was too dangerous. Hod-ya sensed it whenever I was near her, although, thankfully, she never associated me with her sense that something was out of place. I knew she'd eventually suspect the lesser staff, even those under the oath. That's when I discovered a very secret passage and hid it there. I go there without fear of discovery, even daring to make noise and shine its light around. Only a very few know that passage, and of course Hod-ya, who showed it to me. But they never go there."

"How did you, an Ecclessite, come to be under the oath?"

"I wondered when you'd ask."

"When Hod-ya interviewed me," said Jeda, " . . . she looked right through me. She asked if I knew Logon, and since I only knew him under the name Alfomega, I truly said I didn't. If I had known he was Logon then, she'd have known."

"Undoubtedly, considering the close scrutiny she gives all new workers, she'd have had you tortured, and eventually killed. Like you, I was put into service and under the oath before I met Logon or knew anything about him. I seldom spend more than a minute or two in her presence at any one time, and then she's usually preoccupied."

"But I'm to travel to Pitland with her!"

"Jeda, be strong. Logon will work out every detail. We asked him, remember, and even if we hadn't, I suspect he was already providing for your protection. He'll not abandon you."

"But it seems so . . . hopeless."

"That's so you'll have no doubts that it was he who worked it out. He turns our impossible problems around, usually to the point of benefiting us."

"And if not?"

"He's still our master. We trust him to do what he deems best, even if, to our minds, it seems worst."

"I don't know if I can handle that?"

"Not without tolling your sword and listening to the Advisor, you can't. But if you do those things . . . "

Jeda stopped short.

Dancel took two more steps before realizing Jeda had stopped.

"I'm frightened, Dancel," Jeda said through her tears.

"Of course, you are. Who wouldn't be? But you must go through with it. Logon promised safe passage."

"But can't you see it's worse now?" Jeda wept. "Before I met Logon, Hod-ya had nothing to sense. Now she'll know the minute she sees me."

"Jeda, remember who you met tonight. Could he possibly deceive you?"

Jeda shook her head.

"We sought Logon's protection over you. He gave his word. He doesn't take that lightly and doesn't expect you to either. Trust him, Jeda. I can't believe he'd call you home to Splendora so soon. Come, we must keep moving."

Jeda reluctantly followed. "I've heard a lot of talk about Splendora tonight, but have no idea what it is, other than King Elyon's abode. What's it like?"

"Oh, Jeda, better you should ask me how stars hang in the night sky, or why the wind blows. Splendora is . . . is . . . all that's wonderful, and fair, and clean, and . . . and right."

"I thought that's what Ecclessa was like."

"It's what Ecclessa should be. Unfortunately, Lurcan has spread his influence even there, though not as thoroughly as in the empire's nations."

"I thought only those who'd been to Logon's Rock could cross into Ecclessa."

"True, but remember, we were already in Lurcan's service before we changed our allegiance. Some Ecclessites, after being to Logon's Rock, revert back. And don't forget that the empire's phantoms can enter that land on air currents. It seems Lurcan trains his cleverest cusps for sabotage in Ecclessa by subtly implanting lies in vulnerable kingsmen. Some brigades have been rendered useless for missions into Carnalia. Those captains allow stained tunics and dresses, even some leaders have stained their garments."

"That happens—in Ecclessa?"

"Don't think it so strange, Jeda. Unless you continually spend time with Logon, you too, will forget the Advisor's voice and not be led from within. Then it's an easy matter for cusps to trick you."

"This all sounds so . . . dangerous."

"It has been all along, even without your knowing. But now you're aware of the source of those conflicts. Now you've been awakened to the fight against those evil forces. Who knows, there may be some specific reason why Logon wants you to go to Pitland?"

"Me? What can I do? I don't know anything about fighting cusps . . . and things."

"All the more reason to be prepared by regularly talking to Logon and tolling your sword. Logon's intended will is inscribed on his swords. He'll never contradict his runes."

"Hold up there girls," hailed a voice from the shadows as the girls passed a street corner. A woodsman with a crossbow slung over his shoulder staggered out of a darkened doorway where he'd been lurking. He stood silhouetted against a gas lamp's light. "You girls wanna haf some fun wi' ol' Jern?" A carafe swung on a cord from his belt.

Dancel addressed the approaching drunkard, "I doubt if your concept of fun would pass our criteria. I warn you, we are not defenseless."

"Har har har. Won't pass yer criteria eh? Why it'll be my pleasure ter—"

The sudden appearance of a bright blue light piercing the night struck the inebriated Eroton speechless. Even more astonishing was the fact that the source of that light was an Ecclessite sword.

"I'm warning you," said Dancel, a tremor in her voice, holding Jeda's newly acquired sword between them and the encroaching Eroton. "Come nearer and you'll regret it."

"Oooh, whut a purty blue light!" The drunk stretched out his hand. "Now gimme thet afore yer gets—" with surprising agility the man lunged, grabbing the blade, "—hurt."

Taken off-guard, Dancel couldn't avoid his grasping the sword.

As soon as his palm closed around the blade the sword flashed bright red. A hissing filled their ears and the odor of burnt flesh permeated the air. He couldn't release it. He screamed, violently shaking his hand until the sword fell at Dancel's feet.

Clutching his blistered hand, he fell to his knees and looked pleadingly up at the girls. "Now why'd yers go an' do thet ter pore ol' Jern?"

Dancel scooped up the sword and urged, "Let's get out of here!"

She thrust the re-lit sword back into Jeda's hand; instantly the bright blue faded except for the glowing point. The two fled down the street, Jeda fumbled in the folds of her skirt, trying to replace the sword as they ran. Dancel suddenly jerked Jeda sideways into an alley.

The drunk, finally realizing what had happened, staggered to a corner and raised an outcry. Four sharifs nearby on patrol heard him and rushed past Jeda and Dancel who were hidden in an alcove.

"We've got to hurry," Dancel urged, "once they hear that two women defended themselves with a glowing sword, they'll launch an all-out search. We must get back inside the palace and in our beds . . . "

"I'm right behind you."

The two scurried down the street hugging close to buildings, cautiously scanning all around as they half-ran, half-walked toward their haven.

A shrill whistle pierced the night.

"Uh-oh!" Dancel said. "That's the "invader warning." Run for it, we've got nothing to lose now." They picked up their skirts and sprinted toward the castle. When they were still some distance from the secret forge entry, an alarm bell atop the tower walls knelled down the city streets. Within seconds armed guards swarmed the parapets. On the walls smoky fires were ignited under pots of pitch. Drawbridge chains groaned, and the great gears reverberated as the platform came down and the portcullis was lowered. At the same time, sally ports along side streets emitted armed defenders ready to repel invaders.

"We're trapped," Dancel muttered. "There's no way to get to the secret entry we came out by. Those sentries are blocking us."

Dancel stepped into the shadowed alcove of a doorway. Jeda followed. They watched from their covert position as troops deployed along the castle's perimeter, covering every possible approach.

"We're going to get caught, aren't we?" Jeda said dejectedly.

"I think not," responded Dancel, a note of determination in her voice. "I have an idea. Just go along with what I say. Come . . . " With that, she pulled Jeda away from the safety of the doorway and ran to the men guarding the drawbridge.

"Ecclessites! Ecclessites in the city!" Dancel screamed, tugging Jeda along. "Help, help, Ecclessites in the city!"

"Hold there," commanded a tall, lean corporal. The men on the bridge beside him lowered their pikes, preventing Dancel and Jeda from advancing. "What's that you're saying?"

Eyes wide, Dancel pointed up the street, panting breathlessly, "Ecclessites . . . about forty or fifty . . . with swords!"

The corporal studied the girls for a couple of seconds then, grinning ear to ear, murmured, "Now's my chance. Leave me here guarding the walls, will they? I'll show them I'm capable of better things. Where is this band of raiders, missy?"

"Back there. They were leaving a secret meeting place. You'd better hurry, they were going over that way," she pointed off another direction.

"Yeah, up near the Boar's Tooth Pub, eh? Sure, they hates alehouses with a passion. Lemmit, you stay here and watch these two. I'll want to question them later." He winked at the man to whom he had just given orders.

"Aw, Corp, I don't want to miss all the fun."

"I said watch them! And don't let anyone across the bridge. The rest of you, come with me." The corporal took off down the street at a trot, followed by his squad. Only Lemmit remained behind, sulkily watching his comrades disappear into the night.

"He must trust you a great deal to give you such responsibility," Dancel said to Lemmit.

"Sure!" Lemmit replied sarcastically. "He leaves me here to guard a deserted bridge and two girls, while everyone else gets some action. Some trust," he angrily muttered, stalking back and forth.

"No, I'm serious. What if the enemy comes to this bridge; you're the only one left protecting the castle from invasion," Dancel persisted. "Just thinking about that would make me nervous."

Lemmit stopped pacing. "Oh, that's just fine. Leave me all alone to defend the bridge against . . . how many invaders did you see?"

"Forty or fifty, I'd say, wouldn't you?"

Too non-plused to speak, Jeda nodded in agreement.

"We're so vulnerable out here in the street," Dancel continued, " . . . would you let us cross the bridge and stand by the portcullis?"

"I really shouldn't."

"Oh, please?" Dancel implored taking hold of his sleeve and looking beggingly up at him.

"Well," Lemmit coughed nervously and looked back to the gate, " . . . the portcullis is down. I know you'll not raise that by yourselves. And it would help me keep better watch out there, knowing you two are safe by the iron grate . . . Alright. I guess there's no harm. Go ahead—but, don't touch anything."

"Oh, thank you, sir. Come sister." She didn't need to nudge Jeda who was already half-way across. The two entered the shadow under the stone archway where a coal fire in a brazier yielded warmth against the chilly night air. "Lean against that big stone in the wall," whispered Dancel, " . . . and get ready to disappear."

"What?" Jeda asked, with arched eyebrows. Nevertheless, she obeyed.

"Oh, Lemmit?" Dancel called softly to the lone watchman on the far side of the drawbridge.

Annoyed at the interruption, Lemmit asked, "What is it?"

"Do you believe in ghosts?"

"Ghosts?"

"You know, haunts, phantoms. Beings that appear and disappear at will?"

"Well, I . . . I never thought much about it. Why?"

"Oh . . . no particular reason."

Lemmit studied Dancel for a moment, shrugged his shoulders, and turned his attention back to the street. "Crazy women."

"What was all that about?" Jeda asked.

"To explain our disappearance," Dancel whispered.

Without further ado she inserted a key into what appeared to be nothing more than a chink in the wall. The large stone Jeda had been leaning against pivoted soundlessly inward. Dancel grasped Jeda's hands to keep her from tipping over backward and led her into a dark chamber behind the stone. In the fading light Jeda watched Dancel feel around the wall until she found the internal keyhole that restored the stone door to its original position. As the great stone slid silently shut, Dancel peeked through an opening making sure Lemmit hadn't seen them go. A thin line where the stone doorway didn't quite meet the other stones allowed the girls to watch.

Over Dancel's shoulder Jeda noted that Lemmit rigidly observed the street before him as a rowdy crowd approached. Lemmit withdrew his sword from its scabbard and turned to check on the girls. His mouth dropped open. There was no one on the bridge or even in the archway shadow! Forgetting the approaching mob, he dashed across the drawbridge and checked behind the pillars. He rattled the portcullis and found it secure.

"Lemmit, what are you doing? Where are the girls we left in your custody? I've got some questions for them." The noisy crowd turned out to be the corporal returning with his band of guards, two sharifs and a drunk.

Lemmit faced the corporal, hands hanging useless at his side.

"Lemmit!" the corporal snapped.

"Umm, I . . . er . . . that is . . . "

"Quit stalling man. Where are those girls?"

"They, uh," Lemmit swallowed hard, " . . . were, uh, ghosts, Corp."

"Whaddya mean, 'they were ghosts, Corp.'?" demanded the squad leader.

"They just disappeared into thin air," he snapped his fingers to illustrate. "First, they were here, then . . . poof!" His eyes opened wide. "Imagine that, I seen two ghosts appear and then disappear!"

"Imagine nothing," snapped the corporal. "Now, I want to know where those girls are. Explain it to me quick, mister, and make it believable."

"I let them cross the bridge to the portcullis, figuring it'd be easier to keep track of them. I knew you'd want to question them . . . A second later I turned to check, and they were gone!"

"C'mere, let me smell your breath."

Lemmit allowed the Corporal to sniff his breath.

"Ugh! Whatever did you eat that smelled like that?"

"Corp, I'm telling you, they were ghosts. They even teased me."

"Humph! Luckily for you I smell no intoxicants on your breath."

"You were only gone ten minutes. How could I get drunk in that time? I'm telling you, they were—"

"Yeah, yeah, I know. Now, I'm telling you, you're on report for losing two witnesses. Unknown assailants attacked this man, branded his hand with some Ecclessite rune, then ran off into the night. Those two girls you let escape might have seen something that would help us identify the attackers. And you let them get away. We've suspected that a ring of Ecclessites was brazenly operating right here in Cosmopolis, and at last we have proof, but you, you let the only witnesses get away. Ghosts indeed!"

"I didn't let anyone go, Corp. They went across the drawbridge, and poof . . . disappeared."

"I can't even depend on you to do a simple thing like keep watch on two girls." Other soldiers snickered at Lemmit's predicament as the two sharifs and the corporal walked off to further discuss the evening's events.

Safe inside the dark chamber, Jeda and Dancel giggled at Lemmit's predicament despite their own peril. Finally, Dancel whispered, "We'd better go. Let me have your sword again so we can see where we're going. I seldom have occasion to use this portal so I'm not as familiar with this passage. Watch your step; these passages aren't well maintained."

Jeda yielded her sword to Dancel and the light increased, illuminating the narrow tunnel. The passageway was too narrow to walk side by side, so Jeda followed. The going was slow, even with the aid of the sword's light. Adding to their anxiety, strands of cobwebs dangled in their faces as they continued. The two rarely spoke, and then only in hushed whispers. Dancel didn't seem as confident as in other, more familiar tunnels. She often paused, deliberating over optional paths. Her choices, however, were vindicated each time as she discerned the correct tunnel.

"How did you ever learn all these tunnels?" asked Jeda.

"I was very young when Hod-ya brought me to the palace," replied Dancel. She swung the glowing end of the sword in an arc as they passed through another intersection and ventured into a wider tunnel. "Watch out for that hole." She tapped the edge of an opening that was nearly as wide as the passage. "Ah, I know where we are now. Cling to the wall as you edge around this hole."

Jeda pressed her face against the wall and stepped onto a slim ledge. The wall was moist and slimy. She shuddered, sure that her clothing and face were coated with goo. Gurgling sounds like a watercourse rose from the hole. There was, however, none of the odors associated with streams of water, nevertheless, a chill permeated the air over the opening and light from the sword revealed a mist hovering just beneath the lip.

"What's down there?"

"I'm not sure. Sometimes I come here and sit; listening to what sounds like waves rolling up on a shore far below. I do know that whatever water is down there changes direction. When the mist forms at the lip of the hole, like now, and the air above it is cool, the water flows in one direction. When it changes direction, warm air ascends out of the hole, the mist disappears, and sometimes if I peer down, I can see faint greenish lights, way, way down."

"That's all?"

"I only know passages. There is much evil in Lurcan's designs; there's no telling what he plans to do with such mysteries. Come, we dare not loiter. Marga will be wondering what all the commotion is about. She's a light sleeper, and there's a good chance she'll check the dormitory. We still have a long way to go."

"The journey out didn't seem as long."

"It wasn't. We had to come around the far side of the castle because of that drunk. But we did manage to get inside." Dancel giggled.

Safely past the mysterious hole, the two worked their way through more narrow passages, often squeezing through tight doorways. There were stairwells, too, many leading away from the main path, some up and some down, but Dancel ignored them all, only turning at major junctions, which Jeda surmised were turns in the wall. Dancel was more confident. But being inside the dank walls for so long had had a depressing effect on Jeda. At last they stopped at a wooden door, having passed numerous identical doors; but to Dancel's discerning eye, this was the door she sought.

"Go in," Dancel instructed, " . . . wash up at the hand pump, and tidy your hair a bit. Oh, be sure to keep outer garments over your Logon dress. Only Logon needs to know it's there. Go through the rooms on your left and you'll be in the pantry off the main kitchen. Start getting things ready for breakfast. If anyone asks, tell them you couldn't sleep, and decided to get a start on the morning's chores."

"Aren't you coming?"

"No, I've got to remove the dummies from our beds." So saying, Dancel slipped a key into the slot and opened the door for Jeda.

Jeda stepped through, but before the door closed, she turned and asked, "What about my sword?"

"It'll be beneath your sleeping mat." The door thudded softly, and Jeda was alone in the semi-gloom. The soft, inviting glow of torches from the main kitchen calmed Jeda's fears. She washed her face and hands, glad to be rid of the grime. Withdrawing a comb from her pocket she groomed her hair as best she could without a mirror.

Meal sacks were stacked high all around on the floor. The sound of pots and pans clattering in the next room announced someone busily getting things ready, then suddenly Marga's large frame accompanied by a lantern filled the doorway. Jeda froze; it was too late to hide.

"Wha—? Jeda! Up and about already? I must say, that's more like it."

CHAPTER TEN

RUMORS THAT A HORDE OF kingsmen had descended upon Cosmopolis during the night spread like a brushfire, causing much confusion in the city. The home guard stayed deployed at their posts late into the night. Most of the people from the streets that were rounded up for questioning were in various states of inebriation, and although no Ecclessites were found among them, not a few of the inebriated manifested cuts and abrasions which, they claimed, were due to scuffles with raiding kingsmen. The sharifs took statements as matter of course, all the while knowing such injuries were the results of brawling with each other rather than from enemy encounters. Nonetheless, the supposed raid was put to good use—keeping the populace in a state of alarm and anti-Ecclessite fervor. There'd be less resentment about the inconvenience and cost of maintaining the war. Such things were to be endured if the populace expected to be kept safe.

Squads of soldiers searched for dangerous rebels into the wee hours of the morning through Cosmopolis' streets and back alleys, so once they were back in the fortress, they were ravenous.

"How'd you get here so soon?" Marga leaned on some meal sacks.

"Uh, well, I wasn't sleepy, and," Jeda's brow wrinkled at Marga's lack of reaction.

"What should I do?" Glend sleepily stood in the doorway leaning head and shoulder against the doorframe, eyes half closed.

"First thing you do is wake up," snapped Marga. "Go to the hand pump and wash your face. Then the two of you set these sacks over there where the baking crew can easily reach them. I want all these," Marga indicated with her finger, "put out front," she said, tossing a fifty-pound sack clear over to the door to illustrate. "And the rest stacked in rows behind. You're both so scrawny, you'll need to work together." Then Marga hustled away into the kitchen, barking orders, rapping heads with her ladle and clapping hands for effect as she went.

Jeda grasped a meal sack, but unlike Marga who'd easily tossed one to its place, Jeda barely budged it.

Glend, face dripping with water, tied her hair back out of the way, and said, "Wait for me, Jeda. You'll never move it by yourself."

Together they dragged the sack alongside the one Marga had placed. Beads of perspiration broke out on their brows as they lugged the next several burlap sacks. With much huffing and puffing they finally completed the first row.

"Whew," said Jeda, looking at the several dozen remaining sacks. "Marga made it look so easy."

"Now you know why I want to go to Pitland."

Jeda looked down, wishing she could tell Glend about Logon, but she heeded an inner caution. Was it her own fear, or was the Advisor warning her? She was so new to this new life that it was difficult to know the difference. At any rate, she'd exercise caution until she understood the king's ways better. After all, Dancel didn't indiscriminately go around telling everybody about Logon. Wisdom must be exercised. There's no point in needlessly endangering herself.

"I'm telling you Jeda, I'll have it made. I'll be a princess, ruling hearts and controlling destinies, giving orders instead of obeying

them." Glend's arms swept the room as she lorded over invisible subjects. "They'll crawl to my feet, begging, and I'll have the power to
grant or withhold."

"Is that really what you want?"

"Of course! All my life I've been abused, stepped on, pushed around,
ordered here and there, and denied what I wanted—what I deserved!
That's all going to change. I'll be in control. I'll have everything I want."

"I doubt that'll make you happy, Glend."

"Easy for you to say, miss-always-had-everything-her-little-heart-
desired. Besides, who cares about being happy? Happiness is a myth,
like love. All I want is to be served. I'll have power, giving orders,
rewarding, punishing, denying."

"Don't you see that you'll only perpetuate the system that's treated
you and me and others so harshly? If you truly hate the system, why
be part of it?"

"I don't see it that way. I'll be on the controlling end, using the
system for my own benefit, whether I hate it or not. The way you talk,
you make it sound as if there's an alternative."

"Hey, you two, get busy," Marga snapped from the doorway. "We'll
soon be needing that meal, and you're not even half begun." Marga
disappeared as suddenly as she'd appeared.

For the next several minutes the girls wordlessly tugged, pulled
and yanked a few more sacks into place. Three quarters of an hour
later, with only a dozen more sacks to move, they decided it was safe
to take a breather.

"Tell me, Glend, I know you think Pitland will fulfill your desires, but
don't you hate the thought of the cruelty there; not to mention shrines
dedicated to the dreads which are rumored to go there on occasion?"

"My dear, dear Jeda, there are no such things as dreads, cusps, or tophet creatures, except in the minds of the gullible. Those legends serve to keep the ignorant masses in line lest they catch on to reality."

"I once felt much the same way; now I know different."

"Then you're regressing. You need to learn what's real."

"And that is?"

Glend plopped down on a sack of meal. "Well, as Hod-ya explained it: reality of power is the re-education and exploitation of the population using myths and fables. Pitland is where those in charge learn the craft of manipulation. 'Rule by exploitation and manipulation', she called it. There are times when I wonder if the entire concept of Ecclessa and an enemy king isn't just a fabrication. You know, be loyal and support the empire or else the Boogeyman King will get you! That sort of thing. Hod-ya selects only the most promising girls for training. I had to beg for months before Hod-ya accepted me."

"Well, it sounds perfectly awful to me."

"You'd change your mind if you understood."

"I'll not change my mind. I know that Pitland is a defiled place, full of foul people, and I want no part of it!"

"Well, I doubt you'll need to worry about that. Frankly, you're not the type. But all those rumors of your so-called foul people are only part of the grand deception. Anyway, Hod-ya will instruct me more about the real nature of things along the way. I just wish I knew who else is going with me. I hope it isn't some crude beast like Annessa, or dim-wick like Flanner."

Jeda was unsure how to respond. Finally, she simply said, "It's me. I'm your companion. At least, that how it's supposed to be."

Glend stared open mouthed.

"But, when Hod-ya meets us at the coach, things may change."

"You? But, but . . . "

"That's probably why Marga assigned us to the pantry, so we'd be done with our chores early so we could freshen up and prepare for our departure."

"You knew all along, and you let me rattle on. Oh, but you are a clever one, aren't you? Baiting me to say something against Hod-ya, or the emperor so you could report me. Trying to get in tight at my expense, all the while talking about how you hate the thought of manipulation and those foul people in Pitland."

"Glend, you don't understand."

"Humph! You think you're so clever, but I'm on to you now."

"Listen, if I could prove that malevolent beings like dreads, cusps, and tophets really exist would you believe then that I don't want to go?"

"You left out Ecclessites," Glend mocked. "Have you ever met a real Ecclessite?"

Jeda said nothing.

Glend continued, "For that matter, have you ever actually seen the emperor?"

"What are you getting at?"

"I'm simply saying that there is no unseen realm. If they can't be seen, they don't exist. Now I ask again, have you ever seen the emperor?"

"My father has. He works in the Ministry of Re-Education."

"But has he ever had any direct dealings with the emperor? Don't even bother to answer, I already know the answer. Here, grab this, we're nearly done."

Jeda grabbed the end of the sack and leaned all her weight against it. She tried to recall her father saying anything about seeing the emperor.

She knew the truth of the matter but dared not divulge what she'd experienced last night.

"Well it took you long enough," Marga said from the doorway. "Now both of you grab the water yokes and fill the evening B'n'B pot little more than halfway, understand? The idiots who did it last time filled it too full, and we had to set the smelly ingredients by the fireside while we lowered the water level . T'was enough to make a pig puke. Well, what are you waiting for?" Marga's scrunched-up scowl indicated things elsewhere in the kitchen weren't going smoothly and that she was in no mood for poke-alongs. Jeda and Glend scampered out the door.

The water yoke was a simple contrivance of two buckets hanging from both ends of a wooden bar that rested over the neck and shoulders. The buckets held seven gallons apiece with both buckets filled, and then, including the yoke, it would nearly equal the weight of the girl carrying it. Even empty, the weight of the yoke wasn't comfortable.

"Better grab some padding." Glend pulled a couple of towels from a nearby shelf and folded them over. "It'll take at least four trips by my reckoning, and our shoulders will be raw even with padding."

"Are we allowed?"

"Do you only do what's allowed? Don't be so dull, Jeda. They'll never miss these towels. We'll put them back when we're through, okay? Does that suit you?"

"Well, I guess. The water's that heavy?"

"You'd better believe it. Especially climbing back up those stairs for the fourth time."

The two went down the corridor and descended a long, stone stairway, each step a solid granite slab. There was one landing halfway down where smoky torches provided meager light. Four guards were

stationed at that juncture. It occurred to Jeda that on the other side
of the wall was the ramp where Flanner and some other girls would
soon struggle against the weight of the morning B'n'B pot, taking it
to the lower kitchen. Jeda looked past the landing and its four guards
to the bottom of the stairwell, still a long way off. The gray-blue light
of early morning silently snuck through the doorway. She saw more
guards further down. Jeda counted fifty-two steps to the first landing
and guessed that the same number extended to the bottom.

"If they say anything to us, just ignore them," Glend warned as they
approached the guards on the first landing.

"If they say anything? Like what?" Jeda scrutinized the guards
laughing and nudging each other who'd taken sudden interest in the
girl's approach.

Glend turned to Jeda, accidentally clunking her yoke into the yoke
on Jeda's shoulders. "You really have led a sheltered life, haven't you? Are
you unaware of the remarks crude men make to women in Carnalia?"

"Oh, that." Jeda recalled the leers Snetch had given her, and what
he'd hinted at before Gwinnid intervened.

"Yes, that. Just ignore them."

Jeda suddenly realized how vulnerable they were on this isolated,
darkened stairwell. Blood rushed to her face. Each guard had the
same leering gaze as Snetch. If these soldiers had evil intentions,
who would intervene? She'd rather face Annessa. But Glend had an
air about her, a sassy, don't-mess-with-me-or-else attitude. Jeda could
muster none of that. Instead, she felt only fear, until she remembered
Logon. Flan had said she could communicate with Logon anytime,
by speaking out loud, or even, if necessity warranted, by thinking
thoughts to him.

"Logon," she silently thought, "I'm terrified of what these guards might try."

A silent but clear thought came to her mind. "You have nothing to fear, Jeda. I'm with you." But was it the Advisor Logon said he'd given her, or her own wishful thinking? At any rate, she was no longer craven with fear. Frightened, yes, but not paralyzed. "I trust you, Logon. I hope it really is you."

They were close enough to read the men's eyes even in the dim light. All four greedily ogled the girls and spread across the landing to block the path. Glend slowed her pace. One of the guards stepped forward sporting a wide smile, revealing several rotten teeth and gaps where teeth had once been.

"Now hain't yers lovely?" he said. "S'been a long time since they sent sich purty gals ter fetch water. Come down ter pay usn's a visit, did yers? How nice! Hain't thet nice, fellas? Knowed we was lonely, eh?" He stepped up towards the girls who halted half a dozen steps above the landing. The three men behind him winked at each other and grinned.

"I'm glad you gentlemen are here," Jeda said evenly. "You can protect us from the Magician, if he's with that Ecclessite band that invaded our city last night." Jeda was as surprised at what she'd said as Glend was to hear it.

At the mention of the Magician the guards' expressions turned from hunter to prey.

"Magician?" said the foremost guard. "I hain't heard nuthin' bout him bein' wi' the raiders." He turned to his cronies. "Did yers?"

The three shook their heads, but by the way they glanced back and forth, they now considered it a possibility.

Glend caught on, adding, "I may have caught sight of the Magician, last night, in fact, I'm sure I did."

"Naw!" the leader growled. But his eyes betrayed fear as he descended back to his cronies

Jeda took a step down and continued saying, "He might even be disguised as a palace guard, maybe even one of those guards down there. I'm told he can disguise himself as anything or anyone. His voice controls everyone who comes within earshot, doesn't it? Say, isn't that one guard down there unusually large?"

All four guards peered over the balustrade at the lower-landing guards as they stood silhouetted against the gray dawn broaching the doorway.

"Hey, Gershka," said one, "them hain't the usual guards, is they?"

"Yeah, I noticed summat peculiar 'bout 'em, too," joined another.

"Oh my," gasped Jeda, "in that case, would two of you strong men accompany us to the well for protection?"

"Uh, well, we gots orders, see?" The leader rubbed the stubble on his chin, not taking his eyes off the guards below. "We gots ter stay put."

"Oh, please," Glend added.

"No!" the leader was emphatic. "Go an' git yer water by yerselves. We gots guardin' ter do up here."

Jeda and Glend scurried unhindered past the guards, across the landing and down the next flight.

"Jeda," whispered Glend when they were out of earshot, "that was brilliant. Did you see their beady little eyes grow round with fright at the mere mention of the Magician? Now I see why Hod-ya chose you. You seem so, so timid, and unthreatening, and yet can ruthlessly intimidate. I must say, I never expected it from you."

"Glend, I'm not like that, really. It just sort of came to me. It's not like I planned it, or anything." She wished she could tell Glend the whole truth; that the ploy was from Logon, and not herself.

"Oh, I understand. You don't want me to know the real you. Manipulation is easier if unsuspected, but, I'm on to you, girl. Don't even try that cleverness on me now that I've seen you in action." Then changing her tone, "I think we really were in trouble back there, you know. Bad things happen to the water-carriers once in a while and nothing is ever done about it. Your cleverness saved us, do you know that? Erotons don't bluff easily. They meant us ill. My bravado wouldn't have worked. I'm glad you were along. Erotons are the worst. Scummy slugs!"

Jeda lifted her eyes to the overhead vaulted ceiling and silently thanked Logon.

The guards at the bottom weren't menacing but Glend couldn't resist taunting them. "Those guards up there sure are acting unusual. You don't suppose Ecclessites somehow got in the palace or the Magician might be masquerading as a guard, do you?"

The corporal in charge turned to his men. "Magician? Any of you men hear aught about the Magician being near Cosmopolis?"

Two of them immediately said, "No!", but the third paused. "Now that you mention it, I did hear something or other about ghosts, or people disappearing right before a sentry's eyes. Very queer goings on all night, too, I gather."

At that the four turned their attention upward at the dismal stairway to better scrutinize the men on the upper landing.

"They're just standing there looking down at us. Now that's strange."

With a quick wink, Glend nudged Jeda through the gateway into the open courtyard. "That ought to keep all eight of them busy. Now all we have to worry about is toting this water."

At the well both girls disengaged the buckets from their yokes, setting the yokes on the ground next to hollowed-out stone work and then Glend fastened a bucket to the end of a rope coiled around the axel hanging over the middle of the well. Glend pulled the hand-crank pin releasing the bucket into the depths. A man could easily rewind a full bucket back up to the rim in seconds, but it took both girls rewinding the rope by the crank to bring the bucket to the lip again. They set the bucket beside the yoke and sent Glend's other bucket back down into the depths.

It took a while, but all four buckets were finally full, and it was time to make the return. Glend demonstrated how by placing the wadded towels on her shoulders, stooping under the yoke and rising to full height under the load.

Jeda padded her shoulders and positioned herself as Glend had demonstrated and tried to stand. She gasped. How would she walk, let alone climb under this weight?

Glend smiled at her with a knowing smile and started back with small, mincing steps, swaying her buckets rhythmically.

Jeda imitated Glend by taking small steps and found that as the weight shifted, she was able to swing the other bucket and foot forward. The weight shifted again, and she made her next step more confidently.

Arriving at the stairs, Glend said over her shoulder, "Give a little twist from your waist as the bucket swings forward so all you need do is lift your foot; then twist the other way."

Jeda watched, then imitated. About halfway up to the landing her lower back and legs began burning, but the method worked. By the time they gained the first landing both needed a break. The guards scarcely paid them any attention.

"Ere, whut're they constantly lookin' up here fer?" demanded the Eroton corporal.

Though winded, Glend was only too glad to offer, "They wanted to know how well armed you were, and if you looked like you'd had battle experience, or were just recruits."

"They did, eh? Whut'd yer tell 'em?"

"I told them we were just girls and knew nothing about such things."

"Arrgh! Yer shouldda told 'em we was fierce Eroton warriors."

"Oh. I'll be sure to tell them on our next trip. Ready to go, Jeda?"

Jeda sighed and bent under her yoke. They resumed climbing to the top, pausing briefly before passing through the doorway that led to the kitchen. "I don't see how I'll ever make three more trips, Glend. My knees are all aquiver; my back and legs ache."

"Just imagine Marga standing behind you with her head-thumping ladle. That ought to help." Both girls laughed. "You know, I sort of like you Jeda. At first, I didn't, and when you told me that Hod-ya is taking you along, I almost despised you."

"Don't hold that against me. It's not my choice, believe me."

"Well, I don't trust you, even if I do like you a little." Glend picked up her burden, and Jeda followed. They entered the kitchen and went straight to the B'n'B pot.

Marga saw them out of the corner of her eye and snapped "Glend, Jeda, get over here."

The girls set their burdens down and reported to the kitchen mistress. Amidst the hubbub of bakers, cooks, and cleaners rushing to and fro, Jeda noted two soldiers standing beside Marga, but not ordinary Carnalian soldiers.

These were from Hod-ya's personal bodyguard. They wore black from head to foot and had masks covering the upper half of their faces, like executioners. Two eye-slits were in each mask, but try as she did, Jeda discerned no eyes behind the masks. Indeed, had it not been for their cruelly thin-lipped mouths, she would have questioned whether they were even human. They were tall even for men, and lean. Black gauntlets covered their hands past their wrists, black breeches, black chain mail shirt, jerkin, leather arms, neck, and chest protectors with knee-high boots completed the uniform of each, except for the afore-mentioned mask which she now saw was attached to the cape like a half-hood that hung down over their shoulders to mid-calf. The only skin they showed was the lower half of their faces, and that had a pasty pallor, making them look more dead than alive.

The black-guards said nothing, but only stared, first at Glend, then Jeda. Jeda was somewhat daunted by their baleful appearance and the black, curved scimitars dangling from their belts.

"I need to tell you something, Jeda," Marga began. "Brace yourself."

"Yes'm?"

"Hod-ya has given orders, and when she orders, they're not to be questioned, understand? It'll go harshly with you if you resist her will. You're going to Pitland, this morning, with Glend. These are your escorts."

"Yes'm."

Marga cocked her head to one side and asked, "Did you hear me just now? Do you understand what I said?"

"Yes'm. I'm to go to Pitland with Hod-ya and Glend, and these . . . these guards."

Marga's eyebrows arched. "Well, smack me stupid with a frying pan! Who would've believed that? Might as well have told her the sun was coming up today! Well, good! Both of you go to the dorm and get your things and meet these dronnets in the courtyard. I'll assign the rest of your duties to other girls. Your escorts are impatient, wondering where you've been all this time, so don't annoy them by making them wait too long. Oh, yes, Hod-ya, it seems, was called away on urgent business, so she won't be able to accompany you. But these guards will show you what to do and where to go and so forth. See that you obey them without question. They have little patience for questions and none for disobedience." Marga looked each girl full in the face, acting as if she wanted to give them a motherly hug or a kiss or something, or so Jeda thought, but in the end, all she said was, "Be careful, both of you. I hope, for your sake Glend, Pitland is what you expect. Now, git!"

The girls hung their aprons on hooks for the last time. Jeda was light-headed with relief that Hod-ya wasn't accompanying them, though the presence of Hod-ya's grim bodyguards was by no means comforting. Even Glend seemed subdued in their presence. The girls went to the dorm and stuffed their meager belongings into satchels.

"And that's that," exulted Glend, standing in the dormitory doorway for the last time. "From now on Jeda, we're queens of the shrines."

Jeda made no reply, wondering how long it would take before she was discovered. A day? A week? Longer? She remembered the rune,

'Crella'—safe passage. Well, Logon had indeed worked it out so far. And if he could do this much, why not the rest? Logon was going to Pitland with her! There was still much she didn't understand: like, why did he want her, a novice, and a girl at that, to go to Pitland? If there were some quest to accomplish wouldn't a seasoned warrior be better? And more to the point, would she ever return, or would she die there? She could see no other outcome. She must eventually be discovered and executed, yet, if that was what Logon wanted . . . then she remembered her sword.

"Uh, Glend, you go on ahead. I forgot something. It won't take me a minute." Jeda hurried back to her cot. Had Dancel remembered? What if it wasn't there? But slipping her hand beneath the ticking she felt the cool, hard touch of steel.

"You aren't planning to duck out are you?" Glend hadn't left the doorway. "Oh, I'm so excited. Just to finally be on my way is even worth riding with those two scarecrows. Come on, Jeda, what's keeping you?"

How was Jeda to withdraw the sword and hide it in her skirts with Glend standing there? "Uh, I'll be couple of minutes yet, why don't you go on ahead? I promise, I'm not ducking out. Where would I go?"

"Well, okay. But hurry. The sooner we leave this horrid place the better. I'll be in the kitchen saying goodbye to some friends and watching them eat themselves up with envy. While I'm at it I'll see if Marga can spare some fruit, bread, and cheese for the way." At that, Glend turned and fairly flew up the hallway to the kitchen.

Jeda checked the room making sure she was alone before withdrawing her Child of the Stars. She had a deep sense of calm as she gazed at the brightly shining tip and the rune 'Crella' which was still had a faint glimmer.

She smiled. "As you bid, m'lord; to Pitland I go, to live, or die, I know not. But since it's you who asks, I go." With that, she hid her sword in the folds of her skirt. Then, after retrieving her toller, she picked up her satchel and followed Glend.

CHAPTER ELEVEN

FOUR HOURS OF GRUELING, DUSTY travel had taken a toll on the distaff occupants of the six-horse-hitch carriage. The constant jolting and rumble taxed every muscle and joint. A fine layer of dust coated everything: hair, face, hands, clothing, and shoes, muting all colors to a dun patina. Jeda and Glend faced forward sitting directly underneath the driver's perch. Behind them also forward-facing sat the two dronnet bodyguards, or "scarecrows" as Glend mockingly referred to them.

The coach, like almost every other official thing in Carnalia, was all black except for an embossed, silvery dragon on each door's outer panel. From this serpent's mouth issued a stream of coppery fire encompassing a map of the empire. The horses drawing the coach were also black—coal black. These swarthy horses were of a larger and stronger breed than any Jeda had ever seen, for after hours of continuous gallop they seemed no more winded than at the outset of the journey. From time to time the coachman called encouragingly to one or another of his team by name. Seldom did he ply his whip except to crack it in the air. He, too, was dressed in Carnalian black, but on him it didn't seem so sinister. In truth, he looked quite the jovial soul, with a double chin and protruding belly which gave him the appearance of a pumpkin smuggler according to Glend. He'd smiled at the girls as they boarded and when Jeda smiled back, he blushed.

"Ruark," he'd introduced himself. "Please let me know if you lasses have any needs along the way." Then, despite his girth, he nimbly mounted his perch and within seconds a whip cracked, and their trek was underway.

So, it was that four dusty hours and three score miles later Ruark clucked his team to a cool-down pace; a rest stop was near. Leaning out her window and peering ahead Jeda spied a lush roadside pull-off replete with a gurgling brook. It was a welcome relief to the dreary, forested landscape they'd been passing through.

"I think he means to stop up ahead," she commented to Glend.

"Good. If the water's not stagnant, we can wash off some of this dust," Glend patted her sleeve causing a cloud of dust to rise.

"I can't wait to rinse my mouth. My teeth are gritting."

The bodyguards said nothing, remaining silent, as they had the entire trip thus far. For politeness' sake, the girls had tried engaging them in conversation. But the hooded guards only replied with occasional grunts. Otherwise, they sat silent, rigidly upright, staring straight ahead. So, the girls had passed the time in hushed conversation between themselves.

Ruark pulled the coach over to a grassy field, secured the reins, and climbed down. He opened Jeda's side door and bowed awkwardly. His face dripped with perspiration; his waistcoat was open, revealing a bright red vest with gold buttons.

Jeda left the coach's austere interior, stepped out, and arched her back.

Glend followed, teasing the old coachman upon spying his red vest, "Why, Mr. Ruark, is that regulation uniform?"

Ruark's eyes widened and he straightened his posture. "Uh, uh, I meant no harm m'lady. It's just that the coat gets warm on a humid day like this. I didn't think you'd mind since we're away from Cosmopolis." He fumbled with his coat's lower buttons.

Glend seemed delighted at being called "m'lady" and giggled.

Jeda quickly put the man at ease. "Pay her no mind, Mr. Ruark, she's just teasing. You may do as you like, and don't worry about what we say or think."

"Oh, I see. Thank you, m'lady. Uh, please call me Ruark. That's all. No mister, or nothing. Just Ruark."

"Okay, Ruark, and you needn't call us 'm'lady', either."

"Jeda," chided Glend, "I was just getting used to how that sounded. Oh, isn't it marvelous to not be rushing here, there and everywhere for Marga?"

"Well—"

"Come now, certainly you can't say you'd rather be back there?"

"No, of course not. But I'm not so sure this is where I'd choose to be either."

Glend turned to the two dronnets emerging from the coach. "Will one of you please tell her how lucky she is to be going to Pitland?"

The two guards stood ominously silent, staring.

"Come on," she persisted, reaching out to tug one's sleeve.

A growl rose in the bodyguard's throat as he bared his teeth, which, like Hod-ya's, had been filed to sharp points. Glend immediately stepped back.

Jeda tugged Glend away. "That's a sample of what awaits us in Pitland, I fear."

The guards' attention shifted from Glend's impertinence to Ruark, demanding in a raspy voice, "Ho-ow lo-ong stay?"

Ruark shuddered under their dark stare, and his face, which had been flushed, suddenly drained of color. "O-o-only an hour, m'lord. The horses need their midday feeding and rest."

The guard stared at the thick, arboreal canopy above as if he was reading the sun's position; he then nodded to his partner. The hitherto silent one retreated into the coach. Jeda noted that daylight seemed to annoy them. She mustered her courage to ask, "Would it be all right for us to explore the clearing and little brook?"

The one that Glend had reached out to touch approached the girls. He regarded them through eyeless slits for a full minute then hissed, "One hour. No more. Be back here."

The girls nodded at the half-covered visage. He turned and hissed before joining his companion back inside the coach. The two girls, taking advantage of this unexpected liberty, quickly turned toward the brook.

Glend whispered, "Ooh, they give me the creeps. Did you see how pasty their cheeks and chin are? And that high, creaking voice," she giggled, "sounds like he hasn't oiled it in years."

"That's not all, Glend. They have no eyes! I looked carefully when he came over just now. The light hit him full in the face, and I could see nothing but inky blackness where his eyes ought to be."

"Really? What does that mean, do you think?

"I don't know, but I could wish for better escorts."

Glend laughed. "They're probably Hod-ya's idea of respectable."

"I don't know how you can take this so lightly," Jeda knelt by the water's edge and dipped her hand into the clear water. "I just know that something horrible awaits us in Pitland."

"Oh, Jeda, you're taking this too seriously. Do you suppose for one minute if anything sinister was in the offing that those two characters would be teamed with Ruark?"

"Bodyguards are one thing, coachmen another."

"Oh, come on, be realistic. This is all a show for our benefit. Hod-ya assigned two of the most anti-socials she could find to keep Pitland's mystique alive. You'll see, when we get there we'll be treated like queens."

"It's more probable she found the most agreeable bodyguards she could." Jeda splashed water on her face and let it dribble back into the stream, rippling her reflection.

"How your imagination runs on. Oh, look, over there—" Glend pointed at a file of ducklings trailing behind their mother under an overhanging bank. "Let's see how close we can get."

"I don't care to, but you go ahead. I think I'll investigate that copse of trees." At that Jeda headed upstream, periodically glancing back to make sure Glend wasn't following. Glend was hunched over, moving only when the ducks looked elsewhere, stalking the wild waterfowl and her chicks. At least one wary pair of eyes was on her most of the time, so her progress was slow.

Jeda smiled, tempted to join the fun, but a better way to spend the free time beckoned. She entered under the leafy canopy where a cool, refreshing breeze blew her tresses back as well as some of the silt off her dress. She followed the meandering brook deeper into the grove. Ghost-like fish darted away as she walked along the overhanging, mossy banks. Birds flitted overhead, and insects hummed; it was an idyllic setting and Jeda drank in the sights, sounds and aromatic smells of nature enfolding her. Seeing that she'd made a trail of bent grasses, Jeda ducked behind a shrub and waited for several moments to make sure she wasn't followed. She'd have to be careful. She patiently observed the clearing, now far behind. Ruark was tying feedbags on his horses; Glend made little progress stalking her ducks; as for the bodyguards, they were right where they'd been for the past four hours, sitting motionless inside the coach, staring straight ahead. Were they even conscious?

The sword enfolded in her skirts bumped against her calf.

"Dare I?"

She stepped further behind a thick hedgerow and carefully surveyed the tranquil scene. She was alone and far enough away, so she gripped the sword's handle and drew it out admiring the balance and strength of the blade. The raised, etched runes added to its beauty. How ironic that a young woman on her way to Pitland bore an enemy weapon! Even more illogical was the fact that she had no idea how to sharpen, let alone use this splendid weapon. Now only the tip glowed where Logon had last touched the sword, the rest was dull gray. Jeda decided to attempt tolling. She settled down on a rock, laid the sword across her lap and gingerly pushed the toller on the edge just below the shimmering point.

A soft melodic resonance filled her ears. Startled, Jeda caught her breath and frantically searched her surroundings for the music's source. The tone faded. Where had that pleasant tone come from?

She shifted her body to get more comfortable. As she did the toller rubbed the blade. Again, a melodious sound filled the air, soothing, comforting, refreshing. Jeda turned her gaze to the implements in her lap even as the sound faded. She then experimented, gliding the toller across the blade's edge. Again, the glen reverberated with the sweet sound.

"Oh, Logon!" Another cautious touch released yet another pure, sweet strain; a rune halfway down the blade shimmered briefly. It wasn't a raised rune; she wouldn't even have known of its presence had it not begun to glow. Were there other hidden runes on the sword? Jeda tolled by the disappeared rune to see what, if anything, would happen.

Once more the music sounded, and the rune flickered. She felt wrapped in peace, and this time words came to mind accompanying the melody. She closed her eyes and found herself singing along softly as she tolled the sword:

> From darkness and night, Comes freedom and light,
> 'Neath ocean deeps, O'er mountain steeps,
> Rose up the one, Rose up the son,
> Claiming his throne, Redeeming his own,
> Reaping the sown, Re-gathering the thrown,
> Bestowing fair gifts, With zephyrous uplift,
> Thus weak becomes strong, And meek endures long,
> As small becomes great, Let love dominate.

The music stopped abruptly but the thrill of the moment kept Jeda gently swaying, eyes closed.

"Jeda."

Jeda jerked in alarm and opened her eyes. Her toller tumbled to the ground. Before her stood a tall man in a hooded cloak. When she raised her sword defensively, however, she saw that every rune was merrily aglow.

The stranger laughed. "That sword cannot harm me." He threw back his cowl.

"Logon!" Jeda gasped. "You were here all this time? Why didn't I see you?"

"I am ever with you, Jeda, though you're not aware. But you see and hear me now, that's enough. Understand this, I seldom appear openly. But it's necessary for you that I do so at this moment. You journey into great peril, more dangerous than many of my warriors have encountered. You are going where the powerful are schooled in hatred; a place where people learn to manipulate and victimize others with cruelty, pain, and anguish."

Jeda's hands trembled. "I have no desire to go to such a place."

Logon lightly touched her shoulder. "My servants go where I send. Don't fear, for I'm with you. I'll be your courage and strength. Call upon me. I give you authority to use my name and the ability to use the weapon in your lap to resist your enemy. The Advisor will teach you even as he's shown you how to make your sword sing.

"In addition, I now bestow upon you a special ability to perceive things your mind hasn't learned and to make wise decisions beyond your years and experience. These are activities of the Advisor within you, so heed him; he'll lead you as I myself would. Toll your sword every chance you get, for the knowledge and wisdom you need will come as you learn the runes and rune-songs."

Jeda gazed into Logon's eyes.

"Beware of false friends; they can bring harm and tempt you to stain your dress. See to it that your dress stays spotless; stains will hinder you from hearing the Advisor. In days to come you'll need to clearly hear his voice. Do you understand?"

Jeda nodded.

"One more thing, Jeda."

"M'lord?"

"Be ever mindful that I've forgiven you of all."

"Oh, I am."

"Forgiveness is the key to freedom and guarding your freedom will protect you from deception."

Jeda blinked and was suddenly alone.

Had it really happened? Yes, the sword's runes were still alight, though fading. Logon had been there! She snatched up her toller and plied it to her sword, hoping to summon her liege back. But nothing happened. No glowing runes, no melody, nothing. Then she understood; he's not to be summoned like a servant, but rather, she was. She lowered her sword and hummed the runesong she'd just learned, recalling its encouragement:

From darkness and night, Comes freedom and light . . .

Logon had bestowed a gift upon her, like in the runesong— 'Bestowing fair gifts.' To know things she hadn't learned and to be wise beyond her years? But how? And why? How would she know when she received it?

" . . . as you learn the rune-songs," Logon's voice echoed.

Three quarters of an hour had passed. She guessed she wouldn't be missed yet, there was still time to file her sword and light some runes. Reassured of privacy after scanning the woods she settled back with toller in hand, not to conjure up her liege, but to learn. There was no melody, no exquisite sweetness permeating the air, just the dull scrape of iron on steel.

An engraved rune near the tip began glowing. She didn't know how to pronounce it, but the runic lesson was understood: Forgiveness. She'd lived in uncaring ignorance of Logon all her life, yet he was the most spectacular and truest person who'd ever lived. And he forgave. She'd accused him, he forgave; she hated him, he forgave; she rebelled, he forgave; she slandered, betrayed, denied—he forgave! On and on the lesson continued exposing things she'd never realized about herself.

Then another rune began glowing, a raised rune near the same site. As she continued, its lesson also was revealed: all those who follow Logon should expect to be treated harshly and ignored by those they helped; they'd be despised, falsely accused, slandered, hated, misunderstood, rebelled against, betrayed, yet, with Logon's help, they could and must forgive even as they'd been forgiven.

"Forgiveness is the key to freedom," Logon had said, and only now did she begin to comprehend. Clinging to past hurts only imprisoned her, making her a slave to hatred, wounded twice by the same offense. Hate and bitterness would dull one's ears to the Advisor. But forgiveness set people free to not only hear Logon's counsel but also to enjoy reconciliation and restoration. Tears coursed down her cheeks. She must make every effort to not justify resentment against anyone, not even Annessa, or, or Hod-ya! "Logon, oh, Logon, help me. Increase my ability to believe."

She gradually became aware of her name borne on the soft breeze. They were searching for her. She jumped up and tucked the sword and toller beneath her skirts then wiped her face of joyous tears.

Without warning bushes parted and out stepped Ruark, huffing heavily and wiping his brow with a large, red handkerchief.

"Oh. It's here you are, eh, m'lady?" Then he stopped short and scrutinized her. "Oh, you've been—" he looked carefully around, "with him."

Jeda's mouth dropped open. "Wh—what are you talking about?" She smoothed out her skirt, certain that Ruark couldn't possibly have seen either sword or toller.

Ruark cupped one hand to his lips. "Alfomega. I sense his afterglow." He stepped closer.

"Are you going to report me?"

He halted at arm's length. "Report you? Mercy, no." He withdrew a Child of the Stars from beneath his cloak, smiling broadly. Only an inch shone from the tip, but beside certain runes farther on down the blade were glowing splotches.

"But you work for the empire!"

"And I'm taking you to Pitland," countered the coachman.

"But I don't want to go," protested Jeda.

"Nor do I enjoy some aspects of my work, but I'll stay at my task till he shows me otherwise. All I really do is provide transportation. I have nothing to do with why someone goes. There are many other jobs I could do, but this one is harmless in and of itself. Besides, the horses love and trust me so much."

"Hod-ya knows?"

"Knows? That I'm a kingsman? Of course not! It would be my head if she knew. Then who'd care for my wife and feed my six darlings?" Ruark replaced his sword so cleverly and quickly that Jeda had no idea where it was hidden. "My six darlings are the horses, you know. We have no children."

"Oh."

"I said to myself there was something about you, Miss, but I wasn't sure. That's why I traced your steps after seeing to my darlings. I wanted to talk to you and see if I was right. When I saw you take leave of the other girl, I was pretty sure, for only an Ecclessite would seek to be alone on this journey."

"I've never seen a sword sharpened hit and miss like yours. Why do you do it like that?"

"Ah, you betray yourself as a Sharpointer. New recruit, perhaps?"

Jeda smiled sheepishly.

"I was trained in a Runer brigade. The reason my sword is, as you put it, 'hit and miss,' is because we only learn the most necessary runes. There are so many runes that it would be impossible to learn them all. Sharpening the entire blade and learning all the runes would take forever, and then what time would there be to earn a living?"

"I never thought about that. It's taken quite a bit of time and effort for me to light up just half an inch. I can see how selective sharpening would save time. But, how do you know which runes are necessary?"

"I'll show you." Ruark withdrew his sword in the blink of an eye and knelt, laying the sword on the moss. "This one," he pointed to a rune near the handle, "Is the rune of 'Rejoicing.' It teaches us to be joyful in our expectation of going to Splendora after we die."

Jeda's eyes followed as he pointed out more runes he'd illuminated: health, peace of mind, victory over Lurcan, authority in Logon's name, prosperity, and freedom from fear. "When you've learned these major lessons, you'll see you don't really need too much of the rest."

"What about Forgiveness? I see it isn't lit up on yours."

"Forgiveness? Well, of course, we know about it, but it's not something to spend a whole lot of time on, you know. I suppose I once spent some time learning it, but after you've learned it, why spend more time on it? After all, Alfomega has forgiven us, that's his responsibility. Our job is to discover the other promises he gives, like being happy and in good health. Things like that."

"But you've deliberately chosen only runes with nice meanings. What about endurance, hardship and suffering?"

"Now, now, my dear, you mustn't trouble your mind about such things. Alfomega has promised good things, not bad. But you'll see more clearly as you progress. You'd save much time and effort if you'll listen to me now, but do as you like."

Jeda asked, "How many people have you rescued?"

"We—ll," he shot a sidelong glance at her, "not many, exactly. But someday he'll bring people to me who want to know about Logon's promises. Then I'll be glad to show them."

"Um, I admit I'm inexperienced in these things, but it seems to me that you're the one wasting time by only polishing your favorite runes and not getting all of Logon's instruction." Jeda's bluntness surprised even herself, but it was said in sincerity, without criticism, and as such, she saw that Ruark found it hard to justify feeling offended.

"Now see here, Missy. I've been a kingsman nigh unto thirteen years. I should think if either of us knows the way of things, it wouldn't be a novice. But since you're new, I *forgive* your being so forward."

Boldness rose in Jeda, and though she could have foregone speaking, she blurted out, "Not so, Ruark. As time passes, your 'nice, cheery runes' won't enable you to be counted as loyal to Logon when you're put to the test. You'll have nothing to sustain you; it's possible you'd even deny knowing Logon."

Ruark's face reddened. But Jeda's concern was so evident that he could only sputter, "How can you say such things? What makes you, a novice, so sure of yourself?"

Jeda hesitated, then said, "I'm not sure how I know, but deep inside, I know that's what Logon wanted me to say to you. A time of testing will soon come upon you . . . "

It seemed as if Ruark was searching for a hint of haughtiness in her attitude but found only honesty. "We'd best get back; the hour is up, and you'll be missed." He stood and concealed his Child of the Stars.

Jeda secreted her sword away and followed the coachman, wondering how she'd dared to say such things. A phrase from the rune-song came to mind:

Bestowing fair gifts, With zephyrous uplift . . .

The runesong lingered, a sweet melody of hope.

CHAPTER TWELVE

"Wherever did you go?" Glend asked. The steady clop, clop, clop of horse hooves accentuated the coach's rumbling wheels. "When I finally realized I wasn't going to get anywhere with those ducks, I decided to look for you."

"I wasn't far away, Ruark found me easily enough."

"Well I looked and found no sign of you. In fact," Glend whispered in Jeda's ear, "even the 'scarecrows' were getting fidgety, like they were ready to come searching for you."

"Shh! They might hear what you call them."

Glend giggled. "I don't care if they do. Whether you want to admit it or not, we're the privileged class here, not them. Why, if they even rebuke us, severe repercussions will fall on their heads and they know it. The sooner you trust what I say, the sooner you'll enjoy your new station in life."

Jeda gazed at the passing scenery. "Look out there, will you?"

Glend obliged and looked out her window. "So?"

"It's mid-afternoon, but see how dark it is? Either a storm is building, or these woods have gotten very dense."

A grating sound erupted from behind. Jeda turned to see what caused it and realized the hideous noise was Hod-ya's bodyguards laughing! Even Glend looked unnerved by their weird expression of laughter.

The deepening surrounding forest gloom and the bizarre laughter of the bodyguards only served to deepen the oppressive atmosphere.

"What is it?" Jeda challenged the blackguards. "What's so amusing?"

"Ra-Amawl," scratched the more talkative of the duo.

"What was that? Ra— what?"

The sinister guards glanced at each other, then hissed again before the spokesman hoarsely replied, "Ra-Amawl. Forest Ra-Amawl." He pointed out the window, "Dread moot, Ra-Amawl."

"Dreads?" Visions of imaginary terror filled Jeda's mind.

Glend regained her composure. "Oh, they're just trying to scare us." Then turning to face the guards chided, "You really don't have to keep it up. We're not impressed with your little games, see? We know what goes on in Pitland, so you can drop the act."

The guards silently regarded Glend who had to strain looking over her shoulder to stare them down. But with the carriage jostling and the failing light added to the fact she couldn't locate any eyes in the dronnets' masks, she gave up.

"Oh bother." She turned back around darting angry looks at Jeda. "Don't encourage them, at least."

"Scrarth," rattled the much-unused throat of the hitherto silent bodyguard. Both girls turned. "You be Scrarth!" he reiterated, pointing at Glend.

"My name is not Scarth," Glend retorted, purposely mispronouncing it.

"Not name. You become . . . Scrarth."

"I wager her become Avangar," the other pointed at Jeda.

"We're to be given new names?" Jeda asked.

"Not names." Both guards hissed, filling the coach with the horrible noise of their laughter.

Glend was about to scold them again, but Jeda nudged her, advising, "Don't."

Glend wrinkled her nose and turned back around front. "What do you make of 'Scrarth' and 'Avangar'?"

"I have no idea. But something is very, very strange with how they're acting. It's this forest; like it's awakened them."

Glend glanced nervously over her shoulder. Sure enough, an animated change had come over the two blackguards. Prior to this they hardly stirred. They now seemed even more sinister.

"I've figured out their riddle, at least part of it. Do you remember the scary stories your mother told when you were young?" posed Jeda.

"Come on, Jeda, enough is enough. Scary stories indeed! You're playing right into their hands. You can't believe that stuff about the Chimeree."

"No, they're not here now, or there'd be a greater sense of evil in the air if the legends are true. But, when they do meet this is probably where they come, Ramal, den of the ten, the Council of the Ten. Don't you see, Ramal in the old stories must be Ra-Amawl? The Den of the Ten relates to the ten dreads of the gate."

"You believe what you want; as far as I'm concerned this is nothing more than a dense forest." Glend sulkily stared out her window.

There were goosebumps on Glend's arms. And rightly so, mused Jeda, they were heading into perils beyond description and Glend was totally unprepared. Glend must have at least one opportunity to hear about Logon. But, until Glend perceived her need, Jeda could say nothing.

The carriage rumbled the afternoon hours away penetrating deeper into primal forest. By mid-afternoon Jeda took note that they'd passed fewer and fewer intersecting roads. The trees on either side became huge and close-grown, with overhead bowers so tightly woven that the leafy canopy blotted out the sky. In effect, the road seemed more like a tunnel than a highway. The deeper they went the more it seemed the forest was resentful at their intrusion. It was little wonder they'd encountered no foot-travelers. As for horsemen, there were a few; those were mostly messengers pressing on to appointed destinations, never pausing to exchange greetings.

Conversely, the bodyguards' animation increased with the forest's gloom. They whispered frequently to each other and eagerly peered out the windows for landmarks known only to them.

Jeda and Glend, on the other hand, were more subdued.

Ruark slackened his team's pace after several hours of trotting into the ominous weald. The girls shared concerns that they might have to spend the night on the road in spooky Ra-Amawl. The "scarecrows" were exhilarated, however, whispering freely back and forth as if anticipating something deliciously evil.

Ruark slowed the horses to a walk, cooling them as they approached their next rest.

Glend stuck her head out the window and called up to the coachman, "I had hoped we'd rest at an inn for the night instead of this dank old forest."

A slide opened above the girl's heads, revealing Ruark's round, wind-burned face. "I'm sorry, m'lady," he apologized, "I meant to let you know. I don't suppose they'd have told you, but about two miles up the road is Suffer's Tree Inn. We'll stop there for the night. By the way, while we're there you'd be wise to stick close to your bodyguards."

"Why?" demanded Glend, but the portal had already clicked shut.

A gloved finger tapped Jeda's shoulder making her start. The guard pointed to a forest clearing just ahead. Glend also leaned over to see. A notch had been cut, or burned, out of the thick woods. The first thing they noticed was that it was raining heavily. Before this clearing came into view the overhead canopy had been too dense to allow rain to fall to the ground, but here the rain splattered incessantly on rounded, moss-covered rocks that littered a couple of acres of ground.

"How peculiar so many cobblestones are gathered in this field, all the same size. Was this once a fortress or something?" Jeda asked. A clearing opened on the other side of the road, revealing more of the uniformly shaped stones.

The bodyguards hissed for several seconds, then one said, "Look closer."

Jeda squinted, discerning more detail in this unusual field of stones. Suddenly her palm gripped the hand rest and her knuckles went white as she gasped and sat back, silent, shutting her eyes.

Jeda felt Glend's body lean across her lap as she peered closer at the landscape and a moment later recoiled back. Jeda peeked through her fingers and saw that all color had drained from Glend's face.

The dronnets sitting behind them reveled in sighting the expansive field of skulls, as if revisiting a favorite tourist destination. This scene of carnage-past enlivened the bodyguards to an even higher activity level, though it was now but an old woody paddock of moss and lichen-covered bones on the ground.

One of the guards grated, "Great battle. Kingsman fort destroyed. All dead, some eaten alive! Dreads, tophets, cusps. Hod-ya earn great honor here."

Jeda removed her hands from her eyes.

Glend stared at her feet, occasionally looking up to see if they'd passed the horrible sight yet. She finally whispered, "It's only trees now, Jeda."

Jeda looked up with an angry light in her eyes. "Do you still think it's all show?"

Glend's hands trembled. "I, I don't know what to think. Hod-ya wouldn't lie to me."

"Anyone who'd participate—attained great honor— in that, would lie to you."

"I don't believe tophets, or cusps, or, or any of those things really exist. I don't, I can't believe in them."

"You mean you won't," Jeda kept her voice low for only Glend to hear. "You'd better change your mind; this journey is going to end very differently from what you're expecting. We're in danger, but you more so than I."

"Oh? And why is that?" Glend's face reddened. "Just remember which one of us has been getting personal instruction from Hod-ya for weeks, nay, months. You hardly know her. That, back there, was just some ancient battle field, that's all."

Jeda remained silent.

"Scrarth," muttered the blackguard behind Glend.

A brake squeaked, and the carriage lurched to a halt in the court-yard of an inn, announcing an end to this leg of their journey. The horses stomped as if anxious to be unharnessed, groomed, and fed.

Ruark climbed down and greeted a short, stout person running from the shadows of the inn's front stoop to grasp the reins while Ruark attended his passengers. The inn's windows emitted a welcoming candlelight glow promising a friendly environment.

"Out with you now, m'ladies," said Ruark. "You might want to cover your heads against this rain. And mind what I said about staying close to your dronnets. This is a villainous place. Trust no one." He gave each girl a hand down then bustled away to assist the stable lad.

With mild surprise Jeda noted the stable hand was a hunchback. But then, this was Ra-Amawl where the bizarre was normal.

One of the bodyguards exited the coach and beckoned, "Follow," as he headed for the inn's main door. Jeda and Glend followed side by side, carrying their own hand-satchels atop their heads as protection from the rain, glad to finally be out of the coach. The other guard came last.

The inn's musty atmosphere was thick with the combined odors of pipe smoke, stale beer, and unwashed bodies. Candles fluttered in wall sconces every few feet along the length of the room. Wagon-wheel candelabras dribbling wax on the spokes hung suspended from rafters. Inside a crowd, mostly men, sang heartily and drunkenly danced as Jeda and Glend entered. The singing and dancing slowed as all eyes fastened on the two pretty girls entering their grog-garden.

The lead dronnet ignored the attention his charges received and headed toward the far end of the room where a walk-in-fireplace warmed the room with flames licking upward around a mound of logs. An occasional downdraft from the flue puffed billows of blue-gray smoke into the room and across the stained ceiling. A table sat before the fireplace occupied by two husky, bearded men, their faces close in private discussion. Across the room four men tortured musical instruments: a tambourine, a stringed box with an attached fret board, and two flutes, one large and one small—making more of a racket than music. A nearby group of men turned their attention away from Glend and Jeda to resume laughing at each other as they attempted to perform a tricky dance step. Clustered elsewhere around the perimeter of the room were sullen, grim-faced men returning to their gaming tables. Other men sat at the bar aloof from the other societies in the tavern, near attaining their goal of drinking themselves into oblivion. Behind the bar was the bartender, a tall, burly man who offered no greeting as would have been customary anywhere else but in Ra-Amawl. Instead, he stood rooted behind his bar, annoyed at every interruption.

Glend glanced at the hard, unsmiling faces of cruel, dangerous men around the room and sidled closer to Jeda. There wasn't a friendly visage in the lot. What had sounded like merriment from the outside was, in reality, a desperate exercise in dissipation. The leering stairway guards back at the palace were nothing compared to the peril in this hostile place. And Hod-ya had only sent two bodyguards . . .

"An hour?" Jeda whispered to the nearest guard as they tagged along toward the fireplace.

"Overnight," rasped the blackguard. He then motioned for his companion to go to the innkeeper who had done nothing but stare. "Arrange rooms, meals."

The second blackguard nodded and headed toward the bar.

The first bodyguard stood beside the table where the two burly men still discussed their plans. When they paid him no mind other than a quick upward glance, he commanded, "Move."

Like everyone else, these two men had watched with interest as the two pretty girls blundered into this cutthroat lair. At the dronnet's command however, the larger and meaner-looking of the two got to his feet, tipping his chair over in the process. He was as tall as the bodyguard, but broader and with muscular arms and brawny fists.

"Jest who does yer think yer be's, tellin' me an' me comrade ter move? Yer lady friends be's welcome. But yer scrawny bones had best not upset me, see?" He stepped around the table and got nose to nose with the dronnet.

The bodyguard at the bar turned away from the barman for a moment, observed the situation, hissed briefly, and resumed instructions to the barkeep.

The man's companion rose and stood beside his friend. "Hey, Blarn, I heard about these guys. Don't mess with him. These half-hooded guys are in some kind of elite outfit. We'll find another table."

"Humph! Don't look so tough ter me." Blarn grinned maliciously. "Hey boogerman, be's yer tough? Hey, I be's talkin' ter yer. Cain't yer hear wi' thet hood o'er yer ears?"

"Listen to friend," the blackguard's dispassionate tone grated.

"Lissen ter friend," Blarn mocked, rasping his voice purposely. "Hey yer boogerman, Hey." Blarn poked the bodyguard's shoulder with a forefinger. "Hey boogerman, yer hain't learnt how to talk too good, has yer? Hey! And where ats yer eyes, boogerman?"

"Blarn," his friend begged in a quavering voice.

The dronnet slowly raised his right arm, fingers splayed.

Blarn swiped at the inside of the dronnet's arm to knock it aside, but the grasping, gloved hand wasn't swayed an inch from its course. In another instant the hand scrunched the flesh of Blarn's dumbstruck features into one compressed area around his nose. The dronnet then hoisted the ruffian several inches off the floor with one hand.

"Now you move!" The bodyguard's arm dipped, then released like a steel spring.

Blarn landed atop the blazing logs in the walk-in fireplace, sending sparks and a cloud of smoke rolling from under the mantel into the beerhall.

The tavern's other denizens looked on in stunned silence, all that is, except the other bodyguard who hissed loudly.

It took Blarn a few seconds to regain his senses and discover that his breeches were smoldering. With a yelp he rolled out of the fireplace, flailing his arms and legs, shouting, "Trefta! Trefta, put me out!"

Trefta rushed to Blarn's aid, hauling him to his feet and smacking his britches, finally dousing him with a mug of ale. Trefta then gathered their belongings and pulling his stunned friend along by the sleeve vacated the table, pausing just long enough to collect their coats off the hooks by the door as they left the inn.

As soon as the door slammed shut, the revelers returned to their previous pursuits. From time to time glances were cast at the newcomers—only the focus had shifted from Jeda and Glend to their escorts.

The barman suddenly discovered his manners, treating the bodyguard waiting before him with deference. The lead bodyguard righted the overturned chair and sat at the table he'd won, indicating Jeda and Glend to do likewise. He sat with his back to the fire keeping his eyes sweeping the room. Each patron coming under the mysterious blackguard's scrutiny wisely occupied himself with his own business; none daring to stare back. The musicians re-started their music and the men that had been dancing returned to their clumsy stomping but shortly gave up, having lost the spirit for it. All around men broke into small groups, speaking lowly, darting furtive glances at the table in front of the fireplace.

The other blackguard preceded the barman who carried a tray of beverages. The dronnet occupied the remaining chair, whispered briefly into his companion's ear then both leaned back and silently scanned the room.

Jeda was greatly relieved. "I think that our escorts are for our protection more than we realized. Do you still think it's all a show?"

"I have my doubts, nevertheless, I believe the shrine of Psa isn't as malevolent as you forebode."

Steaming mugs were set before the girls while large, foamy tankards were placed in front of the guards.

"What's this?" Jeda had never thought twice about imbibing strong beverages before meeting Logon, and under normal circumstances would have given it little thought; but now she needed to keep her wits about her.

"Who cares?" said Glend. "The stronger the better."

"It's hot cider, Miss," replied the barman uncharacteristically polite. "Will roast duck and vegetables be satisfactory for your dinner?"

"Oh, that would be nice," replied Jeda. Glend nodded vigorous agreement.

The outside door across the room opened and Ruark, dripping wet, stepped in shaking his coattails. Upon spying his party, he made straight for their table. The inn's other guests returned to their own business as soon as they noted the similarity of his uniform to that of the bodyguards.

"Now, that's the most disinterested reception I've ever received here," Ruark commented pulling another chair to the table. "Hullo, Barkeep."

"Hullo yourself, Ruark," returned the barman, waiting for the dronnets to order. "You're traveling with rather sophisticated folk this time, ain'tcha?"

"You've noticed!" A smile tugged at the corners of the coachman's mouth.

"While you were out tending your team, your friends here made quite an impression."

"I did see two men leave a short while ago, putting their coats on as they went. Did they insult the young ladies?"

"Didn't get a chance. The big fella didn't want to give up his seat."

"Oh." Ruark raised his eyebrows, looking to Jeda. "Well, what's for supper? I'm about half starved."

"Roast duck with trimmings."

"Ah, sounds good. Bring me a brew, too, whatever they're having." He indicated the foamy tankards by the guards. "Now you girls understand why I said to stay close to your guards." Ruark looked around. "You'll have nothing to fear from the rascals at this inn, I think."

"You're soaked through! Is it raining that hard?" asked Jeda.

"You don't know the half of it." The portly coachman shucked his cape and hung it over the back of his seat. "It's a downpour the likes of which I've seldom seen! It's ankle deep over the ground. Seems we arrived in the nick of time, else we might've been stranded in the forest until the storm let up."

Glend set her mug on the table and asked, "Is there a danger of flooding?"

"I think not. Such rains seldom last more than half an hour. I should think it'll be clear by the morrow to resume our journey."

"How close are we?" Jeda, gazed at the fire. "To Pitland, I mean?"

"Oh, about four days to the border, with no hindrances, of course," answered Ruark.

"Well then, are we nearly out of this dreadful forest?" Jeda asked. "It's so thick, and dense, and, and like a presence."

"Now, now, Jeda, face facts. You're on your way to Pitland. If the road leading there is gloomy, what do you expect of your destination? Ra-Amawl gets denser, and angrier with each mile. Then, just inside the border of Pitland lies the White Priestess' Castle where the sky is always like night."

"What are you saying?" asked Glend. "That we'll not see the natural light of the sun till we come back?"

"Light of the sun? If light of the sun is what you prefer you should never have ventured on this journey. From this point on, the only natural light we'll have will be the lamps on my coach. If it's light you want, you'll have to provide your own." Ruark winked slyly at Jeda. "Most likely," he turned to Glend, "*if* you return, you'll be more like your guards who see better at night. Most who go this way usually have no love for light, else they wouldn't go. And none who stay more than a couple of days have ever returned without renouncing light." He somberly stared at Jeda.

"Talk too much," said the lead guard. "Food comes. Eat."

The barman arrived with a young girl in tow who had curly, brown hair hanging in bangs to her eyebrows and flowing down her back; both bore laden trays. Despite her cute, pixie face, the girl's brown eyes were forlorn, and her face was etched with the hardness of roadhouse life. Jeda guessed the girl to be but a couple of years younger than herself, but her features bespoke the seamier, rough side of life. Jeda's heart ached for her. If only she could tell her about Logon . . .

The barman placed slices of roast duck with greens, bread, and an apple tart before Ruark, Jeda, and Glend while the girl served the dronnets. For a brief moment the girl's eyes met Jeda's. Jeda gave her a friendly smile.

Hostility flared in the girl's eyes and she quickly turned her head.

"Have a care there, Tressa, or you'll spill something," snapped the barman.

She cringed as if expecting a kick. "Sorry Papa, I'll be more careful." She presented the plates and left without a backward look.

"Little wench!" growled the barman. "Hain't nothing but trouble, that one. I gotta watch her every second or she'll make woe for me."

"Send to Hod-ya," suggested a dronnet. "Fix her."

"What? Give her to that witchy woman? She'd learn her to put curses on me. Then I'd be worse off. There, now, is there anything else you need?"

"Have we rooms for the night?" asked Ruark.

"All taken care of, Ru. Once the gentleman explained your mission, I had no problem securing rooms for you and the ladies. When you're ready I'll have Tressa show you the way."

"Fine, fine. I don't really need a room though. I'll sleep with my darlings in the stable. That way we'll all sleep better," said Ruark, digging into his supper.

CHAPTER THIRTEEN

GLEND ROLLED TO HER SIDE of the creaky bed, pulling most of the coverlet with her.

Jeda lay still, listening to the rain drumming on the inn roof. Thunder rolled incessantly, dull and thudding rather than crashing; thick foliage surrounding the inn probably muted much of the storm's din.

Earlier Jeda overheard customers talking about the storm's unusual intensity and duration. She harbored hope that she could slip away and toll her Child of the Stars. To her dismay the bodyguards stationed themselves in the hallway right outside their door. There'd be no chance to slip away like Dancel did in the palace. Remembering Dancel brought a smile to her lips.

Glend muttered in her sleep, tensed for a moment, sighed, and relaxed.

Deciding it was worth the risk, Jeda slipped out of bed, tip-toed across the room and rummaged through her clothing. She glanced back at Glend, who, thankfully, slept like the dead. Jeda positioned some garments over a chair back shielding her from Glend's view. Then, taking a deep breath, she withdrew her sword and toller. She hesitated a moment before softly applying the toller. The gray edge under the toller sprang to a brilliant keenness. As if there were arms around her Jeda felt wrapped in Logon's love. A hidden rune near the handle, several inches down from where she intended to toll, flickered. She considered for a moment, then stroked the blade by the point again but the rune near the handle flared once more, as if vying for her attention. She resolutely tolled near the point again, and again the remote rune lit brightly. Jeda heard, or rather sensed, words. She looked up and there was a shimmering column of light hovering an arm's length away. An unexpected thought coursed through her mind.

"Toll the rune that beckons."

Was it Logon? Or was it lightning reflecting through the window? It lasted only as long. Flan had advised her to sharpen the sword in a consistent manner, picking up daily where she'd left off. That was why she'd rebuked Ruark who only tolled beside the runes he liked. She wanted to learn all Logon's directives, not just the pleasant ones, and she wanted to learn them in order.

Another flash of lightning and dull thunder rumbled through the un-shuttered window. Again, unbidden thoughts crossed her mind,

"Toll the rune that beckons."

Then the room went dark except for the glow of her sword's tip and the fading rune near the haft.

"Well, what's the harm?" Jeda timidly touched her toller to the deeper etching. The rune flashed brightly casting shadows on wall and ceiling. And this time the glow was sustained. Encouraged, she gave a hearty stroke and her eyes were dazzled with the light. A barely audible vibration rising from the blade became a bittersweet melody. With the melody were words. She closed her eyes as she tolled, savoring the runesong.

"Sing the lament of Ra-Amawl,

Learn the dirge, beauty defiled,
Once so light and fair of promise,
So clean the soil, and waters pure,
Air was sweet, so newly made,
And all things green, alive, and vibrant,
From grassy blades to stalk-ed crop,
Low moss and fern, high flower and tree,
Thus grew the green of Ra-Amawl,
So bright with verdure, Elyon's steps,
And full of good in Elyon's eye.

At peace was she, sweet Ra-Amawl,
No harm nor threat, no thought disturbed,
The dark was light, and light alive,
From ground to sky was open view,
No shame had she, no need to hide,
Unstained earth from roamers gaze,
Then small and furry came the quick,
For harmony midst the green,
Young and beauteous Ra-Amawl.
Her leaf and fruit provided for,
The creepers and the flying ones,
And life abundant grew and teemed,
In and 'round fair Ra-Amawl,
The kine and hare, hart and bear,
Low mouse and Elyon's giants,
Roamed midst the trees, so long ago,
So long ago sweet Ra-Amawl,
So full of good in Elyon's eye.

Then came the three who are the one,
Who made it all, and paused,
And scooped a hand of soft, moist soil,

To form image of himself,
Into lump of fresh, form-ed earth,
Life he blew, and image waked,
To love and tend and watch and keep,
And rule this most beloved place,
Harmless, fruitful, joyous Ra-Amawl,
Dwelling of the form of him,
Who ruled o'er kingdoms vast,
Who walked delighting in her, his work,
And honored her with garden regent,
So full of good in Elyon's eye.

The image named and power bestowed,
To reign with love productive,
And strong she grew, and pleased him much,
This beloved Ra-Amawl,
For sweet commune and friendship true,
Gave all the realm to him,
For the likeness of the one,
Did all things well, for well he loved,
For she, too, bore hint of him,
And well returned his loving touch.
Thus maker, Elyon, oft would come,
Delighted in love's produce,
For 'tis the way of giving out,
Supplies the giver more,
So full of good in Elyon's eye.

Came the cycle, full circle round,
And birthing time was born,
And every legged and rooted thing,
Found how renews the line,
Families formed of groups and kinds,
And types were named by regent,

Thus strong and thriving Ra-Amawl,
Spread from corner of her place,
To turn the barren, lifeless rock,
To living, loving, gentle grace,
For all things seen in Elyon's realm,
For without there was no other,
So full of good in Elyon's eye.

One thing yet lacked,
Said Elyon, the one among the three,
To bring shadow to complete,
In things present, past, to come,
So rib from image taken was,
A helper, wife and bride,
The union blessed and fruit was borne,
And fairer still waxed Ra-Amawl,
Grown fuller, spreading out,
Conquering unliving stone,
For image of image was fairer still,
A thing of glorious wonder,
To him who ruled and dwelt and loved,
And tended sweet, young Ra-Amawl,
So full of good in Elyon's eye.

How came the dark'ning night to be,
The loving turned to hate?
Whence ugliness and not the fair,
How pain instead of grace?
Whence are the creatures gentle, soft,
How grew the fang and claw?
Whence blade and vine so generous,
Grew picker, thorn and spine?
Water, air, once so clean,
Now grudging in their gift?

Created, living, humble things,
So proud their howling raise?
Is nothing left of Ra-Amawl,
The sweet, the tender, kind?
Has all fallen to such estate,
So bitterly despised?
But fit for wrath in Elyon's eye?

Breeding anger seethes within,
Shame has locked her boughs,
She cannot bear for him to see,
How bloodstained now her sod,
Rampant hate, with cruelty strong,
And ruthless, gloating passion,
She moans and groans and hides away,
Dismayed at her confusion,
She bears not well injury done,
So hostile unto her,
When image of the image,
Wrongly rose and led,
Image of the one did naught,
But joined her in her folly,
Thence came the wrath of he who made,
To be as made to be,
Thence fled the love and joy and peace,
And lost was all that once was,
So full of good in Elyon's eye.

Turned now has fair Ra-Amawl,
To den of murderous thieves,
With silent phantoms gliding by,
And seething hate unleashed,
They harbor there, for cover thick,
Has made a hiding place,

Till dawns the day of semblance real,
By fire and water cleansed,
Descends the son to claim his bride,
O'er-riding all that's foul,
Remade will be the garden place,
Re-birthed fair Ra-Amawl,
When kingsmen rise to claim their own,
Done with sour and shame,
White tunics all, and glowing swords,
Invoking words of power,
And comes the heir of all things seen,
And unseen things as well,
To rule his realm in virtuous love,
And Ra-Amawl again,
No longer will be brooding,
But loved and loving, again at peace,
Fulfilling her high mission,
To seed produce and be the first,
Formed image of the image of the image,
And full of good in Elyon's eye!

The melody faded, the lament complete. Visions in her mind's eye conjured by the words ceased. Jeda's toller stilled.

The actual Ra-Amawl she'd seen, now hateful and angry, hadn't always been that way. King Elyon's work began here. Ecclessa was founded later, but originally Ra-Amawl knew the joyous presence of the king. Brida's deception came later, the meteorite-of-offense came later; Ra-Amawl was where Elyon had placed life beginning with his animals, birds, insects, and fish. And from Ra-Amawl's soil mankind was formed. There was much about the runesong Jeda didn't understand, but she grasped the essentials.

Despite appearances, Ra-Amawl wasn't a product of Lurcan's hate; King Elyon had created it. Lurcan's evil had only twisted what Elyon had made. Lurcan had no power other than that of corrupting. The anger that Jeda sensed in the forest was not toward her or even King Elyon, but against Lurcan. Could the forest, in some strange way be her ally? Was help to be found in that dark, brooding forest? Might it be her escape?

Her lips moved imperceptibly asking Logon to explain why he'd brought her this way and why he'd shown her The Lament of Ra-Amawl.

Glend stirred and rolled over but remained asleep.

Outside, a drenching rain continued, though the thunder and lightning had ceased. Jeda continued communing with Logon, offering up inexpressibly deep concerns from within. Artka came to mind, along with the rest of her family, and others, too; Dancel, Gwinnid, Smid, Flan and Jorna . . .

She quietly sang a runesong she'd learned at her first and only brigade meeting.

> *You bring the light into my life,*
> *Yours is the joy, ending all strife,*
> *Desire of the Ages, be close to me,*
> *I need your love, to set me free.*

How aptly the words fit with what she'd just learned about Ra-Amawl. Tears filled Jeda's eyes. She whispered the chorus over and over, receiving hope. Though she was surrounded by hardened, cruel people, it was true, Logon couldn't be kept out of any place his followers went. Now that she was in Ra-Amawl so was Logon!

Footsteps in the outside corridor and a muffled, masculine voice followed by a brief rap on a door just down the corridor broke the quiet. A few seconds later a girl gave a sleepy, muffled reply, then the footsteps retreated, followed by lighter, shuffling steps. Jeda and Glend's door bumped against its jamb as if someone had been leaning against it but suddenly stood away. Looking up Jeda noted gray light filtering through the window.

A fist banged on the door and a blackguard croaked, "Get up." He banged the door once more for effect, then went down the passageway.

Glend rolled over groaning, only then realizing Jeda wasn't in bed. "Jeda? Where are you?"

Jeda had passed the entire night tolling and communing with Logon. "I'm here," she wrapped a petticoat around her sword. It only seemed like minutes, possibly an hour, but certainly not the whole night!

"What are you doing over there? And what was that strange light?"

Jeda covered the petticoat hiding her sword. "I was uncomfortable in bed, so I spent the night here."

"Spending the night on the floor can't be very refreshing."

"Oh, but it is!" She'd never uttered truer words.

A knock on the door was followed by a girl's voice, "Your toiletries, m'ladies."

CHAPTER FOURTEEN

THE TAVERN'S ONLY INHABITANTS THAT morning other than Hod-ya's party were a couple of messengers seeking shelter from the storm. One of these, a raw-boned, good-looking chap sitting alone perked up as Glend and Jeda trailed their guards into the dining room. He was tall and muscular, with bright blue eyes peering from beneath shaggy brows; his half-combed, dark brown hair hung over his collar. He was rough-hewn but had none of the sinister demeanor of the previous evening's revelers. His dress was part military, but more overtly, woodsman. As he wolfed down his breakfast, he didn't take his eyes off the girls, especially Jeda. As a result, bits of egg, bacon, and toast littered his table.

Breakfast fare was ample and tasty unlike the mush she'd been served in Marga's kitchen; Jeda was surprised to find that she liked the simple cuisine of outlanders better than the dainties she'd grown up with in her father's house.

While the girls finished breakfast the messenger approached their table. "I assume you're with Ruark's party?" he addressed the dronnets.

The bodyguards bristled when the stranger made no attempt to hide his staring at the young ladies while pretending to address the guards.

"I'm Juued, courier of the captain of the guard of the White Priestess." Juued then boldly turned and faced Jeda. "And I assume you're the lady in charge of this expedition?"

"Certainly not!" Jeda blushed. "Hod-ya is in charge. My companion and I are being taken to—"

"Say not Pitland." The messenger frowned.

The lead bodyguard hissed like a viper as he slapped a curved knife atop the table. "Tend own business."

Turning his head toward the blackguard Juued retorted, "This is my business if you're on your way to Pitland. During the night I came up the road you must take."

Jeda remembered the thug who'd refused to give up his seat and feared for the young man's safety.

"Ruark asked me to inform you that, in his opinion, the road is too dangerous to travel. I, myself crossed a bridge late last night only a few miles south; even then it was under several inches of water. Ruark fears the bridge's foundations might have washed away so he's gone to investigate. He asked me to let you know. He also asked me to look after the young ladies till he returned. I suppose he knew they'd not get much companionship from the two of you."

Jeda glanced nervously at Glend who likewise looked concerned for the man's welfare.

The guard's hand moved toward the knife handle but just as his fingers wrapped around the weapon, with lightning swift speed Juued whipped out a Child of the Stars!

Jeda gasped.

The dronnets sprang to their feet overturning their chairs.

The other blackguard drew his knife.

Juued smiled and placed the sword on the table. "I know how you must win the right to be in the dronnet corps, in single combat with a Craniantium lion, right? Well, you're not the only warriors away from the front lines. The kingsman I relieved of this prize just a fortnight ago had it glowing clear to here," he indicated the hiltguard's double-winged birds. "You know that this didn't fall easily into my power, either."

For several seconds the three men stared at each other: Juued's dull, un-lighted sword was still on the table but his hand rested firmly on the haft as the blackguards menacingly waved their blades in small circles. The lead guard suddenly sheathed his weapon and motioned for his companion to follow suit. They righted their chairs and sat at table as before.

"An Ecclessite sword," marveled Glend. "This deep in Carnalia! Maybe they do have brigades everywhere. May I see it?"

"Of course." Juued was only too pleased to have the young ladies admire his trophy.

"Fool! Dangerous souvenir," grated the usually quiet blackguard.

"Ah, but I've dominated its power. I took the glow completely out of it; they're only dangerous if they glow." He watched, smiling as Glend's finger traced an etched rune.

"What are these curious markings?" Glend looked up. "I've never seen anything so intricate, so marvelous. It almost makes me think that there is a real king in Ecclessa. Something as fine as this wasn't produced in Carnalia, I'm sure."

"And there you are most certainly correct, Miss—"

"I'm Glend, and she's Jeda."

The lead bodyguard's throat rumbled as Juued bent forward to kiss their hands.

Juued ignored the warning and flashed a winsome smile at them, Jeda in particular. "Very pleased to make your acquaintances. May I?" he asked, pulling a chair from a nearby table.

"No," said a blackguard.

"Please do," Glend with a flip of her hair grinned at the brash interloper.

Juued sat. "Thank you, I believe I will. Besides, we," he pointed at the blackguards, "need to discuss something important. Certain rumors have arisen in the White Priestess' castle that might be of interest to you. But first, I'd like to talk to the ladies. It's been so long since I've been in the company of such rare beauty."

Jeda's face warmed, and as she turned to Glend, saw that her cheeks were rosier than usual. Glend finished her examination of the sword and offered it back.

Juued then extended it toward Jeda, "Perhaps you'd like to examine this magical weapon which I won in mortal combat?"

Jeda recoiled. "Oh no, that's quite all right. I've no need to examine it."

"Really!" It was a comment, not a question. He smiled and winked at her.

"Oh, go ahead, Jeda," urged Glend. "It truly is a remarkable piece of work. You never did tell me about these markings, Juued."

"You're right," He laid the sword on the table. "When a master warrior, like the one I dispatched, earns a sword, their Magician chants fey spells upon the blade which make it glow with an eerie, blue light. This supposedly gives them power over their enemies."

"So that's what that light was by you this morning, Jeda," Glend teased. "I know your secret now. You're an Ecclessite sword-maiden en-route to overthrow the White Priestess with your spells." Glend and Juued laughed gaily.

Jeda's eyes widened as she gulped, "Oh, now you've found me out. And I thought I was keeping my secret so well. I suppose I have no choice but to slay you all."

Glend and Juued found this even more amusing; the blackguards regarded Juued coldly.

Juued then said, "In truth, as I stabled my horse in the wee morning hours, I thought I heard the sound of a file, as is oft heard from Ecclessite encampments before battle. They're obsessed with sharpening their swords before battles. I don't know how they do it, though, for I've tried every file known to man on this sword to no effect. In fact, the file is useless after only a couple of strokes, destroyed by the sword's unusual metal."

"You know, after seeing this magnificent weapon, I do begin to believe there might be an Ecclessite king," reasserted Glend. "I shudder to think how cruel he must be to produce weapons that destroy iron files. But, if his weapons are stronger, wouldn't he be stronger than our emperor?"

"Stupid girl!" erupted the senior bodyguard leaning forward. "Not talk stupid."

"Well, excuse me!" Glend's eyes flashed. "I meant nothing."

The blackguard leaned back and returned his eyeless stare to Juued.

"Why don't you girls join me where we can talk more freely," Juued waved his hand, "over at that table by the window?"

"I'd rather not, but please, Glend, feel free, if you like." Jeda hoped to get alone.

Glend smiled. "I'd be delighted."

"Not go," rasped the lead guard. "Soon leave." He then turned to Juued, demanding, "What business?"

"Eh, business? Oh, yes," he stroked his whiskers "Would you, by any chance, know an Ugen, officer of the dronnets, I believe?"

The blackguards glanced at each other. "We know Ugen."

"Did you know he's been at the White Priestess' castle?"

"Ugen at Insurrecta." stated the senior guard.

"Uh-huh. That's what I thought, too, until I was given a message to take first to Insurrecta, to his second in command, Flarg, if memory serves, who was to put Insurrecta's seal on it and then send it on to Cosmopolis making it look like the message originated in Insurrecta. Imagine my surprise when Ugen himself put the letter in my pouch right there in the White Priestess' castle. He's been there for three months. Now, why am I telling you this? After all, what could a simple messenger care about politics and coups? Understand, I have no political connections or loyalties whatsoever, and I don't really care who supplants or who's removed. But there's a rumor afoot that a strong challenger has arisen for the Scrarth and Avangar tournament, presenting a real threat to Hod-ya, especially if one of her most trusted lieutenants is betraying her."

Both blackguards leaned forward, their attention riveted.

"Yes, I thought that might interest you."

"Who challenges?" grated the spokesman.

"Who indeed? Suppose I mentioned the name of a lady from Craniantium, a very great lady, with strong support who has risen to prominence by capturing Ecclessite fortresses by stealth without shedding blood? Furthermore, rumors abound that this lady is a known consort of a dread, and might even have the ear of the emperor himself?"

"Who?"

"Deparis, and she wields a great deal of influence both in and out of her region. It seems she's been training her own 'Scrarth and Avangar' contestants and plans on issuing her challenge during the recognition of novices. Word has it that the White Priestess will sanction the contest. More importantly, the contest is to be . . . ultimate."

"Scrarth?" asked Glend.

"Avangar?" echoed Jeda.

The dronnet put a finger to Juued's lips. "Hod-ya's orders, they not know."

Juued leaned back stroking his chin. "I've seen Deparis' contestants. They're beautiful indeed, and strong and cruel."

"Just what is this 'Scrarth and Avangar' business?" demanded Glend.

"Meet Hod-ya soon. She tell," replied the usually silent guard.

"But I want to know now." Glend put her fists on the table and stood.

"I'd like to tell you, Miss, but I dare not cross Hod-ya, especially since I think she'll eventually win out. Though I must say the two of you hardly seem the type for that recognition, much less 'Scrarth and Avangar' material. The outcome is in some question."

"Well, you shouldn't bring it up if you can't talk about it in front of us," scolded Jeda.

"You don't fit in here at all, Jeda," said Juued. "I suppose Hod-ya knows what she's doing, but if she's unaware of challengers, especially one secretly in league with one of her own officers, she may be unprepared."

A dronnet's gloved fist slammed the table.

"It's true. Why else is Ugen sending messages as if from Insurrecta and not Pitland? Where, by the way, is Hod-ya now?"

"What you care?"

"As I said, I have no political aspirations or allegiances, but I'd like to retire young and wealthy. I've seen enough of the wars. It's been said that Hod-ya knows how to reward useful information."

"How much?"

"Not so fast. I only bargain with Hod-ya."

"Hod-ya in Pitland."

"She can't be, I've just come from there."

Both guards looked at each other again but said nothing.

"Well, at any rate I'd hoped to meet up with her along this road. When I saw her carriage in the stable last night, I hoped . . . " Juued fell silent.

Jeda excused herself under the pretense of tidying her room. The guards voiced no objections. Glend opted for the company of the dashing messenger.

Jeda gained the first landing and turned to go up the next flight of stairs staying just out of sight, but not earshot. She heard the main door open and Ruark's friendly but unanswered greeting hailing all within. She peeked around the corner.

Ruark entered the inn shivering and drenched to the skin, rivulets trailing a pathway of water behind as he made straight for the hearth's blazing fire. He sniffed and drew a sleeve across his nose. "Blast! Now I've done it. I've caught a chill."

"My good man," exclaimed Juued. "What happened? Did you fall in?"

"I'd probably be drier if I had," the rotund coachman sniffed and complained. "Barkeep," he barked. When the man appeared, he ordered, "Bring me a hot, buttered rum quick as you can."

"Bridge?" asked the lead dronnet.

"Aaaah-chooo! What bridge?"

"Bridge on road." The bodyguard was in no mood for bandying words.

Rubbing his sleeve across his reddened nose, Ruark turned his back to the fire. "Can't tell if it's there or not. I couldn't get close enough.

Too much," he sniffed loudly, "water on the road. We'll have to stay here a couple of days, looks like."

Jeda, still on the landing, had heard enough. She continued up the rickety flight of stairs when a form suddenly loomed before her, causing her to catch her breath. "Oh, you startled me."

It was Tressa, the servant girl. "Are you going to Pitland?"

Jeda attained the top stair and stood face to face with Tressa. The girl was about Glend's size but not quite grown into womanhood. There was a hint of natural beauty in her face, but grime and a hard expression obscured it.

"Well," Jeda replied, "it seems that way. Why?"

"I'd give anything to go with you and be trained to be a 'lady of the powers'. Can you speak to one of the guards and ask if I can go? I'll be no problem, I promise. I'll be your servant. Just don't let my step-father know I've asked."

Jeda studied Tressa. "Come with me."

Jeda led into her chambers; the servant girl followed close behind. After checking the hallway Jeda quietly closed then barricaded the door by wedging a chair under the latch. "Believe me, Tressa, things are worse in Pitland than here."

"Oh, m'lady, nothing could be worse than my life here."

"Tell me."

Tressa's eyes brimmed with tears as she searched Jeda's face for a hint of rejection. "I, I don't know why, but I feel I can trust you. No other Scrarth and Avangar contestants were like you. Not even your friend is like you, and she's no match for most initiates passing through."

"You know about 'Scrarth and Avangar'?"

"The fight to the death? Sure, I know about it, a little, anyway. But, I'm not afraid. Even death would be better than life here."

"Fight to the de—" Jeda's mind reeled. Who, or what, were she and Glend to be teamed against after the initiation? What horrible fate would they face? Oh, Logon, how could this be your intention?

" . . . so when my real father died of the injuries my mother had to accept the first man who'd marry her or else lose the inn." Tressa had been relating her story while Jeda's mind was in a fog, distracted at discovering her own predicament. Realizing that the girl was pouring out her heart, Jeda forced herself to concentrate.

"They said she was kicked by a horse, but I heard them arguing out in the stable the night she died. I'm sure he killed my mother and then blamed it on a horse. Nothing was ever done to any horse as they usually do. Sometimes, I even suspect he was the burglar who broke in the night my father got hurt, which would make him the murderer of both my mother and father." She sobbed quietly, hugging her knees. "He insists I call him Papa, so customers will think I'm his child. Many customers who knew my parents think of me as his daughter now. I hate him. I'd kill him if I could."

"Oh, Tressa, you mustn't let such hatred fill you."

"But he does such evil things." She was unable to continue for several moments. She finally took a deep breath, wiped her eyes. "I dare not say more. I hate him. If I ever get the chance, I'll kill him, just like he killed my parents. That's why I want to be a lady of the powers. Then I could conjure a tophet to rend him limb from limb and slowly devour him as he begs for his life." Tear streaks begrimed her face. "Will you help me?"

Jeda lowered her head. When she raised it again, she looked directly into Tressa's pleading eyes. "Tressa, listen to me carefully."

Tressa nodded.

"Your step-father is a product of the powers governing all Carnalia."

"What are you saying?" Tressa asked suspiciously.

"Revenge will only make you more a victim of the forces that control him, do you understand? You'll become like him if you follow your instincts."

"But he killed my parents, not some vague forces."

"Whatever he did, he did as an unwitting, though not necessarily unwilling, agent of the forces that hold sway over Carnalia. He's responsible for his actions, but, he was only obeying the impulses that control people."

"What do you mean?"

"This is a difficult concept, in fact, much of what I'm telling you is coming to me as I speak. Your urge for revenge is one of the forces the emperor uses to control people. Everyone in Carnalia is driven by unseen powers to destroy either themselves or others. Taking revenge would only make you a slave of those same forces that murdered your parents."

"And just what are these forces?"

"Hod-ya, for one; my own father for another. And on up to the emperor himself, including cusps, dreads, tophets and the like. If you were to become a lady of the powers the tophets and cusps you'd order to do your bidding would eventually control you. Believe it or not, those guards accompanying my companion and myself once had friends and personalities with likes and dislikes and emotions, but since they gave themselves over to the forces of darkness, well you see the results for yourself."

An angry fire blazed in Tressa's eyes. "That would be better than no justice."

"Justice? You don't know what you're asking for. But there is justice to be had."

"Tell me."

"This kind of justice requires putting away all thought of vengeance."

"What kind of justice is that?"

Jeda held a finger to her lips as footsteps approached the door then passed on. "I'm talking about the kind of justice that makes evil flee in fear, begging for mercy."

"Sounds like vengeance to me."

"Revenge springs from a desire to payback evil for evil. The justice I speak of springs from goodness."

"What's the difference? As long as my step-father gets what's coming to him."

"A victim's vengeance increases the power of evil. Righteous justice diminishes evil. But I know a champion who metes out righteous justice."

"Who? How can I contact this champion? Whatever it costs, I'll steal enough to pay him to avenge me."

"First, you must make peace with him yourself, for you've offended him."

Tressa sat back, her brow furrowed. "You play games, m'lady. I'd hoped I could trust you."

"No games, Tressa. I'm in dead earnest." Jeda leaned forward. "What I'm about to tell you could cost me my life, do you understand? You can trust me, but dare I trust you?"

"If you can summon this champion to help me, you can indeed, trust me. But how I've offended him, I haven't the slightest notion. Why, I don't even know him."

Footsteps in the outer corridor again passed their door and Jeda thought it prudent to remove the chair from the door. "Not here, not now. Meet me in the stable in fifteen minutes."

Tressa nodded, stood, and picked up the wash basin she'd left in the room earlier.

The door opened. Glend entered. "We're stranded here a couple of days, Jeda. Isn't that good? You ought to like that. It's the first time rain ever did anything nice for me. Oh, girl, don't forget the towels by the window. Now get along with you. Jeda, that messenger-warrior, or whatever he is, is so charming. Don't you think?"

"I thought him a bit full of himself."

"Indeed?" Glend smiled coyly. "I guess that means I have him all to myself then. He's decided not to run his message to Insurrecta. Instead, he's going to accompany us to Pitland taking his chances that Hod-ya will win out. If Hod-ya loses, at least according to him, we'll all be in danger. Somehow, it's all tied up in the outcome of that 'Scrarth and Avangar' thing. Oh well, 'Live for the Moment' and all that."

Tressa left the room casting a quick backward glance at Jeda.

"What are you going to do, Jeda, since we're not going anywhere for a couple of days? You're quite sure you have no interests in Juued?" Glend persisted.

"Quite sure. I think I'll explore a bit, get to know the place. What are our guards doing?"

Glend giggled. "You mean the vultures? Just sitting motionless, waiting for something to die so they can pounce and eat it. I sometimes wonder if they share the same world with us. They only seem alive when something sinister is afoot, like with that bully last night."

"Or when they pass the scene of a massacre. They're in the same world all right, but as what?"

"Scarecrows!" Glend volunteered brightly.

"Indeed," muttered Jeda, donning her wrap.

"You can't be thinking of going outside. It's pouring! Ruark said tree limbs are breaking under the weight of the rain falling from the skies. You'll drown standing up."

"I'll stay within sight of the inn. I simply have to get some fresh air."

"You'd be more comfortable sitting at a table with Juued and me, listening to his fascinating tales. He's been about everywhere, done about everything, and at such a young age, too."

"Enjoy yourself but trust him only in the presence of our guards, or Ruark."

"Oh, that reminds me, Ruark has come down with a bad cold. He's even decided to take a room in the inn away from his precious darlings in the stable."

"He's that bad? Ruark wouldn't part from his horses unless it was necessary."

Glend primped and tidied herself in the looking glass, intending to bedazzle the worldly-wise Juued.

As Jeda went down the hall she heard breathy snuffling accompanied by the heavy step of someone laboriously climbing the stairway. "Ruark. Are you all right?"

"Huh? Oh, it's you is it, Miss Jeda?" He sniffed. "Oh, I've gone and done it now. I'm hoping to put myself to bed with a quarter-keg of rum and find myself sober and well three days hence. If not . . . if I'm not better by then, I suppose you'll have to find a new coachman. Anyway, the road will be impassable for at least that long, so make the best of your time." Another sniff overtook him. He then leaned close and whispered, "Don't be careless with your you-know-what." His breath was saturated with the sweet redolence of rum.

Jeda backed away, gasping for air. "I'll be careful. And I'll mention you, too."

"Eh? Oh, yes, that would be fine. Now, if you'll excuse me . . . " With another loud sniff, he trudged toward his room at the end of the hallway.

Jeda descended to the landing and as she turned the corner espied a shadowy form lurking at the bottom step.

"Ah, Miss Jeda. What a delightful surprise." Juued half bowed. "It appears you're intent upon going outside."

"I want some solitude, and outside seems to be the only place to achieve that."

"In such a drencher? But then, Psa's novitiates aren't brought hither for their common sense, are they? Nevertheless, I wouldn't wander about Suffer's Tree Inn without an escort."

"Isn't Glend expecting more tales of daring-do? You wouldn't want to disappoint her, would you?"

"Why light a candle when a lantern is near?"

Jeda tried to push past. "I have no use for flatterers, sir. Nor for those who manipulate people in an effort to get to others. Now, kindly let me pass."

"Truly you misjudge my intentions. My sole concern is for your safety."

"I think no villains would be about in such a downpour, nor so early in the morning. I am in no need of protection. In fact, I'll be safest alone, despite such noble company."

"Ah, it's because you don't trust your own heart to be with me, isn't it?"

"It's because I don't trust you at all."

"Or, could it be that you trust not the sword hidden in your skirts to keep itself quiet?"

Jeda retreated a step. "Wha-what do you mean?"

"Allow me to tell a tale of daring-do. I know a certain traveler who, upon being forced by harsh weather to put up at an inn very late one night, after stabling his horse, got misdirected in the heavy rains and found himself on the backside of said inn. There, above the noise of thunder and rain, he heard a melodic sound peculiar to Ecclessa. And he saw a blue light emanating from a window above and knew for certain that an enemy of the empire was sequestered in the inn."

Jeda remained expressionless.

"After Glend teased you about a strange, blue light and you refused to touch my captured sword, I knew I'd found my Ecclessite." He smiled triumphantly, as if expecting congratulations for being so clever.

"What are you going to do?"

"Like I said, you misjudge me. I have no thought but for your safety, m'lady."

"You, you aren't a kingsman, are you?" Jeda asked.

"Me? Oh no! Don't misjudge me that way either. Were you a man, I'd challenge you to a duel. But what glory is there in defeating a woman?

But you're a worthy opponent, it would seem. How ever did you manage to fool Hod-ya?"

"I didn't. She selected me before I met Lo—"

Juued put his finger to Jeda's lips. "Hush! Say not that name aloud if you intend to carry off your masquerade. So, here you are, a novice, all alone in enemy territory. Your superiors have less heart and courage than you, if not more brains. They must be desperate to send a woman on such a mission. You do know, I hope, that you can't possibly survive, let alone succeed?"

Jeda leaned against the wall and stared at her feet. "As far as I know, I have no mission. I'm just caught up in circumstances, but I trust my liege to do his will."

"You need an escort more than I thought. Had you been properly escorted all along, you'd not be in this evil strait now. Well, at the least, this should prove interesting as it unfolds. I've decided to disobey orders and throw in my lot with Hod-ya. I hope you don't mind, but even if you do, I'm going to Pitland with you." He lifted her face with his fingers under her chin, so their eyes met. "I promise you this, I'll not betray your secret, not even if it crumbles the empire. In fact," he clicked his heels together, "I hereby pledge you my assistance against any and all enemies."

"You mock me."

"Well, maybe a little. But I promise I'll not interfere. Face it; you really must trust someone; why not me?"

"Your choices are your own, I hold you to none of your words. And I still want to be left alone now."

Juued studied her, still holding her chin. "Perhaps I'll allow you to pierce my heart. I think you already have." He released her.

Jeda swished past him hoping he'd not caught her blush.

Juued made no move to follow but merely watched as she headed for the doorway. The blackguards stared icily as she crossed the room, leaning forward as if intending to follow her.

She paused before exiting, explaining, "Umm, I'm going to check on Ruark's horses. It'll help him rest easy if he's assured they're being properly looked after. And I'd like some time alone, as well. Any problem with that?"

They conferred briefly, then the leader sat back and with a flick of his wrist dismissed her. The other guard leaned back as well.

Jeda exhaled in relief.

Juued settled into a chair by the hearth, but not too close to Hodya's bodyguards, sending a wink and smile that only Jeda caught.

CHAPTER FIFTEEN

WATER CASCADED OFF THE INN'S roof daring Jeda to proceed as she stood in the open doorway. The dronnets' hissing filled the tavern behind her. Determined, Jeda tugged her hood over her head and leaned forward to ward off the cataract as she tugged the door shut silencing the mockery behind. Taking a deep breath, she launched off the stoop and across the inn yard which was a couple of inches of mud rather than firm footing. The pelting rain felt as though she was being assailed by naughty boys throwing gravel. The stable, barely visible through the foggy downpour, loomed like a dark cave across the yard. She made straight for the largest, darkest part of the stable hoping it was the door. She didn't anticipate encountering horse-length risers hidden beneath the watery surface; she caught her foot and stumbled to the next riser, hands outspread in front to prevent falling face-first. She came to a halt just inside the gloom-filled, musty doorway and uncovered her head then stood still. The only sound was rain hammering the roof.

A horse snorted.

Jeda's eyes gradually adjusted to the dim lighting and she noted how well-ordered and dry the stable was. Several horses were tethered in individual cubicles that were well ventilated from a panel overhead. Each horse had access to a rack of hay, a feed trough with salt cube and a small reservoir of water fed by a pipe that ran through the stalls.

Jeda turned and searched the yard outside for Tressa. Could the girl get away unnoticed? If so, what could she possibly say to this woeful child? Jeda had no choice but to reveal herself as an Ecclessite. Would Tressa turn her in or keep her secret? One thing was certain, only Logon could help the poor girl. But dare Jeda even suggest such a thing this deep in Carnalia?

"Logon, help me know what to do."

Flan's voice echoed in her mind, "*Though we keep our existence secret, we should seek out those Logon has selected. Logon's own will know him when he calls. Our part, no matter how dangerous, is to reveal him to potential followers.*"

"Okay, Logon, despite the consequences, I want to give Tressa a chance to follow you."

"Miss Jeda, who are you talking to?"

Jeda whirled around.

Tressa emerged from beneath an overburdened hayloft; and . . . someone else skulked in the shadows behind Tressa.

"Oh, Tressa! You startled me!" Jeda's heart thudded. Had they heard her utter Logon's name? "Who, who's with you?"

At Tressa's prodding, the hunchback stable boy stepped out of the shadows. Jeda noted one of his eyes was discolored and half-closed. He was no taller than Tressa but gave the appearance of being a couple of years older. His clothes were tattered and threadbare. He stood shyly, eyeing Jeda.

"This is Filke, my brother."

"Brother?"

"No one knows except you, Miss Jeda. When I told him of an avenger who would hear our cause, he insisted we take you fully into our confidence. Our own parents always treated him like a stable boy anyway, 'cause they thought it would hurt business if it was known that a huncher was born to the family."

"I see."

"Don't misunderstand," Tressa defensively rejoined, "they loved him as much as they loved me even though they kept him in the stables. Even my stepfather doesn't know. He assumes Filke came with the stable when he inherited the inn. If he had any idea of the truth, Filke's life would be in danger."

Jeda glanced around. "Is anyone else here?"

"No, just us. Now, tell us about your avenger."

Filke nodded.

"Don't mind him, he can talk, but doesn't like to. He's not very good at words."

"Let's sit over there, out of the doorway yet close enough to keep an eye out if anyone comes?

"Of course." Tressa nodded, anxious to please. "Filke, put some hay bales where we can see out, but not be seen."

Filke took a bale in each hand and plopped them beside the doorpost. Jeda sat on one while Tressa and Filke sat facing her on the other.

Satisfied they'd spot intruders, Jeda began. "You both shared your secret, so it's only right that I share my secret."

They nodded.

They were so young, so abused, so embittered. Jeda felt inadequate to share even the little she knew about Logon. She was a couple of years older than they but had known nothing of the hardships foisted upon them; yet, their situation was no less dire than her own.

"We won't betray you, Miss Jeda, no matter what your secret is. Only tell us about this avenger." Filke nodded.

"Well, he's not merely an avenger, he's The Righteous Avenger. To receive his help, you must be sorry for all the hurt you've done to others."

Filke broke his silence, his words slow, his voice strained. "Tressa not hurt anyone. Why say her did? Filke done lots bad things, hurt people, but not Tressa."

"I felt that way, too, about myself, Filke. Look, to understand how all three of us have injured and offended this Righteous Avenger, we must understand that he doesn't want to take vengeance on us or anyone."

Both of them tilted their heads, pursed their lips, and furrowed their brows exactly the same way.

"Maybe if I put it in this context; Carnalia is at war, right?"

"Everyone knows that." Tressa brushed some hayseeds off her apron.

"What if you were a soldier and you suddenly discovered that the things you were fighting against were really what you should be defending?"

Defiance flared in Tressa's eyes. "If you're trying to say we're wrong about our stepfather, forget it! He's an evil man. Look what he did to Filke for no reason except a guest asked if the stable roof leaked." Tressa turned Filke's head so that the bruise came fully to light. Even in the gloom Jeda made out a purplish palm print on the boy's cheek. "It's not wrong to hate him."

"I'm not suggesting that. Here let me . . . " Jeda stood and turned to the side in order to extract her sword, "tell you my secret." She turned back pointing her Child of the Stars at them. Several runes were aglow; runes she'd never worked on, nor indeed had even known were on the blade. The portion near the point she'd so diligently labored over also glowed illuminating the alarmed faces before her. "Don't be frightened, I'll not hurt you. In fact, I'm in more danger of you than you are of me."

Filke spoke first. "You, you're one of them!" A smile spread across his face. "Now Filke understand."

"I don't!" protested Tressa rising to her feet. "You're one of them! You're far worse than any of us!"

"Do you really believe that?" challenged Jeda. "Is that what I seem to you?"

"It's the king, isn't it?" Filke beamed. "The king is Righteous Avenger?"

"His son, Logon Xychirion, the Alfomega is," said Jeda. "You see, I discovered which side is the right side, and which is the wrong side."

"Filke, too!" grinned the stable boy.

"What?" said Jeda, startled.

"What are you talking about?" Tressa snapped at her brother. Then, in frustration to Jeda, "You have nothing to offer, *kingswoman*."

Filke grabbed his sister's arm before she had a chance to rush out the door. "Tressa, listen; her right."

Tressa quit struggling and looked disbelievingly at her brother. "Wha-what do you know of such things, Filke? You're here in the stables with horses all the time. I'm in there," she pointed toward the inn "where I hear the horrible talk of war, and how cruel Ecclessites are, and tales of the Magician driving men mad. How could you possibly know anything about the outer world?"

Filke extended his hand toward Jeda's sword, asking "Give, just for minute?"

Jeda reluctantly handed her sword to Filke.

As soon as Filke touched the handle the glow receded from the runes and all light vanished from the blade except for the very tip.

Jeda gasped.

Wordlessly, Filke unbuttoned his shirt to mid-chest, revealing a stained tunic. This he undid from neck to mid-chest, too, revealing a scar over his heart.

"I don't believe this!" exclaimed Tressa. "My own brother? How long?"

"Couple years."

"Oh, Filke, you betrayed me. Why?"

"Nice man and lady talk to Filke. They were different, nice. Filke ask why. Them tell Filke that Alfomega make all problems go away. Filke want all problems go away, ask Alfomega to help, live in heart. Now Filke go live with Alfomega when die. Then have no more trouble."

"Why did you never tell me? We always shared everything."

"Tressa be angry, call Filke 'stupid boy'."

Tressa shook her head.

"Don't be angry, Tressa," said Jeda. "Filke has done the right thing, only not enough of it. Didn't Logon give you a sword, Filke?"

"Lost it."

"May I have mine back?"

Filke relinquished the sword and it resumed its glow as previously. "You should've sharpened it every day, Filke. Then it would shine like mine, even brighter. Then, Filke, you would be a great warrior."

"Filke not smart, too dumb. Hide sword, not sure where." His eyes wandered round the stable, avoiding Jeda's penetrating look.

"But Logon gave the Advisor to you to help you learn. Don't you miss Logon?"

"What are you two talking about? Advisor, Logon? What is all this?"

"Your brother met Logon Xychirion, the Prince of Splendora, two years ago, as evidenced by that scar on his chest. That wound was made by a sword exactly like this one. Logon healed him with a touch and then he put the Advisor inside to help him understand and obey Logon's runes and to be free from the emperor."

"We ain't never served the emperor."

"The emperor wants people to hate and kill; isn't that your plan, to kill your stepfather?"

"Well, he deserves it."

"If you got your wish, how would you be any different from him?"

Tressa was silent.

"That's all it takes to serve the emperor. Living for the moment includes revenge. If you obey someone's commands, you're their servant. Since the emperor commands 'live for the moment', and you obey by plotting revenge, are you not his servant?"

"But our stepfather deserves to die."

"Okay, so he's more a slave of the emperor than you. That doesn't change the fact that you're a slave, too. All the emperor's servants will receive the same fate when the king and his brights descend upon the empire to end the rebellion."

"That's just what you want to believe. The emperor is too powerful to be defeated."

Jeda pursed her lips making a squeaky sound. How was she to answer Tressa? Her glance fell upon the glowing runes. She withdrew her toller and placed it in Tressa's hands. "Here, see for yourself. Rub this file over the blade, right here by this rune. I'll hold the sword."

Tressa blinked in astonishment but asked, "How? Like this?" She rubbed the toller across the sword.

Immediately a low-pitched, steady vibration emitted from the sword. Tressa dropped the toller to the floor. "I hear dreadful words of doom, fury, and torment! Make it stop."

"The song won't hurt you, Tressa, but you must hear its message. Please, pick up the toller and do it again before the tone fades. Yes, that's it, and keep stroking till the message stops."

"I'm afraid."

Filke took the toller from his sister's hand and was going to stroke the blade for her, his eyes wide with wonder, but Jeda stayed his hand. "She has to do this herself, Filke, or she won't believe it."

Filke turned to his sister, insisting, "Take."

She reluctantly received the toller again. "Is this really necessary?" The tone faded.

"There, it stopped. It's too late now."

"I don't think so, for the rune still glows. This rune is a warning to those who, after hearing of the amnesty he offers, continue serving the emperor. You must toll it, so you'll know the runesong is true."

"How do I know this sword sings the truth?"

"How many other swords do you know of that sing?"

"There's some magic spell upon this sword."

As if for the sake of honesty, Filke felt obliged to state, "Filke's sword not sing."

"You didn't toll it long enough. Logon expects more of you than to be content to live with him someday in Splendora, Filke, he wants your service now. But you can only be of use to him if you prepare by sharpening your sword."

Then Jeda turned back to Tressa. "The king and his son never use magic; they don't need to, for they're the power that created and holds all existence together. They have no need of cheap magic. The power in this sword is the power of their word. They cannot lie, so whatever the sword says is absolutely true, forever. To call the sword false without even hearing what it says is the same as calling the king a liar. Now, toll the blade and see what awaits those who reject Logon Xychirion."

Tressa considered for a moment, then applying the file with a hearty thrust, filled the stable's confines with the ominous tone again, deadening the din of the torrential downpour. Unbidden words filled the thoughts of all present as Tressa filed. It was more a chant than song, yet haunting in its air, conveying sorrow, grief and loss more than wrath and judgment.

Jeda sang aloud as brother and sister trembled at the import of the message:

> "A lake of pitch, sulfurous hot,
> A place where hope abideth not,
> Dwells rebellious, violent lot,
> A lake of pitch, sulfurous hot.
>
> Depart from me ye cursed, go flee,
> Go to this molten, bubbling sea,
> Reap your wage eternally,
> Depart from me ye cursed, go flee.
>
> Firewind and molten mount,
> Brights avenge every count,
> Mete to each the full amount,
> Firewind and molten mount.
>
> The host of Elyon rides in power,
> Hate's dark night has passed its hour,
> The Evil snared in his own tower,
> The host of Elyon rides in power.
>
> Wail aloud and gnash the teeth,
> Fiery grief doth boil and seethe,
> From lowest slave to highest wreath,
> Wail aloud and gnash the teeth.

All offense is taken low,
The land is cleansed by fiery blow,
Burned to ash is Elyon's foe,
All offense is taken low.

And which the ones who make a stay?
What strength can stand that awful day?
With swords aglow, in white array,
And which the ones who make a stay?

The son will ride and conquer all,
The vanquished drink a bitter gall,
From dragon great to lizard small,
The son will ride and conquer all.

Phantom lords and tophet beasts,
Cusp and irk, from great to least,
And human slaves become the feast,
Of phantom lords and tophet beasts.

As in the end the specter's hate,
Becomes the same as human fate,
All locked within torment's gate,
As in the end the specter's hate."

Visions of writhing people tormented in flames yet not consumed, never dying, filled their minds. Continuous, eternal torment! It was overwhelming, even for Jeda. They sat quietly on their respective bales long after the tone subsided, and the rune ceased glowing.

Filke finally broke the silence. "Filke not burn! Live with Logon." He tapped his chest as he spoke.

"But . . . but I don't deserve that," objected Tressa, her attitude much subdued.

"Elyon's enemies do." Jeda tapped another glowing rune. "Try this one."

Tressa cautiously touched the file to the rune and suddenly dazzling flashes of color sprang from the sword. Jeda checked the inn yard, for the flashing lights must attract attention if anyone was there to see. But the deluge continued unabated; no one cared to venture out-of-doors yet. Tressa filed slowly, thoughtfully. For several moments, only the rasping of the toller was heard, but she kept filing expectantly. Finally, a soft, pleasing tune sweetened the air; the rune glowed a different color for a few seconds, then shifted to another color, then another, and so on. Their huddled faces took on whatever hue happened to be glowing at any particular moment. Again, words filled their minds accompanying the melody, and Jeda sang as Filke hummed:

> *"His blood flowed brightest red,*
> *Wounded was the royal head,*
> *Suffering in our rightful stead.*
>
> *Astray we ran o'er meadows green,*
> *That turned to deserts, cruel and mean,*
> *And death, our foe, didst stalk unseen.*
>
> *Our brazen leaders like headstrong rams,*
> *And we all followed like ewes and lambs,*
> *Astray we went like floods o'er dams.*
>
> *Flowers copper, silver, gold,*
> *Drawn aside, our hearts turned cold,*
> *And snared our feet, though we'd been told.*

Then came death all dressed in black,
And lured us to the butcher's shack,
The knife did boast 'I give not back'.

Fled we our shepherd to this end?
Though he was our constant friend,
Too late for us our lives to mend.

Dare we expect that hope could stay,
Sentence of death's gray day?
But hope did come, and death waylay!

His own to save, the shepherd came,
To yield his life to death's dark claim,
He freed his own in his own name.

His broken frame has wrought release,
The flock is freed in life's new lease,
In Elyon's pasture to find his peace."

Tears streamed down Tressa's cheeks, though not a sound did she make. Even Filke's eyes watered as he seemed to remember the love he'd forgotten.

"One more rune glows, Tressa, it's for you alone to hear."

"I'm afraid, Miss Jeda, I fear this rune, for I think it knows my heart, and I'm afraid to see what's really there."

"And well you should be," said Jeda. "Nevertheless, you must toll it, or experience the fire-rune prophecy. Which do you fear more?"

Tressa touched the toller by the last glowing rune. Immediately a bittersweet melody, barely audible to Jeda or Filke, taught Tressa the contents of her own heart. The song was short; no words occurred to any save Tressa alone.

When the song ended, she said, "I'm ready. Pierce my heart, Miss Jeda, for I myself am guilty of the Righteous Avenger's blood. I don't deserve to live, as this last rune declares. Slay me."

Solemnly lifting her Child of the Stars, Jeda said, "A life for the king," and gently touched her sword to Tressa's chest, watching in awe as the point passed through clothing, skin, bone, and into the heart. Jeda had never done this before and hoped she wasn't doing anything wrong. She withdrew the sword only when sure the work was done.

Tressa sobbed bitterly and fell to her knees. "Yes, m'lord," she said as if answering someone.

Her weeping stopped, and from her kneeling position she extended her hand, as if touching something. She shuddered a moment, then rolled onto her side as if dead. A beautiful white, though simple garment suddenly appeared upon her and mystically "sank" through her outer clothing to be next to her flesh. She then was raised to a standing position, though still unconscious—or dead. The wound in her chest shimmered briefly, and Tressa gasped for air.

"And how did I get up here m'lord?" Tressa asked, eyes still closed. "And my brother? Miss Jeda, too? Oh yes, I'd like that very much, only I'm so unworthy." She then tilted her head as if looking down at herself with eyes still closed.

Jeda's eyes glistened, recalling the exhilaration of looking into those eyes, that healing touch, his words of love and acceptance.

Tressa continued, " . . . and I'm forgiven? But must I forgive even him? Yes, I know. I tugged you down on that stake. My rebellion pulled you deeper, I saw my desire for vengeance as the extra tug pulling you down farther. Yes," Tears coursed down her face as she wept, "I forgive, for your sake, if you help me."

Jeda felt a tug on her sleeve. The stable boy whispered, "Filke miss Logon."

Tressa slipped to her knees and then with head high, extended her hand. A fully glowing sword appeared in it. Every rune flashed brightly as well as the edge, illuminating the entire stable. But the glow quickly faded, and the blade turned a dull gray, all except for the very tip. Tressa extended her other hand; a toller appeared. "I will, m'lord. You are?" She became excited, elated. "How soon? Oh, I will, I will." Then her eyes opened, and she blinked in wonderment.

Filke's eyes suddenly opened wide as he stared at a seemingly vacant spot. "Oh no, m'lord, I lost, yes, you right. I hid it. Yes, you did. So, it has. I, I sorry m'lord. Yes, the two of us. That be better. And Miss Jeda? Oh, is she? Yes, Filke fetch it right now and learn." Then he blinked, and his eyes darted back and forth as if searching for something.

"Well done, Jeda." Logon stood directly before her. "You counted not your own safety above the needs of others. The gifts I gave you aren't wasted. Therefore, you shall grow stronger in them. You'll need them, for greater danger lies in your path. Seek me and I will use you. Heed the Advisor and you'll accomplish my purpose. I send you where no army can go; I delight using the weak and despised, the rejected and helpless to accomplish my ends. Strengthen yourself in me, and you'll see enemies fall before you."

He was gone as suddenly as he'd appeared. Jeda blinked, vainly looking about for the gray-hooded visitor.

Filke was at the other end of the stable prying up some floorboards.

Tressa stared at the sword and toller in her lap as tears coursed down her face.

Jeda was the first to notice. "The rain, it's stopped!"

Sure enough, rain no longer drummed on the roof. The inn door opened and Hod-ya's bodyguards emerged, followed by Juued and the barman. At first, they made no attempt to assay out into the ankle-deep mud and water but remained on the inn steps looking at the sky. A ray of sunshine broke through the clouds striking the four men where they stood, spreading diamond-like sparkles off the rippling waters. The blackguards recoiled and went back into the gloom of Suffer's Tree Inn. The other men seemed glad for the sunshine. Juued looked across the inn yard to the dark, leafy bowers of the forest beyond, then quickly glanced at the stable door where Jeda stood.

With a start Jeda realized her sword was fully exposed, its blue point shining like a beacon. She retreated behind the posts, secreting her sword away as she did so.

"Quick, Tressa, hide your sword and toller, like this," she demonstrated. "The men will be here any second."

Tressa did as Jeda showed her. There was a light in her eyes and peace upon her face. "Miss Jeda. I never knew life could be so wonderful!"

Jeda impulsively gave the girl a hug. "Be careful."

"I will."

"Filke find it!" cried the stable boy, running up and brandishing a sword that was dull and lifeless except for the very tip. "Now I please Logon. Toll much, be ready."

"Oh, Filke, that's good, but hide it now, the men are coming."

"Men coming? Filke hide it, but not forget where this time."

"Hello?" Juued's voice intruded. "Anybody in there?" His footsteps splashed noisily across the water of the innyard.

Jeda stepped into the sunlight. "Just us, me and Tressa, and of course Filke, the stable boy."

Juued and the barman were nearly at the steps. "It's stopped raining," announced the messenger.

"We've noticed, oh, watch out for that first step!"

Jeda's warning came too late. Juued tripped on the underwater step. His other boot caught fast, and he fell headlong on the next step.

Unable to stop themselves, Tressa, Jeda, and Filke burst out laughing.

The barman growled, "Here now, I'll not have you mocking my guests. How long have you been out here wasting time with these horses instead of serving guests, wench? And you boy, you'd better not be bothering the Missy, or you'll feel the bite of leather. I'm sorry, Miss, if these two bothered you." He went to Juued's assistance.

"Sorry, Papa, I'm on my way." Tressa lifted her skirts and waded through the ankle-deep waters toward the inn.

The innkeeper stared after Tressa, then turned a curious eye on Jeda. "What's been going on out here? Have you been spellbinding these children? I'll not have you practicing dark arts in my inn. I don't care if you are under Hod-ya's protection, I won't have it."

Juued, back on his feet, wiped his hands on his breeches and looked keenly at Jeda, remarking, "I doubt she's been up to any real mischief, Ralal, look at her. She's not the type, if you know what I mean."

"No master, Miss Jeda do nothing wrong," pleaded Filke from the doorway.

Ralal, the barman, stared open-mouthed at Filke, then said, "Isn't the type, eh? That boy hasn't said more than three words at a time since I've known him, but to defend this witchling, he's put out a whole sentence."

"Hardly what I'd call loquacious, but is it so unusual for a stable lad to defend a beautiful maiden?"

"Hmm, there's something mighty singular going on here."

"Well, to tell you the truth, if I felt that way, I'd take a humbler approach." Juued winked at Jeda. "After all, being selected by Hod-ya, and if I might say so, being the more beautiful of the two, she may have powers you don't want to arouse."

A gasp of indignation escaped Glend's lips. She'd waded out behind Juued and Ralal and overheard every word spoken in Jeda's behalf. Glend narrowed her eyes, spitting out, "You'd best guard your own heart and mind, Juued. She does indeed cast spells, and in such an innocent way, no one would suspect. You should've seen her cast a spell on some Eroton guards. Hod-ya has selected you well, 'witchling'." Glend turned in a huff and sloshed back to the inn.

"I apologize, Jeda, I didn't know she was there."

"Well, I've seen and heard enough," said Ralal. "There'll be no more of your black arts around here, understand? If word gets out, it'll be bad for business."

"Ralal, where else is anyone going to go for refreshment in these parts? Think about it."

Jeda wanted to defend herself but knew doing so would be useless. The changes in Tressa and Filke were too obvious. It was simpler to let him believe what he wished. "I understand. There'll be no trouble from me."

The barman nodded and started back across the inn yard.

"Jeda, quick," called Juued, "while he's not looking, change him into a goose."

Ralal cast a baleful eye over his shoulder at Juued as he trudged toward the lodge.

"Juued, stop it. You're only making things worse," Jeda chided.

Juued laughed. "Look at him look. He's afraid you might do it." Then he spoke quietly, "Just what did go on out here?"

"Oh, I thought you knew. My associates and I were plotting Lurcan's overthrow."

"Okay, be sarcastic, but a stable boy and a scullery maid will be of no assistance should you be discovered. You need a warrior, one not unlike myself, to protect you."

"And who will protect me from the likes of you?" Jeda brushed past and made for the inn.

Juued fell into step beside her. "Isn't your precious liege powerful enough to protect you from the likes of me?"

Without slowing her steps or even deigning to look at him she replied, "Indeed he is, though I know you don't believe it."

"Oh ho, but I do."

Jeda halted and faced Juued. "You do?"

"Of course. I've seen too many unexplained things that could only be Logon's hand. I know full well that he stands for goodness and truth and will eventually defeat his enemy."

"Then, why don't you follow him?"

"I will, someday. I'm just not ready yet. I haven't done everything I want to do yet, things I doubt he'd allow."

"You're worse than I first thought. How can you obey Lurcan when you know Logon is true?"

"Just goes to show what a rascal I am, doesn't it?" Juued grinned and raised his eyebrows.

"It proves how despicable you are, knowing Logon died to rescue you, yet you want to have some more Lurcanish fun before yielding to him." Jeda turned and hurried toward the inn.

"Jeda, wait!"

"No. I can't abide someone who'd treat my liege so."

"All right, pierce my heart then," he said, opening his shirt. "I didn't mean to offend you."

"Well you did. You don't really want your heart pierced."

"Yes, I do."

"No, you just want me to accept you."

"Is that so bad?"

"Yes."

"But Jeda, can't you tell I'm falling in love with you?"

"You dare speak of love? You despise one who loves you so much that he died for you, yet profess love for me? He's my heart's love, and since you reject him, I could never give you all my love. He's all my life, all that matters. If he's not the same to you, you could never understand or love me. It's not me you're in love with, you love yourself too much to love anything else. I just represent another fun part of your life. He's the life of all his followers, as the runes say."

"Ahh, the runes. Who's to say the runes weren't inscribed by some over-idealistic generals? Sure, I believe Elyon exists, and Logon, but who can say more with certainty?"

"That's a matter of the heart. The mind will always have another question, but the heart knows when it's found truth. Don't waste your time and mine by trying to win my affections."

"Well, at any rate we'd better quit standing out here in ankle deep water arguing or they'll think we're up to something."

CHAPTER SIXTEEN

THE NEXT TWO DAYS AT Suffers Tree Inn were spent lazily, for although the sun shone brightly the chilly air that rushed in behind the storm did little to evaporate the floodwaters. Roads were little more than muddy wallows.

On the morning of the third day after the storm's abatement, Ruark emerged from his self-imposed quarantine to check on his darlings.

Jeda, who consistently avoided Juued, was relieved that the coachman was indeed recovered, despite the hangover, from his cold due to his unique method of cure.

Hod-ya's dronnets had barely stirred the whole time except to attend to bodily needs and to take turns standing guard outside the girls' sleeping chambers at night.

Tressa was seen only at a distance, and Filke not at all. It little mattered, for Jeda purposed to stay away from them. Brief glimpses of Tressa convinced Jeda that Logon had indeed met with the serving girl; there was hope in her eyes and peace upon her countenance. In fact, her face had lost its hardened look and was becoming soft and gentle, more appropriate to her age and gender.

Glend presented the most difficulty. She was no longer friendly being convinced that Jeda was quite accomplished at spell-binding. She was only somewhat appeased that Jeda avoided any and all contact with Juued.

Jeda spent what time she could communing with Logon and tolling her sword, though it was usually late at night in a corner of the room behind furniture or underneath blankets. She didn't always feel Logon's presence, nevertheless she clung to his promises.

If Ralal, the innkeeper, had reported his suspicions about Jeda to the bodyguards, nothing came of it. All that mattered to them was getting underway again, especially since Hod-ya's position and title were threatened.

Juued stayed true to his decision to disobey orders, though it wasn't out of loyalty to Hod-ya but rather his interest in Jeda. He vainly sought occasions to be with her, believing persistence would eventually wear down her resistance, but she seemingly had limitless resources against his most winsome efforts. This seemed to perplex him; it was as if no maiden had ever resisted him so completely before. No amount of flattery, begging or cajoling affected her.

Thus, it was that on the third day, Ruark, coming in from checking his team, saw Jeda sitting at a table all alone. This was the first day that the inn's regulars reappeared. Road conditions had prevented clientele from the trip but now droves of thirsty men braved the drying sloughs with the intention of deferring said thirst no longer. Thus, most tables and the bar were filled with earnest drinkers.

Ruark approached Jeda. "Jeda."

Jeda looked up and smelled the evidence of his medicine on his breath.

"I see you've been busy."

Jeda furrowed her brow.

"The stable lad."

"Oh? Is he doing well?"

"Better than I ever saw him."

"I'm glad to hear that."

"You've got pluck, girl. I'll say that. Not much sense, but pluck!"

"I've been sent here for a reason, Ruark. It's not the road I'd have chosen, but it seems, it's been chosen for me. My part is to do what I've been sent to do. I don't think pluck has anything to do with it. I do what I do because I love the one who sent me."

"Yes, well it works for you, so far. But please, exercise a little caution. If you get yourself into trouble, you're on your own. I don't dare jeopardize my livelihood by coming to your aid. I hope you understand; my wife and darlings depend on me."

Jeda studied Ruark. What priorities did he live by?

"That's all I'm going to say on the matter. Now, if they agree," Ruark nodded toward the bodyguards, "we'll resume our journey this afternoon. By traveling all night, we can be at the Four Horses Inn by midday or early afternoon. Two days after that we'll arrive at Willow House where guest quarters are reserved for those on official business. That's just a day's ride from the White Priestess' Castle."

"I'll gather my things." Jeda started to rise.

"Best wait till I clear it with them." His hand on Jeda's shoulder stayed her. "It's a bad business going through this next section of Ra-Amawl at night and they have to decide if the risks are worth making up lost time."

"Dangerous for them?" Jeda wondered aloud. How great was the peril of crossing those woods?

"Ra-Amawl is no ally of Lurcan's. I've only driven that section at night once, carrying the Lady Hod-ya herself, else I wouldn't have done it. Even then, I was thoroughly unnerved."

"What happened?"

"I'd rather not say. It was only my you-know-what that gave me courage to face those night horrors."

"Ruark," Jeda said in mock surprise, "there's hope for you yet."

"Be not sassy with me, Miss. You're too young to understand. I admire your zeal, but you shouldn't think poorly of others who have more to lose than you."

"Ruark," grated the chief dronnet from across the room.

Ruark straightened up and waved.

Jeda said, "I'm sorry; of course, you're right, I guess. I'm new to all this. There's so much I need to learn."

"There, there, that's all right. Just do what Lo— er, he wants you to do, and don't go around criticizing just because others happen to see things differently."

"Ruark," grated the raspy voice again.

"Coming," he hailed back, nodded and left Jeda.

"Oh, Logon," Jeda whispered, "help me understand your ways. Forgive me for thinking myself braver than Ruark."

At the dronnets' table Ruark took a step back at what they said. He glanced about the room. "Juued?" he said loud enough to clue Jeda in. Then he approached them and bent over to keep the conversation private. After some debate, he shrugged, announcing, "I'll take no responsibility. I'll do as I'm told, but I think it foolish. I doubt Hod-ya would approve."

Leaning both hands on the table the lead bodyguard growled, "Just do as told. Not matter if you like."

"Well, I said I would, didn't I? But I don't like it, not one bit." With that he stomped away purposely passing Jeda's table and whispering,

"Trouble's a-brewing." He then headed back outside to prepare the harness and carriage.

The bodyguards got to their feet and strode across the room. "Get things; leaving," the quiet one muttered as they passed Jeda.

Jeda rose and made for the stairs.

"Tell other girl," the leader said over his shoulder.

"I will."

Jeda heard Glend and Juued laughing as she approached her room. Glend greeted Jeda's arrival with a chilly, appraising look, but Juued's eyes brightened. Jeda ignored Juued, speaking only to Glend. "The guards said we're leaving as soon as Ruark gets his horses hitched."

Juued jumped up from the window seat. "I've got to gather my things and saddle my horse."

Glend, still on the window seat, said, "You weren't teasing then? You really are coming?"

"Could I deceive such a fair maiden?"

Jeda feigned a cough but Glend drank in every word. With a few other affectionate, parting words, some of which were spoken with his eyes directed at Jeda, Juued departed.

"I hope you don't take him seriously, Glend."

"What's it to you if I do?"

"I just don't want you getting hurt."

"And you're an expert in such matters, I suppose?"

Jeda blushed. Glend had struck a telling point. She was far from experienced in romantic things. She turned her face away, gathering her belongings. "You know I'm not. Nevertheless, I have good reason to believe he'll come to no good end, and so will anyone who follows him."

Glend paused packing. "How can you say such a thing?"

"I just feel it, that's all." Jeda noted the fleeting look of fear on Glend's face. "No, it's not what you think. I have no powers that tell the future."

"Then what makes you so certain?"

Jeda looked Glend square in the eye. "I wish I could tell you. Maybe someday, but not yet."

Glend jammed another garment into her hand-satchel, sending jealous darts with her eyes at Jeda.

Jeda understood; she was Glend's rival, not only in Juued's affections, but also in Hod-ya's esteem. And Glend seemed to think Jeda had the upper hand on all counts. Would that jealousy flare into hatred, perhaps even violence?

"Quick," grated the second dronnet from the open doorway. Both girls tied their bags shut, entered the hallway, then went down the stairs and through the inn as they'd come, carrying their own baggage. They again had become the center of attention to the pub's patrons, but upon seeing the escorts most imbibers returned to catching up on three lost days of grog consumption.

Ruark pulled the carriage around to the front steps just as the party emerged. Behind the coach trotted an impressive white stallion bedecked in war harness and saddle. Juued sat atop the steed smiling broadly. Ruark relieved the girls of their satchels and opened the carriage door. After the girls were seated the lead blackguard disappeared back inside the inn while the other stood with arms crossed outside the open coach door, staring expectantly toward the inn's doorway.

A chilly wind kicked up; Jeda drew her cloak tightly about her shoulders. Movement in the inn's portal drew her attention. It wasn't the awaited guard, but Tressa, carrying a basket covered with a cloth napkin. She walked around the far side of the coach to Jeda's side, avoiding both the bodyguard and Glend. "Here, m'lady, the master sends these with his wishes for a safe and prosperous journey." She smiled and winked.

Jeda received the proffered basket and peeked under the dishcloth revealing fresh baked biscuits, a round of cheese, pastries, and a few apples. "Tell your master we're grateful."

Tressa's eyes were clear and bright, the hardness of her face had softened noticeably since their first encounter.

"I wish you well, Tressa. Mind, pay attention to your cutlery."

Tressa's face lit up. "I will." Then whispering so only Jeda could hear, "I'm not alone."

Jeda nodded. "I know."

Tressa shook her head. "No, no. Not just that. There are more," she said tapping her skirt where her Child of the Stars was stashed.

Jeda gradually understood Tressa's meaning. "What, even here?"

The serving girl nodded. "A beam of light from the point led us through the forest, and we found a secret—"

"Just what are you two plotting?" challenged Glend, leaning over.

Jeda jerked upright, aware of how Glend would perceive their whispering. But before she could reply, the lead bodyguard emerged with the innkeeper on his heels, insisting, " . . . it will be, it will be. I assure you Gragnold, all will be in readiness should she come this way."

"Not forget message," rattled Gragnold, the senior guard.

"A contender arises; the right hand is untrustworthy," quoted the barman. "But, what's the meaning of it?"

A nasty hiss greeted the innkeeper's question, and both guards took seats behind the girls.

Tressa drew away from Jeda's window but not before mouthing "King's road to you."

Ruark clucked and the coach lurched down the ill-omened road. The pace was quick despite a few muddied wallows, to the liking of all except Jeda. She dreaded the challenges in her path yet was resigned to obey Logon. She wished she could have spent more time with Tressa and Filke, especially since it seemed that they'd found a secret brigade even in Ra-Amawl. Would wonders never cease?

Before meeting Logon, life had had its ups and downs, but was basically settled and predictable. But now every day was an adventure. To be sure it required great daring and trust to continue, and he never guaranteed the outcome, yet to disobey was unthinkable. Safety, such as it was, was a nebulous part of her past life. She would never be safe in the old way again. Yet, never had she felt more secure! She was a living paradox. True life came only after despairing of finding it; by surrendering, she became a conqueror; in constant danger she was never more protected; seeking peace and safety would be the most perilous thing she could do.

"Ah, Logon, how strange are your ways," she murmured under her breath. So, while Glend napped Jeda passed many miles sweetly pondering her liege's wonders.

Some hours later, jolted by a bump in the road, Glend awoke in a foul mood. Her voice disrupted Jeda's reverie. "Why are you smiling? Aren't you supposed to be reluctant about this journey to Pitland?"

Jeda replied, "Oh, nothing, except that I've made peace with it."

Just after sundown, which in Ra-Amawl was all but indiscernible anyway, Juued spurred his steed outside Jeda's coach window. "We're coming to a perilous region of the forest where bizarre, manlike creatures and savage beasts roam unhindered. Ruark will stop to briefly rest the team, douse the lanterns, and perhaps pad his horses' feet and grease the carriage springs and axles to keep noise of our passing at a minimum. It wouldn't do to announce our presence through this upcoming section of forest by any careless talking, so please, keep your thoughts to yourselves, or if you must communicate, whisper. This sector is dangerous enough in the daytime, but at night . . . Unless I miss my guess, our bravery will be sorely tested before we emerge on the other side. When you hear the waterfall, we'll have gotten past the worst."

No sooner had Juued ended his warning than Ruark slowed his darlings and brought them to a standstill in the roadway. Before the portly driver had a chance to descend, Gragnold, the lead dronnet, was already out the door, peering ahead and around into the forest on either side.

Ruark landed with a soft thud, walked to the foremost horses and sniffed the air, then busied himself unwrapping six sets of leather hoof-boots he'd extracted from a nook under the driver's perch. Talking gently, he quieted each horse as he came to them, stroking their shoulders and flanks as he shod their feet.

Gragnold's dusky face suddenly appeared in Jeda's window, growling to his partner, "Sevrid, go, smell, look, listen." His gloved finger pointed to the road ahead.

The other dronnet wordlessly climbed out the rear door and soundless as a cat walked ahead, listening, sniffing, cocking his head, checking either side as he disappeared into the dark.

"Here now, Ruark, my good man, you wouldn't happen to have an extra set of those horse boots, would you?" Juued whispered.

"I've got to keep what spares I have in case one falls off or wears through. Sorry."

"So, what am I supposed to do? I know better than to go clip-clopping through this stretch of Ra-Amawl after dark." Then turning to the dronnet, said, "Look Gragnold, you agreed it was a good idea for me to come along; now you make that fat coachman lend me those extra boots."

Gragnold's reply was a hiss. In fact, there seemed to be a hint of glee in his prolonged hissing.

Juued sounded angry and fearful as he said, "Well, what then? Should I ride in, or perhaps on, the coach, and send my horse back? Just what do you expect me to do? Surely you knew this situation would arise; have you no contingency?"

Gragnold hissed again.

"Now look here!" Panic was in Juued's tone. "I don't like the idea, but I'm willing to part with my horse; taking him on this stretch of road at night will most certainly draw attention. You can't be unaware of that. Just what is it I should do?"

"Scout ahead," rattled the blackguard.

"You can't be serious! Why you half-breed scion-of-a-tophet, I'd rather—"

A red glow flared in Gragnold's eye slits. Even in the fading twilight under the thick, leafy canopy, Jeda noted Juued's stunned features.

Gragnold pointed in the direction of his companion. "Show ladies bravery; take point, send Sevrid back."

Wordlessly, Juued unslung his crossbow, cocked it, and loaded a dart. He then grimly stared at Gragnold as if contemplating using his weapon then and there. Choosing wisely, he clucked to his mount and sullenly clip-clopped up the road to relieve the advance dronnet.

Glend leaned close to Jeda. "Now I'm worried. They intended all along to use Juued as bait. That's so unfair, and I just noticed, they're using names. Gragnold, Sevrid. What do you make of that?"

"Why Glend, you're right. I hadn't noticed. What does that mean?"

"Umm, maybe we've passed a point of no return, so it's safe to let us know more about themselves, do you think?"

Jeda shrugged.

Ruark finished booting the last of his darlings, then applied additional grease to every moving part of the coach and undercarriage, including doors, hinges and latches, working the grease in by swinging the doors open and shut several times. "From this point on, ladies," he poked his head inside the coach, "no loud noises, and don't speak above a whisper. And put your lantern out as I extinguish these outside the coach. If you sense anything the least bit strange, tell Gragnold immediately."

Glend touched the coachman's arm, asking, "Why such precautions?"

"You don't know? These woods are a main thoroughfare for all manner of creatures: cusps, tophets, even dreads on the prowl, and that's only non-blooded beasts. It's also infested with irks."

"All this for fanciful monsters? I find that hard to swallow. Tell me of the blooded beasts, for I find more merit in their existence than goblins," said Glend.

Ruark sized the girl up as if for the first time. "So, you don't believe in cusps and what-not? Before this night's journey is over, I warrant you'll believe! As to the blooded-beasts, lions big as a house, bats that drain every drop of blood from your body as you sleep, wolves and bears twice normal size and four times as fierce. Then there's half-men, all covered in hair, with fangs this long," he splayed thumb and fore-finger, "and madmen and ghouls of every sort."

"Enough," interrupted Gragnold. "Sevrid here. We go."

Ruark apologized, "I'm sorry. I got carried away. I didn't mean to frighten you. But you must believe that this is a very dangerous passage, so be silent. Every nightmare you've ever had has its origin here. The next thirty miles are the most perilous of the entire journey."

Glend sat back and swallowed hard. "Well, I'm not sure I believe all this, Ruark, but I do believe you wouldn't take such cautions with-out need, especially since we're pressed for time. Nor would Juued, valiant and bold as he is, have quailed at taking the point without reason. We are safe though, aren't we? I mean if we keep silent and stay to the path?"

Ruark glanced furtively at the dark forest. "We won't know safety until mid-to-late-morning, which will be dim, indeed. Even the noon hour is dusky under these resentful boughs. You'd best steel yourselves not to cry out at sudden frights, else you'll draw trouble down on us."

"Perhaps re-lighting lanterns would cause fear in these creatures of night," suggested Jeda.

"A suggestion I'd expect from you. But on this nighttime trail light attracts unwanted attention, as much, if not more, than noise. Any light, if you catch my meaning, Miss Jeda."

Jeda nodded.

Jeda peered into the outside gloom. Ruark, barely discernible, as-cended his driver's perch and released the brake. Gragnold climbed up behind him, his scimitar unsheathed and at the ready. Sevrid climbed into the coach, resuming his seat behind the girls, his knife unsheathed and on his lap.

The girls leaned back; there was nothing to be said, though they were bursting with anticipation and all the more so as darkness descended like a blanket obliterating all visibility. A sense of helpless vulnerability settled on them. Even the usually comforting, rhythmic hoof-beats of Ruark's darlings were no longer audible. Only faint vibrations within the carriage gave evidence that they were even underway. There was little of substance to talk about, yet at the same time so much Jeda wanted to say out of sheer nervousness. She slid her hand across the seat and found Glend's.

Glend gratefully squeezed back in return.

A distant whinny followed by shouting shattered the silence. Jeda tensed, thinking of Juued cruelly betrayed into riding point. More shouting, followed by several loud pops.

Then all was silent.

Ruark halted the carriage and whispered something to Gragnold. Two full minutes passed before he received a reply. Sevrid, still seated behind Jeda, leaned forward between the girls, turning his ear first to one window, then the other, then back again.

Jeda whispered, "Do you see anything?"

Sevrid turned his head to the other side of the coach. "Not see; sense."

Ruark half-climbed, half-fell to the ground and moved beside Glend's door. The popping noises started again, but there were no screams or shouts. "It doesn't look good, m'ladies," Ruark whispered.

Glend asked, "What's that popping?"

"Well," Ruark considered, "There's no point deceiving you. You might as well know what we face. What I mentioned a while ago, the half-men, roam in packs like wolves and are carnivorous. We're too far away to hear their growls but the pops you heard likely indicate Juued has met his end. And his horse, as well. You heard his cries for help. Knowing the valiant warrior he was, he probably killed some of them before—"

"But what were the pops?" persisted Glend, squeezing Jeda's hand.

"Bones pop like that when ripped from their sockets. They must be eating their own dead as well; it's not likely much remains of Juued or his horse."

Both Glend and Jeda bit their knuckles.

Suddenly the coach rocked to one side.

Gragnold sprang from up top to the road and dashed to the front of the horses. There was a thud, an inhuman scream, then silence.

CHAPTER SEVENTEEN

RUARK STOOD STOCK-STILL BESIDE THE coach door.

Jeda wondered if Gragnold was still alive.

Hurried hoofbeats were heard rushing toward the coach.

Ruark jumped and gave a yelp.

"Sssss, fool. Bring death."

"Sorry. Oh, I'm sorry. I didn't think you were that close. What did you intercept?"

"Sssss." Gragnold cocked his head listening to the rustling leaves surrounding them.

A sudden snort caused Jeda and Glend to start.

Gragnold sniffed. "Juued's horse; blood on saddle."

Susurration in the forest increased.

Jeda ducked down so only her eyes showed above the window sill. "What's all that commotion?"

"Sssss," hushed Sevrid. "Stupid question."

"Ruark, get up," Gragnold commanded. "I ride horse; you bring coach quick."

Gragnold mounted Juued's horse preparing to dash up the road. Ruark clambered atop his seat, seized the reins and released the brake. His darlings snorted and tossed their heads, impatient to flee the unknown shadows creeping through the hedges lining the road.

The coach lurched forward.

Jeda thought she spied lightning-quick flashes of light out of the corner of her eye. "Sevrid, see those flashes?"

"Fireflies."

Glend whispered in Jeda's ear, "I saw them, too, and they didn't look like fireflies."

Juued's horse whinnied; seconds later several thuds rocked the coach as something leapt from the darkness and clung to the outside of the chassis, clawing for a crevice by which to tear open the doors. The terrified girls hugged each other. Jeda's door bulged inward, threatening to buckle. Sevrid pushed back from the inside. Up top they heard Ruark give a yelp.

Gragnold's wolf-like howl split the night.

Juued's horse whinnied again just before several thuds too numerous to count bombarded each side of the coach. Sevrid threw all his might against the door. For several moments he kept whatever creatures were pressing inward at bay. The door was nigh splintering under the opposing forces. Without warning all external pressure was gone. Sevrid's outward force tore the door loose from its hinges with a loud crack and propelled him out into the night.

Seconds later rough hands (or were they grasping paws?) pulled first Jeda, then Glend, through the shattered portal to spill out onto the roadway. Jeda's arms were immediately pinioned to her sides preventing her from reaching her Child of the Stars. Another hand clamped over her mouth stopping any outcry, then a rag was tied over her mouth Why, oh why hadn't she gotten her sword out? How pitiful! Taken without a struggle. Now it was too late.

A voice urged, "Slit their throats and be done with 'em."

Another, more authoritarian, voice replied, "Sharn, that's not our way, and you know it. Besides, it isn't the Psa woman after all. Just two frightened girls who don't know what they've gotten into."

"They're on their way to become Psa witches though. We can't just let them go," advised yet another.

"True enough, besides, it would be cruel to abandon them here. On or off the road, they'd not last the night," answered the authority. "As I see it, we have only one option."

"You can't be serious," challenged another. Several murmured in agreement.

Jeda struggled against the arms holding her to no avail. A gruff voice growled, "Be still, lass."

"I am serious, and more than that, I'm in charge. If you think my decision unwise, you know the protocols to challenge me back at camp. Until we get back from patrol, I'm in command. We take them prisoner and let Varter decide what to do. Sack 'em."

A rough fabric slid down over Jeda's face and shoulders past her knees. A staff rapped painfully behind both her knees, knocking her off balance as ungentle hands dropped her on the ground. Drawstrings were pulled tight, closing the sack around her ankles. She wasn't even able to kick, thus confined in the stuffy sack she still couldn't reach her sword. After a few moments of wriggling she resigned herself to her fate.

Glend didn't fare as well. Gasps and squeals mingled with grunts from her captors indicated she hadn't capitulated. A light thud followed, and the squealing stopped. A husky voice said, "Now then, Missy, ye'll git worse if'n ye dinnae quiet doon."

Glend whimpered.

Jeda was slung over a shoulder, and the patrol, quite sizable by the sound of their footfalls, set off into the mysterious depths of Ra-Amawl. The air was knocked out of her several times before she learned to time her breathing to her mount's pace. Her entire frame was jolted, her muscles cramped, blood rushed to her head. Never had she known such discomfort. It felt like she was being slowly beaten up. Occasional low hanging tree limbs smacked her as well, raising welts and bruises even through the burlap.

After an interminable stretch of time she was traded off to a fresh mount and had to learn his unique style of dodging brush and branches all over again.

So, the journey continued, transferred to a fresh mount whenever the one carrying her wearied. Her insides ached from the jouncing. She was glad she that she hadn't partaken much from the basket Tressa had given her; with all this jouncing, and in this stuffy sack . . .

But would this torment never end? Twice more she was traded to fresh shoulders. All she could think about was getting relief from the constant pounding.

Glend had whimpered only once more at the outset of the trek, but stopped immediately when a gruff voice threatened, "Hush up lass. Do ye no ken beasties be's aprowlin'?"

That was sufficient. Glend fell silent.

Jeda felt like weeping but it would only make her estate worse. So, instead of dwelling on her misery, she tried to think of Logon. But instead of joyful communion, doubts vexed her. How could this be Logon's plan? Had he forgotten to keep track of her? She knew such questions were wrong, and yet, the circumstances offered no other explanation. How could it be Logon's will for unknown assailants to drag her into Ra-Amawl's depths? What possible good would her death deep in the forest accomplish?

Despair settled on her, she silently cried out, "Logon, I want to trust you, but—"

Then she remembered his eyes. Those eyes so full of understanding, acceptance, forgiveness, mercy; and above all, love. She was comforted, even if these bandits, or half-men, or whatever they were, killed and devoured her, it would never be senseless. Nor could it be that he'd forgotten her. She had to trust that this raid hadn't taken him by surprise. Nothing caught him unawares; the runes on his sword couldn't deceive. Logon was trustworthy, even now.

A faint roar echoed through the forest and the column halted abruptly. Everything suddenly was silent as a graveyard. Then another roar, louder and closer, sounded from behind.

A nervous voice whispered, "We're between them."

Another added, "Sounds as if they haven't eaten lately."

"Shhh."

More silence.

"They've scented us!"

"Shhh."

"Please let me out," Glend's muffled voice whimpered softly. "Don't just drop me and run."

The same thought had occurred to Jeda. Now that Glend had given voice to the thought it seemed a frighteningly real possibility. Simple logic necessitated dropping cumbersome loads, so their captors could flee. Were they about to become fodder for some loathsome, half-starved predator?

A third roar blasted over the patrol from head-on and very close.

"We're surrounded, Bonu."

"Right," replied the leader's voice. "We fight. Weapons out." The ring of scabbards yielding their contents filled the air.

"What about the captives?"

"Un-sack them. I doubt they'll run off."

Jeda's feet tingled painfully as she landed on the ground with a thump. Her sack was untied and roughly removed. She tottered a moment, struggling to regain balance on her awakening legs. She tore the gag off her mouth and saw that all around her were bright blue splotches of light dangling or swinging as if in mid-air. "You, you're kingsmen!"

No one paid her attention as they scurried to defensive positions.

"Hey, I'm one of yo—" She was elbowed aside by a large man hurrying to his post.

"Words of the word." She extracted her sword from the folds of her skirt and held it aloft. The two glowing inches of her sword joined the light of the other swords. All her captors' swords had identical runes aglow with the exception of one sword which had a semi-sheen halfway up the blade as well as identical runes to the others.

Astonished gasps escaped the lips of her captors as her sword joined the common defense.

Glend's eyes popped round and her jaw dropped as she was more than a little taken aback.

Bonu, leader of the patrol and owner of the half-glowing sword, was the first to recover. "Well, look what we have here! And you blokes wanted to turn her loose to her fate." He turned to Glend, "Are you one of us, too?"

Glend, slack-jawed and too astonished to respond, just blinked.

Jeda answered for her, "No, she's not."

"I see. And just what's a Sharpointer kingswoman doing in the Psa woman's coach?"

"I'm not exactly sure of that myself. But I know Logon has led me thus far. Since I've been captured, er, liberated by you, it may be this is what he intended."

"Hmmm, we'll see, later. Right now, we've got some hungry Craniantium lions to dissuade. Have you much battle experience?"

"None to speak of."

"In that case, hopefully, you'll not be needed. If the battle comes your way, you've got enough light on your weapon, if not the proper runes."

"What about her?" Jeda indicated Glend.

"Without the light of Logon, she's on her own. We'll do the best we can, but . . . "

Glend found her voice. "What does that mean?"

Bonu ignored her, having turned to the more urgent business of setting up a perimeter defense.

"What does that mean?" Glend demanded. "Does that mean I'm lion fodder if you traitors all flee?"

"No one will desert you, Glend." Jeda stepped close to her traveling companion.

"Oh sure, words of loyalty from a traitor! That's a lot of comfort."

"Look, I'm trying to be helpful."

"Who needs your help, kingsman. You deceived me, the bodyguards, even Hod-ya! How you managed that I'd like to know. You and I are mortal enemies; don't think I'll trust anything you ever say. For all I know, you'll stab me in the back with that thing when I'm not looking. To think I once wondered if Ecclessites dared live in Carnalia. What a fool I've been!"

An angry roar accompanied by shouting erupted on the right. Blue arcs flashed in the darkness illuminating saucer-sized, leonine eyes and dirk-sized, teeth.

"Fill that gap," Bonu cried out from the fore of the circle.

Several rushed to the spot, but a huge lion, some twenty-feet long, had broken through the first line, and threatened to rampage to the interior where it could maul at will. Bonu, silhouetted against the backdrop of blue light, garbled his words as he charged an invading feline, recklessly throwing himself in front of the great beast, followed closely by other sword-wielding warriors.

Jeda pointed her sword at the battle unfolding in the dimly-lit scene as she stepped protectively in front of Glend.

Shouting and roars broke out on the left flank, further evidence, if any was needed, that a pride of lions surrounded the patrol and was intent on wearing them down. Snarls, growls, shouts, and screams of mortal conflict filled the night. Another lion attacked from the rear.

Then a savage, pain-filled roar burst into the darkness. Bonu's sword had struck a vital spot. The lion whirled around and swatted Bonu who was sent flying. He picked himself up off the ground, checking for injuries. Except for superficial scratches and bruises, he was unhurt. He retrieved his weapon from the turf and sprang again. Again, he was knocked sprawling, this time still clutching his sword. The beast pounced. From underneath Bonu's Child of the Stars found its mark as he gave a mighty, upward thrust into the soft underbelly of the great cat. The lion reared on hind legs, snarling in outrage, its entrails bulging from the slit. It darted away, into the recesses of Ra-Amawl.

The other attackers suddenly withdrew.

Jeda wanted to cheer but noted that no one else celebrated. Wiping blood off his blade, Bonu approached Jeda and Glend.

"Is it over, are they gone?" Jeda asked.

"Too soon to tell. With lions, especially Craniantium lions, you're never sure if you've beaten them, or if they're just regrouping. Those beasts are unusually intelligent. They almost order their attacks like men."

"Bonu, sir. I think they've gone," said an approaching form out of the dark.

"We'll wait," responded Bonu.

"I'd be glad to scout, if you like, sir," ventured the voice.

"Go ahead, Etel. But use care. Take someone reliable with you."

"Right. Hanell, up for some adventure?"

An affirmative grunt greeted him, and the two left the circle of men dressing wounds and regrouping for another attack.

"Knarsh," Bonu called.

A man ran up, panting. "Yessir?"

"Casualties?"

"Yessir." And he disappeared into the jungle's obscurity as quickly as he'd appeared.

Bonu took the girls aside. "We've got some time; now we can talk. No sense whispering either. That battle announced our presence to everything within a mile. Now, tell me, how is it that a Sharpointer is riding in the Psa woman's coach?"

"It's a long story."

"Time is what we have at the moment."

Jeda briefly recounted being disowned by her parents, how she discovered Smid's sword, was delivered to the castle, interviewed by

Hod-ya, met Dancel, snuck out to a secret brigade meeting, had her heart pierced, and was selected by Hod-ya for Psa's shrine on the basis of her first interview.

Glend faced Jeda with cold eyes. "So-oo, Dancel is one of you, too,"

"Oh dear, I shouldn't have revealed that."

"Am I to understand that Glend didn't know your true loyalties?" intruded Bonu.

"Not until I pulled out my Child of the Stars during the lion attack."

"Amazing such a bright light remained hidden so long. No one else knew?"

"Well," Jeda looked dubiously at Glend.

"Might as well tell," said Glend with saucy toss of her head. "What harm can I do out here, captive to your king and his lackeys, doomed to a more horrible fate than if I'd stayed a scullery maid in Marga's kitchen. Even if I escaped, which I am loath to do in this evil forest, I'd never find my way to warn Hod-ya of all the infidels in her ranks."

"Miss, I promise no harm will come to you. I'm sure you understand why we dare not give you freedom ever again, unless, hopefully in time, you let your heart be pierced and yield allegiance to Logon Xychirion."

"Why don't you hold your breath until I do," retorted Glend. "So, please tell us Jeda, who are your fellow conspirators. Juued?"

"He knew but wasn't an Ecclessite himself."

"Juued?" asked Bonu.

"The man, the noble warrior, you rebels pulled limb from limb to make us think you were half-men," spat Glend.

"What?"

"We heard the popping noises," explained Jeda.

"Popping noi—Oh, Juued was your advance guard? Ha ha. Rest assured he wasn't popped limb from limb. The pops you heard were tree limbs being broken to make a cage for his protection. We had him off his horse and bound before he even knew we were there. He did manage to shout once or twice before we gagged him. That's how we knew you were back there. His Ecclessite sword puzzled us a little, though it had no glow until we handled it. We figured it for a souvenir."

"Juued is alive and well?" Glend asked.

"Settle for alive. He was pretty much cramped in that cage. We suspended it high enough to protect him from most prowling beasts. It'll take a couple of hours to unknot him when he's found."

"And Ruark, our coachman?" Jeda pried.

"Ah now, that plump fellow, being what he was and yet willingly doing what he was doing . . . "

Glend got face to face with Jeda. "Being what he was? What was he?"

Ignoring Glend, Jeda explained, "I tried talking to him, but he always had a rationalization. I finally gave up, wondering if I was being too critical. What's become of him?"

"You mean, no, it can't be, he's one of you, too?" Glend sat back, incredulity in every line of her face.

Bonu ignored Glend. "We exposed his barely glowing sword before those blackguards, so he's revealed now and has nowhere to run but to us. A couple of men are watching him this very moment, waiting to bring him to safety when he decides he wants it."

"Knarsh reporting, sir," interrupted a soldier coming up behind Bonu. "No serious or disabling injuries. About two dozen with scratches, some that will need attending; and a couple were bitten, but not much blood. As far as I know, a few sprains, but no broken bones."

"Logon was with us. Thank the king, it wasn't bad at all. Thank you, Knarsh. You may return."

"Did you kill the bodyguards?" asked Jeda.

"Your sword point has enough light on it for you to know that that's not Logon's way, girl."

Jeda rankled at his condescension. "Well, yes, but, they're so evil."

"No one is beyond being pierced by Logon's swords; if they can be pierced, they can be rescued."

"Etel and Hanell reporting in, sir," came another voice out of the nearby darkness.

"Yes?"

"All seems clear. We found one lion, dead of wounds received. We think it's the one you disemboweled."

"Yeah, it felt like a vital spot. Okay, pass the word to form up."

"The, uh, captives?"

"Will go under their own power."

Etel and Hanell vanished. Feet shuffled all around the girls as word was passed and the troop gathered their gear.

"Stay right behind me," Bonu instructed. "Jeda, you're responsible to keep Glend in line. Use your sword to illumine the path. There's no sense cloaking our presence anymore. Speed, not stealth, is our ally now."

Bonu rose from his haunches. "Right, then, men. Let your blades gleam to warn any predators that we're not to be trifled with. Onward."

A column of blue lights tagged after Bonu as he led the Runer patrol back to camp. Jeda was grateful to be on her own legs rather than jouncing along on someone's shoulders. She was also thankful to be among kingsmen.

Glend glumly plodded along.

CHAPTER EIGHTEEN

TRUDGING FOR HOURS UP AND down hillocks littered with boulders, around or over fallen trees, and through cocklebur bushes took a toll on Jeda and Glend. Their skirts frequently snagged bringing contemptuous looks from Bonu, to their dismay. When the patrol finally took a rest, Jeda trimmed the larger tatters from their hems with her sword.

"Leave no threads," warned Bonu as he stood over them, "they'd make a fine trail to our encampment. We're in the general region of our camp now and need to be extra cautious."

Jeda swept her sword point near the ground to make sure she hadn't dropped any threads.

"How much farther?" Jeda frowned quizzically at Glend's sly smile but then thought better of her suspicions and turned her attention to Bonu.

"Well, it'll be light, so to speak, in another hour. Then about another half-hour's trek. All in all, about two hours."

"I'd hoped we were closer."

"It won't seem so long, you'll see." Bonu pursed his lips and chirred like a cricket. The patrol rose to their feet.

Jeda followed Bonu, sweeping her sword to light the path. Glend followed Jeda, taking cues from Jeda's dodging and weaving to avoid obstacles.

It was exhausting for Jeda to meticulously place her feet where they wouldn't snap twigs or rustle in the dried leaves. Now that they were closer to camp Bonu stressed stealth more than speed. Jeda soon discovered that Bonu's concept of stealth was vastly different than her own. Bonu kept turning and holding a finger to his lips even when Jeda took special pains to be quiet. Bonu finally gave in to a more accommodating pace but still glanced back in exasperation, saying nothing, apparently realizing further admonishments were a waste of breath.

Jeda, in turn, was annoyed at his unrealistic expectations. Couldn't he see she was trying her best?

Jeda's mood darkened despite having much reason to rejoice, after all she was no longer on her way to Pitland but rescued by Ecclessites, and she was no longer in that stuffy sack fighting nausea. She was surprised at herself for harboring such animosity against Bonu. Sure, every muscle in her back and legs ached, the soles of her feet were sore, and nothing suited Bonu; but why this inappropriate anger? Making matters worse, she owed Bonu a debt of gratitude for insisting on doing the right thing by taking the girls, burden that they were, to their campsite in Ra-Amawl instead of letting them fend for themselves.

A sword tip touched Jeda, stinging behind her right ear. Her fingers reflexively went to the spot and were smeared in blood. Enough was enough! She turned to swat her tormentor, but Bonu reached back blocking her strike.

"He intentionally nicked me with his sword," Jeda breathed out hotly, displaying a bloody finger.

Hanell, the man behind her, bowed his head. "Pardon, Miss, but you were irked."

"So, poking me with your sword is going to improve my attitude? Maybe you don't know it, but this has been a trying day, what with being sacked and forced to jog miles on end over terrain a deer would find difficult. Please explain how my being disturbed gives you the right to slit my throat."

"No, no, you don't understand. You were being 'irked', you know, by irks." Hanell held his sword up for Jeda's inspection, as if that was self-explanatory.

"What?" she snapped.

"Irks." Hanell took a finger-nail-sized insect off his blade and held it up to her face. It was round with eight legs sticking out and a long, needle-thin snout. "Haven't you ever seen an irk before?"

Jeda scrunched her features and pulled back. "Ugh! What a disgusting—"

"It was sucking your blood. There, behind you ear, see?"

"It was sucking my—Eww!"

"Good thing I got it when I did, too. It was fixing to bore in."

Jeda's eyes widened and her lips parted at the prospect of that filthy bug crawling into her.

Bonu dabbed her wound and then her finger with a clean piece of cloth. "Irks dwell on trees as well as the ground in Ra-Amawl. When something warm-blooded passes underneath they drop onto it claiming it as a host and then poke their snouts into tender skin, usually just below or behind the ear. They're a lot like ticks and such, except they burrow under your skin to lay eggs."

"But I never felt the bite."

"No, of course not. They desensitize your feelings. You might feel a slight itch when they first land, but often not even that if you're distracted. The best way we've learned to detect irk bites is by a sullen, angry attitude coming over us for no apparent reason."

"Oh."

"They're a lower form of lurcanish agent that do his bidding as surely as tophets and cusps."

"Well, I was feeling miffed, but did you have to cut me?"

"I didn't cut you," said Hanell. "I merely touched the irk with the flat of my blade, that's all. The sting you felt was its snout ripping out and blood running down your neck because I touched my sword to it. You'll be alright now."

"Ooh, check me, too," pleaded Glend.

"I already did. No sign of 'em."

"What would have happened if it had burrowed in and laid eggs?" Jeda gingerly touched the swelling behind her right ear.

"Best not to talk about such things right now," advised Bonu. "If dark thoughts cross your mind again, have one of us check you. Ready to move on?"

"Wait a minute. Isn't there something I can do to protect myself?"

"Oh, I thought you understood. Keep a rune in your mind, one that recently taught you something about Logon. That usually prevents them from attaching."

"Are you serious? Just thinking about one of the runes will keep them from biting me? How?"

"Oh, they may bite, but as soon as they break the skin, they'll sense Logon's presence if your thoughts are on him. They'll drop off so fast you'd think a cinder was put to them."

"Are there," Glend gulped and compulsively checked her ears, neck and throat again. "many of them?"

"They abound everywhere, especially in dark places like this forest. Ready to go?"

Glend drew her hood strings tight as the troop resumed its journey.

At long last the dark of night showed signs of passing as a muted light filtered through the interlocked branches overhead. Jeda wondered how long daylight had been abroad before penetrating beneath Ra-Amawl's verdant bowers?

A slight sensation, almost an itch near her earlobe startled her. She slapped her neck. Upon examining her fingers, she found a squashed mosquito.

Bonu stopped and examined the parasite. "Good thing you got him!"

"Why?" Jeda asked, alarmed at the potential danger even ordinary things like bugs and mosquitos posed under Ra-Amawl's dark influence. "What do they do?"

"Suck your blood."

Was there a smirk on his face as he turned around? Sure, go ahead, make a joke! Then, aware of her attitude, Jeda cautiously re-checked her neck but found nothing. Her resentment was her own this time. She plodded on, using her sword less as daylight grew. To Jeda's eye there was no trail, but, as Dancel knew each doorway in the palace maze, Bonu seemed acquainted with each tree and bush. His lead never faltered; he never stopped to reconsider his direction but confidently led onward.

Of the entire party, Jeda and Glend made the only discernible noise, irritating Jeda all the more; she wanted to prove to Bonu, who was so full of himself, so confident in his ability, that she was quite capable of taking care of herself. The more she thought about it, the more piqued she became.

A light thwack on the left side of her neck along with the familiar sting interrupted her thoughts.

"Not again!"

"Afraid so." Hanell withdrew his sword. "You must keep your mind on Logon or a rune. It's the mind they affect first. They're able to sense what your mind is dwelling on. Their venom will produce all manner of smoldering grudges against others. Carnalians are like that anyway, so irk bites don't always have an immediate effect on them, for their thoughts are already lurcanish in nature."

"Do you mean I have been perspiring under this hood when I didn't have to?" moaned Glend. "Well, I like that! Why didn't anyone tell me?"

Ignoring Glend, Hanell continued, "We Ecclessites will have a different perspective on things as long as we keep Logon-like thoughts in our minds. If we allow those annoying little beasties under our skin, which they can achieve quickly, they'll lay eggs that hatch into worms, which in turn, will infect more of our thinking making it difficult to toll swords or get along with each other. Many kingsmen become unreasonable, unteachable, and opinionated, thus becoming useless to Logon."

"All that from a little bug bite?"

"Well, I've described the worst case, but why go through even a little of that, if you don't have to?"

"Once the eggs are laid, can anything be done?"

"It's difficult, but yes. The infested person must constantly be watchful; every time a grumpy or critical thought arises, they must immediately recognize and counter it with a rune or runesong. That usually drives out or kills the hatched worm, but each hatchling must be dealt with individually, and you're never quite sure when they're all gone. So, like I said, be safe and don't dwell on *irky* things."

"I'll be more careful."

"Seems like Carnalians have all the advantages, eh?" Glend mocked.

Hanell dropped back to walk alongside Glend. "I didn't say irks never bite Carnalians, but when they do, their end is worse than any Ecclessite's."

"How's that?" Glend was less cocky, but still defiant.

"Unchecked, the worms inhabit the heart after taking over the mind, making them impenetrable to all but the most determined application of runes from a Child of the Stars."

"Doesn't sound so bad to me."

"Ahh, it would if you knew where that path leads."

"Okay, so tell me."

"Yes, Hanell. I think the time has come. Tell her," Bonu said over his shoulder.

"Well, all right," agreed Hanell. "If you refuse to allow Logon Xychirion's words to enter your heart, you prevent him from giving you his life."

"Ugh! Stop right there. Who wants the life of someone else in them? This whole fantasy is too disgusting to listen to."

"But you already have another's life in you, living out its will through you, dominating your nature, and you don't even know it."

"Not likely! I know who I am and am in complete control of my own wits."

"Live for the moment, die for the empire," quoted Jeda.

"Lurcan and his ilk live out their desires through you, and not only you, but millions of others just like you. You think you control your life, but in actuality you're a puppet, a slave to the greed and passions Lurcan casts upon you. He vicariously continues his rebellion, evil, hatred, and cruelty through his slaves."

"I see, and the way to liberation is to let you stick cold steel right into my heart, right? Well, no thanks! Even if what you said was true, I'd rather be Lurcan's slave than fools like all of you. Your king isn't even strong enough to protect his servants and soldiers from butchery."

"We passed the field of skulls on the way to Suffers Tree Inn," Jeda explained.

"Ah, and no doubt you think that was a victory for Lurcan?" said Hanell.

"Oh no-oo," mocked Glend, "anyone could see what a great victory that was for you kingsmen."

"It truly was," returned Hanell.

"Then the dead are better off than the living."

"If they die in loyal service to the king, they are," Hanell said, unperturbed by Glend's caustic taunts. "Victory lies not solely on the battlefield, but by what has been won in the heart. You'll meet some survivors of that battle back at camp; they can tell you what they gained better than I."

"But we were told there were no survivors." Jeda paused mid-step.

"Yes, Lurcan's agents claim that, but Lurcan is a liar, therefore all his servants are deceived and spread his lies. The kingsmen that died in that massacre won the greater battle of giving Elyon glory at the cost of their instinct for self-preservation. Messengers had been sent to the gates to persuade Ecclessites to save their lives by renouncing allegiance to Logon. They were promised their lives would be spared, but none went out of the fortress, choosing instead to renounce all ties to Lurcan, dying to the moment so they might live to the eternal."

"May all the king's soldiers have such victories." Glend stomped on a branch.

"You're a hard one, aren't you? Nevertheless, and bear this in mind, all lives end someday. Those who live and die in Logon's service will be rewarded with good things that will never end."

"And just how is that supposed to happen to the dead and dis-membered? Can't you see how foolish this sounds? You win battles by being killed; you live forever by dying; you believe death is the ultimate fulfillment of life, so why don't you all just commit suicide and achieve your desired end?"

"There are two kinds of death, Glend. We who follow Logon escape the second, and by far the worst, death. The first death is but a shadow of the second death, just as this life is but a shadow of the second life, which those who obey Logon will receive in Splendora. But you'll never know the second life unless you first escape the second death."

"You're cusp-touched."

"Do you want to hear about the second death?"

"Not really. You don't believe all this first-life, second-death stuff, do you Jeda?"

"Well I . . . I haven't applied my toller to all the runes that reveal those things, but I see no reason to doubt these men. I've seen some of the runes that apply, like the Bubbling Sea of Pitch."

Hanell quick-stepped to catch up to Bonu. "Can we take a halt? I think a few minutes looking at some runes would be well spent."

Bonu's hand went up, signifying a pause rather than a complete rest. "You and Plenk fall out with the girls. The rest of us will press on to camp since we're so close. I want to make my report without delay, though I see the advantage of bringing only kingsmen into the enclosure if you have success with her. I think we're safe enough now. Will the two of you be enough?"

"I'm sure. Besides, where could she go?"

Bonu nodded and Plenk fell out as the patrol continued. Bonu left without another word or even a backward glance at Jeda. How could he be so, so, inconsiderate? Jeda's hand went to her neck but found nothing. Well then, if he was just going to ignore her . . . fine. She'd just ignore him, too.

The patrol passed silently on, leaving the four examining the rune in question. Glend wasn't exactly excited to have to hear the runes explained, but both girls were glad for the rest, knowing that Bonu's "almost there" probably meant another hour of hard hiking.

"The rune *Pur* teaches intense suffering as a result or consequence,'" Hanell laid his sword across his lap and tolled by a rune. "It doesn't, however, mean that the infraction will ever be adjudged as paid for, for the infractions that incur this penalty are of the greatest magnitude. Since the only pardon available has been rejected, nothing is left but punishment of the highest magnitude—torment forever in the 'flames of regret'."

"Whatever are you talking about? Who here has committed the crime of the highest magnitude? Because if you're insinuating I did, I've got news for you. I'm the victim of crimes, and whatever crimes I can return won't begin to make up for what I've suffered." The hardness of Glend's face revealed that she spoke from a deep-rooted bitterness. "All these trumped-up threats of eternal torment don't move me. Number one, it doesn't exist, and number two, if it did exist, with all your talk about Elyon being loving, just and true, he'd avenge me, not condemn me!"

Hanell sighed. "It doesn't work that way. All Carnalia, indeed all nations of the empire, are enslaved to Lurcan. Since Lurcan is the king's enemy, when he's overthrown, and rest assured he will be, he'll be tried for crimes of treason against King Elyon and Logon Xychirion. After the evidence is examined, he'll be judged and sentenced to the 'flames of regret' forever. So will all that follow him instead of seeking Logon's amnesty. Logon Xychirion seeks to pardon all who will turn away from Lurcan to follow him."

"So, if I don't turn traitor against my emperor, and he loses the war, I'll be punished for his crimes, even though my crimes are far less than his? What kind of justice is that?"

"You'll be held accountable for murdering the king's son: treason of the highest magnitude."

"I never murdered anyone, much less the king's son!"

"He gave his life to pardon your crimes against him. As long as you refuse that pardon you treat his blood as common dirt. Acting as if Logon's sacrifice is of no importance is the same as contributing to his murder. Persisting in that attitude will give the king no choice but to allow the consequences you've chosen. Thus, you reject the only possible pardon. By serving Lurcan, who instigated Logon's murder, you, his servant, are complicit in the crime and deserve the same penalty."

"Well, I don't see it that way. Besides, look around. Does it seem as if Lurcan is about to be overthrown by a ragtag bunch of misfits such as yourselves? I think not."

"Glend, don't be so stubborn," urged Jeda. "Listen to him. He speaks the truth."

"Humph! The witchy powers I've seen you use don't exactly make you a credible witness for their side. You claim to be for Logon, and may have duped such as these, but I've seen your powers. Such wiles can only come from the dreads of the gate!"

"What's she talking about?" asked Plenk who had been silent until Glend leveled this accusation.

"Some Eroton soldiers were menacing us," Jeda explained. "Logon gave me wisdom that turned our enemies' focus on each other. She thinks I charmed them."

"Don't forget how you charmed Juued, and the spell you cast on the children at the inn. Who knows how many other spells you've cast? Could an ordinary Ecclessite come all this way without those two dronnets knowing?"

"I thought you didn't believe such things," countered Jeda.

"Well, maybe you've opened my eyes. Obviously, I believe there are kingsmen in Carnalia. Who knows but that before all this is over, you'll turn out to be a tophet yourself?"

Hanell regarded Jeda suspiciously. "These are serious charges, Miss. I hope you have good answers. I'm afraid we need to look deeper into this. Our existence is too precarious to take anyone at face value. I'm sure you understand why we need to keep you under close scrutiny and not let either of you have the run of the camp until we're certain of your loyalties."

"I understand. I'm too weary to wander about, anyway. All I want to do when I get to your camp is sleep," said Jeda.

"Let's be on our way then," Hanell stood. "It seems we've gained nothing for our efforts; indeed, we may have more problems than we originally thought. Plenk, take care of Glend, I'll guard Jeda. Let's go."

Though frustrated at having to prove herself, Jeda arose and followed, too weary to voice her emotions, hoping that camp would soon be reached, and all these ridiculous questions put to rest. A rune came to mind:

The King's follower is delivered from all danger,
The wicked will inherit it in their stead.

She was comforted, and although she'd not tolled the rune herself, she understood.

CHAPTER NINETEEN

THEY WALKED ANOTHER HALF-HOUR UPON a bed of moss permitting Jeda to walk less carefully. Glend also clumped along, relieved, too, from the hours of stalking stealthily within the primal forest. Walking on the moss seemed more like floating on air after such a long night's trek over rough terrain. They were once again able to swing their hands freely and relieve aches as they gawked at the ancient timberland surrounding them. Immense boles covered with lichen rose into the heights, fern beds stood waist high, mushrooms like stepstools littered the ground in circles, and shelf fungi extruded like ladders on various trees as if inviting one to scale into the heights and have a look around.

An obscenely loud crackling disrupted the silence; both Jeda and Glend yelped in fright. The moss bed that had lulled them into carelessness had abruptly become a bed of dried twigs, a warning hazard surrounding the kingsmen encampment. They were within hailing distance.

The two escorts suppressed laughter at the panic-induced knee-high prancing of the girls in reaction to their fright and dismay at being the source of the racket.

Controlling his mirth, Hanell pointed and advised, "Use the stones."

Miffed, Jeda followed Hanell's point. Sure enough, flat stepping stones were set at regular intervals crossing the noise hazard. "You might have warned us."

The girls trailed single file after Hanell, Plenk brought up the rear.

"I expected," said Hanell in his own defense, "that you were placing your feet in my tracks."

"Well, we weren't."

"Anyway," Plenk added, "you now see one of our alarms against invaders."

Hanell added, "See that hedgerow ahead?"

Jeda glanced ahead, trying not to miss the rock his foot had just vacated. A twelve-foot-high hedge loomed with interwoven branches tighter than Ra-Amawl's overhead boughs. "Yes, I see it. So?" Drawing nearer Jeda also saw three-inch thorns dispersed throughout. "Surely you don't intend to crawl through that!"

Hanell chirped a short, high-pitched note like a finch.

"No need for that, Hanell," a voice came apparently out of nowhere. "We heard you stomping on the crackle hazard and knew it must be you. That's why we didn't rouse the camp."

A five-foot wide section of the hedge slid noiselessly to one side.

Upon entering the compound Jeda discovered that the entire hedge was only two feet thick though from the outside it appeared to be an impenetrable thorn thicket. The sliding "gate" was suspended by tree vines. It was an impressive display of camouflage engineering. Anyone just outside would never suspect an encampment of Ecclessites lay merely feet away.

Inside the campgrounds the earth was bare; void of dry leaves and twigs and anything that would make a noise. Walking quietly would be no problem. Looking upward Jeda espied several archers concealed in the treetops. Others stood at intervals along the wall equipped with bows and even some with crossbows, peering out of arrow loops.

"Arrows?" Jeda raised her eyebrows. "I wasn't aware kingsmen defended themselves by killing. Does Logon approve?"

"Calm down, Miss," said Plenk. "Carnalians aren't the only invaders we worry about, you know."

"Oh, yes, of course, lions."

"And half-men, wolves, and—"

"Enough Plenk. They've already seen too much of our defenses. The captain needs to determine what to do with them."

Glend was subdued as they were led through the camp. Jeda wondered if she was finally accepting the futility of resistance, or was she up to something?

They were taken to a tent with one door flap tied open. Captain Varter sat at a table poring over a doeskin map spread out before him. Candles flickered as the other tent flap was lifted to admit the stragglers.

Varter looked up, his eyes red from prolonged scrutiny of rivers, canebrakes, swamps, marshes, ridges, and valleys scribed on the map. He blinked, rubbed his eyes with his knuckles and stared at the intruders. "What is it?"

"Uh, sir, these are the girls I told you about," said Bonu, who was standing just off to the side. "Did you have any success, Hanell?"

"Not even when we revealed the rune *Pur*. In fact, as we discoursed, some interesting facts came to light about this other young lady, as well."

"Such as?" The captain rose to full height and stretched his back muscles. He was well over six feet, broad-shouldered, and trim at the waist. His steel-gray eyes were kindly, though there was an air about him that signaled that he wasn't to be trifled with. His tunic, worn as an outer garment, was clean and white. A sword hanging from his belt swung in tiny arcs as the captain stretched from side to side. The entire length of the blade was aglow, albeit, faintly, but certain runes here and there glowed brightly.

"Well, sir, it seems this one has accused her companion that has the Child of the Stars of sorcery." Hanell nudged Jeda forward.

Captain Varter's eyes rested on Jeda for a long moment, studying her. "You possess a sword? Hold it up; Jeda, is it?"

Jeda nodded and rested the glowing point of her sword on the desk. She studied Captain Varter as he bent over and examined her sword. His hair was unkempt, and longer than military men usually wore it, especially those of rank. Deep lines creased his brow and he had wrinkles around the eyes; a black and gray-flecked mustache and beard completed her examination of his face. She thought him to be a fair man, though capable of deep anger if pushed.

He suddenly yanked the sword from Jeda's grasp.

Light sprang along the whole outer edge with his own familiar runes being the brighter spots. "Well, it's genuine, and I surmise so is she, even if she is a Sharpointer."

"I found the girl trustworthy, sir," said Bonu from the shadows.

The girl! He referred to her as "the girl"! Jeda bit the inside of her cheek to keep her tongue from setting him straight. How dare he refer to her as a mere girl after all she'd been through?

Captain Varter glanced at Glend and asked, "And this one?"

"I believe this young lady, on the other hand, should definitely be under restriction. If given the chance she'd betray us quicker than a viper strike." Bonu stepped back.

So, Glend was "this young lady" while Jeda only rated "the girl." Well, Mister Bonu, Jeda thought, you can just mind your own business and treat me like a "girl," if that's what you think. Then her lips parted slightly and Jeda discretely checked her neck for irks.

" . . . in the Psa woman's coach?"

Captain Varter expected her to answer.

"Uh, I'm sorry, sir. I was distracted. Could you repeat the question?"

"I asked, why were you in the Psa woman's coach? I mean, it's not every day we raid Hod-ya's personal coach, let alone discover an Ecclessite on her way to Pitland. How do you explain that?"

"I'm not sure I can. I'm so weary, I can't seem to think straight."

"Poor thing, she's had a trying time of it, captain," ventured Bonu.

"I don't need you to defend me!" Jeda snapped. "Oh, please excuse me, captain. I don't know why I did that. Perhaps it is those irk bites."

"Hmmm, I think not." Varter gave Jeda's sword back.

"Captain Varter, I'm very tired. Could you—?"

"Yes, of course. Plenk, take these young women to their quarters."

"Yessir! Follow me, ladies." Plenk led outside and turned toward some larger tents manifesting signs of domestic life: laundry drying on lines, cooking pots over small, smokeless fires, and a few crude child's toys scattered about. Plenk led to a large tent at the end of the row hard by the camouflaged back wall surrounding the camp. "Those tents over there are for single men, then over here are the married quarters," Plenk indicated with a sweep of his arm. "And these over here at this end are for single women like yourselves." Plenk turned and called, "Vawella?"

An attractive, dark-haired girl stuck her head out of a nearby tent.

"Your father said to assign cots to these two. This one, Glend, is to be guarded at all times. She has not been to Logon's Rock and has no inclination to go as of yet. Jeda here, is one of us, though there was some suspicion, but your father trusts her."

Vawella emerged from the tent. She was tall and sturdy with no excess weight. Like her father, Vawella's tunic was white and visible under the opening of her outer garment. "Hi," she offered after a quick perusal of the new inhabitants. "You look exhausted."

"They're what we netted from the raid. It seems someone misunderstood his hunch."

"What? You captured them from the inn road and marched them all the way here in one night? Who's responsible for that decision?"

"Bonu."

"Well he ought to know better." Then to Jeda and Glend, "I'm afraid . . . never mind. Uh, Glend, you can have the first cot inside the door. Jeda, yours will be all the way at the back end. That's the best we can do for now, but if you're as exhausted as you look, where your cot is won't matter."

Jeda was already through the tent flap searching for an empty cot.

Glend wearily said to Vawella, "Don't mind at all," and collapsed on her cot, not even removing her shoes. Within a minute she was breathing deeply.

Twelve cots intervened between Glend's and Jeda's, all perfectly made without a wrinkle. Underneath each bed was someone's belongings set in orderly array. Jeda plopped down on the edge of her cot and kicked off her shoes. Outside she heard voices.

"But, Vawella, where will you sleep?"

"I'll work something out. Meanwhile, Hanell, please go and alert a couple of my charges that I need to see them. I think you'll find them over at the mess tent."

"Sure, no problem. Have you, er, told your father, about, you know?"

"He's been so busy receiving scouting reports that I didn't want to burden him. The time will come, soon, Hanell. Please, be patient."

Jeda's head hit the pillow and her eyes closed as the voices receded. Other sounds of the camp blurred together into a hum as sleep overtook her.

CHAPTER TWENTY

"JEDA," A VOICE INTRUDED ON her dream, "time to rise and help prepare our evening meal."

Jeda rolled over and sat up acutely aware of her aching muscles.

Vawella stood over her smiling. "You'll catch up on sleep after the meal and the evening assembly."

Jeda stretched her arms overhead. "Ooh-ahh, how long have I been asleep?"

"Since mid-morning, about six hours."

Jeda yawned and arched her back.

"You can freshen up out back; there's an enclosure that will afford privacy as you tend to your needs. Uh, you may find these clothes more suitable to wilderness living than those."

Jeda surveyed her tattered, wine-red, velvet gown. How pitiful it looked, once so gay and attractive, the desire of all the girls who saw it; even Velnu and Cornil had designs on it despite their own closets bursting with fashionable trousseau, which is why, out of pettiness, she'd kept it. How foolish. But she didn't know Logon then, nor that she'd receive a Logon dress that put all their rags to shame even though it was the simplest of garments. She should have let Cornil have the gown. Such grandiose things were of little use in Logon's service.

How wonderful it felt to be amongst kingsmen! So, this is what Logon had in mind when he sent her on such a dangerous mission. It was puzzling, for Logon warned she'd encounter dangers and malevolent creatures plotting against Ecclessa and people victimizing each other. That warning seemed so remote now.

"After you're refreshed go to the wooden building; it's the only one in the compound. That's where we take our meals, hold rune instruction, and receive daily assignments. Tonight, Bonu will relate your rescue. You're expected to say a few words, an explanation of why you were where you were. So, be prepared." Vawella went to the front of the tent to wake Glend who still slept soundly. There was a stake in the ground with a chain that went under Glend's covers.

"Is that necessary?" Jeda rose from the cot.

"It does look severe, I'm afraid, but it's necessary. If we're discovered, it will mean annihilation. We can take no chances." Before waking Glend Vawella unlocked the padded ankle shackle.

Jeda went outside.

People scurried cheerfully to and fro quietly greeting one another. She found the latrine enclosure satisfactory though crude and sparse as bathhouses went. There was a wooden barrel half-full of tepid water. Bars of soap rendered from wood ash and animal fat lay on a nearby shelf alongside a soft chamois for drying.

"Well, this is more like it. Even the inn didn't afford the luxury of a bath," she said aloud climbing in for a good soak.

She rinsed her face and neck and settled back, letting the warm water soothe her aching muscles.

Glend entered. "Well here you are! I suppose this is all to your liking, isn't it?"

"Well, I—"

"I bet they didn't chain you down, did they? Did you know they shackled me? As if there was anywhere I could escape to."

"Can you blame them? After all, you choose to continue being their—our enemy."

"Sure, go ahead, side with them. You probably cast some spell on that captain 'Varmint', making him think you're an Ecclessite."

"I am an Ecclessite, Glend. If you still think I charmed those Erotons you should know that Logon protects his followers. That's how we were protected, not by spells."

"Save it, Jeda, Logon didn't protect that fortress along the road, so why should he protect you? Hey, hurry up will you, I'm stinky and sticky. Haven't you been in there long enough?"

"Okay, I'm done. Hand me a chamois, will you"

As Jeda dried herself, Glend clambered into the barrel, sloshing water to the floor. "Look, Jeda, you're content to be here, but I'm not. I can't stand these people; they make my flesh crawl. I'm terrified they'll tie me up and stick a sword through me. You can't let that happen. Help me escape, I'm begging you. We've been through too much for you to abandon me now. You owe me."

"It's not like that, Glend. You must be willing to allow Logon's blade to pierce your heart, else nothing will come of it. Besides, where could you go? You must see yourself as you are, not how you imagine yourself."

"I'm not the one living in an imaginary world."

Footsteps in the outer entry disrupted their conversation. Jeda hastily pulled on her Logon dress as Glend hunched below the barrel's edge.

Two girls about Jeda's age rounded the corner. Their Logon dresses were worn beneath rugged, outer clothing. Swords dangled from their leather belts. Both girls were pretty, with shoulder-length brown hair and sparkling green eyes.

"Which of you is Glend?" asked one.

"She is." Without hesitation Glend pointed at Jeda.

Jeda's arm was half raised to point at Glend. It took only a second for her to recover. "No! She's Glend."

"This is easily settled you know," said the other girl. "All we have to do is touch you with a sword. So, who is Glend?"

Glend moodily rinsed her hair as Jeda reiterated, "She is."

"Aha! Well, Glend, as long as you're in camp, Ble-ana and I will be at your side. My name is Dacey. Don't let our appearance fool you; we're trained guards and will use whatever force is necessary. If you co-operate, you'll discover we can be nice, too."

"Are you going to chain me?"

"That depends. If you don't give us any trouble, I doubt that'll be necessary, except at night."

"Oh, Jeda, don't leave me."

"Now, now, you're not trying very hard to find out what good company we can be," Ble-ana wagged her finger at Glend.

"And we do have much to talk about," added Dacey.

Glend disappeared beneath the water and came up huffing loudly, clearing her nostrils and mouth. "Like what?"

"Like how we each met Logon and how much he loves you and wants you to meet him."

"Pitland! I'd rather be irk bit. Jeda, you can't leave me alone with them."

"Jeda has her orders. She couldn't stay even if she wanted to."

"I have orders?" Jeda hadn't thought she'd be put in service so quickly. "What are they?"

"Vawella, servant of the unmarried women, will assign you," said Dacey.

"But I just left her a short while ago before coming to bathe; she said nothing about orders."

"Are you sure? That's not like her."

"She told me I could come here and freshen up, and then, if I liked, go to the wooden building. Oh, she also suggested I prepare some explanation for tonight about how I got involved in this adventure."

"My dear," said Ble-ana, "when Vawella suggests something, it's an order."

"Oh, I see. Well, in that case, I'd better go. Uh, how do I fasten my sword to this belt? I only know how to conceal it in the folds of my skirt, and this skirt isn't long enough to hide all of it."

"Hmmm, start by loosening this strap, see, like this, and slip it around the wings of your hand guard, that's it. Now, tie it back . . . no, not like that or you'll never get it loose in a hurry." Ble-ana took hold of the strap and demonstrated a simple knot that was secure yet could be released with a mere tug. "There, now you try it. Yes, you've got it."

"It feels so different."

"You'll get used to it. In fact, you'll prefer this method to hiding it 'neath the folds of a skirt."

"Yes, I can see that, if it doesn't trip me, swinging like that when I walk. Thank you."

"It can't cause you to stumble, Jeda, just like it won't harm a loyal kingsman in battle or practice."

"Well, I'd better go."

"No, Jeda!" Glend cried plaintively.

Dacey winked at Jeda and Ble-ana laughed. "She'll be all right. You should go like Vawella suggested. She's probably waiting."

"I do hope you're not going to prove difficult, Glend." Dacey placed her hands on the sides of the barrel. "The last time someone proved difficult we had to keep her tied and gagged four weeks before she finally surrendered."

"Oh, Jeda," Glend sank beneath the water's surface with a pitiful wail that turned into bubbles.

Jeda exited combing out her hair as she went. She stood at the outside entry of the tent and searched for the central building.

A masculine voice hailed from behind, "Jeda, Jeda, wait up."

Turning, she saw Bonu jogging toward her. She bit her lower lip. What did he want?

"I'm glad I chanced to see you." He stopped beside her, noting, "Took a bath, I see. That's good." He stared into her eyes, blushing slightly.

"Oh? Was I," Jeda turned away, continuing toward the lodge, "so offensive?"

"What? Oh, no! Not at all." Bonu fell into step beside her. "I just thought, oh, never mind. You've heard about tonight's meeting?"

"Yes, and I suppose I have you to thank that I need to prepare some sort of explanation."

"No, that was Captain Varter's idea. It's his way of introducing newcomers. But I'm personally looking forward to a more detailed account."

"I hate speaking to groups of people, especially when I don't know them."

"Awww, it's not so bad. You'll get used to it. Want some help preparing?"

"Not really. I'd rather be alone just now, if you don't mind."

His face fell; the twinkle disappeared from his eyes. "Oh. I'm sorry. I didn't mean to intrude. Suppose I just get lost, or something."

"Well, maybe that would be best, at least, for now."

Oh, bother! Why had she included that 'for now'? Now he'd cling to some hope. What was it about him that infuriated her? He really seemed a nice sort, so why all this resentment? Now, on top of that, she'd hurt his feelings. She despised herself for being so cold towards him.

Then in a flash Jeda understood her reaction: he was taken with her!

Bonu turned away, head bowed, shoulders slumped. "Guess I'll see you later. I've got some things to attend to before tonight, anyway."

"Bonu, I—yes, I'll see you later, then." She watched the dejected lieutenant walk away, angry with herself, angry with him. She checked for irks but found none.

The main lodge was constructed of felled trees painstakingly hewn to fit without chinking. Jeda cupped her hands and peered inside through an opening. It was clean and orderly despite having a dirt-packed floor. Trestle tables and benches made up the dominant furniture covering the entire space. In the rear of the dining hall young women scurried about setting dishes, tankards, tableware, breads, meats, vegetables, puddings, pies and cakes on a central counter. Overhead joists a foot square and a hundred feet long crisscrossed the building, supported by equally impressive pillars placed at strategic intervals. All that rafter and truss infrastructure supported a thatched roof with moss and thickets growing atop. It took genius to conceal a brigade of some three hundred people in this forest. Adding to the illusion was the fact that everyone went about their business in near silence; very little noise carried to the outside perimeter camouflage wall. From without, this encampment appeared to be nothing more than a dense, tangled thicket of briars. Whenever fires were lit smokeless wood was used. Conversations were kept low and shouting was outright banned, even from children. Communication over distances were accomplished by hand signals or various natural woodland sounds: bird calls, squirrels chattering, duck quacks, goose honks, insect chirps and buzzes, each with its own distinct meaning. Would she ever be able to learn all those different signals?

"Jeda," Vawella leaned out another opening. "I'm so glad you came. Would you mind terribly giving us a hand in the kitchen?"

"Be happy to, uh, how do I get in?"

"Go around that corner and you'll see the door. All doors are catty-corner so that in the event of attack we can make a stand. Hurry 'round, I'll meet you there."

Jeda passed more pane-less windows with shutters latched against swinging in the breeze. Arriving at the corner she found, as Vawella had indicated, a heavy, hardwood door, oak or hickory she guessed, reinforced with heavy bars on the inside against battering rams. There were slits in the walls on either side through which swords and darts could afflict any hostiles who approached.

The heavy door swung open and Vawella greeted, "Come in, come in. We really need your help. Do you have any kitchen experience? Not that it really matters."

"Some. I worked in the palace kitchen for a little while."

"Indeed? What palace was that?"

"In Cosmopolis, the emperor's palace."

"The emp—that palace? My goodness! I had no idea. Maybe you can show us how a real kitchen operates." Vawella lead toward the rear of the lodge.

"I was only there a short time, so I don't think—"

"Whatever you can share will be appreciated if it makes our work-load lighter." Another of Vawella's suggestions. "I'll introduce you to Kyleah, the kitchen servant."

Jeda obediently, albeit unenthusiastically, followed. Kitchen work wasn't exactly what she wanted to do. She'd had her fill of it and hoped she'd left that drudgery behind. Other girls burdened with trays eyed her curiously. Some smiled shyly, others politely nodded. This was a far cry from Annessa's welcome in Marga's kitchen. Maybe this wouldn't be so bad after all.

Vawella led behind a walled partition which, upon first entering the lodge, Jeda had mistaken as the rearmost wall. The familiar, steamy smells and moist atmosphere of cooking enveloped her, awakening memories of her short-lived service. But though the sights, smells, and sounds were similar, there was no contention, jealousy, or rivalry. All personnel pleasantly pursued their duties, politely yielding to and assisting each other. Jeda stood transfixed; this was so unlike the palace kitchen. Even the nastiest job could be endured, if not enjoyed, in such an atmosphere.

"Kyleah?" Vawella called.

A slim, round-faced woman in her mid-forties raised her head out of a flour barrel. White smudges mottled her face, arms, and hair which stuck oddly out from beneath a kerchief. She wore her Logon dress as an outer garment, and it was spotless. She flashed a toothy grin at Vawella and clapped her hands sending billows of flour dust into the air, then headed toward Jeda. As she drew near, Jeda noted that the white in Kyleah's dark hair wasn't all from the flour bin.

"Are you so short-handed you have to scrape the barrel sides your-self?" Vawella asked.

"Eh? No, I just don't like making anyone do someting I wouldn't do myself. Who's this?" Her sharp eyes scrutinized Jeda from head to foot in less time than it takes to crack an egg.

"This is Jeda. She's not been assigned yet, if indeed, we're to keep her. She came into our hands when the Psa woman's coach was way-laid. I thought, until they decide where to put her, you could use another pair of hands. She was in the emperor's palace kitchen for a short while."

"I sure can. I'll take good care of her."

"She needs time to prepare a small speech for the meeting tonight. Bonu is reporting on his raid, and she's the only one who can fill in certain details."

"Understood. Come with me, Jeda. Thanks, Vawella."

Jeda followed Kyleah through the kitchen's maze of tables, barrels, basins, and drains, taking it all in.

"Kyleah?" interposed a pert brunette with a turned up, button nose and reddish freckles. "Did I hear Bonu is speaking to the meeting tonight?"

Kyleah sighed and turned to Jeda. "He's the most eligible bachelor in camp. Rugged good looks, brawny frame, clear blue eyes an' a coura-geous, single-hearted devotion ter Logon and duty. Every single girl in camp dreams he'll take a fancy to her."

Then to the inquirer, "Yes, Leezle, he's gonna address the assembly tonight. Now get on with you an' tell your friends too, so you can all work faster and get yer jobs done so as ter pick seats up front afore they're all taken. Now shoo!"

With a big grin Leezle scampered away at the news, if the light beaming from her face was any indication.

"Bother! That lieutenant is all these girls think about. I do wish he'd pick one and marry her. Then maybe we could hold a decent conversation hereabouts without his name croppin' up all the time. Well, here we are."

Jeda found herself in front of a large wooden barrel.

"You look a mite thin girl, but I suppose you're sturdy enough if you trekked all night through the forest. Ever used one of these afore?" Kyleah held up a water-yoke, similar to what she and Glend had used to haul water the day they left Cosmopolis."

"Some."

"Good! And have you used buckets like these, too?"

"Aren't they all the same?"

"Not hardly. Take a closer look. See? These have trap-doors in the bottom. You just plop the bucket in the water, the trap-door lifts and the bucket fills. To close the trap door all you need do is lift, and it seals shut again. Just make sure these cords are kept untangled, cause when you empty them you pull the cord to lift the trap door. Understand?"

"I'll figure it out." Unlike Vawella, this woman had such a condescending tone that Jeda felt it necessary to assert herself.

A smile played briefly at the corner of Kyleah's lips. She opened the inset door and pointed toward a slow-flowing stream fifty feet away. "Follow the footpath to the stream; you'll find seven steps going down into the stream bed, it's what we call the dry trench. It's a path into the midst o' the stream. A mixed stone and clay wall keeps it dry, so you can walk in and out easily enough as you fill the buckets. All you do is walk out with the buckets hanging over each side till they touch the water surface and begin to fill. There's a couple of crotched sticks set in mortar, so you can rest the yoke on them while you turn around to come back. When you get back just dump them in here," she indicated the large, wooden barrel.

"And when I'm done?"

Again, a smile crossed Kyleah's mouth. "Just replenish as needed. You can use the rest of your time to organize your thoughts for your *speechifyin*.'"

"That's it?"

"Yep." With that, the kitchen servant headed off to attend other matters.

Jeda turned her attention to her duties, glad to contribute. She looked about for pads to cushion her shoulders, like Glend had shown her back in the emperor's palace. She was about to ask Kyleah where the pads were when she caught sight of the water yoke. It was already padded with a soft, furry animal skin.

"It would be like this in Logon's domains," she chided herself. "The same work needs to be done, but, what a difference in how." Her heart leapt in gratitude as she knelt under the yoke. "What a difference!"

She passed easily through the wide doorway and found the inlaid, stone pathway leading down into the water. As Kyleah had described, the pathway descended into the stream, but she stayed dry by virtue of the dike on either side abutting and ending at a huge boulder. She was fascinated by the unique, water level view of the river as the buckets filled. She settled the yoke with its buckets into the crotched branches and momentarily stepped free of her burden to face the other way.

She observed the quiet, but active bustle of the covert brigade going about their business: men engaged in quiet conversations, sword drills or sport; women and children chatting or playing; young-teen girls serving the needs of the camp by helping mothers with their toddlers. How peaceful and marvelous, deep behind enemy lines, in such an inhospitable jungle, a small, impoverished community thrived on Logon's love. It was a precarious existence, to be sure, always in jeopardy, living hand to mouth off the sparse forage afforded by the forest. Absent were luxuries such as she'd known growing up, yet no one seemed to mind. And why should they? What more did anyone really need other than food, shelter, trusted friends and Logon's companionship?

A bucket clunked against the stone dike reminding Jeda of her responsibilities. She bent under her burden, straightened her knees, and assumed the weight of the yoke. She felt, rather than heard the trap doors close as she stood to full height. By the third step Jeda remembered to employ the swinging motion required to ascend stairs. Once out of the trench she fell into a natural rhythm and covered the short path to the lodge in no time.

Once inside, however, she stood by the reservoir barrel unsure how to empty the buckets. Both buckets couldn't be suspended over the barrel at the same time, so simultaneous discharge of the contents was out of the question. To empty only one would tilt her off balance, spilling the other bucket. There must be some trick Kyleah hadn't told her—ahh, if only she hadn't been so smug. Now she understood Kyleah's fleeting smile.

Jeda thought she heard whispering; craning her neck around she briefly caught sight of Kyleah cupping her hand over another girl's ears. The girl nodded and came around a stack of baskets straight to Jeda. "Hi, I'm Leezle."

"Oh, yes, I remember, from before."

"Want some advice?"

Jeda smiled, and said, "Please. I have no idea what I'm doing. The buckets don't appear to detach from the yoke, but I'm afraid I'll spill one if I empty the other."

Leezle smiled knowingly. "Look up."

"Excuse me?"

"Look up," repeated the brunette. "See that rope with a hook?"

Jeda looked up. "Uh-huh."

"Pull it down, slip the hook into the ring on the yoke. Then step free."

Doing as instructed, Jeda was delighted that the weight of the yoke was lifted off her shoulders; she could now manipulate the buckets one at at time over the barrel. The cord to the trap door was within reach, and when centered over the reservoir, she released its contents with a splash. The other bucket dipped low, but stayed upright, and then was also easily maneuvered over the barrel.

"That's all there is to it."

"Ingenious, wonderful. Do all kingsmen brigades practice this technique?"

"I don't think so. Bonu watched us tote water for a couple of days, then proposed building the dry trench and the trap-door buckets and rafter hook. Isn't he wonderful?"

"Bonu did that?"

Leezle dipped her pitcher into the crystal-clear liquid. "Well, see you later."

Jeda returned to her assignment, making several more trips. Workers drew water for drinking, boiling or washing, lowering the level almost as fast as she refilled it, but at last she was caught up and a little ahead of demand. She was tired and achy, yet overall, felt good.

Settling down on an unused countertop she outlined her explanation aloud to herself. "They'll likely want to know how an Ecclessite could travel undetected among so many Carnalians," she mused. "So,

I'll just say 'how can a brigade remain secret in the bowels of Ra-Amawl?'" Thus, she rehearsed, recalling details to lend credibility.

At some point she was distracted by a smallish girl, more petite than Glend, struggling to carry a stack of wooden platters. Jeda jumped and took the top half of the stack, helping the girl distribute them to each table in the main room. Later she saw another girl laboriously scrubbing burnt material out of a pan and went to hold it still for her. When returning from that she noticed the water level had dropped and made more trips to the stream. Thus, she passed the afternoon working on her presentation, re-filling the water reservoir, and helping wherever she could.

Jeda was startled from her meditation by the scree of a nighthawk echoing over the darkening camp, followed by the hoot of an owl.

"Meal call," Leezle explained.

Kyleah sauntered over to the girls. "Captain Varter requests yer ter sit wi' his family and officers, Jeda. S'quite a honor."

"Oh, I can't, I'm all sweaty, and, and mussed and—"

"Tut, tut, child. Yer looks fine. Besides, it' a honor to be grimy from servin' yer brothers an' sisters. I seen how yer kept hoppin' up all the time ter help out. Yer be's a true kingswoman, even if'n yer be's a Sharpointer," chuckled the kitchen servant. "Now gimme thet apron an' go fix yer hair. I arranged it fer Bonu ter sit next ter yer."

CHAPTER TWENTY-ONE

JEDA TOOK HER SEAT AT Captain Varter's table and sent a sharp look toward the lieutenant at the captain's right hand, warning him in no uncertain terms that though she was placed beside him, she had no interest in anything but polite conversation.

Bonu apparently received the message for he buried his head in concentrated consumption of woodland salad, only occasionally contributing to the conversation.

Seated on the captain's left were his wife, Vefta, his daughter Vawella, and a young man who, throughout the meal, unsuccessfully vied for Vawella's attention.

Vawella was distracted by the goings-on at a table that was the site of tittering laughter. Nevertheless, the young man beside Vawella held forth about his exploits, accomplishments, dreams and hopes as if his dinner partner shared his enthusiasm.

On the captain's right sat Bonu, then Jeda, and two senior officers, designated as captains by chevrons on their sleeves. They were retired from active duty, Bonu explained, due to their advanced years, though they were still useful for training recruits and were expected to help in the common defense should the need arise. "One never quite retires from Logon's service until arrival in Splendora," said the lieutenant.

The meal progressed uneventfully. Jeda enjoyed the simple but delicious fare of the forest: various nuts grated over edible leaves and roots, dollops of honey countering the bitterroot flavor, altogether making for a delightful taste experience. The water was cold and clear, with a hint of mineral aftertaste. The main meal consisted of various steamed vegetables mixed with ground meat, which Jeda guessed to be venison, and baked to the consistency of bread dough. It was tasty and filling. Condiments such as pepper would have been nice, but such elements were luxuries in the wilderness. A dessert of puddings, pies, and cakes followed the main course, astounding Jeda that the ingredients for such things could be found in Ra-Amawl.

The retired captain to Jeda's left told her that kingsmen patrols disguised as half-men sometimes raided enemy supply trains in order to refill the larder with difficult-to-find foodstuffs.

These people eked a marvelous existence from almost nothing, Jeda mused. Why had Logon placed them here? What purpose could a secret brigade so distant from the front lines be? And, what role could she possibly have among these self-sufficient people, she who was pampered and raised grasping a silver spoon, who, only in the last few weeks learned the strain, pain and stiffness of physical labor. What could she add to them?

After a round of fruit and nuts the kitchen staff cleared tables away and swept the floor. The job was quickly finished, and benches were arranged in rows as tables were stacked to the rear.

Captain Varter climbed up on a table, clapped his hands and beckoned everyone to come to the fore of the room. The assembly eagerly awaited the evening's field reports and rune study.

Jeda felt conspicuous sitting next to Bonu, drawing the envious stare of many a serving girl on the kitchen staff.

"As many of you know," Captain Varter began, "Bonu's raid ended differently than we had expected. We, er, have a guest, with, I suspect, an unusual tale."

Jeda dropped her eyes to avoid curious stares.

"So, before we get to the rune study, Lieutenant Bonu, the meeting is yours."

Bonu straightened his tunic, ascended the table top and cleared his throat. "As many of you know, a week ago, Kyleah, head of the kitchen staff, received a message that Logon wanted the Psa woman's carriage detained and the occupant brought to camp. We assumed we were to capture the Psa woman. Who else would be riding in the Psa Woman's coach? So, we prepared ourselves to capture the dangerous and powerful Hod-ya Kar Psa."

A murmur ran through the crowd.

"Instead, we found two young ladies on their way to Pitland for the rites of Scrarth and Avangar, one of the most sinister plots ever foisted upon womankind."

Another murmur rolled across the hall.

"To our surprise and, I speak for myself, delight, we discovered one of the young ladies being transported to Psa's shrine was one of our own, er, not one of our own from this brigade, but one of our own, as in Ecclessite. Miss Jeda of the House of Kway, taken by unfortunate circumstance from her father's house to the emperor's service. Logon rescued her in her darkest hour. But I'm telling her story. Let me introduce her. I ask that afterward you make her feel welcome, for I suspect she's been sent by Logon to become a vital part of our brigade. Jeda . . . "

A polite ripple of applause rustled like a breeze throughout the gathering, greeting Jeda as Bonu jumped down, and without asking, placed his hands about her waist and hoisted her up on the table.

She narrowed her eyes at Bonu, then looked up and swallowed a lump in her throat as she beheld their expectant faces. "I, uh, I tried to prepare something, uh, to say what I thought, uh, you wanted to know, but I forgot everything I planned to say." She shrugged with a bashful smile.

Nervous laughter came from the sea of faces, comforting her, accepting her.

Bonu, misunderstanding the rapport Jeda was building, bounded up beside her, and defensively put his arm about her. Her annoyed glance caused him to step back without uttering a word.

Certain girls in the audience took note how this comely, young lady wanted no part of Bonu's protection, and not a few kitchen staff workers' faces brightened.

Bonu's face, on the other hand, turned crimson. Embarrassed, he stepped down off the table.

Jeda watched him go with a strange pang in her heart, but then looked up and continued, "Perhaps, if you just ask me what you'd like to know . . . "

Captain Varter was first. "How is it that you, an Ecclessite from a Sharpointer Brigade got selected by Hod-ya to go to Pitland in the first place?"

Smiling gratefully, Jeda replied, "When I arrived at the emperor's palace, I didn't know Logon. In fact, I didn't even know him as Logon. Two of my father's servants secretly told me about Alfomega, and the password, 'words of the word', which would protect me if I repeated them." Thus, Jeda related the experiences she thought relevant, mentioning Dancel, Flan, Ruark, the blackguards, meeting Logon by the brook, the intense rain storm, Juued, Filke, and Tressa.

When finished, questions flew from all directions, including one from Leezle about whether she had a beau.

Jeda laughed. "No, Leezle, not yet, if ever. But if you're interested, I have a brother, Artka, who may some day, I trust, meet with Logon. I'll be glad to introduce you." Leezle blushed as her friends prodded her ribs, tickling her, and laughing in merriment.

Jeda felt comfortable, even up on the table before this crowd. These dear people openly, warmly accepted her at face value, though they had reason to be suspicious. She knew then and there where she belonged.

She moved to the edge of the table and Bonu extended his hands to lift her down, but before she stepped into his waiting hands a commotion at the rear of the lodge drew everyone's attention. Jeda, still atop the table, had the best view.

Three men entered the lodge. The middle one caught Jeda's immediate attention, for between two tall patrol members waddled a short, stout man, stripped to his breeches and Logon tunic, which was badly stained. He huffed and puffed as they half-dragged him, one on either side like prison guards.

One of the soldiers addressed Captain Varter as they made their way through the crowd, "Sir, we have him. It took some doing, but here he is. Even when his own life was in desperate peril he didn't want to leave. So, we abducted him." The short man stood before the three captains.

Jeda's hand went to her lip as she muttered, "Ruark?"

The exhausted coachman turned to see who spoke his name. "Miss Jeda! You're alive! I never expected to see you again. What are they going to do with us, do you know?"

Captain Varter seized Ruark's shoulder and turned him around. "How dare you call yourself an Ecclessite and come here with such a filthy tunic? Have you lost your love for Logon? And what business do Ecclessites have in willingly serving the mistress of a dread? Have you lost your senses? Give answer." Captain Varter glowered at the coachman.

Ruark wilted, muttering meaningless half phrases. "I, er, that is, what good would it be if, oh, but that is too late now. What I mean is, you have no idea how hard it's been for, no that won't do either. I'm afraid I can't, uh, let me put it this way, er—"

"Quit babbling, man. Give an answer."

Bonu assisted Jeda down from the tabletop as the entire assembly listened intently to Ruark's answers.

Ruark snuffled and blew his nose. "You have no right to question me. I'm of a different brigade. We don't live by your rules."

"Obviously! I wouldn't want to stand before Logon as an officer of your brigade, giving account of you. Have your servants lost their respect and fear of Elyon to let you run amok?"

"What need we fear of Elyon? His son died for us. So, it matters not whether we follow all his rules exactly. I'm assured of going to Splendora, that's the main thing isn't it? You have no right to judge me. In fact, your men had no right to bring me here. I demand to be returned. I can convince them it was all a mistake and be reinstated."

Jeda was aghast. She'd never seen Ruark so angry, so rebellious, or so frightened.

"You foolish, foolish man," chided Captain Varter. Then, Varter asked of the soldiers who brought Ruark in, "Where's his sword?"

"We couldn't find one."

"What did you do with your sword, man?" Captain Varter was impatient. "Did you turn coward and throw it away?"

"If they'd discovered it on me, I'd be dead."

"You'd be in Splendora, and better off than you are at this moment, I dare say. You have all the earmarks of a man who'd deny knowing Logon just to prolong your miserable life." The captain withdrew his sword and held it under Ruark's dripping nose. "Do you see this rune? Speak up man, do you see the rune?"

"Ye-es." Ruark trembled.

"Read it."

Ruark glanced at it, then turned his eyes away.

"Out loud. Read it out loud."

Ruark slowly pronounced the difficult words,

"Sunapeth anomen suzasomen,

Hupomenomen sumbasilusomen,

Apnumetha apnesethai,

Apnasthai heaton hunatai."

"Do you know what it means?"

"I never tolled that far."

Varter continued, "The rough interpretation is: 'If we endure, we will reign, If we deny, he will deny, If we break covenant and fall away, he will yet be faithful to his father.' In short, it means we must stay faithful to our part of the covenant, with the Advisor's help. Were he to bring anyone to his father after that individual denied him, he would be breaking the covenant he made to only bring the loyal to

Splendora. You are close to that act of denial. We'll do what we can to undo the damage. Take him to the men's baths. I put you on notice, Ruark, only you can cleanse your tunic, by going to Logon yourself. I advise you to waste no time."

The soldiers hustled the coachman back through the murmuring crowd and out the door as abruptly as they'd entered.

Jeda was dumbfounded. She already knew that Ruark was foolish and made compromises in order to keep his job, but this brigade took the matter very seriously, as if his very being and future rewards in Splendora depended on maintaining a loyal relationship with Logon.

Bonu clambered back up on the table cooing like a mourning dove to quell the murmurs. "Getting back to the purpose of tonight's meeting . . . "

The crowd settled.

"Five days ago, fifty of us set out to waylay the Psa woman's coach. We expected rough going and weren't disappointed. We ventured out during a torrential rain and before we'd gone fifteen miles numerous cusps and tophets attacked. I think they were hunting our encampment, so it's a good thing we took a circuitous route. The battle lasted hours, and we were giving way to fatigue. Our swords moved heavily in our hands; at times barely able to defend ourselves, so intense was the attack. If Logon hadn't sent roamers, you'd be hearing a very different account. When the enemy was finally driven off, since the hour was late, we camped for the night. Some wanted to return and forget the exploit, but we held council and decided that when Logon speaks definitively through a seer, in this case, Kyleah, that we should expect opposition and not be dissuaded from our mission."

A murmur of approval swept through the assembly. Leezle slid beside Jeda on the bench, smiled, and then turned her full attention to the man on the table.

"Logon said," Bonu continued, "to 'apprehend the vehicle used of the daughter of wickedness, and bring the captive hither', as I remember the utterance."

Jeda leaned over to Leezle, asking, "How did Logon send that message? Did he appear and say it, or send a bright?"

"He spoke through Kyleah." It was stated so matter-of-factly that Jeda felt patronized.

"What do you mean, 'spoke through Kyleah?'"

"Shh, I'll tell you later. I don't want to miss any of this." Leezle turned her full attention back on Bonu.

Jeda sat back as her rescuer told of his mission. He told it simply, even self-effacingly, yet Jeda felt as if all her clumsiness and inexperience was exposed, if not magnified by his tale.

Vawella sidled up on Jeda's other side, smiling, leaning close to whisper, "We've decided to put you on forage detail tomorrow. I think you'll like that. Now, listen to Bonu. He went through a lot to get you here. You should at least know what it cost him to be the agent of your escape."

"The half-men tore up our supplies, roughing up some of our guards. It's a good thing there were only four or five, else we would've been delayed and might have missed the coach.

"After driving off the half-men we encountered no more obstacles. There was some discussion about where to situate the ambush. Finally, we settled under cover in a gulley to await the carriage. If Kyleah hadn't been established as a seer we wouldn't have dared lay in wait as long as we did, for the risk of discovery was imminent. The enemy's agents use that conduit with regularity, and they're keen to sense their enemy's presence within their precincts. But because Kyleah has proven so reliable in the past, we kept to our mission.

"And so, we waited; there was little traffic on the road that night. Even then, we were almost caught unawares. The coach was cleverly silenced as a precaution against the denizens of Ra-Amawl. If one of their party hadn't been riding a horse without boots on its hooves intruding on the silence of those hushed, lightless lairs, we would've missed the passing coach altogether, thinking it nothing more than stirring breezes. But a messenger preceded them on horseback. We gagged and bound him and for his own protection, deposited him in a hastily constructed cage and hung it from a high tree. Then several of us hastened toward the carriage.

"There we found two of the feared Dronnet kar Bones corps, Hodya's personal bodyguard, protecting the young lasses. The blackguards had so hardened their hearts that there was no other choice but to bludgeon them senseless lest they do us great harm, for their powers are strong. But first we exposed that unfortunate coachman as an Ecclessite to the dronnets before we rendered them unconscious. Anyway, that's not my tale, but another's."

A murmur of approval rose from the assembly.

"When we broke into the coach, we found not the Psa woman, which caused some doubting the word of Kyleah, but rather these two, charming, but duped girls."

Jeda "humphed" loudly enough to be heard several rows back.

Bonu seemed not to notice, continuing, "Unsure what to do, I decided to sack them and bring them along into the forest. We couldn't leave them on their own, helpless as they were."

Another "humph" ensued but was likewise ignored by Bonu.

"Because they'd have been eaten. On the way back, we were surrounded by a pride of Craniantium lions."

A gasp went up from the whole assembly.

"Yes, evidently they've returned. As I was saying, we were surrounded and attacked, and that was when we learned that one of our captives was a kingswoman, for when we unsacked the girls to let them have a running chance should things go badly, Jeda came out of her sack swinging her sword, ready to battle the lions with us!"

A delighted ripple of applause and happy chuckles greeted this pronouncement, but Jeda was implacable. Bonu seemed intent on having fun at her expense, making her look quite the fool.

"She valiantly protected her unpierced friend while we carried the battle to the felines, driving them back into the forest licking their wounds. From that point on, because the melee made so much commotion, we no longer concealed our swords but used them to guide our path. Nonetheless, since we had inexperienced trekkers with us, we had to slow down to their pace."

Jeda's face flushed.

"The swords can't be seen far away through that dense undergrowth, but the noise these girls made, no doubt, was heard so we were hindered anyway. But thanks to Logon, here we are, none the worse for wear. There is a sad note however, for my cousin, Harru, was lost in the fight with the dronnets, whether killed or just missing is yet unknown. We searched the roadside as long as we dared but had to leave off looking." Bonu briefly hung his head, then regaining his composure, said, "He'll be missed, but those of you who bore his burden will carry on his work, as will I." Then he jumped off the table and stood beside Jeda, embarrassed at all the kudos for such a daring raid.

"Bonu," Jeda whispered, "I, I'm sorry about your cousin. I never knew. Why didn't you say something?"

"What difference would it have made? Anyway, he was the only casualty, so our mission was successful, you were rescued from Pitland's grasp, and Logon is glorified."

Captain Varter was again atop the table with raised hands, silencing the whispers. "Beloved, there are many things to consider in tonight's report, and, I think, some of special concern. We've also learned that Hod-ya has a rising challenger who is also en-route to Pitland, perhaps by way of Ra-Amawl, which means opportunity might exist for us to launch another rescue mission. These are times of great opportunity if we be not faint-hearted."

All around the room men and women pulled swords and tollers out. Jeda followed their cue. Bonu settled on the bench between Jeda and Leezle, causing Leezle's eyes to widen.

Jeda shifted away, focusing her attention on Captain Varter, but Leezle was flustered by Bonu choosing to sit next to her.

Bonu, on the other hand, was solely concerned with Jeda's welfare.

Out of the corner of her eye Jeda kept check on the insufferable lieutenant, wishing he'd just go away.

When Leezle asked Bonu a question, and Bonu answered, Jeda felt uneasy. It couldn't be jealousy, could it? Of course not!

" . . . much we cannot understand about these things, because they've not yet been revealed. But as the time draws nearer for all things to begin anew, more information about the mystery runes will be unveiled to Logon's bonded-servants."

Jeda knew the term bonded-servant only too well.

"It's said that many will leave the path of truth by ignoring, or even despising, Logon's swords. Those who haven't discovered the warrunes won't know how to fight the battles that lay ahead. Indeed, many won't even know the final war has begun until they face the searing hatred of Lurcan himself, newly cast out of the nether realm. That which is only ghostly now will take on substance, revealed as they are, not as they represent themselves. Will you be ready? Are you sharpening by the warrunes?

"Tonight, you heard that Bonu and his patrol encountered tophets, and how after hours of battle they were weary; their swords keeping up the fight even though they were physically drained by the battle. And these are the strongest, best prepared among us! How will you fare, you who are lazy and not tolling your swords?"

An uneasy silence filled the dining hall; apparently not a few had been slothful.

Captain Varter's eyes searched the assembly, finally resting on Jeda's sword, which wasn't splotchy like Runer swords but glowed brightly a full three inches from the tip. "Jeda, show us your sword."

Stunned, Jeda rose and willed her feet to approach Captain Varter. Firm hands hoisted her to the tabletop. The sea of eager faces looked up expectantly. Jeda feared she was going to be made an example of how not to sharpen a sword.

"Jeda, hold your sword aloft, so all can see."

"I've not been an Ecclessite all that long . . . " She was sure her face was bright crimson as she complied.

Varter smiled at her. "Now look here, everyone; turn it sideways, Jeda, so they can see, that's it, see how the first few inches glow brightly? We all have the first inch sharpened like hers, but then, as Runers, we've been trained to skip over runes to toll by those we're more familiar with, bypassing portions of the blade." Captain Varter held his own sword beside Jeda's. "As you can see, lately I've been sharpening those vacant spots on my blade. In comparison to Jeda's, my sword is dull after the point; and I see runes on hers that I have no knowledge of, nor indeed even suspected were there. The Runer Brigade HQ where I trained never mentioned these runes, so neither my predecessors, nor I could train you in them. Now, however, I suspect there's more to Logon's swords than we've known. By sharpening more, I've discovered more about Logon; I appreciate and know him better and am more sensitive to his instructions."

Murmuring filled the assembly.

One of the retired captains rose to his feet. "Look here, Varter, what's your point? Are you suggesting we become Sharpointers, like the young lass, here?"

"No, Blegash, I'm not. I think they, too, have too limited an understanding. I believe that the entire blade needs to be aglow—brightly aglow, so the whole counsel of Logon can be understood."

Several rose to their feet quietly clamoring; others pled for silence so Varter could finish his point.

Captain Varter stomped a boot heel, silencing the crowd. "Sit down, sit down, all of you, sit down. Let me finish."

The crowd quieted, each cautioning his neighbor about the outcry.

Jeda was unnerved. This charming, friendly brigade had quickly, alarmingly become quite agitated.

They all sat, except Blegash.

"Blegash, please, take your seat. Hear me out. I didn't reach this conclusion lightly. Nor did the appearance of this charming young lady affect me in any way except to confirm what I'd already suspected."

"Very well, Varter, I sit. But, bear in mind that I only relinquished full command a fortnight ago, with the stipulation that if you proved unworthy, I'd take my authority back. So, your explanation had better be good. There's nothing worse than denying one's training; remember that." The elderly, retired officer took his seat to the ripple of applause.

"Your point is well taken, Blegash. Should the council so determine that I'm unfit, I'll step down. But it must be the council, not you or any dissidents who merely want to follow Runer traditions. What I'm about to present isn't new, but old, so old it'll seem original. I've revealed a rune that challenges the teaching that limits sharpening the entire swords."

Murmuring again filled the room.

Captain Varter called for order, flashing angry eyes at the most antagonistic protesters. "Let me finish! Haven't you ever asked your-selves if there wasn't anything of importance on the blade between the runes we toll? Sure, the runes we know are useful, but haven't you ever felt there might be more? I've begun tolling the dull parts of my blade to see what would happen, and I assure you, there is more, much more.

"You all know the history of Logon dwelling amongst men, and how his generals waged legendary campaigns against Lurcan's empire. Those runes are plainly etched and need not be tolled overly much to comprehend. But, what if they're more than historical stories? What if they're patterns for us to imitate today? What if the traditions and training methods laid down by Logon's first generals are still meant for us to use these many generations later? Do we not rob ourselves by treating our heritage as only that, heritage, rather than examples of how to live and rescue lives to the king?"

Here and there people nodded in agreement.

"Place your tollers here," Varter demonstrated, "and pass it over this seemingly empty spot on your blade."

To Jeda he said, "Dear, you may resume your seat."

As Jeda descended with Bonu's assistance, scraping of files on swords was heard, the brigade, for the moment, giving their captain the benefit of the doubt.

"See it? It's the 'Rune of Foundations'. It reads:

> *"Will Elyon change, or his son ask why?*
> *Is he a man that he should lie?*
> *Is the future dark to him who knows,*
> *End from beginning, friends from foes?*
> *Engraved by servants tried and true,*
> *The runes change not, nor need review,*
> *Keep that which from beginning came,*
> *Aglow and sharp, a holy flame,*
> *What is given will surely keep,*
> *And harvest rich will he reap.*
> *To those who add will come sore plague,*
> *Those who reduce and make truth vague,*
> *Will find their name removed from page,*
> *Of Logon's book who found life's wage.*
> *These runes aglow, this blade of light,*
> *Above man's wisdom, power and might,*
> *Breathed by Elyon so strong and pure,*
> *Will train his warriors to endure.*
> *So search out word, rune and song,*

Content not just to get along,
With merest scrap of information,
For Logon builds a mighty nation."

Captain Varter studied his audience. Many still scraped, finishing the stanza, pondering the mystery. When all looked to him, he confessed, "I admit, there's much I don't comprehend, such as this line: 'So search out word, rune and song,' I've not discovered music in my blade, but, as you can see, I've begun sharpening both edges, with the goal of leaving no empty spots from tip to haft. I'm only half way, albeit, dim. Even so, my understanding of Logon's person has increased and my trust in him is surer. It hasn't harmed me to explore the unknown parts of my blade in any way, in fact, it's helped."

Blegash was instantly on his feet, scowling. "You're learning more because you carry the responsibility of leadership now. It has nothing to do with sharpening more of your sword. And though you don't see it, you've wasted valuable time putting a glow on unnecessary parts of your sword that are no longer relevant; time which should've been used to put your own house in order. When you came to us from Ecclessa you knew all you needed to know. What you're learning now will only cause division. I warn you, you're on a dangerous pathway. For instance, that phrase about 'seeking word, rune and song,' is based on a superstition that some 'special warriors' can make their swords sing! It borders on Psacraft, and you'll be guilty of leading a whole brigade astray if you continue down that unadvised trail."

"Oh, no," Jeda rose up, surprised at herself. "The sword does sing, aloud, and it takes no one special, just someone who loves Logon more than anything."

"Are you insinuating that because my sword has never sung that I don't love Logon more than you do?" Blegash retorted.

"Jeda, your sword . . . sang?" Captain Varter asked looking down at her.

Before she answered the kitchen's main door burst open and a soldier rushed in. "Enemies!" he hoarsely whispered. "Setting up camp just beyond the hazard barrier. Three, maybe four regiments. There are several dronnets, too."

CHAPTER TWENTY-TWO

OVER THE NEXT TWO DAYS the brigade lived a hushed existence; mothers with small children remained sequestered in the lodge to muffle inadvertent noises; men, older boys and unmarried women stealthily carried on with only the most pressing of chores; fires were banned as was all verbal communication. All external patrols ceased. Those patrols stranded outside remained afield; there was no way to let them in without exposing the camouflage ruse.

Watchmen peered for hours on end through spy ports, monitoring Carnalian positions, comings and goings of significant personnel. Changing of the kingsman guard was scheduled to coincide with the Carnalian changing of the guard to offset any noises. Victuals were brought to watchmen on duty. As to weaponry, only swords were kept ready; these foes were human, there was no evidence of beasts mixing with empire troops to attack.

Carnalian scouting patrols streamed in and out at all hours of the day and night, each led by a member of Hod-ya's fierce dronnet corps. Enemy movements, it was noted, were conducted in a search-grid pattern all around the outskirts of the hidden campsite; it seemed as if they intended to cover every square furlong in the vicinity.

Jeda and Leezle brought Bonu a meal of uncooked roots and dried venison jerky.

Bonu whispered as he received his share of the fare, "They're searching for the lost Scrarth and Avangar contestants. But how did they know to start here?" Bonu gnawed off a bite of venison. The other soldiers stationed with Bonu said nothing but nodded gratefully as they accepted the proffered food.

Jeda inwardly feared that she might have left some telltale sign, ruing her ineptitude that might have exposed the entire brigade to discovery and assault. Or, had Glend done something? At any rate, Jeda felt responsible.

Leezle guided Jeda along a pathway of imbedded stones to the next guard station, demonstrating how to utilize the large, flat rocks soundlessly from outpost to outpost. Thus, the meals were delivered to those on guard duty, cold and tasteless as it was. After completing the rounds Leezle and Jeda reported back to Vawella.

Vawella spied Jeda and Leezle as they entered the lodge, asking with her hands, "Did all go well?"

Leezle replied in kind that all was well.

Vawella sighed. They were the last food-runners to return, and their delay had been the cause of some anxiety. The leadership was still somewhat concerned with Jeda's unfamiliarity with the brigade's silent-mode operations.

For Jeda's sake Vawella whispered to Leezle, "You and Jeda go to the bathhouse and relieve Derter and Famala. They've had a double shift and are wearing out. Your friend has proven quite a handful, Jeda. No wonder Hod-ya selected her. There's more grit to that girl than appears at first glance."

Leezle nodded and motioned Jeda to follow.

They crossed the yard and entered the dimly lit bath hut to behold a pitiful sight. Derter and Famala sat side by side along a wall, clearly exhausted, hair disheveled, clothes rumpled, scratched on arms and faces. Underneath them lay a small form bound hand and foot and gagged. Above the gag two hate-filled eyes promised revenge. Jeda had never seen Glend in such a wild, unmanageable state.

"Oh, Glend, what's become of you?"

"Better you should ask what's become of us!" whispered the brunette. The auburn-haired girl nodded in agreement. Derter continued, "This witchling has tried our patience until we're ready to strangle her. I hope you're our relief. I don't think I can stand much more."

The bundle under their legs squirmed.

Both girls simultaneously hoisted themselves upward then thumped down hard on Glend.

A muffled grunt emitted from the trussed body.

"Go get some rest," said Leezle. "We'll take over."

"Don't, under any circumstances, remove her gag, or her bonds as long as the situation exists. She must be kept immobile and silent—Captain Varter's orders." With that, the two weary girls lifted themselves off their prisoner and exited.

"Glend, it's me, Jeda."

The bundle on the floor rolled over, facing away.

"And I'm Leezle. We're going to be with you for the next few hours. I know you don't understand what's going on, and I'm afraid we can't tell you why we must keep you tied up like this, but we do so only because it's absolutely necessary. If you prove trustworthy, we'll prove gentle companions. But I warn you, I've already had a long trying day, as has Jeda, and we're in no mood for trouble. One hint of inappropriate behavior . . . " she picked up a stick of firewood and rapped it against her palm, "and goodnight!" She meant it, as was evident in her tone and the look in her eye.

Glend stared at the wall.

"Well, that will do just fine. Jeda, let's have a seat. This will probably be a long wait." She then sat on a barrel lying on its side.

Jeda found a small wooden footstool that sat low to the ground. "Do you think it would be safe to toll our swords?"

Leezle cocked her head and considered for a moment. "Well, can you keep it real, real quiet?"

"I'll try."

"Oh, go ahead, but file slowly."

Jeda withdrew her toller and sword, finding where she'd left off; even within the confines of the shed the scrape was barely audible.

Leezle relaxed, leaned back against the wall and closed her eyes.

Jeda tolled for several minutes, letting the blaze of a new rune instruct her about Logon's goodness, bringing needed comfort. She felt refreshed despite the tension and extra duty. She needed this more than sleep.

Was that ever-so-slight sound coming from Glend? Jeda looked over at their prisoner. Was there a change in her position? She couldn't be sure . . . ; Leezle's breathing became deep and regular. Jeda eagerly returned to poring over her sword, drinking in knowledge about Logon.

Half an hour passed. Jeda moved her neck side to side, momentarily lifting her gaze off her sword. When she met Glend's eyes both girls were locked in visual combat. Had Jeda not just been tolling her Child of the Stars she'd have cowered, for the look that challenged her had telltale red dots like when she first stood before Hod-ya. Was Psa in possession of Glend?

Despite the chill creeping down her spine and the knocking of her knees Jeda slowly lifted her sword and pointed it at Glend, whispering hoarsely, "Lee-eezle, wake up."

Glend averted her eyes away from the small but brilliant glowing patch on the sword.

Leezle drew another deep breath and continued snoozing.

"Leezle, get up. This isn't Glend anymore! Oh, Leezle, please get up." Jeda drew her feet under her preparing to stand, still aiming her sword directly at the monstrous entity glaring at her through Glend's eyes.

A hiss emitted from beneath Glend's gag; she began writhing like a snake, her fingers worked loose and began tearing at her bonds. She violently twisted around and thrust her bound legs outward, knocking the barrel from under Leezle; it crashed into the wall. Leezle toppled over backward landing on her head and shoulders with a cry of pain. Her collarbone protruded abnormally.

Jeda scrambled backward away from Glend's thrashing feet but snagged her heel on the edge of the barrel and fell to the floor. Her sword skittered out of reach across the room.

Glend's feet rose high then came down forcefully on Leezle. Leezle screamed, further shattering the silence. One of Glend's hands slipped free of its bonds and tore savagely at the remaining cords. The bonds snapped one by one as if they were thread. Then, to Jeda's horror, both Glend's hands were suddenly free and clawing at the bonds around Glend's ankles, tearing skin and ropes alike.

In another swoop of her hand the layers of cloth stuffed into her mouth were gone, setting her voice free. What came out wasn't Glend's voice.

A cold wind swept through the little bath hut; the voice sounded like stones in a rockslide, yet forming words:

"Pretty little beauty, thinks escape has come,
But she owes her duty, and now she'll pay it some,
Kar Hod-ya owns you dearie, and Psa will have his way,
Be you strong or weary, you will rue this day!"

Jeda rolled over lunging for her sword. She finally grasped her Child of the Stars and raising up on one knee held it out defensively as she watched Glend rip asunder her final fetter.

Glend was on her feet in a flash and advanced, hateful, red dots overtaking each eye entirely.

~

The fracas in the bath hut was heard throughout both encampments.

Ecclessite soldiers peering out through the camouflage wall spun around at the thuds, screams, and voices erupting from the hut.

Bonu bolted from his post heedless of mandated cautions, barely touching the ground as he charged straight for the bath hut, knowing Jeda had been sent there.

At the same time Captain Varter emerged from his tent and beckoned a dozen guards to head toward the bathhouse. Other guards stationed on the perimeter tensed, checking over their shoulders to see if the compound had been breeched behind them. Captain Varter himself hustled to the nearest outpost to check on the enemy's reaction.

~

Across the intervening woodland the Carnalian camp also froze at the disturbance. The accompanying thuds and voices drew their attention to the impenetrable thicket before them. Out of the Carnalian HQ tent stepped a squat officer adorned in the usual garb, black with crimson trim, trailing a cape that dragged the ground behind him.

~

Captain Varter, peered through a spy hole and instantly recognized Mileer and sadly shook his head. "Captain Mileer, as vindictive and ruthless a cutthroat as ever lived." Then Varter's blood chilled, for in Mileer's train came a tall, black-garbed woman. Even at that distance it was impossible to mistake her lean form and pasty complexion: Hod-ya Kar Psa! There was no longer any question as to why Carnalians were stomping through this region of Ra-Amawl's recesses. Four dronnets deployed behind Hod-ya as she and Mileer observed, as if for the first time, the thicket opposite them. She mumbled something to Captain Mileer then returned her gaze across the expanse between the two enemy camps. Captain Mileer immediately retreated, barking orders left and right, sending soldiers scurrying.

Captain Varter hooted like an owl; a warning for the camp to prepare for attack?

But instead of attack, empire soldiers began dismantling the camp. Tents were taken down and packed up in record time and all fires were doused.

Captain Varter withdrew from the spyhole when a column of twinkling lights drifted right in front of his peephole. Going back to the aperture he saw another column pass by, and another. Soon the forested expanse was populated with columns of hovering, twinkly lights.

Hod-ya's undivided concentration was fixed on them, not the camouflage barricade beyond. These sparkling lights under the dark haunts of Ra-Amawl posed a clear and present threat to the Carnalian task force, prompting Hod-ya to break camp. Runners were immediately dispatched to recall search parties and patrols so as to leave no stragglers behind.

"Are, are they roamers, captain?" a guard whispered in Varter's ear.

"I believe they are, son, I believe they are. I've never seen one before, but from what I understand, that's what they must be. Logon sent help just when we needed it most."

~

Across the way Captain Mileer sidled-up alongside Hod-ya, his Carnalian sword drawn, a blood-red ruby ensconced in the handle. "Brights?" he asked.

"Umm. But, why, way out here? And why aren't they attacking?" Hod-ya turned to observe the preparations behind her. "Mileer, have you recalled all patrols?"

"I've sent runners out, but it's too soon for any to report back."

"And the main battle group?"

"Still too far away. Progress is difficult in these thick woods, especially with such a large contingent. Quicksand, impenetrable briar patches, detours around swamps, it takes time to cut a pathway through or find safe ground, not to mention hindrances like clouds of mosquitoes, carnivorous plants, marauding lions, wolves and half-men. The last messenger from regiment said that a whole brigade wandered into an unknown swath of jungle and hasn't been heard from since. Say, you aren't thinking of putting up a fight, are you?"

"Do you take me for a fool? Of course not! But these threads didn't grow out here on their own, either." Hod-ya's fingers held half a dozen threads. "These match the dress last seen on one of my contestants, and I must have her back, at least. Hopefully both of them, but I must have at least one. If I can impute my power into one, then I can face the challenger."

"But other than those threads found two days ago, we have no assurance this is even the area—"

"My master assures me; this is the area."

"Yeah, well, if he's so wise, why'd he have us camp beside a nest of brights?"

"Don't be insolent. Content yourself to relocate to a safer location, leave the planning to me. There's more here than meets the eye."

"Well, I should think so. Not a few of my men have wondered why three advance brigades, followed by a battalion, plus half of your bodyguard, is needed to find two girls lost in the woods—who are probably dead anyway."

"Just see to it that you maintain order among the troops by giving them plausible answers, Mileer. Keep in mind, if I fall, you fall with me."

At that moment another scream rent the air, shriller than before, more desperate, anguished. Carnalians stood alertly watching, apprehensive. The inner bowels of Ra-Amawl had made a deep impression on these soldiers, especially recruits. The dronnets feared none of the things Carnalian regulars did, but stood ready to battle whatever human, beast or apparition had caused such hideous screams. In fact, their appetites were whetted, for the last scream had the sound of blood mingled with terror.

Hod-ya suddenly went rigid, unaware that she was gouging her sharpened nails into her palms and her pointed teeth piercing her lower lip, drawing bloody splotches. Suddenly she gasped and staggered backward into Captain Mileer, sending both sprawling to the mossy bed. Hod-ya's mouth foamed and she began writhing. A voice, unlike anything Captain Mileer had ever heard, deep and malignant, rolled from Hod-ya's mouth:

"Move away from cursed place,
Set afire all this wood,
Remove from trees this open space,
Kill all soldiers of the good."

"She's incoherent," Mileer said to attendants as he picked himself off the ground. "There's no open space or soldiers of the good nearby. Carry her. We must get her away quickly, else we'll all share her fate. The brights are driving her mad."

One of the dronnets picked Hod-ya's quivering form up in his arms and, contradicting Mileer, turned and said, "Not brights; Psa."

"Whatever. But we leave now. Understand? Now!" He turned and approached his regulars who were more uneasy than ever. The bodyguard carried his mistress who still muttered the same quatrain over and over.

Mileer wasn't prepared to battle brights, especially with only three brigades and a handful of blackguards. No one, not even Hod-ya, could expect that. The others grimly followed, reluctantly obeying the captain, though they suspected Psa and Hod-ya wanted them to set the forest afire. Mileer's hasty retreat left supplies and foodstuffs behind that would hinder their flight. He took only a spare moment to post notices for the stranded patrols, detailing where they could rejoin the main body.

~

Captain Varter found it difficult to believe his eyes. Mileer's forces were in full retreat. Varter automatically plotted how to waylay any straggling Carnalian patrols. But first, he must discover what caused those blood-curdling screams. He set off for the bath hut.

Nearly there, Varter encountered his own elite bodyguard, the dozen warriors he'd dispatched to investigate at the first scream, lying beside the trail in various states of consciousness. He slowed his pace, pondering what could have caused such a complete disabling of such stalwart men.

Upon entering the dimly lit bathhouse he stumbled over Bonu's inert form lying spread eagle, face down. He rolled Bonu over and was relieved to find him breathing. A large, discolored lump covered his entire forehead. A shadow filled the doorway behind, blotting out what little light came in. Varter instinctively rolled to the side swinging his sword to ward off an attack. A splotched, blue sword met his, checking his swipe in midair.

"Father, it's me."

"Vawella?"

"I came as soon as I could. What happened?"

"I, I don't know yet. Who was guarding the Carnalian girl?"

"Leezle and Jeda. Oh no! Oh no!"

Dreading what he might find, Captain Varter entered the inner passage, his sword lighting the way before him. Vawella followed close behind. Coming around a stanchion he espied shattered barrel staves and metallic hoops spread hap-hazard across the floor. Amidst the staves was a bloodstained cloth and several rope fragments. Leezle lay against the wall whimpering incoherently, partially conscious. Across from her Jeda sprawled atop Glend. Neither girl moved. From the splatter of blood on the walls, floor, and garments, Varter doubted either was alive.

CHAPTER TWENTY-THREE

"JEDA?" CAPTAIN VARTER WHISPERED. "JEDA?" He touched her throat and was relieved to feel a steady throb. "She's alive, thank Logon."

Vawella gently rolled Jeda over, removing her from atop Glend's inert form. Vawella knowingly probed Jeda for wounds and broken bones but found none. Glend, on the other hand, had been stabbed in the chest, her legs suffered savage claw marks and her right hand was discolored and swollen. Vawella then turned her attention to Leezle who babbled nonsense through a haze of pain. Her collarbone appeared broken and she had a nasty bump on the back of her head; other than that, she didn't seem critically injured.

Other kingsmen arrived anxious to discover what had happened.

Leezle, Jeda, and Glend were quickly, quietly transferred to the medical shelter for a more thorough examination. Varter demanded to be apprised of any change in the girls' condition.

Bonu sat on the floor, head between his knees, groaning. Varter placed a hand on Bonu's shoulder. "What happened, Bonu? Can you shed any light on what took place? Who knocked you on the head?"

"Uh, ooh! Sorry, Captain, ooh! I don't remember. I heard a woman's voice, it must have been Jeda, fending off . . . using Logon's name; then, there was a scream and a blast of thick, black smoke. That's about all I remember."

"Okay, well, we'll get you fixed up. Should you remember any more—"

"You'll be the first to know."

Captain Varter issued orders for officers to attend an emergency meeting in his HQ within the hour to decide what to do in light of the fact that Mileer and Hod-ya couldn't possibly be ignorant of their presence any more.

A constant guard was set over Glend, for though she bore a chest wound, no Logon dress appeared. The wound might or might not have been caused by Jeda's sword, and Varter wasn't taking any chances.

In attendance on the meeting in the captain's quarters were lieutenants, both retired captains, a few higher-ranking sergeants as well as Kyleah, seer and head of the kitchen staff.

The meeting came to order, those who were younger settled on the dirt floor allowing the older men to occupy whatever seating could be provided.

Blegash rose to his feet from a tripod stool in the corner, cleared his throat and said, "Whereas Captain Varter and I are known to be at odds in certain matters . . . I want it clearly understood that there is no dispute between Varter and myself in this crisis. I support him fully and urge any who have doubts to put them away and submit to his leadership. It's of utmost importance we be united." Blegash took his seat again.

Here and there muted voices uttered, "Well said!" and "Here, here!"

"I'm honored," responded Captain Varter, rising to his feet and nodding deferentially to the former captain. "We desperately need Logon's guidance; he provided roamers for our defense, so I'm sure he'll provide instruction to us. Perhaps this is the call to the last battle—the

Tremendum—which we've been anticipating. Or, perhaps that's not to happen for generations. Whatever the case, we need to discern Logon's will and dare not make a move without it." At that he unrolled a map suspended from the ceiling at the rear of his tent revealing a rough topography of their immediate section of Ra-Amawl. The present kingsman campsite was marked in charcoal with an 'X'. The perimeter of dry sticks was denoted by tiny slash marks; various other markings depicted depressions, elevations, bogs, thickets, trenches and quicksand as well as other forest features. Secret trails for food-gathering, ambuscades or trails to other resources in various sectors of the forest were shown as series of dashes. Known areas of danger, such as the haunts of the half-men or paths used by Carnalian regulars were also marked.

"We need to locate the enemy's new camp before we relocate our camp. We can, as most of you know, dismantle our camouflage shrubbery and reconstruct it anywhere we choose. No one knows the interior of Ra-Amawl like we do, so it's not likely anyone will notice a dense thicket changing locations." Several chuckles greeted his announcement. "But, like I said, we need to ascertain Logon's guidance before doing anything."

"Captain, may I suggest," ventured Bonu, who'd been sitting off to one side, "that we take every precaution against dread attack." He winced and tilted his head to the side. The bandage wrapped around his forehead seemed to do little to suppress the headache.

"Dreads, Bonu? Don't you think that's a bit fantastic?" Blegash tugged his beard. "I mean, tophets are no strangers to these parts, same with cusps, and though dreads have been known to venture here in times past, recent historical record—as long as we've been a brigade which is since I was a lad—hasn't mentioned dreads."

"If what I ran into in the bath hut, and if what others saw drifting over our camp wasn't a disembodied dread, we are being confronted by another order of enemy of which the runes yield no knowledge."

"But disembodied tophets flee back to the haunts of their formation in fireballs," protested a sergeant beside Bonu. "This thing didn't flee, but leisurely drifted through our compound."

"Exactly," agreed Bonu. "That is why I believe it wasn't any kind of tophet, but something of greater power. You saw it, right, Sergeant Kirp?"

The sergeant nodded.

"Would you recount what you saw, for the benefit of those who weren't there to see?" Captain Varter asked. "I'm sure Bonu would like to know what he missed."

"I may have missed it, but it didn't miss me, sir," replied Bonu, gingerly touching his forehead.

"Sir?" said sergeant Kirp.

"Go ahead, son, but stand up and speak clearly so all can hear."

Kirp rose to his feet. "I was assigned to the wall facing the enemy camp. I heard the thud and scream coming from behind me and spun around thinking one of our walls had been breached. I saw Lieutenant Bonu race toward the bath hut followed at some distance by your own bodyguard, sir. Then I heard the second scream and more thrashing sounds. I wanted to assist, but daren't leave, for I was the only one at that post. I checked outside and saw that the Carnalians were frozen by the sounds coming from what they'd assumed was a dense thicket. Then I heard a noise like rocks tumbling together, followed by that last, loud, piercing scream. I turned just in time to see Bonu dash into the bath hut gangway.

"Within a minute, certainly no longer, a massive, roiling cloud of dense, black smoke poured out the gangway. It was huge, without definite shape, about thirty or forty feet long, rising in the air as it drifted contrary to the prevailing breeze, following its own will, as it were. Then it descended upon your bodyguard. When it lifted they were all strewn on the ground. It turned and drifted toward the fence close by my station. I gripped my sword and called on Logon, but it apparently had no interest in assaulting me, for it passed straight through the wall. I watched through my peephole as the roamers cleared a path, letting it pass unhindered. The last I saw, it was settling upon the Black Lady!" Kirp looked around the tent waiting for questions, but none came. He re-settled cross-legged to the floor.

"Thank you, sergeant. Any comments or questions?"

Blegash rose to his feet again, saying, "As to what that apparition was, I have no idea, but as to its being one of the ten dreads, I'm afraid there has never been a recorded incident, either on the swords or in the annals of history that a dread left its physical form and drifted about like an errant thunderstorm. You probably witnessed a higher echelon tophet, or a lord of the cusps or some such, sergeant."

"Bonu?" Captain Varter responded to the lieutenant's raised hand.

"Thank you, sir. I know my own encounter was brief, very brief, but, I had a profound sense of malignant evil, much stronger than any tophet or cusp I ever encountered. In my humble opinion, it can be none other than one of the ten Chimeree, disembodied or otherwise."

"Does it really make a difference? It might be a dread or only a tophet. Evil has come upon us," ventured a lieutenant from the other side of the tent. "It knows we're here, and it'll only be a short time before it communicates that information."

Others murmured in agreement.

At that, the oldest, other retired captain, Bainch, rose to his feet leaning heavily on his staff. He held up a hand for quiet. His voice was high-pitched due to advanced age. "Brothers, it's of the utmost importance to accurately identify our enemy, for only by knowing him can we approximate not only his objective, but where we are in the prophetic scheme of things. If it's merely a tophet, as some suggest, this enemy camp was a search party for two lost girls; but, if, as I begin to suspect, it was a dread of the gate, we've crossed the threshold into a more serious era. It's foretold in the warrunes that when the ten dreads travel wide and begin to dwindle, the final battles of the war will quickly follow. Therefore, if a dread has entered Ra-Amawl on some mission from Cosmopolis, it is quite a significant event, for that means the other dreads have also been released from the gates where they've been locked by Elyon's command. There's a rune that reads:

> "Last of days, least of dreads, under roof of Ra-Amawl,
> Fiercely as this warrior treads, thus begins the end of all."

"Bainch, you quote the mysterious runes?" Blegash earnestly searched his peer's face. "They're beyond the allowed runes. You agree with Varter then, about tolling the whole blade?"

The white-haired officer sighed deeply. "I, too, for some time now, have had my doubts about not sharpening the entire sword. I said nothing, because I didn't want to influence anyone, not even you, my friend. I've spent much time recently on the mysterious runes, however, and believe Logon has given me a little insight, insight that would now be better shared than kept private."

"Please sit, Captain Bainch, don't weary yourself by standing, but we would like to hear those insights," urged Captain Varter.

The eldest brigade member gratefully re-seated himself in a make-shift, rustic chair "I was a young man, a servant on forage detail, when the brigade first came to Ra-Amawl and established a secretive campsite. We had four captains back then, powerful warriors of Logon, very sensitive to the Advisor. Ahh, those were days of renown." Bainch fell silent, head tilted slightly back as he stared at the tent's ceiling, remembering.

"Captain Bainch?" Varter quietly recalled the elder back to the present. "You were about to relate something about the mysterious runes?"

"Eh? Oh yes, the mysterious runes." The old man apparently felt no shame at lapsing into reminiscence, for these were his children in Logon. He'd seen each of them pierced and washed, stumbling and growing; and so, felt no unease at his own awkwardness. "As you know, the mystery runes are most difficult to untangle. What they portray, the images conjured, the proclamation of judgment and doom, blessing and bliss, mixed so none can easily decipher them, all intended to reveal, in time, the masterful way Logon conceals his intentions from the idly curious, not to mention his enemies. Only his committed servants will perceive those truths, and few, even among officers, have attained that knowledge.

"A few weeks ago, I recalled a dream I'd dreamt years earlier. I pondered this memory of a long-forgotten dream many days. It stays vividly etched in my mind, occupying my thoughts. I determined to know if it was from Logon. In times past, he spoke in such ways, but I wasn't sure he still did so nowadays, since we have his runes engraved on the swords. I sought answers in my daily tolling and I gradually understood the dream's symbolism."

"And what was the message?" asked Blegash.

"I recall every detail, color, word, image . . . In the dream I stood upon a hill with little children playing at my feet. I was responsible for them, like a shepherd. I originally had this dream when I was merely a servant on forage detail, mind you. I saw a firestorm sweeping through the valley, sending billows of smoke into the air, threatening to sweep over the hill where I guarded the children. Behind me was a noise like howling wolves. Turning, I saw half-men on a rampage, killing every living thing in their path, heading up the other side of my hill. Then a thunderstorm broke out right over top of us, but instead of thunder, curses and threats rained down. The children huddled close to me, and I feebly held my sword aloft to fend off the onslaught. In the midst of this assault my sword began pulsing with a beautiful melody. I won't offend you by trying to sing the melody, but the words went:

> More, more, more, yet more,
> Light is needed on this sword,
> Learn, learn, learn, yet learn,
> Before the wrath begins to burn.
> Runes, runes, runes, more runes,
> Your foe is strong his trail makes ruins,
> Strokes, strokes, strokes, learn strokes,
> To stand against the dreadful hoax.

"I believe the memory of that dream was restored to me warning us of the days now descending upon us. When the young lass with the sword glowing beyond the point came into our assembly, I understood the message of the dream. She, in her short time of knowing Logon, knows him at least as well as many in our midst who've been with us for years. Didn't you see her face radiate his love and peace? I knew then that we'd been short-changed in our regimented brigade training. Kingsmen need to sharpen the entire sword.

"Varter, I'm pleased you said what you did the other night, though many were offended. You were right to take such a stand. Ah, but, that's not my concern now. You want to know about the runes, the mysterious runes, for their proper interpretation reveals whether we're in the last days of the age or not."

Several around the room withdrew swords and tollers.

"Up near the hilt, where the head of the dove and eagle meet the runes are boldly embossed, yet inscrutable, as if the rune maker dared anyone to interpret them. I don't have much understanding, but I believe a tiny portion has been revealed to me. Ply your tollers by the almost indiscernible rune beneath the largest one." He demonstrated by scraping a long, deliberate stroke. "This is the chronicle of the dreads.

Lurcan banished from the ether, cast from Splendora's henge,
Drew his rabble close beside and plotted out his dark revenge,
Vile and violent gathered, mutated by their fall,
Sheltering frightened 'neath his wings, unsure of fate's last call,
For Elyon's power and scope unknown, surely must defend his own.

Given leave to make a stand, Lurcan chose a battleground,
The sands and seas, lands and meas in man's home new found,
Quickly set, his kingdom patterned from what he knew before,
And tophets, cusps and wily beasts worried mankind to the floor,
Deceiving and destroying, and blinding to the truth,
Great lords ten, with dreadful power, defiled horn and hoof,
Darkness reigned and siege began 'neath Lurcan's brooding hate,
The times were set, the court would sit, let justice come, but late.

For Elyon, Logon, and Advisor, the hidden would reveal,
And all would know of Lurcan's woe caused by selfish zeal,
That such ways bring disease, unrest, and crowded graves,
Though long it tarries, when wrath comes, will swell in tidal waves,

It hastes, it hastes, a short work done, when harvest is grown nigh,
Look to your swords, they point the way, as stars fall from the sky.

Midst their fall, Reltar, prince, will open smoking pits,
Unleashing fiery biters to give all mankind fits,
Broack prowls to forge dark, fell swords anew,
So roam the twins, Neask, Zindrad, unleashing ruin's few,
Though Zindrad prevail, Neask's own tongue will fall,
And ten begin to dwindle, each to find a bitter gall,
Mambu the foul, the lord of cusps, will turn upon his friend.
Deh-Ropec the final one, remains until the end,
And Psa, deceiver of womankind, first to taste of death,
Ponthy the fair, deceiver, pretender, kills with sweetened breath,
While Laroc, beauty, colors beckon, drinks blood from all his prey,
And Prive tyrant, tophet leader, leads hordes in vile array,
Be on your guard all servants bonded, look to your swords, be brave,
Fear not, for when these times begin, Logon rides to save.

Beastly creatures, forms defiled, dragons, monsters, horned,
Lions, leopards, eyes and crowns, speaking vile, forewarned,
Roamers clash with trumpets blare, earthquake, fire and famine,
Frogs and locusts, lice and flood, stars like falling mammon,
Mountains spewing out raw blood, rivers run polluted,
Carnalia's empire is undone, Lurcan's realm is looted.

Who can stand? Who must fight? Who will live? Who leads the way?
Only Logon's faithful find strength and power that day."

The old man sat silent for a moment, then said, "I think we're in that day of the dreads being loosed, to be followed closely by Logon cleansing the earth of all villainy. Now look closely under that rune, ahh, it glows on all our swords. See, more information is revealed individually about the dreads. I don't fully know what's referred to, such as what it says about Neask:

Neask—
The day you seek the untrained warrior,
Will be the day you rue,
Selecting spy beyond your reach,
Boastful tongue—away it flew!

"What that's all about I have no hint, but consider what it says about Psa:

Psa—
Women swoon under your spell,
Control o'er men through them you sell,
But fire and wood, flood and slough,
Your end will come 'neath leaf and bough,
Your door will crash upon your flight,
Your peers assisting will draw the night,
Quickly down in one fell stroke,
Comes a conqueror to break your yoke.

"Where else is 'leaf and bough' as thick as Ra-Amawl? Why would Logon place a brigade here except to battle Psa in fulfillment of prophecy if and when that monster comes to Ra-Amawl? I believe Bonu and the others did encounter a dread outside his nearly-invincible, physical form. Take note, not just any dread, but Psa, setting the stage for fulfillment of prophecy."

"Hold on there," interrupted Blegash. "You put a lot of weight on a dream's interpretation. Before we think of challenging that Carnalian force invading Ra-Amawl, or that huge, black cloud of whatever origin, we'd better be certain."

Several men erupted in hushed dispute, some pro, some con, most questioning.

Captain Varter held his hands up for silence. "That was amazing Captain Bainch. I'm not sure what to make of it. I have very little knowledge of the mysterious runes myself, and like Captain Blegash, am hesitant to pursue any endeavors with so much at stake. Kyleah, we haven't heard anything from you. What do you say about this since it was your word that set this chain of events in motion?"

Kyleah blushed. It was bad enough that Captain Varter had insisted upon her attendance in this meeting. She was just a kitchen servant, and happy to remain that. She never expected Logon to use her for anything special and was as surprised as anyone when Logon gave her special encouragement for individuals and sometimes the group at large. This was a Runer brigade, and one of the runes they tolled encouraged such activities; nevertheless, they were all surprised when Kyleah's gift surfaced in the brigade. Many comforting words, and not a few exhortations, even mild rebukes came through her, all of which were carefully scrutinized and confirmed as in line with Logon's runes. Thus, when she gave the word to raid the Psa Woman's coach, though it was very unusual, not to mention a dangerous course, Captain Varter regarded it as Logon's command, not Kyleah's suggestion.

All eyes rested on her, the only woman invited to the council. It was an opportunity to appear important, useful, to be recognized by the leadership. But Kyleah wanted no glory. Indeed, she'd have been happier if she could give her epiphanies anonymously. She shrugged, apologizing, "I, I have nothing to add."

"Very well. It would be wrong of us to force an opinion from you. However, if a word comes, don't hesitate to interrupt."

Kyleah shyly nodded.

"So, where does that leave us?" asked Blegash.

"I say this," ventured Bainch, "if we discover that what Bonu and Kirp suppose is true, I think we have our orders."

Approving murmurs greeted this decision.

Captain Varter saw the logic. "But, to think that fulfillment of prophecy is up to us. Well, let's see if Logon gives confirmation, as the rune says:

'Let everything be proven by two or three.'

The tent flap opened and Hanell entered.

Bonu chided, "Hanell, this is a private meeting. Officers only."

"Begging your pardon, sirs, the captain left word that if the girls' condition changed—"

"Yes, man, what is it?" Captain Varter stood, both fists on his desk.

"One of them hovers near death, sir."

"Which one?" demanded Varter.

Bonu jumped to his feet and nearly blacked out from the sudden pain.

Hanell's eyes widened and his jaw went slack as he replied, "I'm not sure. I don't think they said."

"Jeda!" Bonu uttered and was out the door and rushing toward the medical tent despite his throbbing head.

CHAPTER TWENTY-FOUR

OUT OF BREATH AND WITH a drum pounding in his head, Bonu burst into the medical tent fearful of what he'd find. He headed straight for the critical care section, striding past rows of unoccupied cots. Pulling back the curtain he encountered a beehive of activity; attendants bustled about carrying various gourds or surgical implements and several were clustered around one raised table, working furiously on a patient. So many were crowded into that section of the tent that Bonu was unable to identify the patient they were working on. He paused in the entry so not to disrupt the workers.

A hand touched his shoulder. Captain Varter whispered, "Let me through, lieutenant, as soon as I know anything, I'll let you know."

"Captain, please, if it's Jeda, let me know how she fares."

Captain Varter looked Bonu full in the face for a quick, analytical moment. "Indeed, lieutenant? Your interest surpasses military matters, I take it?"

Bonu's cheeks flushed.

"I see. Hmm, I should've known." He pushed past some attendants and made his way to Kraga, the chief medical officer.

By the stern faces surrounding the patient Bonu surmised that the patient's condition was urgent. Captain Varter looked up from the huddle straight at Bonu and gravely shook his head. Bonu's hands went cold; his knees buckled; all went black.

When Bonu opened his eyes, he found himself on a cot. He was embarrassed at having become a distraction when others needed the attention. Captain Varter's broad face gradually came into focus.

The commotion around the operating table was still at fever pitch.

"Tut, tut, just lay back, Bonu," said Varter. "I think you misunderstood. I shook my head to say it wasn't Jeda, but Glend. You must have thought I was saying Jeda wasn't going to make it, didn't you?"

"Not Jeda? She's okay?" Relief swept over him like a wave of cool water. "Captain, I—"

"Save your strength. It turns out you're in worse condition than we thought. Whether that black cloud you encountered was a dread or not it must have injected some kind of poison into you. Everyone it touched received a dose. Not to worry though, Kraga assures me the effects will soon wear off. So, for now, remain here under supervision. Rest assured, Jeda is sleeping peacefully right over there."

Bonu followed Captain Varter's point across the aisle.

Jeda was asleep on a cot, head propped on a pillow, face drawn, her usually rosy cheeks were sallow. Bonu studied Jeda as she slept off the effects of what?

Captain Varter, returned to the more pressing business of Glend's situation.

Bonu lay back on his pillow. The captain was right; he needed rest. But what was that black cloud that he, Jeda, and the captain's bodyguard encountered if not a disembodied dread? Some of those soldiers had already returned to duty; others remained under watchful care, their symptoms little improved.

He closed his eyes trying to reconstruct the final, hectic moments of that eerie encounter. He remembered dashing into the bath hut through the portal. He heard a voice, a woman's voice, Jeda's? Possibly. What did the voice say?

"Touch me not with that! No, no, touch me no-ooeeeeaaahhh!"

That accounted for the second loud, inhuman scream. Now that he thought about it, it didn't sound at all like Jeda. Oh, poor Jeda, what horror did she face alone, not knowing help was but a step away? Hmmph! Some help he brought!

After that piercing scream the black cloud descended and over-whelmed him. In a delirium he thought the hut was afire. He charged into the swirling smoke to rescue Jeda. That was all he remembered except a quick glimpse of a wooden beam about eye level and a cruel, feminine voice sneering, "Did you think you could help?"

Bonu sat upright. "Captain, I remembered something."

Varter turned from beside Kraga, eyebrows raised.

"It may be important, or it may be just delusion."

Varter acknowledged Bonu with a nod, then returned his attention to the person on the table. The technicians were waiting for a word from Captain Varter whether to continue the struggle or let Glend go. Even Kraga waited for Varter's decision. Kraga's word usually took precedence in these matters but this decision he yielded to Varter.

At long last Captain Varter said, "Leave her alone. It's between Glend and Logon now. There's nothing more we can do. If that wound is from Jeda's sword, and Glend isn't willing, it will end badly."

Everyone stepped back. Glend would receive the consequence of her choice; there was nothing anyone could do to help. Hands that had busily tried everything to keep her from slipping away now hung helpless at their sides.

Several tense moments passed. Glend, barely breathing, was the color of the sheets she lay upon. Her chest barely rose as she took a final, shallow breath, exhaled and became still. Her spirit was somewhere between earthly and nether regions. She hadn't allowed Logon to heal her heart. No greater tragedy could befall a person than to come that close, and yet defer.

Minutes passed, yet none of the attendants left; all clung to hope beyond reason.

Finally, Captain Varter intoned, "It's been too long, there's nothing more we can do. Go about your duties and know that you tried your best. Try not to let this discourage you."

Bonu watched the workers move away from Glend's prone form with heavy hearts, leaving only Kraga and Varter staring down upon Glend. Captain Varter turned to leave but Kraga suddenly seized his hand, staying him.

Bonu elevated himself to his elbows and watched with renewed anticipation as a green glow surrounded Glend's bed. Then a dress appeared upon her form and sank beneath the coverlet; the Logon dress was simple, yet elegant in design and of luxuriant fabric. A rosy blush sprang to Glend's cheeks, her chest heaved as she inhaled a draught of air. Varter and Kraga hugged each other. Servants who were cleaning up and others that hadn't yet gone to other responsibilities were drawn back.

Glend mumbled unintelligibly, talking to the greatest physician.

"What is it? What's all the commotion?" came from the cot opposite.

Bonu's head spun around so fast he lost his equilibrium. When his vision cleared, he saw Jeda sitting upright, staring inquisitively, watching the gathering around Glend.

"Jeda! You, you're awake?"

"What's going on? Who are they so concerned about?"

"Glend. She just received her Logon dress. Uh, how are you feeling?"

"Glend! You're kidding! Who pierced her heart?"

"Didn't you? She had a chest wound. We all assumed you, but, if you didn't, who did?"

"Jeda, my dear, you're awake, and in the flush of health it would seem," Kraga stepped between Bonu and Jeda. "Please lay back and let me check your injuries."

Captain Varter moved in behind him, anxious to question Jeda.

Kraga turned to Varter. "I'm sorry captain, but I insist your questions wait until I've seen to the state of my patient."

"Captain," Bonu called softly.

Varter turned around.

"I remembered something, I think, and it's just been confirmed by Jeda, sort of. There might have been someone else in the hut."

"Yes, Leezle was there."

"I don't think Leezle, in her condition, could have pierced Glend's heart; and Jeda says she didn't. There must have been someone else!"

"Lieutenant, how could there be? There's only one entry to the bath hut, and you blocked the egress yourself, though unconscious. I wasn't but a minute behind you and encountered no one coming out. Witnesses attest that no one left the building before I arrived except that black cloud. Inside we found only Glend, Leezle, Jeda, and you. So how could anyone else have been there?"

"I heard a voice, a woman's voice, saying 'Don't touch me with that thing!'"

"Jeda's voice?"

"No, she was already unconscious, and it didn't sound like her. Just before I lost consciousness the same voice said to me, 'Did you think you could help?' Now Jeda just told me she didn't pierce Glend's heart, so, who did?"

Furrows lined Varter's forehead.

"Okay, Captain," said Kraga as he tapped Varter's shoulder, "she seems to be in the rosy bloom of health, though fatigued. You may ask questions, but please, be mindful that she's still weak." The physician stepped back but not away, as Captain Varter turned his attention to Jeda.

"Jeda?"

"Yes, sir?" Jeda's eyes opened and then widened with recognition as Captain Varter leaned close.

"Can you tell me what happened in the bath hut?"

"The bath hut? Oh, well, I guess, I'll try. We, uh Leezle and I, were guarding Glend. She began to writhe free . . . " Jeda sat up again. "Captain, I saw the same phantom in Glend that I saw when I was interviewed by Hod-ya. I saw Psa!"

Captain Varter stood erect. "Psa? Jeda, are you quite sure? Psa, one of the dreads of the gate?"

"The same. It used Glend to kick the barrel out from under Lee—Leezle! How is she? Is she, did she get—?"

"Leezle has a broken collarbone and a headache and some effects left over from inhaling the same noxious fumes as you and Bonu, but in time she'll be fine. Now, about Psa. How do you know it was Psa?"

"I remember seeing," Jeda rubbed her temples, "red dots in her eyes, growing larger, filling the whole eye socket. I was terrified. If I hadn't just been sharpening my sword, I would have fainted dead away. It chanted at me, I don't recall what it said, but I was frightened, for it knew me." Jeda shuddered and closed her eyes.

"Jeda," interrupted Kraga, "if this is too difficult—"

"No! I need to talk about it. I've had dreams of it threatening to get me, to take me to Hod-ya." A tear dripped from the corner of her eye. "It was Psa."

The certainty in her voice seemed to convince Captain Varter. "Thank you, Jeda, you've been quite helpful." He stroked his beard thoughtfully as he walked away.

Bonu watched him leave, careful to not disturb his thoughts; the fate of the encampment rested on Varter's shoulders. Bonu had, at other times, seen him thus absorbed to the exclusion of his surroundings until he finally reached a decision. Then he would act with daring certainty, often taking the most dangerous role himself to make sure his plan was faithfully executed.

"Bonu, why are you here?"

Bonu turned his attention to the girl occupying the cot across the way.

Kraga, recognizing he was no longer needed, smiled at the two then assigned himself other duties.

"Your forehead, it's so discolored. What happened?"

Jeda seemed genuinely concerned.

"I, uh, ran into your Psa, I think."

"You were there? In the bath hut? I didn't see you."

"I came as soon as I heard your scream, or was it Leezle? Anyway, when I entered, you were already unconscious. All I remember is a thick, black cloud enveloping me as I bumped into a rafter. Next thing I knew Captain Varter was turning me over. Oh, yes, and I heard a voice saying something about 'not touching' . . . or something like that."

Jeda closed her eyes. "I remember hearing those words, too! Although it seemed at a great distance. It was a feminine voice, but not Leezle's. And certainly not mine. It must have been Psa, crying out, 'touch me not with that thing!' What thing could it have meant?"

"Psa spoke?"

"It was speaking in an unusual sound, like stones tumbling over and over on each other. It was horrible. It said nasty things to me, threatening me." Jeda wiped away a tear. "I never felt so frightened in all my life. It inhabited Glend, using her limbs, glaring through her eyes even as it came for me, boasting about taking me back to Hod-ya. I stumbled and dropped my sword . . . I reached my hand out to retrieve it and suddenly it was in my hand. I put it between myself and Glend and struggled to my feet. Suddenly Glend was free of her bonds. She lunged, teeth bared, fingers splayed like talons. Darkness overwhelmed me before I could aim it at her."

"It's over now, Jeda. You're safe. Captain Varter is making plans to move the camp to a more secure location so the Carnalian task force can't find us. That means Psa won't know where we went either. He'll never find you again."

"It, it seemed so certain, promising to take me to Hod-ya. Why it didn't seize me when I passed out I'll never know."

"Jeda, brace yourself for some more bad news. Hod-ya was right outside our wall."

Jeda's eyebrows rose. "You saw her?"

"I'm not sure. Before the scream that brought me running, I saw a woman across the clearing, tall and lean, dressed in black from head to foot, fitting the description I've heard of her. Captain Varter is certain he recognized her, though, for he's had dealings with her before she rose to power. Of course, we all know her by reputation."

"Then you were right, they're seeking Glend and me. I still don't quite know what Scrarth and Avangar is. What can you tell me?"

"I don't know much, except that it's a duel to the death. Two contestants pitted against beasts or half men, or some loathsome creature to prove their worthiness to continue training in Pitland's service. Survivors are rigorously indoctrinated with mystical and secret rites. More than that I don't want to say. Just be glad you escaped."

"Oh, I am, I am. You know, seeing you like this, abed and in a weak state, I could begin to kind of like you. You're not so conceited when all your girlfriend admirers aren't around." She smiled, making his soul soar. "I think I could endure your presence—on a limited basis, that is. I still think you're proud. And the way you treated me on the trek from the road . . . "

"What, what are you talking about? I never treated you badly. I only did what was necessary for your safety."

Jeda's smile disappeared and her brows lowered. "What is it with you? Why can't you just be nice? Why are you always putting me in my place, exposing my flaws?" She slumped back down on her pillow and turned away. "I thought you were, that we could, oh, never mind. I guess I don't like you very much, after all, Bonu. It's just a personality thing. Logon commands us to love each other, so I will endeavor my utmost to abide your presence in Ecclessite love, but I doubt we'll ever be close friends."

Bonu's mouth drooped and his eyes descended to the dirt floor. Jeda was the only girl he'd ever met that held any attraction for him.

She was intent upon following Logon, as was he, and she wasn't silly like so many other girls—primping and vainly making themselves outwardly attractive by adorning their natural features. To be sure, Jeda was beautiful, perhaps the most beautiful girl he'd ever set eyes on, yet her inner beauty outshone her exterior features; there was something Logon-like about her, making her irresistible. For a brief moment he hoped she was beginning to like him, that maybe she would develop feelings for him. Then she dashed all hope! It was clear that she could barely tolerate him. The only woman he ever thought was "the one," couldn't stand the sight of him.

"Ah Logon, with what grief have I been pierced?" he muttered as he rolled over. "Help me not seek anything but what you would give."

Although Jeda rolled away, too, and faced the tent wall, Bonu faintly heard Jeda muttering to herself, "Thinks he's a gift to women? Wants to trifle with my affections like all those others, does he? Thinks he's the best soldier afield, too, no doubt. What conceit! What arrogance! Of all the men I've ever known, and I've known some 'bell-ringers,' this man annoys me the most!"

"Well, well, how are you two getting on?" asked Vawella, apparently having heard the news about Glend and come fresh from her duties. She looked pleasantly surprised to find Jeda awake and conversant. "I should think you two have a lot to talk about."

"Well, we don't," snapped Jeda.

Taken aback, Vawella looked from one to the other. "Indeed? I thought you two made a lovely couple."

"Uh, I think, uh, I'd better quit lazing about and see if I can't be useful somewhere," said Bonu, swinging his legs over the cot. It took a moment for the dizziness swimming in his head to clear. "I'm feeling better, I think. There's much to do if we're breaking camp. I'm, uh, sure Captain Varter can find a use for me." He took a couple of faltering steps and paused until his legs stabilized, then made his way outside.

~

"Jeda?" queried the captain's daughter.

"Oh, I know. He means no harm."

"Do you know what I think?"

"About what?"

"About you and Bonu."

"About me and—! Oh, you've got to be jesting."

"The enchantment is as plain as the bark on a grizzle tree."

"Well, I thought so, poor man. He doesn't realize I have no interest in him. I try not to encourage him, but he's so persistent."

"I'm not talking about him."

Jeda looked up blankly.

"Do I have to make the obvious plain? Yes, I can see that I do. Jeda, you're quite fascinated with Bonu."

"Hold on, Vawella. Just because you and every other nubile female in camp think he's the most—"

"Don't protest too much. You may not recognize it, but you top the list of those who are dreamy over him."

"Fiddle-faddle!"

"Think about it, girl. Why do you suppose you're so upset over the treatment you received from him on the trek from the road? And the way you resented his leaping up beside you when you gave your report. Why are you constantly rehearsing all his characteristics trying to find fault, so you don't have to admit you really like him?"

"Because he always puts me in a bad light."

"No, Jeda, I think not. Even the short time you've been with us I've seen you bear patiently with others who offended you. I must admit, at first I was puzzled why the camp's most eligible bachelor was spurned by the newest marriageable young woman, and now I believe I have the answer."

"It's simple, I'm not attracted in the least to him."

"Oh, but you are. I watched you both at dinner the other night. I saw how your eyes followed his every move, how your ears strained for every word he spoke, how your faced flushed when he paid attention to Leezle's questions."

"I was just concerned."

"Yes? Concerned that she had his attention, attention you wanted, though when he did pay you attention, you gave him the brush-off. Come now, Jeda, that's no way to treat an eligible suitor. The sooner you admit it to yourself, and explore whether such a relationship has Logon's approval, the sooner you'll know whether to pursue the relationship. No doubt you've denied it because you don't think Logon wants marriage for you, and you want to spare yourself the hurt. But you'll never know Logon's will until you acknowledge and own up to your own feelings. Once you identify your true feelings, you'll be able to clearly discern whether it's Logon's will. Don't be afraid to risk being hurt either; only Logon can comfort us anyway, and you'll never discover his solace unless you're willing to be vulnerable."

Jeda blinked away the tears that confirmed Vawella's perceptions. "You don't know that! You're just guessing!" Her face flushed, and her cheeks grew hot.

"Well, if I wasn't sure before, I am now." Vawella laughed lightly and stood akimbo. "You ought to see your face."

"Oh!" Jeda pulled the sheets over her head "Leave me alone."

"Very well. I'll just check on Glend first. But think about it. You're in love girl, like it or not."

Jeda mumbled unintelligible noises. Jeda peeked out from under her coverlet.

~

Vawella turned her attention to the girl sleeping peacefully a few paces away. "Glend, can you hear me?"

"Mmmmph?" An eye opened a fraction of an inch. "Whozzat?" she asked.

"Glend, it's Vawella. Do you remember me?"

"Vawella? Oh, yes." Both eyes opened, and she stared up into the gentle face of the young leader of women. "He said you'd help me."

"He?"

"Logo—!" She groped the scar on her chest. "It really happened. I'm one of them, er, you, er, us. The monster was driven out!"

"I really met him! Oh Vawella! He's wonderful. I never knew how much I needed him, how he was what I longed for. Jeda! Is that you over there? Oh, Jeda, I met him! Why didn't you ever tell me how wonderful he was?"

"I did, remember?" Jeda sat up. "Several times."

"Well, yes, but, but you didn't say he was that wonderful!"

Vawella and Jeda laughed.

Glend tried to sit up. "I don't remember coming here, though. When did that happen, ooh! My head!"

"Here, just lay back and rest. You've been through an ordeal. You need time to recuperate. You're under strict orders to rest until further notice. I'll come by from time to time to check on you and see

how you're doing. Don't try to get up. If you need anything, call for
an attendant. They'll be glad to meet your needs." With that, Vawella
returned to her regular duties.

~

Jeda sat upright. "Glend?"

Glend's eyes opened again as she turned to see who addressed her.
"Oh, it's you, Jeda."

"You really met him, Logon I mean?"

"Mmm-mmm. I wish I'd have listened to you sooner."

Jeda lay back down and stared at the ceiling of the tent. "And do
you remember your conversation with him?"

"I think so. He said as I sharpen my sword, oh, where is it?" She
patted the bed while casting her eyes about the tent. "Ahh, here it is."
She touched the bedding alongside her leg where two lumps rumpled
the sheets. "He said as I sharpen my sword I'd recall more of our conversation. And that Vawella would help me learn to use the toller and
adjust to Ecclessite ways. Isn't that wonderful?"

"Glend, I'm so glad for you. Do you recall the fight in the bath hut?"

"Fight in the bath hut? I remember being tied and gagged, then a
sweet voice, enchanting, feminine, promising me power. Who could
that have been? Why was I tied?"

"I wasn't in on the decision to tie you, but I doubt I'd have had little
impact on their decision anyway. Carnalian forces surrounded us;
Hod-ya's bodyguards were searching for us. Bonu tells me that Hod-ya
was with them. The kingsmen didn't want you to cry out giving away
our hiding place. That's why they bound and gagged you."

"Oh. No wonder I felt outraged. Now I understand. But when
that voice, that sweet, syrupy voice suggested I summon the forces

of Lurcan with my mind, I desired the power it promised. I have to confess, I wanted to pluck your eyes from their sockets and tear you limb from limb, and—"

"Enough, Glend. Don't dwell on those thoughts. Be glad you're free of that hate."

"I'm so sorry I attacked you. It's kind of hazy, like I was off to one side watching instead of participating."

"It was Psa, Glend. Not the engraved image on the backside of the palace gates, but the spirit lord himself. He took control of you, your face, your hands, your voice. When you came at me, I held up my sword, but I don't remember striking a blow."

"Jeda, what I must tell you doesn't come easy. True, there was an evil being in me that wanted to hurt you, but . . . but I also wanted to kill you. There was a moment, just the briefest lapse, that the entity needed my permission to fully be in control." Glend searched Jeda's eyes for any sign of recrimination. "I whole-heartedly agreed to destroy you. I never hated anyone as much as I hated you in that moment. You stood for everything I loathed, you had to be destroyed. To be sure, the force inhabiting my mind hated you, too, and I was aware that it hatred you, but it hated you no worse than it hated others here. But I did. If Logon hadn't intervened, I'd have killed you."

"Logon intervened?"

"You don't know?"

"How? When?"

"I felt Psa's awesome power surge through me, the power that I'd craved since before coming to the palace staff, remember? I let that power have control, to reign in my body and carry out its evil design. Your eyes were round with fright, yet you bravely thrust your sword as I approached. Your strength was no match for mine, that is, the strength of the thing in me. I was about to crush you, then he appeared. You went limp, but your sword arm stayed rigid, pointed right at me! For an instant my eyes were opened, and I saw Logon, and I saw the hideous monstrosity within my own flesh. Logon's gaze pierced through me as his eyes bored into Psa, challenging it in some mystical language.

"Psa cowered, letting me collect my own wits. Logon's eyes, so full of fury for Psa, held my gaze, filled with love and tenderness as he spoke: 'This is your last chance to avail yourself of my mercy, Glend. Allow me to pierce your heart and drive that fallen bright out of you, else, the next time we meet, I'll be your adversary!' I suddenly dreaded him more than anything. It would indeed be a horrible thing to fall into the hands of him that had died, yet still lives. All I had to do was look in his eyes and he knew my heart before I spoke. He struck me with your sword, your hand still upon the haft, though you were unconscious. I swooned, but a violent scream erupted from my lips as Psa was driven out.

"The next thing I knew I was at the base of a cliff. Logon towered over me, standing atop the cliff in all his majesty, patiently gazing at me, waiting for me to do something."

"Logon's Rock."

"I knew he wanted me to touch the rock, though he said nothing. I instinctively knew that by touching the rock wall I'd be admitting my complicity in his death. But, I couldn't, I was afraid of his wrath if I owned up to all my crimes against him. I was unwilling to relinquish my hopes of dominating others, afraid to not be in control. Silly isn't it, I had absolutely no control anyway, yet wanted to cling to empty hopes and futile schemes rather than his promises. How long I hesitated I can't say. It seemed days."

"It was. In fact, you almost waited too long."

"I know. Just before I finally touched it, I felt myself fading, yet when I touched the rock cliff and opened my eyes, I found myself more alive than ever, standing with him atop his rock. He told me how close I'd come to perishing. To be wounded by his sword, to have the knowledge of his offer of amnesty and not respond ends in a worse fate than never being wounded at all."

Footsteps scurrying down the aisle toward their little nook interrupted them. Vawella's face poked through a curtain. "We're moving. Can you two travel, or will you need to be borne on litters?"

CHAPTER TWENTY-FIVE

SCOUTS REPORTED TO CAPTAIN VARTER saying they'd found a safe, protected site ideal for setting up the camouflage fortress. Captain Varter agreed to move the camp without seeing the new location. The site was enclosed in a real thicket bordered on three sides by a swift-running tributary of the Figolive River. Treacherous white water comprised the border of the new settlement providing a defense that bespoke watery disaster for any enemy attempting to ford the rapids. Additionally, the roar of rushing water would cover any inadvertent campground noises. The trade-off was that they would likewise be hindered hearing enemies approach.

It was with a heavy heart that Varter decided on this move, for they had been safe in their present locus nearly a decade; but the safety of people under his command necessitated the move. Within hours the tents, lean-tos, and dining lodge would be dismantled. A work crew removed the walk-in-trench from the creek, disposing of any telltale signs that a camp had ever been there. Another crew carefully disassembled sections of the lightweight, camouflage wall, toting them to the new location where another crew was at work clearing the ground in preparation for setting up the wall again. By the time the main population arrived a large section of the wall would already be in place.

The brigade was divided into four columns; patrols of thirty stalwart fighters would escort each of these columns to the new site. So, it was that the Ecclessites vacated the hollow where they'd spent many secure years, heading yet deeper into the unknown, ominous jungle, a safer distance from their enemy yet more distant from their mission of rescuing lives for the king.

The four columns would travel different routes through the forest but would converge at the new site thus avoiding tell-tale signs for Carnalian trackers.

The idea haunted Captain Varter that Hod-ya, with her dronnets and Carnalian regulars, were nearer than they'd ever been to their camp. Nor did it escape Varter's notice that Psa now knew their camouflage strategy and would surely communicate it through Hod-ya. He also marveled that he'd lived to see the day the dreads of the gates issued forth as the ancient runes foretold. But . . . just what did the prophecies foretell? There were obscure runes:

. . . end will come 'neath leaf and bough . . .

How could a dread come to an end? Weren't they everlasting creations of Elyon? Even in their rebellion their essence hadn't been taken from them; they'd corrupted themselves into defiled forms, but Elyon hadn't yet entered fully into judgment with them except to bind them to land and sea lest they roam the ether realms spreading their toxic rebellion. Ah, such answers would have to come in due time. For now, his duty was to relocate the camp. As long as their camouflage was down, and their warriors scattered, they were vulnerable. Splitting up was a defensive tactic, though a weak one; if one column got raided, the others would hopefully be spared.

"Logon, please send roamers to protect and guide us to our new home. Confuse and distract our enemy while we escape. And please show me how we are to fight a dread."

"Captain?" Lieutenant Bonu had come up just behind Varter.

"Lieutenant, what are you doing up and about? You should be resting, getting to know that remarkable young lady."

"I'm fit enough for duty, sir. There's much that needs doing, and I don't feel right about being inactive. As for that remarkable young lady, well, I don't think there's much future in pursuing that, sir."

"Hmmm, very well lieutenant, I'm sure I can find some detail for you to look after. You sure you're fit for duty?"

"Yes, sir. If I may, I'd like to scout around a bit?"

"Come now, man; you're still recovering. After all, you did just pass out not an hour gone by. It's good you want to be active, but don't take so much upon yourself."

"I'll be freer to move about on solitary patrol; maybe I can spy out the enemy's camp, or prowl around for the lairs of half-men or Craniantium Lions, or something. I'm quite fit, sir. Besides, I need some time to sort things out. I'll use extreme caution, I promise."

Varter rested his hand on Bonu's shoulder and peered into the younger man's eyes. "You're a good man, Bonu. I'd hate to lose you, even if only for a short while. But, I understand your needs, too. As it happens, except for lending an extra pair of hands to a work detail, there isn't much for you to do right now. Go ahead, but, for Splendora's sake, be careful."

"Besides," the captain blinked away the moisture threatening to dampen his cheek, "I'd like to know what that witch woman is up to, if you feel so led. King's road to you."

"Thank you, sir. I'll leave as soon as I gather supplies. Where's the new campsite?"

"Half a day's march, following three points off south by southwest, where the edge of the forest thickens into jungle. There's a thicket already established, and white water surrounds it on three sides."

"Ah, I know the place. I've often hunted there and thought it would make an excellent campsite. I'll be gone about a week, maybe two, unless I learn something urgent, whereupon I'll return and advise you. King's road to you." He saluted his superior and turned smartly on his heel, not necessary in this protocol-relaxed brigade, but appreciated nonetheless as Varter watched the junior officer depart.

"Captain, Captain," huffed a soldier running up. "Blegash sent me to ask about the food stores we can't carry. Should we destroy them? Or will you send a detail to bring it along later?"

"No, no, don't destroy them. Bury them where the kitchen used to be and mark the spot with Logon's secret sign in case any kingsmen happen by and need sustenance." The messenger saluted and retreated.

Captain Varter was busy the next hour and a half overseeing the dismantling of the camp. "Father?"

Varter looked up from securing a bundle of tent posts. "What is it, Vawella? Can't you see I'm in a bit of a hurry to get things done?" He let out a long sigh as he picked the bundle up and placed it squarely on a lad's shoulders. "There, got it?"

The boy grunted an affirmative and trotted off to join the third column as the tail end disappeared into the forest.

"Have you seen Bonu about?" Vawella asked. "I have someone here who wants a few words with him." Jeda stood slightly behind the captain's daughter, smiling, peering shyly over Vawella's shoulder.

"Eh? Bonu? Oh, Bonu." He looked about before asking "Have you checked—"

"Everywhere. His lodgings, the kitchen, the outposts, the stream, everywhere. He doesn't seem to be in the compound. It's important that Jeda speak to him, for there's been a misunderstanding."

"He must've left already. Asked permission to spy about. Said he'd be gone about two weeks. But I doubt there's any misunderstanding. He's quite aware of how he's bothered you Miss and wants to be alone to work things out in his heart."

Jeda started to protest. "But I—"

"Oh, don't you fret. He'll be all right; he's a good man, that one. Pity you two couldn't see eye to eye, you'd have made a lovely couple. You both seem to be called into similar service."

"Excuse me, Father, Jeda realizes she's made a mistake. She does have strong feelings for him after all. How long ago did he leave? Do you think we can catch up to him, or at least send a messenger after him?"

"I'm sorry girls, I have no idea how long ago he left, or even which direction. I really can't spare any workers just now. Truth is, I didn't want him to go, but I could see he was in such anguish that he needed time alone. I reluctantly gave permission. You'll just have to trust him to Logon."

Another brigade member intruded, drawing the captain's attention.

~

"Well, Jeda, it shouldn't be hard to spend time speaking to Logon about him. At least you can do that," Vawella consoled as they departed from Varter.

"Perhaps that's the most I can do. If I trust him to Logon, he'll be in better care than if I were with him myself." Turning her face skyward she said, "Logon, please watch over Bonu and don't let him despair. Don't let him take any unnecessary risks, I ask you."

"Now, little sister," Vawella stepped up her pace, "let's see how Glend fares. No doubt she'll need to lean on one or the other of us once the last column gets underway. What a joy that she's become one of us, and especially since we don't have to keep her under guard anymore."

"I've been wondering," Jeda mused, "Logon warned that I was going into great danger, yet here I am safe in a brigade. Oh, Vawella, why is it so confusing? When I first followed Logon, everything seemed clear and simple—just obey. Now, things are complicated."

"There are many reasons, Jeda. Our hearts desire normal things of life. Then, too, Logon stretches our ability to hear him and learn to obey by letting us face challenges. That's how we become stronger. We start following him as children in our understanding, but he's not content to let us remain in that phase. He wants us to mature into useful servants and warriors. That kind of growth only happens when our patience, trust, and endurance are tested."

"He said the Advisor would give me a gift to help."

"Then he will, only it might not be what you expect, and it'll require commitment to obey his runes over the desires of your heart."

"I still don't understand. It seems so time-consuming. Couldn't he just make me become what he wants all at once?"

"It takes time for the deeper, hidden desires of our hearts to surface. That's one of the reasons he gives us the Advisor, to reveal our false feelings for what they are, a real and present danger to our getting close to him. Our minds try to rationalize these desires as harmless. I've learned that my own heart will deceive me into un-Logon-like wants even while pretending to seek him. Ah, look, there's Glend. Is she tolling? She is, she's tolling her sword!" Jeda and Vawella hurried over and settled beside Glend on a log, giving her pointers on tolling for maximum effect.

~

A league away Bonu knelt to examine a depression on the ground; he'd found the spoor of a Carnalian patrol. Upon investigating the Carnalian campground he found a hastily-scrawled note nailed to a tree:

BEWARE

BRIGHTS IN VICINITY

ENEMY FORCES AT WORK

RETURN TO FORMER CAMPSITE

Captain Mileer

Bonu destroyed the note then loaded a dart into his crossbow. He wouldn't cock it until necessary. He pressed his fingers into the footprint of a very large soldier, emitting a low whistle. The man was huge, possibly seven feet tall. The patrol wasn't being too careful about leaving footprints. Bonu pored over the marks around the base of a tree, gleaning information on the squad. As near as he could tell, there were only five Carnalians, including the giant. He'd be the most formidable if it came to hand to hand combat, but, Bonu was only fact-gathering.

They were the first and only patrol to arrive at the Carnalian camp-site so far as Bonu could discern. Without Mileer's posted notice, other returning patrols would have no clue as to what to do. If he erased the patrol's trail, the other stranded patrols would be bewildered and perhaps stumble into one of Varter's companies and be confronted with Logon's offer of amnesty. Bonu expertly removed all trace of the Carnalian patrol's trail within a hundred paces then set off after the lost patrol.

For the next two hours he went through dense undergrowth, at times forced to crawl so as not to miss even the slightest sign. The Carnalian patrol was tiring, especially the big fellow; his footprints were closer together, and deeper, manifesting trudging rather than walking. With his bulk, he'd have the rougher time pushing through this undergrowth. But the others were being careless as well, bending reeds, snapping twigs—indicative of exhaustion. They'd soon stop for the night.

Bonu estimated that he was half-an-hour behind his quarry, maybe nearer if they stopped before the light failed altogether. He didn't want to accidentally overtake them in the dark.

On the other hand, if he lay up somewhere for the night, all alone with his dashed hopes . . . he wasn't yet ready to deal with the pain of Jeda's rejection. He must press on, focus on tracking, on pursuit, on anything but Jeda. An image of her face floated in his mind's eye; her countenance so clear and sparkling, her lips pursed in a half-smile, her silky blonde hair caught in a breeze and blown gently across her cheek.

He stifled a moan, he never thought his heart could ache so. Jeda was the only one. There could never be another. "Ahh, Logon, have you no cure for this agony?"

Bonu bent to the ground, forcing himself to find the next telltale mark: a scuff on a tree trunk, a stone turned dirty side up, a missing flower petal. Wait, what was this? Blood? He touched the droplet with his forefinger. The outer covering was congealed, but the inside was still fluid. Whatever was bleeding had been here recently. He lifted the drop of blood to his nostril and sniffed. There was no discernible odor, so it wasn't animal blood. He knew and could easily identify each forest animal's scent, but being human, the smell of man eluded him. He concluded that one of the Carnalians must be bleeding.

In the failing light the trail became increasingly difficult to follow, but he knew the general direction they were headed. Their probable objective was the waterfall by the cliff. If so, they were going a round-about way. By going straight over the ridge, he could be at the waterfall in twenty minutes; and if his guess was wrong, or they hadn't arrived yet, he could scale the cliff and hide in the niche of the rock ledge that overlooked the hillside and glen down below. Bonu quickened his pace, guided by infrequent flashes from his sword as he covered the uneven ground. The only sound he made was the labored breathing of his rapid pace as he leapt over fallen logs, circumvented brambles, side-stepped saplings, waded across bogs and swampy sloughs to arrive at a creek bank landmark. A cheery, musical ripple from the lapping waters along the bank greeted his ears. Though this was his favorite hunting ground he found little to be cheery about tonight. His pace slowed as he tested the air, then, satisfied it was safe, pressed on up-stream, toward the falls.

The falls weren't a great cataract, but merely the drop-off of a stream that meandered through the plateau, delightfully splashing fifty feet to the forest floor below. A pool had formed at the bottom of the cliff where large, edible fish and crawdads lived. Best of all, sunlight bathed the pool during the day, one of the few spots in Ra-Amawl where foliage didn't block out the light. As a result, various kinds of flowers crowded around the pool, providing a colorful break from shades of green, brown, and gray that dominated all else within Ra-Amawl.

Bonu slowed to a stealthy pace and concealed his Child of the Stars. Unobstructed moonlight filtered through the thinned canopy illuminating his path. He paused several times to listen. Any patrol camped nearby would make enough noise for him to detect. They'd have no reason to suspect they were being spied upon; furthermore, the legends about Ra-Amawl should make them nervous enough to need each other's chatter as a calming influence.

Upon reaching the base of the waterfall Bonu concluded no enemy was near. Perhaps they hadn't come this way after all. Or, perhaps they'd gotten bogged down and made camp where convenient. At any rate, he'd pick up their trail first thing in the morning.

He scaled part of the way up the cliff feeling the cool, moist splatter of the nearby cascade on his face, then paused to once more scan the dark scene below. All was quiet except for the persistent plashing of the waterfall. He climbed another twenty feet and checked below again. Still nothing, except something beside the pool was illumined in the moonlight; there seemed to be some large object, like a huge tree trunk or massive rock at the far end of the pool standing like a silent sentinel, one that he didn't recall being there prior. But scudding clouds covered the face of the moon making the hillside and pool splotchy with shadow; it was difficult to be sure. His imagination might be playing tricks on him. He knew the glade well; normally there was no such object there. Why, the thing must be near thirty feet high and seven or more feet wide! That was absurd, for nothing but a Craniantium Lion came close to those dimensions, and it would have to be standing on its hind legs.

He shrugged off his misgivings and ascended the rest of the way to his small cave, a place he'd sheltered in during many a storm while hunting in the vicinity. He'd discovered it by accident when hunting peccary. He'd tracked the wild pig to this pool, shot it with his crossbow and was in the middle of field dressing it when a brown bear poked its hungry head out of a bush and charged. Bonu cleared several feet up the cliff in one bound, and since his weapons, sword included, had been laid on the mossy turf as he dressed the varmint, he could do nothing else but climb. That's how he stumbled into a crevice that widened to a small, albeit comfy cave. From this lofty perch he was granted a commanding view of the lay of the land beneath the plateau, from which he watched the bear devour his game.

Bonu smiled at the memory. Logon had sent that brown bear, though at the time, he wasn't too pleased at having lost the food meant for the brigade. He'd never explored the back parts of the cave, choosing to stay in this cozy, main room, which tapered to a narrow funnel at the back.

Bonu crawled in, flashing his sword about to make sure the cave was empty. As high as it was in the cliff, it was unlikely anything, but birds or bats would use it, and indeed, there was evidence that a bird of prey had been there. He grabbed tinder and a few sticks of the firewood he'd previously stacked and built a fire. In times past, he'd lit fires at night and went outside, both up on the plateau and down to the hillside by the waterfall just to see if his fire was visible. It wasn't, even though he knew where to look, for the entry crevice was small and faced straight up. The smoke from his campfire drafted out through a cranny in the back of the cave and wouldn't betray his presence should he desire a fire, and tonight, he so desired.

The pleasant crackling and popping of the fruity-wood fire filled the chamber with a sweet aroma; its flickering light comforted his loneliness. He stretched out on his bedroll, satisfied with the day's accomplishments, able to not think about . . . One thing yet remained—Logon. He took out his toller, sat cross-legged, and began to toll as he communed with his liege. This was a meeting he seldom defaulted on, for Logon was his chief joy and love.

After meditating in the runes, he lay his sword by his side, tucked his toller away, and positioned himself to stare into the flickering flame playing hide-and-seek beneath and around the larger chunks of wood. He was only somewhat unburdened by the time spent with Logon, and so, fell asleep still aching for Jeda.

An hour later his sleep was disrupted by angry shouts. He groggily shook his head and noted the fire was down to coals. He cautiously hoisted himself up out of the cave and peered down over the cliff at the wooded field gradually stretching away uphill.

There was a raging campfire half-way down the hillside, surrounded by eight men. Four stood with their backs to the fire, bows and crossbows pointed defensively out at the night.

"Put on a larger piece, Scung. Make it light up the dark," commanded one. Bonu noted a huge man, nearly seven feet tall, dropping a small tree trunk on the fire. "Right, that oughtta keep the beasties at bay. Look sharp lads, them noises couldda been anything."

A tall, lean figure squatted by the fire, warming his hands; a low hiss emitted from his throat. A chill tingled Bonu's spine as he recognized the thin, black-garbed man was a dronnet. In fact, there were two dronnets. Undoubtedly this was the patrol he'd trailed, but he hadn't taken into account a dronnet's ability to leave sparse tracks. That oversight would have proven fatal had he stumbled into the patrol. Another man was laid out by the fire and seemed to be wounded, offering no voice, not helping guard, not tending the fire. He probably accounted for the drops of blood Bonu had found.

"Says you," shouted the Carnalian squad leader sassily. "Let a dronnet tag along and he thinks he knows everything. Well, following you got us lost, didn't it?"

Another hiss greeted the man's retort but the dronnet stayed on his haunches, hands extended toward the fire.

"Maybe he's right, Dornt," suggested another of the men. "They can see in the dark like we see in the day, you know. I say he's probably right, that that noise was only a varmint scurrying to his den. No use keeping us up all night for the sake of a varmint, is there?"

A rumble of agreement emitted from the others.

Recognizing a potential mutiny, the squad leader judiciously backed off.

Bonu watched long enough to know that the motion to relax their guard carried; the corporal was overruled. The party would sleep with only two pickets. Bonu dropped back into his cave, glad he was sheltered and warm, with little likelihood of intruders. Down there anything might suddenly surprise them. But then, they had dronnets, so they weren't too badly off.

A flutter of wings brushed past him and an ornery "Hoo-oot, hoot," brought him instantly awake again. The great white owl didn't care for this invasion of his lodge and made his feelings known—from a safe distance. A dead rabbit lay at the owl's feet, as yet untorn. The owl flapped his wings and blustered to scare the trespasser out of his residence; he was somewhat unnerved that his bluffs weren't working. He hooted again, opened his beak wide and flapped his wings causing a stir of dust, fur and feathers to rise off the cave floor.

Bonu brandished his sword.

The owl spluttered some more and backed awkwardly under the opening.

Bonu rose to his knees and made a feint at the bird.

The owl decided he was overmatched. With a "Hoo-oot!" it spread its wings and flew into the graying sky.

Bonu picked up the rabbit and felt its body heat. "Thank you, Logon, for a fresh breakfast. Oh, yes, and you, too, friend owl." He stirred the coals of his fire, skinned, gutted, and spitted the rabbit on a long stick, then leaned comfortably against the wall and waited while breakfast cooked.

The Tantalizing aroma of meat whet his appetite, but he forced himself to wait until the meat was fully cooked before snatching the spit from over the hot coals and tearing a hind leg from the carcass. After gnawing the meat off the last leg bone, he resumed surveillance on the Carnalian patrol; all were sleeping, even the pickets.

Due to the diminished treetop canopy around the pool, day dawned brighter than elsewhere in Ra-Amawl. As daylight increased the nighttime's obscure forms became recognizable as various trees, hedgerows, rock formations, lone boulders, clumps of grass all resolved into familiar shaped objects except for that odd, oversized thing on the edge of the pool he'd noted last night. It wasn't any more discernible in the misty dawn as it stood at the far end of the pool, well away from the slumbering Carnalians, motionless, as it had been last night. Somehow a sense of menace emanated from it. Of course, it was probably just a tangle of trees tossed there by some storm, all leaning in upon one main support, yet, there was this persistent, malevolent feeling.

Bah! His imagination was getting the better of him. He hadn't expected dronnets, and that, combined with his recent brush with Psa's black cloud made him prone to the jitters.

"Waugh!" The huge man by the Carnalians' fire-ring cried out suddenly and sat up. His massive fist slugged the sleeping form beside him.

The man cried out and doubled up under his blanket. Everyone else in the camp jumped out of their bedrolls, weapons in hand ready for a fight.

"What is it? What's going on?" demanded the corporal.

One of the dronnets hissed. The corporal heard and must have understood, for he replied, "Oh, bad dream again, eh, Scung?"

The giant rubbed his face. "Yeah, I guesses so. Whut be's fer breakfast?"

The man under the blanket groaned then threw back his cover and came out of his bedroll with knife in hand. "By Pitland I'll skewer you this time!"

The shaggy giant merely stuck his foot out and the attacker sprawled headlong. "Later, Blepit, later. Usn's play later, okay. Right now, I wants food. Whut be's left o' supplies?"

"Nothing's left," replied one of the men. "We ate the last bit up last night. We'll have to forage."

A moan from all greeted this report, but they resolutely set about packing their gear.

Then suddenly the two dronnets jerked straight as ramrods and stared at the lower end of the pool.

The others ceased their labors to see what had alarmed the dronnets. Bonu, too, up in his cave, shifted his gaze from the awakening camp to the object he himself had been trying to identify.

A small gleam of sunlight filtered through a break in the leaves and splayed upon the object. Bonu saw it for what it was. Still as stone, silent as death, watching the pool and those beside it stood the inert form of a dread! Bonu's blood ran cold. It had been there all night, just several dozen yards from his hideaway!

CHAPTER TWENTY-SIX

A PERKY, TEEN-AGED GIRL RELIEVED Jeda of her bundle; tramping through the jungle was taking a toll, especially since Jeda was still somewhat under the effects of encountering Psa. "Thank you, Spoena, I thought I'd be able to handle my own things, but I guess not."

"Was it really Psa?" asked the bright-eyed girl walking beside her new friend. She was about sixteen, long-legged with strong, squared shoulders from wilderness life, the eldest of six sisters. Her dark-brown hair was neatly tied in a bun that sported a polished stick keeping it in place; her face was youthfully round with freckles and a turned-up nose.

"Oh, I'm certain." Jeda smiled as the girl's eyes widened. "Don't worry. If Captain Varter thought there was any imminent danger, he'd move us out of Ra-Amawl altogether. If he has confidence in the new location, it must be secure."

"Oh, Jeda, I hope so." Spoena shouldered Jeda's things with ease, and Glend's as well. Despite a strong physique from doing woodland chores, Spoena maintained an obvious, blooming femininity as well as a gentle spirit. "Sometimes at night, when I think about living in hiding, I tremble, what with cusps, irks, and occasional tophet creatures sniffing about—not to mention lions, Carnalian soldiers, half-men, and now a dread."

Jeda paused to catch her breath. "You must trust Logon. He'll not allow anything to harm us unless it's his will and for our best."

"We mustn't stop." Spoena stepped around Jeda. "This part of the forest isn't safe; there are predators. And we mustn't talk too loud either. But I know what you're saying. I guess I haven't learned to trust Logon enough. I haven't spent the time getting to know him."

Jeda resumed the pace. "When we settle in the new camp come over to my tent and we'll toll our swords together, okay?"

"I'd like that. Ever since mama died it's been hard for papa to keep us girls in line, forage, provide our needs, and teach us sword runes, too. We just kind of let that go since other needs are more pressing. Sharpened swords don't seem as necessary when you're cold or hungry."

Jeda hiked her skirt up to step over a log. "Until you get attacked."

"Yes, until you get attacked. As soon as I'm done helping papa, I'll be over. You're staying in Vawella's tent, right?"

"Uh-huh. Maybe Glend will join us, too."

"It's amazing how she was so set against Logon, and about to die, and then suddenly she's one of us. The whole brigade is abuzz about it."

Glend had been borne ahead on a litter supported by four lads. For the first hour Glend gamely struggled on foot, leaning on Vawella or one of the other girls. But, with dodging limbs and vines and climbing over obstacles, her strength was quickly sapped; she had no choice but to let others assist her.

In times past Jeda and Artka had often talked about an idyllic lifestyle where the weak were protected and cared for by the strong, not preyed upon. Low and behold, it was the culture of Ecclessa they'd been longing for but didn't know it!

Artka. Where was he now? Had he been in any battles? Was there a chance he'd met Logon? Oh, if only he'd give some Ecclessite a chance to explain the way of the king.

The fourth column, in which Jeda traveled, was two hours into their journey, making good time, though not as efficiently as other columns. Captain Varter led this segment taking the shortest route. The three swifter columns had departed earlier taking roundabout ways to throw off any empire trackers and so, the slower column of the infirmary, younger children, and the elderly would be less impeded with diversionary tactics.

Thick undergrowth swished as Jeda pushed her way through the tangle of leaves and branches. Brigaders following her kept a respectful distance, avoiding the backlash.

Spoena outpaced Jeda even though she bore the burdens of three. It wasn't so much that Spoena was fast, but rather that Jeda lagged. Two more women soundlessly by-passed Jeda.

Jeda lifted her eyes just in time to see the back-swinging branch that slapped her face. Her cheek smarted; putting her hand to it she found a trickle of blood.

A strong arm encircled her waist. She turned and looked up into Vawella's face. "I'm the last one, Jeda, beside the rearmost guards. Lean on me. Maybe we should've gotten a litter for you, too, eh?"

"I'm sorry to be such a burden. I really thought I'd be able to handle the trek. Are there any rests soon?"

"Hmmm, maybe one, but that's at least another hour off, perhaps two. Can you keep going?"

"I . . . I think so."

"Well if you can't, I'll commandeer a couple of guards to carry you. Let me know if leaning on me isn't enough."

"I will. I'll keep at it. I don't want to slow the column down."

~

The great cat slumbering under an outcropping rock opened an eye and twitched his nose at the tantalizing scent of blood drifting on the breeze. The spoor was human. His ears pricked forward, detecting slight rustling sounds half a mile away. Ordinarily his nap wouldn't have been disturbed by such slight noises but coupled with the redolence of blood meant wounded prey was near. Fanga's stomach growled; he hadn't eaten for several days except a few paltry mice and a groundhog. He extended his forepaws and raised his haunches in a stretch. A sharp pain in his rear leg interrupted his pre-hunt ritual. He bent around to lick the wound where an arrow shaft still protruded. Infection had set in; the festering leg wouldn't bear much strain, hence his poor hunting.

Due to pain and hunger he was also in a bad temper. Manlings! They'd ruined him. He recalled the attack he and five other lions made on the human patrol and how they'd beaten his pride back. His mate had "stopped running" as a result. He, himself, was badly injured and unable to keep up with the pride. Now he was famished, abandoned, incapable of supplying his own needs. His ribs were visible through his once sleek, black hide, and he winded easily. He was unable to give chase due to the excruciating pain in his wounded leg. He licked the oozing pus and congealed blood by his wound. It wasn't healing.

He had no desire for vengeance. Unless desperate for food, cornered or hunted down, the great Craniantium lions avoided contact with humans as much as possible. He instinctively knew humans were to be feared, though, in a pinch, could be a source for food. But Fanga was half-starved and would attack anything that couldn't swiftly flee. He limped down the slope on three legs following the blood odor. As he slunk through the undergrowth, he analyzed the lingering scent of many humans. A large party of humans had recently passed, many very young and vulnerable, as well as older infirm beings amidst the strong. His saliva glands were primed with drool, driving the cat onward despite the throbbing pain. His sore leg began bleeding afresh, but he must ignore it.

He stopped to sniff a branch with a drop of blood, and then licked it. With head lowered, he began his stalk, hobbling, gradually increasing weight on his injured limb. His discriminating nose kept him intent upon the essence of the wounded human, forcing pain to the hinder part of his mind. He would not be denied this kill.

The black shadow slipped through the trees, drawing ever closer to the column's rear echelon. Fanga heard humans, their voices a murmur, their footsteps clumsily treading and scuffing. Even through the flora his skilled eyes detected movement some fifty strides ahead. A breeze blew toward his quarry; other prey would take note and flee but humans were stupid, careless, never testing the air as other creatures knew to do. He scrunched low to the ground; a stinging pang reminded him of his wound, but he was too focused on a tantalizingly easy kill.

Twenty yards, ten; Fanga discerned four men and two women following the tail of the column. The two women leaned against each other, and one of them was the one that had left blood on the branch. The lion licked his lips; his incisors eager to penetrate flesh and crunch bone . . . He fixed his eyes on the weaker of the two women and prepared to engulf her head and torso in one bite, crushing the shoulders, arms and ribcage, suffocating the life out in mere seconds.

His claws dug into the leafy turf as he began his approach. He burst between the rearmost of the men, stunning and knocking them aside. With an ear-splitting, throaty roar he sprang. One of the guards feebly swung a sword even as he was brushed aside, but the lion's reflexes were too quick. The prey was his. In seconds her blood would fill his mouth with a warm, coppery taste . . .

The prey didn't even dodge but stood gawking over her shoulder, mouth agape, paralyzed in fear.

Suddenly something seized his injured leg bringing excruciating pain, halting his deadly pounce in midair. He turned to swipe at the hindrance. His claws, extended to the full raked through something tangible but invisible. The huge cat crashed to the turf in pain and confusion.

Slowly appearing over him was a human-shaped warrior as tall as a Craniantium lion is long. This defender sparkled with shimmering colors and flashes of light. It was a roamer that clenched the cat's leg in his hand.

One of the kingsmen guards overcoming his initial shock, charged and swung a sword at the lion, seemingly unaware of the roamer's presence and assistance. The man gritted his teeth and plunged his weapon into the feline's injured leg.

The lion convulsed and roared in outrage.

The man stabbed again, this time striking the lower abdomen.

Other guards turned and upon seeing the great cat joined the attack.

The sparkling roamer still wouldn't release his grip, allowing the men to attack at will.

The warrior spoke to the lion, "It's not her time; you are forfeit."

~

A sword bore swiftly down on the cat's skull, splitting it open. Vawella withdrew her blade. "Thanks be to Logon!"

Jeda was on hands and knees retching, staring at the brained, twitching beast a mere arm's length away. She could still feel the hot, sticky, befouled, suffocating breath. It had come that close. Only Logon knew why it was abruptly suspended in mid-spring, but she was grateful. The beast's mouth was cavernous. It could've swallowed her whole. Had it not been stopped she'd be the one losing her life! Jeda's palms were clammy and she suddenly felt light-headed; the landscape tilted, all went dark.

The first thing she saw upon opening her eyes was Captain Varter staring down at her, along with a host of soldiers flanking him. Vawella knelt beside her, anxiously patting Jeda's hand.

"Are you all right, Jeda?" the captain asked.

For a brief instant he reminded her of the father she'd wished for all her life.

"Your color's coming back, but you'd better lie still."

Bushes parted, and a scout appeared, standing beside Jeda. "He was alone, sir. His wounded leg must have caused the rest of the pride to abandon him. Looks like one of the beasties that attacked lieutenant Bonu's patrol. If so, he's been suffering with that gangrenous wound for a long time. Putting him out of his misery was a mercy. Well done, Vawella."

"I really can't take credit. It was the roamer. If he hadn't told me to strike, I'd probably still be gawking. I was as frozen as Jeda. Trembu should really get the credit. It was his sword-stroke that slowed the cat."

Trembu protested, "I can take no credit either, sir. Whether or not there was a roamer, I can't say. But something suspended that great cat in mid-air for two or three seconds while I collected my wits enough to strike. Vawella finished him off by splitting his head open. I say the credit and the robe goes to her."

"Well, Daughter, looks like you qualify for the company of dronnets," teased Captain Varter. "You killed a Craniantium lion in hand to paw combat, a rare feat."

"Don't even joke about that, Father. I tell you, there was a roamer, a bright, sparkling thing, standing by the lion's rear leg, saying, 'Strike the beast's head with the sure word of your prince.' I couldn't have disobeyed if I'd wanted to, well, practically."

"He was a beautiful thing, wasn't he? Powerful, sleek, black as char, fierce, strong rippling muscles. Too bad we had to kill it."

Jeda also studied the great carnivore, his eight-inch canines gleaming brightly even in the shaded verdure of Ra-Amawl. As Vawella said, he was magnificent once upon a time. But she was glad he was dead!

Captain Varter ordered, "Trembu, you and Garshick prepare a branch-litter and carry Jeda. The rest of you return to your positions and tell everybody there's nothing to fear; the lion was alone and now he's dead. Lieutenant Huy, I'll stay with the rear guard and my daughter, the dronnet," he teased. "I'd like you to take the point."

Vawella bristled, but Huy said, "Might as well accept it, Vaw, it was a remarkable feat that will encourage the whole camp. You'll be a celebrity, at least for a while. Sir, if anything of note occurs, I'll send word immediately." He saluted, winked at Vawella, and disappeared into the undergrowth with such agility that barely a leaf stirred.

"Huy is right, you know," Varter said. "You'll have to endure some good-natured teasing for a while, I suspect, and not a little admiration. Think you can handle the fame?"

"But I did nothing. The roamer held the beast, so it couldn't fight back. All I did was strike the final blow."

"You're the lion-slayer, Vawella. Give the glory to Logon, as you should, but acknowledge his use of you to accomplish his purpose. Be honest; true humility can acknowledge being used without taking credit. At least you don't have that false humility so many feign, trying to gain recognition while appearing to give Logon the glory."

"I wouldn't do that, Father."

"I know. I just wanted to remind you. As for the robe trophy, I'm afraid we don't have time to skin the beast. I'm sorry, it would have made an ideal cover for your tent floor. Hopefully, scavengers will consume the carcass before enemy trackers come across it. We don't need any telltale signs exposing our path."

Father and daughter together backtracked a short distance covering traces of the trail, although nearly seventy people had passed by. Except for the lion's carcass, the forest appeared undisturbed.

Alert to the journey's dangers the mood in the column was more cautious: guards swung out wider, scouts probed a little farther ahead, unwilling to let potential harm near the column again. In the vanguard people were quieter, more watchful.

The rocking motion of the improvised litter hoisted between the guards caused Jeda to nod off. When she awoke the column was just arriving at the new campsite. Most of the camo-wall was already up as well as many living-quarters tents. A kitchen/dining hall/lodge was under construction and a submerged, invisible walkway across the rapids had already been established and was being learned by latecomers. This, the fourth column, was the last to arrive, as expected. None of the other columns had encountered any difficulty, the camp's mood was optimistic, though wary when informed of the lion attack.

Jeda sat beside Glend and related the lion attack in detail as people all around staked-out tent sites. The two young women were under orders to not do anything strenuous, and so were confined to watching. Glend had fared the journey well enough. She was glad to sit quietly and toll her sword and listen to Jeda's tale.

Captain Varter strode about offering helpful hints or issuing commands where needed, overseeing the establishment of their new location. By the time darkness enveloped the campsite setting up was complete except for the kitchen and dining hall. Those would take a few days to construct. One of the other columns had toted the heavy iron stove and huge kettles, along with other irreplaceable items. Jeda was amazed at what people could do when they had to.

Vawella approached the girls. "Want to see your new home?"

"It's ready?" Glend asked.

"All it needs is residents."

"Well then, let's go," agreed Jeda.

Vawella led to a small tent beside a larger one. "This is where I'll be, with the girls I'm training," she said, indicating the larger of the two tents. "And this," she pointed to the smaller tent, "is where you two, along with Leezle and Spoena will sleep. You're older and don't need supervision as do my other girls, so, I thought you'd enjoy a little more privacy than you'd get in my twenty-person tent."

"Spoena? I thought she was staying with her father to help look after her sisters?"

Vawella smiled. "Apparently, somewhere along the trail, her dad asked Kyleah to marry him, and she accepted! Isn't that great?"

"What, just like that?" Glend asked.

"Well, it seems there's been something going on there for some time, though none of us knew."

"How is Spoena taking the news?" Jeda asked.

"Seems to be fine with the idea, but just the same, I invited her to join you unmarried women if she felt uncomfortable in her father's abode. She readily accepted."

"And Leezle? She's well enough to be out of the hospital tents?"

"Not really, but the hospital isn't functional yet, and the care she needs can be met by the three of you. She doesn't require medical expertise, just assistance, like getting dressed. Things like that."

Jeda answered, "Well, if you think we're up to it."

"I do. In fact, it's exactly what you need, someone to serve, and therein your devotion to Logon will grow. It's settled then. Ah, here comes Spoena. I guess it's time for me to tend to my other charges. Goodnight, ladies."

"Jeda, Glend, I hope you don't mind." Spoena shyly stood in the doorway. "Vawella asked me to join you."

"Mind? Of course not, come in, come in," invited Glend, acting like a barracks monitor. Jeda noted how friendly and at home Glend had become. "Uh, I guess you can choose any cot, you don't mind do you, Jeda?"

Jeda shook her head wearily and said, "As long as I get to sleep somewhere, and soon. I'm exhausted."

Each girl chose a cot and rummaged through the stack of blankets and skins Vawella had deposited with them, outfitting their cots and situating their meager belongings underneath. The four cots occupied most of the space, allowing only a narrow aisle down the tent's center. Each girl gladly settled in earlier than usual, but then, the whole camp was settling down for the night.

Half an hour later Vawella softly called from outside, "Jeda, are you awake?"

"Almost," Jeda stifled a yawn. "Why? What's happening?"

Vawella poked her head inside the flap. "I've just been alerted that the entire area is infested with irks. Check yourselves and each other thoroughly before you turn-in, and your beds, and your belongings, and your—"

"We get it," said Glend, swinging her legs over the edge of her cot. "Get up girls, let's check each other; and everything else."

"I hate irks," grumbled Spoena.

"Me, too. Make sure you fall asleep thinking of Logon," advised Vawella. "He'll protect you through the night."

Two irks were discovered, both in Spoena's bundle. They were summarily smashed with their sword pommels. The rest of the tent seemed clear, so they put everything back and took to their cots again.

Jeda fell asleep listening to Spoena and Glend trade life stories, the latter's being the more exciting.

When Jeda woke in the morning, her first thoughts to Logon were of Bonu.

~

Bonu was too engrossed in the scene below to think about Jeda. The dronnets had prostrated themselves upon discovering the dread's image at the edge of the pool. When the other soldiers caught sight of the dread, they wailed and fell to their knees, folding their hands in supplication, one of them chanting:

"Oh mighty Psa, bane of kings and princes,
Swift death to all enemies of the empire,
Servant of the great Lurcan, spare us!
We did not know we trespassed your sacred pool! Have mercy!"

Scung, the large man, remained on his knees as the others fell groveling to their faces. Even the dronnets exhibited reverence. Upon first spotting him they fell headlong to the ground, arms extended, afraid to look up and behold their mistress' master, for they recognized the great dread, Psa.

Bonu was puzzled. No doubt remained in his mind about it being a dread, and probably Psa—the disembodied spirit he'd already encountered. The figure wasn't absolutely still, for it slowly inhaled and exhaled about once every two minutes. Last night it couldn't have missed him climbing to his hidden rock chamber. It didn't attack. Why?

As daylight strengthened Bonu made out more detail. The creature looked hideous, with a longish snout that sprouted a horn, no, two horns, though the second was dwarfed by the first, and nearly hidden behind it. Psa's eyes weren't fiery red as he'd heard, but rather a dull gray, moving slowly, as if between looking at the groveling men and then turning toward Bonu's hideout. Other than that, it remained still as stone. It stood beneath an alder tree thick with leaf and bough. His armor-plated shoulders were ten feet across, from which sprouted stubby arms, muscled and taut. Its hands clutched weapons: in his left was a cross-bow fashioned from an ash's trunk. Fitted in the slot was a straight, narrow dart crafted from a sapling and tipped with a sharp flint-stone; his right hand cuddled the handle of a massive scythe, the blade of which rested on the ground beside his feet. From his head a mane of black, shiny hair flowed to his waist. His brow was thick, but that might have been due to the helmet bunched down over his forehead. His legs were like oak trunks up as far as the shirt of mail that covered halfway to his knees. All in all, he was a fearsome sight.

But, why was he so inanimate? That he was aware of Bonu's location was certain, for his eyes traveled to Bonu's lair at regular intervals, then back to the Carnalian camp. A shiver ran down Bonu's spine as he realized that, though paralyzed, the dread was signaling his presence with his eyes to the obsequious Carnalians.

"'Ere now, summat be's wrong," said the large Eroton, refusing to humble himself any longer. "He ain't actin' right."

"Fool, get down on your face before you get us all killed. He doesn't care how many Ecclessites you've dispatched," growled the corporal, "he's a dread, and not easily impressed."

But the Eroton rose to his feet. "Nah, he'd o' done summat to us'ns long afore now if'n he was gonna." He walked slowly toward the towering abomination.

"Scung, it'll kill you!" warned another, raising his mud-smudged face.

The Eroton paid no heed, but ambled along the pool's marshy edge, his feet making sucking noises with each step. The others rose to their knees, watching, enthralled by Scung's audacity.

The gray eyes now fixed upon the Eroton. Though daunted, Scung took another step. Scung called over his shoulder, "It's eyes be's movin' back'n'forth ter the cliff." Scung turned and looked briefly at the rock cliff but evidently saw nothing of note and shrugged at his comrades.

He took another cautious step, then another, and finally was within arm's length.

The squad's corporal leapt to his feet, cupped his hands and shouted, "Don't touch it. It'll suck your soul out of you!"

Due to the morning stillness Bonu clearly heard the conversations echoing up to him.

Scung heeded the advice and backed away.

It breathed, very slowly. And its eyes kept shifting between Scung and the cliff. Scung backed away, then circled the nightmarish monster, scrutinizing it carefully. He scuffed his boots in some dried leaves near its feet and avoided trampling a fairy-ring that had sprung up in the creature's shadow.

He came around to the fore again and called out, "I dunno, but they's summat powerful amiss. C'mon an' take a look."

The Carnalians slowly rose to their feet seeing that their champion had suffered no harm. The dronnets, too, seemed amazed that Scung dared act so brazenly, but then, it was widely agreed that Erotons lacked some basic intelligence factors. The dronnets and Carnalian regulars walked around the pool to the far side where Scung and Psa waited, leaving unattended the inert form of the wounded man by the fire-ring.

Perhaps Psa was in a dormant state and would awaken at any moment in an outrage and stomp them all into oblivion. Or, perhaps he was in some kind of distress, if dreads experienced such things.

Such were Bonu's thoughts as he watched from his hideout. He could no longer hear what they were saying since they went around the pool and were out of range. If they awoke Psa, he'd assault Bonu's hideout and eat him alive! As that possibility grew more probable, Bonu felt his chances of escape fading. It would take some doing, but he must scale the remainder of the cliff without being seen and high-tail it over the plateau. He'd scaled it before, though now it would be almost impossible to do unseen.

Bonu hoisted his knapsack to a shoulder and crawled up and out the entry. He crouched behind a meager shrub that had its roots lodged securely in a fissure, checking to see that the patrol remained preoccupied with their dark champion and not the waterfall cliff. Satisfied, he stood, grasped an outcropping ledge and hoisted himself up. He gained a higher ridge and was about to grasp the next outcropping rock when crashing noises filled the hillside.

Bonu froze and peered over his shoulder.

Across the sparsely wooded tract a dozen dronnets marched at the fore of a company of Carnalians, stomping downhill toward the pool, carrying on a litter the prone form of a woman dressed in black. The woman babbled incessantly, incoherently, shouting in a gravelly voice that fluctuated from bass to soprano: "Get me back in my body. Haste, before its too late. There's danger! He sees. The prophecy, the prophecy!"

CHAPTER TWENTY-SEVEN

BONU FROZE; STAYING STOCK STILL was his safest ploy. The Carnalians were preoccupied afresh with Hod-ya's approach way up-hill; Bonu didn't dare scale the cliff now. Even if he gained the plateau, there'd be no haven, for the dronnets would give chase. He could easily elude Carnalian regulars, but dronnets? Bonu had the utmost respect for their abilities. If he caught their attention he'd be as good as dead. So, clinging to the cliff face, with barely a toehold, he craned his neck around to watch.

Down to the clearing four dronnets carried Hod-ya on a hastily constructed litter of branches broken off trees. Behind them trailed a disordered assembly of Carnalian regulars interspersed with ragtag Erotons and a few Craniantiumites.

The patrol at the dread's feet stared dumbfounded at the oncoming muddle.

Hod-ya screamed hoarsely, "Don't you fools see him? Kill him! Kill him. The prophecy! Restore me to my body; I'll show you how to deal with those who presume to fulfill prophecies!"

But her raving was treated as nonsense, the mystical ranting of one under the influence of spiritual forces. Hod-ya herself was exhausted. Even at that distance Bonu could see her usually dark and sinister eyes were deep hollows and her lips were covered with a foamy mixture of slaver and blood. She was strapped to her litter lest her thrashing cast her upon the ground. One dronnet, by his insignias the leader, walked casually alongside, hissing soothingly in her ear, but with little success.

Bonu also identified Captain Mileer's stubby form traipsing behind the dronnets, at the head of the hodgepodge of empire troops. Bonu's lips pursed as he wondered whatever had possessed Mileer to go on such a fool's venture with the Psa woman. Mileer had a reputation for being wiser than this.

The two dronnets from the original patrol met the approaching company, bowed, then fell in at the rear of the newly arrived black-guards. Scung and his mates backed away to a respectful distance. There was no point antagonizing dronnets, much less Hod-ya. Their inspection of the dread could be interpreted as meddling in affairs way beyond their scope.

All Carnalian eyes dwelt on the spectacle of Hod-ya babbling away, affording Bonu an opportunity to drop from his precarious hold on the cliff to a shelf and scurry behind a bush that was rooted in a crevice. He intended to observe just a little while longer before dodging back into his cave. Bonu crammed dried jerky into his mouth and slowly let his saliva re-hydrate the morsel. Should he be discovered there'd be an all-out effort to catch him. Whether he went up over the cliff and fled via the plateau or delved into the unknown depths of the cavern of his little hideout, he'd have precious little time for food then.

The bush's leaves rustled as if in a breeze, but there was no breeze. It also shimmered for a second as if in sunlight, but it was too early for the sun to shine upon the hidden glen.

"Bonu," a wispy voice entered his ear.

He nearly choked on the pemmican and prepared to climb as fast as hands and feet could propel him.

"Be at peace, don't flee."

"Wh-o said that?" He whispered, furtively glancing over his shoulders.

The leaves rustled again, and a hushed voice continued, "It'll go badly if I reveal my presence. I have a message from Logon: 'Do as the runes foretell. Take no thought for your own safety. Great events hinge upon your obedience.'"

"Runes? What events?"

There was no answer. The glow had vanished.

"Hey, where'd you go? I want some answers."

The dronnets in the clearing formed themselves in a mystical, five-pointed pattern and began chanting.

Bonu argued, "If you think I know what you're talking about—"

Suddenly the confab in Captain Varter's tent came to mind: In his mind's eye he saw Captain Bainch leaning upon his cane, addressing the meeting. He remembered snatches of conversation concerning the mysterious runes and Psa:

Psa—

Women swoon 'neath your spell,

Control o'er men through them you sell,

But fire and wood, flood and slough,

Your end will come 'neath leaf and bough . . .

"Your end will come 'neath leaf and bough . . . "

"But, how?"

Two dronnets laid their mistress on the turf before the dread's statue-like body. They chanted in a language that Bonu had never before heard, nor ever cared to hear again. The company of Carnalian regulars fell out around the pool to watch. Only the dronnets stayed on their feet. The patrol Bonu had followed the previous day was gathered off to one side taking in the dronnet ritual with great interest.

The pair that had rejoined the patrol were taken aside for interrogation by the lead dronnet. The corporal denied having done anything to the thirty-foot-tall dread, insisting that they'd only discovered its presence a few minutes prior.

Scung was then singled out and brought over for questioning. Bonu heard his loud protestations and intermingled oaths as he exclaimed, "No, I moved nuthin'. I didn't even touch it. An' even if'n I was gonna, I didn't git no chance. Yer must think I be's summat kinda foof-foof bird ter think I'd be goin' about touchin' dreads whut be's standin' 'round forest pools."

The lead dronnet conferred with his subordinates, then snarled at Scung, who made no reply but stepped back to his companions.

Captain Mileer watched quietly until the dronnet finished interrogating Scung then said, "It'll take longer since there's only a dozen, and they're not able to summon their usual helpers of cusps, tophets, and the like."

Hod-ya lay face up, babbling incoherently and straining against her bonds. Blackguards took positions at each of her limbs, pinning her down. The lead dronnet addressed Mileer's company, but Bonu couldn't discern what was said. With groans and complaints, the company prostrated themselves, all except Captain Mileer. The lead dronnet hissed at him.

Mileer indignantly replied, "Oh, come now, I've seen this ritual dozens of times. Hod-ya doesn't care that I watch."

The dronnet reverted to plain speech and with a thin, wavering voice said, "No ordinary re-entering. Psa never outside this long. There are difficulties."

"Difficulties? You talk about difficulties after I bring a battalion into this forsaken forest? And I suppose my laying face down in the dirt will ease those difficulties? Look here, you may be an officer in her bodyguard, but I'm a commander of the emperor's legions and I'll not be humiliated. Besides, I begin to think Hod-ya is becoming unhinged. Babbling all night about some Ecclessite prophecy, she's lost her mind. I think she's used up. Psa might even choose another vessel when he wants to go traipsing around out of body. I hear there's a challenger."

The dronnet drew back his hand as if to slap Mileer, but then thought better of it. "Fool, know nothing. Your scouts never discover kingsmen without Psa leaving body. Now, you must lay prostrate, or face consequences."

"Says you. If Hod-ya is okay, she'll protect me; if she isn't, Psa needs my troops to protect him while his shade re-enters, for that's when he's vulnerable. We'll soon enough see, won't we? So, get started."

A brief staring match ensued, but Mileer finally won the contest of wills. The dronnet returned to Hod-ya's side and waved his hands over her to begin the ritual.

Hod-ya suddenly ceased murmuring. The dronnet lowered his arms, spun around and stared straight at Bonu, announcing, "An enemy!"

"Uh-ohhh," Bonu uttered under his breath.

A hundred heads simultaneously lifted off the ground and followed the dronnet's stare to the cliff.

Captain Mileer spun around and drew his sword. "Archers!"

Several men scrambled to their feet.

Mileer 's eyes searched the cliff face. "Where, Scrimmit? I see nothing."

The dronnet stretched a gloved finger toward Bonu, saying, "There, next to the falls. What is that?"

"Archers!" Bonu mumbled. "Well, scaling the cliff is out." He prepared to drop down into his chamber.

The bush rustled again and a column of twinkly lights appeared ten feet to Bonu's left. A voice said, "There is only one thing to do, obey the runes while you can." Then the column of lights floated down off the ledge to drift over the shoreline flashing different colors, drawing all eyes to itself. Then it meandered right through the stunned Carnalian company. Panic ensued: men fled from the bright. A few dared to loose arrows, which passed harmlessly through but nicked some unfortunate comrades-in-arms on the other side.

"Obey the runes?" Bonu pondered.

"Fools," Hod-ya croaked, "that bright can't stop the process. Never mind it. Get on with the ceremony. It's a diversion, the real danger is still up there. Get on with it!"

Scrimmit returned to the matter at hand. He was about to lift his hands again when Hod-ya, still pinned down, exclaimed in her own voice, "You've already done that. Commence the removal."

The chagrined dronnet touched his scimitar point to Hod-ya's belt buckle. A crackling belch of flame erupted, turning into a dense, roiling black cloud. It soared upward like a gigantic serpent, winding round and round the inert dread, spiraling until it reached the dread's nostrils, where it hovered, awaiting the next inhalation. The rest of the smoky trail coiled around the dread's form; still more black smoke flowed from Hod-ya's belt buckle until it resembled a fifty-foot boa constrictor. The dronnets meanwhile struggled to keep Hod-ya's body from levitating off the ground as the serpentine smoke column belched from her buckle.

The panic caused by the roamer diminished as it continued uphill. Soldiers again fell on their faces, as fearful of the disembodied dread as they were of a departing bright.

A couple of feet of the hovering smoke was drafted into the dread's snout on the next inhalation. The eyes briefly glowed red.

Terror mingled with fascination as Bonu watched another several sections of the undulating black column disappear inside the nostrils. The great monster shook his head side to side and yawned. And smoke still billowed from Hod-ya's buckle, adding to the coils wrapping around the towering monster. Psa inhaled again; another few feet of the smoky coil disappeared inside the creature's nose. Psa flexed his shoulders and swiveled his neck.

Captain Mileer stood off to the side, arms crossed, slightly bored.

Bonu muttered, "It needs its spirit to move . . . it vacated its physical form beside the pool thinking it a safe place that no one would stumble across. A remnant of itself must have remained behind to signal should an enemy appear. When I arrived last night, it recognized me as an enemy, especially here where leaf and bough abound."

But, what did Logon expect Bonu to do? Was he to attack while the dread was incapacitated? No, charging through an entire company of Carnalians would be suicidal.

"Take no thought for your own safety," was part of the roamer's message.

The monster inhaled again and flexed his arms and curled his fingers around his weapons. The final trailer of smoke trickled out of

Hod-ya's belt buckle to hover near Psa's ankles. Hod-ya went limp, she was conscious, but exhausted.

Another sniff from the dread inducted a few more feet of smoke; the upper torso twisted and leaned forward.

Bonu realized with a start that only another three, or at most, four, inhalations would complete Psa's re-entry. Something must be done now; another couple of minutes would be too late. But it would take at least five minutes to climb down the cliff, dodging arrows, crossbow darts, and spears all the way, then he'd have to charge a hundred-yard gauntlet around the pool, fighting off defenders all the while, just to get to the dread.

And when he got to it—then what? Even were the dread still incapacitated, what weapon could possibly have any effect on his stony hide? There was just no way. If only the roamer been more explicit? What did Logon expect? He wasn't sufficient for these things.

But there was no other option. He must attack or die trying. Could it be that Logon had brought him to this place long ago in preparation for this day's combat? And now the hour had come.

"Take no thought for your own safety."

Eight dronnets were still on hands and knees, gasping for breath, exhausted from keeping Hod-ya on the ground against the pull of the dread's spirit.

Hod-ya lay motionless.

Carnalian regulars were scattered over the forest, faces in the dirt. Only Mileer was alert, the sole obstacle between Bonu and the dread. An irrational urge to jump off the cliff into the pool below stole over him. Ridiculous! He didn't even know if the water in the pool was deep enough to cushion his jump. It might be only two or three feet deep and he'd surely break both legs, if not worse. Nevertheless, if he did nothing, the dread would soon regain use of all his faculties and would spare no effort pursuing him. In fact, even at that moment the hateful, fiery red eyes were fixed on him, sending a chill down his backbone.

Gripping his sword and crossbow tightly, Bonu took a deep breath and leapt off his ledge.

Hod-ya bolted upright. As he descended Bonu saw that she'd seen him leap and tried to raise the alarm.

Water suddenly inundated Bonu. The force of entering the water had swept the crossbow from his hand; at the same time, he renewed his grip on his Child of the Stars. He sank deep. Would he have enough breath to surface? His feet touched bottom and he propelled himself upward, kicking and one-arm-paddling until his feet touched sand. He broke surface and waded with long strides to the shallows brandishing his sword.

Captain Mileer spun around to investigate the loud splash in the middle of the pool and was dumbfounded to behold a dripping-wet Ecclessite warrior rising out of the waters with determination in his eye, a war chant upon his lips, and swinging a glowing sword.

~

Jeda was on one side of Glend while Spoena supported the other. Glend's condition had taken a turn for the worse during the night; she felt weak, headachy. They checked her for irk bites but found none, and upon deciding she hadn't eaten enough, led her to the mess tent for breakfast. Jeda mused aloud for the sake of conversation, "I wonder if he's thinking of me at all."

"Who?" asked Spoena.

Glend smiled and said, "Bonu, of course. Didn't you know? I thought the whole camp knew."

Jeda blushed.

"I'll bet he's got nothing else on his mind but you," said Vawella, catching up from behind. "What's the matter, Glend?"

"Oh, Vawella, I, I don't know. When I woke this morning, my legs were so stiff I could hardly move them, and my back and shoulders, too. If these two weren't holding me up, I'd fall over."

"Hmmm, stiff from yesterday's journey, do you suppose?"

"Yes, I'm sure that's it. I'll be all right after some breakfast. I'm really famished. All I ate yesterday were some nuts and mushrooms, and other tidbits I foraged along the way."

"Mushrooms? You ate mushrooms along the trail?" Vawella was suddenly serious.

"Uh-huh. Was that wrong? I mean, I was taught which mushrooms to pick and which to avoid."

"Yes, I'm sure you were, for any other forest. But this is Ra-Amawl. Nothing is to be taken for granted in Ra-Amawl. Yesterday we passed through a region known as Lurcan's Footprints; his toxic effect is still in evidence even in the plants that grow there. We'd better get you to the healers before breakfast. Eating may worsen your condition. I remember when I was a little girl and the brigade moved to Ra-Amawl there were a lot of paralyzed people in camp. It was discovered that they'd eaten some tainted fish."

"What happened to them?" Jeda asked, trying to remember if she'd eaten anything on the journey other than a couple of handfuls of berries.

"Some recovered I think, maybe all of them. Anyway, the healers will know what to do, Glend, so don't worry. It's my fault; I should have warned you. I forgot that you new-comers need to learn things the rest of us take as a matter of course."

Vawella assigned one of the girls following her to take charge in her stead at the kitchen while she escorted Glend to the hospital tent.

The camp's perimeter walls were successfully integrated into the lay of the land by work crews that labored all night putting finishing touches on their project. A good portion of the kitchen was completed and operating satisfactorily except that it wasn't convenient to water. Others finished placing sod and vegetation on the roof making the kitchen and mess hall appear like a hill in the midst of a thicket. The camouflage, although flawless, would afford little protection against attack if detected. It was a trade-off: invisibility as opposed to fortified walls. A fort of walls and redoubts would attract attention, come under siege and eventually fall to Lurcan's armies. Yet displaying Logon's wisdom rather than their own, this brigade had evaded discovery for almost a generation.

The girls were admitted to the hospital tent by a duly concerned woman who immediately summoned Kraga, the chief medical officer. After assuring Jeda and Spoena that Glend was in good hands and things weren't as serious as they could've been, the nurse sent them to their duties with an invitation to check back after morning chores.

CHAPTER TWENTY-EIGHT

JEDA GLADLY HELPED PREPARE BREAKFAST for the work crews. The men engaged in setting up the rustic, albeit necessary conveniences to community life, worked tirelessly at their tasks.

"I truly feel like I belong here," Jeda commented to Artil, Spoena's younger sister beside her doling out a mash of boiled grain to hungry workers. "I love the people; I love our situation, precarious as it is; I love Logon, his swords, our captain—"

"His lieutenants?" Artil teased.

Jeda playfully retorted, "Never you mind, nosey! Just watch that you don't spill hot mush on anyone while you're snooping in other people's business." She laughed to mask her embarrassment, wondering if the blush rising to her cheeks was visible.

Yes, she could freely admit it now; she had strong feelings, special feelings for Bonu and not the way she loved everyone else. Bonu's mannerisms, courage, genuineness, and sensitivity put him in a class by himself. But most of all his heart was set to follow Logon even above his own personal interests. That trait might threaten some women; they'd constantly seek reassurance of their husband's love; but Jeda was also intent upon following Logon no matter what that entailed. She would allow her husband—wait a minute! Was she already thinking marriage? This was so sudden and herself unprepared for that eventuality.

Did Logon intend for them to become man and wife? Could that be why he'd gone to such lengths to bring her to the middle of nowhere? And she'd thought it was about some dangerous mission. What a relief! Marriage was what Logon wanted instead of throwing her life upon the spears and swords of evil doers in the hideous Scrarth and Avangar duels. Of course, she would still seek Logon's will to ascertain it. She smiled.

"Jeda, are you going to fill those bowls or are you going to hold them over the pot all day?" asked a freckle-faced lad waiting in line.

"Leave her alone, Gogar; can't you see she's meditating on something, er, someone important?" giggled Artil.

Jeda poked Artil's ribs with an elbow but hastily scooped some mush from the steaming caldron. Those waiting in line grinned. Did everyone know? Jeda's blush deepened as she posed, "Is there anyone who doesn't know?"

"Only Bonu," someone in line lamely joked.

No one laughed.

"Uh, I'm sorry, Jeda; I wasn't thinking."

"That's okay. I just wish he, that is, I, oh, I don't mind." But she did mind, very much. Not about the joke, but that Bonu was on a dangerous mission in the wilds of Ra-Amawl and not safely in camp due to her rebuffs. How foolish not to have been honest with herself. As soon as Bonu returned she'd reveal her true feelings. 'Two weeks,' he'd told Captain Varter. Could she wait that long without bursting? What if he was delayed? Oh, she didn't dare consider that. Jeda didn't mind the teasing. For Bonu's sake she could endure any amount of kidding, or worse, if necessary.

Would you interpose your life for his?

The question startled her, so unexpected, so encompassing in scope. "Logon wouldn't ask that, not now."

"I'm sorry, Jeda, I missed that. What'd you say?" asked Artil, turning to her friend. Artil was obviously Spoena's younger sister, the family resemblance was easily noted: same shaped face, hair color, eyes, strong legs and arms, and mischievous attitude.

"Uh, I was just thinking out loud."

"Oh."

The question remained: would she interpose her life to save Bonu's? Whether or not the thought came from Logon, the question was valid and demanded an answer. Would she? She'd found someone who loved her for herself, as Logon did, and wanted to make her happy and wanted to follow Logon. Would she, for his sake, yield her own life and any chance of happiness with Bonu so he might live? After all, isn't that the essence of love? Anything else would be just infatuation—a boost to the ego, a love of self and not true love for the one who made her feel good about herself.

"I suppose you've heard about my dad?" Artil intruded on Jeda's thoughts, taking advantage of a lull in the line. "They're already married; barely moved into the new campsite and got hitched. What do you think of that?"

"I heard. Kyleah, isn't it? Well, I don't know either of them, but I suppose—"

"Do you think loneliness drove him to it?"

"Loneliness? With six girls to look after? I doubt loneliness is the reason. If anything, desperation for assistance would be more a factor."

Artil didn't smile.

"This is really weighing on you, Artil. I'm sorry, I didn't mean to make light of your feelings."

"I don't want my dad to have to take a wife because we're too much for him." Artil's usually jubilant face sobered. "If we all had pitched in more, we could've taken care of things without an outsider's help."

"Artil, there are things about growing up that you don't yet understand. I'm sure your father considered all aspects of this decision and wouldn't have gone through with it if he didn't feel it was best. His concern for you and your sisters was only part of his decision. I'm sure he also considered what was best for Kyleah, don't you?"

"She was doing fine without a husband. Now she's living with us, and Spoena had to move out."

"Ah, you feel your family will never be the same again."

Artil's expression confirmed Jeda's suspicion.

Jeda continued, "And you're right. But, Kyleah's coming didn't change your family, your mother's death did. The replacement only caused you to feel the loss more keenly. You were faced with the realization that you had to accept the change as permanent; isn't that true?"

Artil said, "Maybe, I'm not sure. My mother was so pretty, so in love with my father, and he with her. It just doesn't seem right. And why did Spoena have to move out?"

"Spoena's nearly grown, Artil, as you'll soon be, too. True, she's a bit young to leave home, but it's not the same as going out on her own. She's still part of the camp; she'll see you every day. As for your father, he's a respected warrior, a man that Captain Varter seeks out for advice. I trust he knows what's best. He loves you no less, even as he takes a new wife. You and your sisters will always be special to him. I think

Logon brings changes into our lives because we need to keep adapting lest we become stagnant in our comforts."

"I don't know if I trust Logon any more. First, he takes my mother to Splendora, now a strange woman moves in and my sister moves out."

"Logon is revealing that you only trust him when things are going the way you want. But if things go contrary, that's when you find out whether you're trusting Logon or your own plans."

"But I'm only twelve. Why would Logon be so stern with me?"

"Who knows what the future holds, Artil? In my opinion, you're too young for these heart-breaking lessons; but Logon knows what's ahead in your lifepath. If you resist his changes, when the tough times come, you'll not be prepared to face them. You mustn't resent whatever Logon allows, but rather, thank and trust him."

Tears brimmed in Artil's eyes. "Seems harsh using hurt and pain to prepare someone."

Jeda put an arm around the young girl. "I know, I know. These things do hurt. But they'll only hurt more if you resist them. Let Logon do what he deems best; accept the grief and pain; let them do their work. I know a girl, not much older than you, who suffered under a cruel stepfather . . ." Jeda continued relating Tressa's story and the peace and joy that came with trusting Logon and accepting her lot in life.

The clean-up crew under Vawella's supervision took over the kitchen chores; those who had served during breakfast were released. Jeda accompanied Artil to her father's tent. Jeda whispered as they approached, "Give Kyleah a chance, Artil. She loves Logon and has been given a useful gift. Maybe Logon will use her to teach you things no one else could."

Kyleah greeted them with a warm smile as she shook out wet laundry. "Artil, you got up so early this morning, I missed seeing you off. Hello, Jeda."

"Hi," returned Jeda.

Artil avoided Kyleah's eyes, but replied, "I woke early, and thought maybe I could help serve breakfast."

Kyleah's eyes glistened, but there was a quiet wisdom in her kindly expression as she nodded and returned to her work. "I'm glad you took the opportunity since I was needed here."

"Jeda, Jeda," a voice called from behind. It was Spoena. "Oh, I've found you. Come quickly, work crews are being assigned, and there's a chance we can go on the forage detail, harvesting food from the forest. It's one of the more interesting jobs. Come on before the best spots are taken. Hi, Artil, Kyleah. Everyone okay?"

Artil nodded glumly, but Kyleah greeted, "Spoena! Oh, take a minute and tell me how you're getting on. Your father and sisters miss you so."

"I . . . I really can't right now, Kyleah. But, I will later, this afternoon. Vawella says I should get to know you better, and, I think I'd like that."

"I'd like that, too," said Kyleah. "Jeda, thank you for walking Artil back. You three had better hurry now, those foraging openings won't last long. Go on now." She smiled and made a brushing-off motion with her hands.

~

Bonu waded out of the thigh-deep waters wielding his sword and bellowing a war chant for all he was worth. He let the melody and words flow that came to mind:

"Sons of Mada turn from your empty way,
Your rulers all despise you, their hatred is disguised,
Void of love and care, they use you and discard,
Devouring you at will when their purpose served.

The promised joys and pleasures will crumble and decay,
Vain, fancied power corrupted, frail, despised,
The path you found so easy will turn bitter, hard,
All who tread this dark trail, soon become unnerved!

Sons of Mada seek the one who gives you hope alway,
Logon's blood is shed for you, for you are highly prized,
Seek Elyon's amnesty, for you his form was marred,
Mercy is a gift from him, though all undeserved."

Mileer was in no mood for such invitations. With a growl he lunged, brandishing his ruby-studded, Carnalian sword in one hand and a, rubied dirk in the other. The swords clashed; each man's strength pitted against the other's.

Mileer's dirk savagely whooshed past Bonu's exposed underbelly, scoring his leather vest, painfully scraping the skin underneath.

Bonu retreated before the dirk slashed again. A welt rose but the skin wasn't broken. Carnalian dirks were often poisoned; but the tunic hadn't torn. Bonu attacked again, ducking beneath the black sword's roundhouse, warily watching the dirk as he probed for Mileer's vulnerability. There was none, for the dirk turned the glowing point of the Child of the Stars aside to pass through Mileer's sleeve and scrape his coat of mail. Bonu dodged, but not quickly enough.

Mileer's broadside glanced off Bonu's shoulder, sending a tingle to his fingertips. Mileer withdrew to inspect his tattered sleeve.

Bonu took the break to glance beyond his opponent to Psa who inhaled another draught of the serpentine column of smoke. Only two more breaths remained before the monstrosity would be fully resident and invincible. Dueling with Mileer wasted time: Psa, partially un-housed and vulnerable, was the target.

Mileer angered at having his expensive uniform slashed, rushed Bonu, sword and dirk leveled straight out. Whichever weapon Bonu parried, the other was sure to find its mark. But Bonu feinted left, then right; indecision slowing Mileer. Bonu suddenly knelt before the crafty fighter holding his sword straight up.

Mileer's weapons parted to either side. Mileer smirked as he said, "Kingsman, think you can pierce my chest with that short sword? I've got a nasty surprise for you if you do."

Quicker than the eye could follow the Child of the Stars flicked to the left, deflecting the long sword, then to the right, knocking the dirk aside as well, then Bonu purposely fell on his back. Mileer, thrown off balance by the maneuver, couldn't avoid tripping over the prone form; his momentum sent him headlong into the pool's rippling waters where his shirt of mail dragged him out of sight.

Bonu jumped to his feet and charged full tilt at Psa.

Soldiers, aware of the intruder, slowly clambered to their feet.

Hod-ya was purple from shouting.

The monster's fiery eyes fixated on Bonu; the immense creature seemed to be trying to inhale faster. Another section of the dense, roiling cloud disappeared. The scythe lifted off the turf; fingers flexed around the crossbow. A tremble went through the scaly feet.

Thirty yards lay between Bonu and Psa; only one inhalation of cloud remained.

Bonu scanned his opponent searching for a chink in his armor. Even a partially paralyzed dread presented a formidable problem: covered head to foot in iron armor and thick leather, not to mention stony scales that comprised his skin. Maybe, if he had all day to go round and round, probing, experimenting . . . But Bonu had no such luxury.

In another breath the dread would be fully empowered, and it would come for him. As if that wasn't enough, a hundred Carnalians had picked themselves off the ground and were bearing down on him, intending to rend him savagely limb from limb.

"Logon, what do I do?"

Powerful arms wrapped around Bonu's thighs and threw him face down to the turf. Bonu's sword was pressed hard against his face and his arms were pinioned underneath. He kicked his right leg and connected with a face. Then he was free. Bonu rolled over and found that it was the giant Eroton who'd tackled him and was now sitting just behind nursing a bloody nose.

"Owww! Now yer done it, yer Ecclessite scum! I be's gonna break yer in half." Bonu grabbed desperately for his sword as the Eroton rose to pounce.

The surrounding Carnalian patrol respectfully allowed the Eroton room to finish his kill.

Psa started inhaling his final draught with a look of triumph.

Scung growled like a bear and sprang atop Bonu.

Bonu gripped and defensively thrust his sword up into the chest wall of the descending warrior.

A look of astonishment crossed the giant's face just before he collapsed.

"A life for the king!" Bonu muttered, wriggling from underneath the fallen champion.

The smoke trail, but for a wisp, had disappeared into the monster's nostrils, his feet lifted and stomped the ground, crunching his way toward Bonu.

The clamor of soldiers surrounding Bonu rushed with grasping fingers as they closed in.

In an act of desperation Bonu hurled his sword at the approaching dread.

It tumbled end over end toward the monster.

Bonu was seized by the swarming hands of a score of attackers.

CHAPTER TWENTY-NINE

THE PATROL OF BURDENED, BASKET-BEARING girls, fifteen in number, slowly probed beneath root, leaf and stem for edible plants and grubs. Their baskets, ideal for garnering nature's bounty, were of tightly woven and dried marsh reeds. The line of foraging girls was escorted by an equal number of crossbow-armed young men sweeping the region for rabbits, squirrels, and game birds. The harvest of flora and fauna yielded a plentiful supply for those who knew what to look for, augmenting the staples secured by raids.

Artil and Spoena communicated with Jeda in whispers instead of signs, animal sounds, and birdcalls. Jeda had to receive special allowance to be on foraging detail because not knowing sign language made her a liability. Permission was granted provided she stay close to her guides. All the brigade's women needed to learn foraging. Jeda reveled in discovering how much food was available in the wild, even though the search was tinged with danger. For the first time since leaving home, maybe in her life, Jeda reveled in the thought that she belonged with these people, that she was part of this brigade. The fact that Captain Varter urged everyone to sharpen the entire sword, not merely certain runes, was confirmation that Logon wanted her here. Jeda smiled at her foolish worries.

"Oh, look," whispered Spoena, pointing to a type of tree. "I'll bet manu grows there."

"What's manu?" Jeda whispered, trailing just behind Spoena, ducking to avoid a back-swishing branch.

Before Spoena answered, a rolling, thunderous boom reverberated through the forest. The foraging party froze in place.

"That's odd," mused Spoena, resuming her task after nothing else followed, "it doesn't feel like rain is approaching. That's one thing about Ra-Amawl that I wish was different. We seldom, if ever, see the sky; we can't tell what the weather's going to do. Anyway, about manu, it's a type of food that King Elyon sent to sustain the descendants of Baram, father of Laffer and grandfather of Suplan, when they wandered over Psychanan. It was plentiful in those days. It was their only food source, well, almost. I thought you knew these things?" They started toward the tree.

"Don't forget, I'm new to all this," replied Jeda. "I've barely begun sharpening my sword. There's so much to learn; I want to study all about Logon before I learn about the days before Logon walked the earth. So, you're saying that manu is some kind of ready-to-eat bread that grows out here?"

"Not exactly." They reached the tree in question and Spoena's hand deftly scooped the crotches of the lower branches. She turned, holding a white, web-like substance in her fingers. "It sort of forms, somehow. Actually, nobody knows how, but in these spike trees whenever Elyon's people have need, Logon sends manu. All you do is gather it; some add water; some cook it, but you don't have to do either. It's sweet and filling. You can eat it as is. Want some?"

"Well, I—"

"Oh, go ahead. You'll like it."

Overcoming the repulsive sensation that she was eating a ball of spider webs, Jeda took a pinch on the tip of her tongue. It thickened as soon as it touched saliva; it was sweet but not overly so, more a hint of sweetness. There were subtle hints of other flavors as well; it was a veritable banquet of flavors in one bite.

"Like it?"

"Mmmm, delicious."

"I told you so. There's more. Give me a hand up, will you? Looks like Logon has provided a special treat for us. It complements whatever you serve with it."

"I tasted many subtle flavors. What kind of tree is this? You say it grows only on this kind of tree?"

"Not grows. Forms, like dew. This is called a spike tree."

"Unusual name."

Artil joined them. "It's the kind of tree Lurcan fashioned into the spike that impaled Logon."

"Oh." Jeda beheld the tree reverently. "And manu only forms on this type of tree?"

Spoena and Artil nodded. Artil added, "Gogar says, because of the thunder, we should return to camp in case it rains and floods like it did a couple of weeks ago. Let's gather what manu we can off the lower limbs and catch up to the others. They've started back already."

"It doesn't feel like rain. What do you think, Jeda?"

"I haven't lived in the jungle long enough to know the feel of rain, but I heard the thunder. We all heard it, so it must be going to rain whether you feel it or not, right?"

"Haven't heard any thunder since; nor has the wind picked up in the treetops," argued Spoena. "Something's odd. Here, hoist me up so I can gather a little more manu before we head back. There's no hurry; it's not going to rain, at least for a while. It's Gogar's first time leading and he's just being extra cautious."

"I don't know, Spoena," cautioned her younger sister. "I don't feel safe away from the hunters."

"Nonsense! This'll just take a minute if you two will give me a boost; then we'll hustle and catch up to the others."

Being the best trail finder, Spoena was obviously not going to guide them until she'd harvested more manu.

Artil and Jeda boosted Spoena up. Artil's eyes were wide with worry.

"Hurry, will you, Spoena?" pleaded Jeda.

"Sssh! Not so loud. Remember to keep your voice—" She froze in mid-sentence.

Jeda and Artil looked up anxiously.

Spoena dropped almost soundlessly to the ground, pulling the other two down beside her. Her face had gone pale and her breathing was shallow. "Half-men."

~

"He be's mine!" Scung bellowed amid the mass confusion. Soldiers were knocked aside as if they were ragdolls as he scooped the unconscious Ecclessite around the middle and secured him with a brawny arm. "I catched him, I gits ter eat his heart!"

Several Carnalians and a few Erotons opposed his retreat.

"Not so fast, Eroton," hissed a dronnet, pushing his way through the ring surrounding the Eroton. "He's to be questioned. We want to know where his brigade has moved. So, the sooner we extricate the answers from him the sooner you can have what's left of him when we're finished if, you can beat off all the others who want a piece of him." Four other dronnets flanked the speaker.

Scung scanned the angry mob who were awaiting his answer. He often relied on his reputation for being highly skilled in battle, but taking on five dronnets? Scung, "The Scourge of the Southland," was renowned for once fighting forty kingsmen at one time, killing some and maiming most of the rest. He was a famous warrior. But dronnets were a class by themselves, and five at once? This was almost as amazing as the foolish Ecclessite attacking the dread by merely throwing his sword. What tales would be sung of today's events.

Realizing the hopelessness of his situation, Scung scowled darkly, muttering with a rasp, "Come git him, if'n yer dares." His black, curved scimitar wavered under the dronnet's noses. "I ain't afeered o' yers, but yer'd best be afeered o' me?" A glint in the Eroton's eye bespoke reckless daring.

The dronnets cast sideways glances at each other. What was the Eroton up to? Everything had been thrown into confusion, and with their lady still babbling semi-conscious on the ground, they were unsure what to do. Any other day they would've made mincemeat of the audacious Eroton, but this was not any other day. Mileer, coughing and sputtering, just being hauled out of the pond, was despised by dronnets; they wouldn't even consider asking him to order the Eroton to relinquish his prey.

~

In that moment of hesitation, Psa spied the sword that had bounced harmlessly off his nose, now lying on the moss. He'd watched as Carnalian soldiers pummeled the kingsman into oblivion. The Ecclessite had acted in desperation by hurling his sword, twirling end over end to barely miss the tail end of Psa's unclothed shade as it was sucked in. Had the sword touched his dark spirit, Psa would be but a sheet of flame winging toward Cosmopolis in defeat, announcing the beginning fulfillment of Elyon's prophecies that foretold the imminent end of Lurcan. The prophecies decreed that he, Psa, would be the first to pay the price of rebellion since he'd been the first to rally to Lurcan's side. The sword flung at him had come close, but he managed to suck in the last little trailer of smoke just as the point of the shiny sword bounced off his scaly nose. In fact, it struck the very nostril the smoke had entered a millisecond late! The prophecy would go unfulfilled.

Strength surged into Psa's limbs. He flexed his muscles impressing the lackeys gawking at him. That's when he spied the kingsman's sword, the hated, shiny needle, laying where it had fallen. He raised his heel to grind it to fragments. His first stomp bent the gray metal slightly and caused the eagle-dove haft to crack, nevertheless it held together.

Soldiers watching the confrontation between Scung and the dronnets turned to see why the ground trembled. Amused, they heard the dread laugh scornfully and stomp the sword again. This time the haft jammed down into the ground, leaving the point sticking straight up. In the shadow of the monster's heel several runes suddenly flared bright yellow, but the dread didn't see.

Instead, he boastfully announced, "I show the weakness of this annoying little needle as I, Psa the Defiler, break its power." Matching his proud words, his foot descended.

~

Hod-ya stopped ranting and sat up exhausted, but nonetheless, conscious, all but forgotten in the pandemonium. Out of the corner of her eye she saw Psa lift his foot to stomp on the sword. She rasped in alarm, "No! The runes blaze colors!"

Psa's foot crashed down with earth-shaking force. Hod-ya watched in terror as, instead of shattering, the sword penetrated the scaly bottom of beast's arch, driving deep into the titan's foot.

The dread's eyes popped wide open; his mouth gaped exposing serrated teeth as he bellowed his outrage.

Black, gooey tar spurted like blood from Psa's foot. Everything touched by that effluent burst into flames; everyone immediately blistered if they got sprayed. Seasoned veterans and recruits alike howled and ran pell-mell up the hill or down into the forest to avoid the hopping, maddened monster as he tried to extricate the cause of his agony. His clumsy pawing pushed the last bit of the sword's haft deeper. The giant scythe and crossbow slammed into the ground as in a rage he toppled over and cursed, crushing men beneath his writhing hulk.

Psa's leg burst into flames from the knee down. Thick, murky fumes billowed into the air. All who inhaled it fell to the ground eyes bulging and clutching their throats. Panicking, Psa rolled over several times in an attempt to douse the flames; failing that, he rose and limped headlong for the pool below the waterfall. An inferno now engulfed his entire leg, spreading in turn to his mid-section, his other leg, and his upper torso.

The thirty-foot conflagration dove into the crystalline pool. Around him water boiled angrily into steam and mixed with the heavy, black smoke sending a dense fog over the pool. The pond boiled away until almost naught was left but marine vegetation, mud, bare rocks, flopping fish and the smoldering carcass of Psa. The front half of the dread's bulk had burrowed into the silty bottom of the pool leaving only his charred feet sticking out on the bank

Chaos reigned all around. Men scattered in every direction, some rolling in the dried leaves on the forest floor trying to douse the fires Psa's blood had ignited. Others, in the wake of their champion's demise, attacked one another in a savage, insane frenzy.

Scung made good his escape from the madness, still lugging Bonu under one arm, wildly waving his scimitar at anyone who approached.

~

The forest was ablaze from the dread's blood as well as from the men trying to extinguish their clothing. A whipping wind drove the flames up the hillside and into the forest. Small creatures scampered for their lives; men caught in front of the fire line dropped their burdens and weapons as they fled. Those near the pool jumped into what little water and mud remained after the dread boiled most of the moisture away, scalding themselves. Others ran helter-skelter in desperation, seeking any escape.

Scung turned around watching, and through a rift in the smoke and flames decided the cliff was the only viable escape. He slung Bonu over a shoulder and effortlessly climbed, locating adequate footholds and dangling vines alongside the gentle cascade that still merrily plunged off the plateau to the scene of devastation below. He eventually found it hard going, but handholds suddenly appeared where none seemed to be a moment prior.

A little more than halfway up the cliff face he spied a ledge and a small crevice leading to a cave. He shifted his burden, angled toward the opening and slipped Bonu's feet inside first, gently lowering him as far as he could, then released his catch. The Eroton then squeezed into the same hole, barely fitting inside the tight orifice. He dropped to the floor then poked his head back up and out the entrance to observe the panic below. With a two-handed grip he wrestled a large stone out of the entry enlarging the opening to his suiting. The rock gave way in a shower of dirt and small stones. He then placed the rock on the cave floor beside Bonu. Finding he fit easily into the entry now, he hoisted himself up and watched the events taking place below.

The scene was indescribable horror. He'd never, even in his entire, violent life, beheld such butchery of men who were on the same side! A fire raged in a growing ring some fifty or sixty yards away; sparks from burning trees allowed flames to race along root networks and fallen treetrunks, endangering all living things. Men lost their bearings and dashed back into the very holocaust they fled, savagely striking at any who dared try to turn them, hewing heads and limbs with abandon.

Amid all that was self-destructing, the tall, lean form of Hod-ya headed for Psa's charred carcass. Water tumbling off the plateau had already restored a tiny reservoir in the deeper regions of the pool. Adding to Scung's amazement were all that remained of the dronnet corps cowering underneath the burned-out dread and a mere half dozen or so bedraggled Carnalian regulars. Hod-ya picked her way across the body-ridden, burnt clearing towards the survivors, but instead of joining them under their cover as they invited, she gestured as if demanding them to come out. Surprisingly, most of them obeyed and climbed from under their fire-shelter and followed her to the cliff where it looked like they intended to scale the rock and leave via the plateau.

A shock wave and tremendous explosion suddenly rocked the glen. Scung was knocked back into the cave. A sheet of flame arched up and away from the pond, scorching its way through what tatters were left of the leafy canopy. Reverberations of that blast resounded deafeningly up and down the plateau wall, echoing outward for miles into the surrounding jungle. The concussion extinguished most of the fires. What flames remained were driven backward as a back-rushing wind compensated for the fireball's vacuum.

Scung, ears ringing, re-examined the enclosure, making sure it was sound after such a tremendous explosion. He again stood upon the rock and peered down.

Hod-ya, and what was left of her bodyguard had tumbled off the cliff face and lay strewn around the base. Elsewhere survivors sat, those that were still alive, holding their heads or sticking fingers in their ears trying to unplug them. The veteran fighting force of three brigades and a platoon of dronnets was obliterated—by the brazen attack of a lone kingsman. Scung noted that Captain Mileer had survived and was crawling out of the brackish mud hole dripping with slime.

But where was Psa? A crater, twice the size of the original pool had formed at the bottom of the waterfall, but there was no dread's carcass. Had Hod-ya known that the dread's corpse was going to explode, bringing even more destruction in his death throes?

The emperor's forces would keenly feel the loss. This had been a veteran, hard-core unit, and though numerically small, its destruction signaled a dismal omen as the first of Lurcan's mighty henchmen fell victim to a single, determined kingsman. The prophecies could not be thwarted!

~

Bonu groaned and rolled over, every muscle screaming.

Scung stepped down off his rock. "Ah, yer be's alive arter all?"

Bonu cracked his eyes open a slit. "No, I don't think so." He made an effort to sit up. Through his grogginess it appeared as if the Eroton he'd killed was up in his hideaway with him. "Help me up, will you?"

"If'n thet's whut yer wants." Strong hands seized Bonu under the armpits and hoisted him against the wall. "'Ere, I found this blanket in some fella's knapsack." He placed it behind Bonu to ward off the chill of the stone wall.

Bonu gingerly tested his limbs. The pain everywhere made it difficult to tell whether anything was broken or just severely bruised. "Who are you?" he asked the huge form kneeling in front of him.

"Thet be's hard ter answer, laddie. I was 'Scung, Scourge of the Southland'. But whut I done in rescuin' the likes o' yer hain't summat Scung the Scourge wouldda done."

Bonu forced his eyes open. "This isn't a dream, is it?"

"I be's the one yer stabbed, remember?"

"It is you, then? Why, where, how?"

Scung opened his Carnalian leather breastplate to reveal a white tunic which he also undid at the chest revealing a freshly healed scar. "Soon as yer shiny sword cut through me skin I seen a man standin' right alongside yer. He says ter me, 'Scung, yer must come wi' me, we gots much ter talk about.' Afore I could say aye or nay, he grabs me hand an' I finds myself at the bottom of a huge rock whut looks like a skull, alongside a swift river, lookin' up at him on top."

"Logon's Rock."

"Yup, Logon's Rock. An' he says ter me, 'Yer gots ter die, an' I gots ter live!' he says. Just like thet, 'Yer gots ter die, an' I gots ter live.' Then I looked down an' seen this wound yer put in me chest, an' instantly I kenned he were offerin' me his life."

Bonu chuckled, then groaned.

"Did I say summat funny?" Scung scowled.

"Ooh, it hurts when I laugh. No, ooh! I'm sorry, Scung. You didn't say anything funny. It's just that Logon never ceases to amaze me. Who'd have thought . . . here I am, still alive after foolishly jumping off a cliff, charging through a whole company of Carnalian regulars to get at a dread and the next thing I know I've been rescued by you, my enemy, turned brother!"

"Thet's whut Logon said, thet when I was 'back', I should rescue me brother. Then he dressed me in this here tunic, an' give me a sword with a tiny blue dot at the point. He said a bunch o' words, and suddenly I was back on the moss bed in time ter see yer fling yer sword. Then a whole company o' me mates pounced on yer."

Bonu sat silently, considering this turn of events. "Did you know that I kept watch on your patrol last night from this hideaway?"

"Yer did? Yer must be a mighty warrior, ter attempt such a daring raid, single-handedly."

"A mighty fool, is more like it. Do I look like a mighty warrior to you?"

Bonu considered what Scung must see: his new comrade-at-arms had every inch of exposed skin turned purple and blue, his face swollen, especially about the eyes and nose, which felt to be broken, and he was bloodied from numerous small cuts and abrasions with his outer clothing torn.

The new Ecclessite recruit replied, "Aye, yer looks like a grand warrior."

"Well, I'm not. I'm a fool, thinking Logon sent me on such an errand. How did you ever manage to get me away?"

"Yer doesn't ken whut happent, does yer?" said Scung. With that he gently picked Bonu up by the armpits and held his head above the cave's opening.

"Hey! What are you doing? Oww! That hurts." As soon as his head cleared the enlarged crevice all protestations stopped. Bonu was awed into silence. Finally, he muttered, "Enough. Enough, Scung, let me down."

The Eroton complied, setting the lieutenant softly back atop his blanket.

Bonu wiped his eyes and shook his head. "All those lives, all those lives, and the dread escaped."

"Psa hain't escaped. Didn't yer see thet crater at the bottom o' the waterfall? He exploded inter a skillion smithereens! An' his shade turned inter fire and fled ter Cosmopolis. Yer won a great victory. Psa be's no more! Mileer's regiment be's decimated! Yer'll be awarded fer this, I be's a guessin'."

"Not likely, Scung. Logon's ways are different. Logon rescues lives, not takes them. What a fool I've been. Why did I think I could fulfill prophecy? Look at the harm my foolishness has done."

"Well, I be's rescued."

Bonu lifted his head and observed his cave mate. "Yes, my friend, you were rescued. Mayhap you were the only one whose heart wasn't too hard. I don't know. It's a shame so many were lost without hearing about Logon's amnesty. But I thank Logon for you."

Scung rose from his haunches and leaned a brawny hand against the wall. "They's summat I doesn't ken, now thet yer brings it up. Why me? Whut have I ever done ter make Logon wanna rescue me?"

"Nothing."

"But, must be summat I done oncet. I been bad, real bad, lieutenant."

"Bonu, call me Bonu. My rank's not important, at least when away from the brigade."

"Bonu, I don't deserve ter be cleaned off and have Logon's Advisor in me heart. I be's afeered he's gonna find out thet he made a mistake and abandon me."

Bonu attempted to rise but he was too stiff and bruised; he settled back with a gasp. When the spasm passed, he said, "Scung, you did nothing to earn his love and forgiveness in the first place, and, as long as you desire to serve Logon, there is nothing you can do to earn his disfavor."

"But, it be's too easy. If I'd a kenned afore how easy it be's ter git Logon's fergiveness, I'd a done it a long time ago."

"That's why kingsmen wage war, not against men but against the rulers of darkness who deceived such as you. Did you never wonder why kingsmen never kill or wound anyone?"

"No, never. We seen the casualties, an' assumed they was dead by yer hands. Now thet I thinks about it, them thet died, died o' freak accidents, mostly. In fact, me own wounds was due ter me carelessness, an' not a kingsman. Ain't thet summat? I never thunk 'bout thet afore."

"Our enemy is also Carnalia's enemy, though Carnalians don't know it. Logon is the rightful ruler of Carnalia as well as all the lands of the empire, not Lurcan. Lurcan is a usurper who uses mankind to get back at King Elyon. In the end, Lurcan consumes even his own forces, destroying them."

"Yeah, I seen thet happen lots. I seen Psa hisself turn an' breathe fire on fourteen men whut had just won him a battle. He said ter those o' us lookin' on thet they was enterin' a better life as a reward."

"Unending torment is more like it," said Bonu. "Well, you're on the right side now, Scung. Do you have a Child of the Stars?"

"Yer means this sword?" he asked pulling it out of hiding. "I doesn't ken how ter use it. It ain't sharp, except on the very point. So, I used me trusty scimitar when I rescued yer."

"Scung, you must never use Carnalian weapons again. They have no place in Logon's kingdom. You'd best destroy them. I'll instruct you how to sharpen and use your new sword."

"Do I hafta?" the Eroton whined like a child who was unwilling to give up his favorite toy. "Me an' these weapons been through a lot."

"If you want to follow Logon, they must be put aside, every last one of them."

Scung frowned, then a smile lit his face. "Fer Logon I'd do anythin'. I'd even go an' spit in Hod-ya's face!"

Bonu laughed. "I doubt he'll ask you to do that."

Out of Scung's vest pockets, boots, belt, cloak, in fact from every Eroton vestment he wore came an assortment of weapons: his long, curved scimitar with a ruby in the handle, two dirks, a knife from each of his boots, a thin garroting cord, a small, cudgel weighted with an iron bar, a mace and chain, two hatchets, a double-bit war axe without a handle, several poisoned darts and blow gun and a spear head which also had no shaft. He lay them one by one on a pile that looked more like armaments for a squad than a single man.

"Is that it?" asked Bonu, incredulous that one man could carry all these and still move with agility.

"Oh, awright," Scung emptied his knapsack of a sling and several round stones, four cross-bow darts, ten arrowheads not yet fitted to shafts, and a pretty, sparkling dagger. "There, thet be's it."

Bonu reached across the pile and picked up the dagger. "I've heard of these, but never, until now, have seen one. Where'd you get it?"

"About a year ago, off'n a poor excuse fer a kingsman warrior. Tried ter stab me leg wi' it, but I ended his career quick. I only kept it cause it be's purty."

"May I have this? I'd like to show it to Captain Varter."

"I give 'em all up. Take whut yer likes. Keep 'em all if'n yer likes, I don't care."

"No, just this. I feel this has significance. Now, if you'll look a little deeper in my rucksack, I believe you'll find some food. It's dry and tough but it'll stave off hunger. After we eat I'll teach you about your sword."

Scung rummaged in the side pockets of Bonu's sack and found dried venison jerky. "No hurry. After we eat, yer'd best git some sleep. I'll stand watch, just in case."

CHAPTER THIRTY

THE HAIRY FEET OF SEVERAL bipeds padded into view not twenty yards from where Jeda, Artil, and Spoena scarcely breathed underneath the drooping branches of a spike tree. They watched as the beasts effortlessly ripped several green branches from trees and shaped them into makeshift beds on the ground then nestled into them.

The girls' faces had gotten smudged from pressing face down into the dirt, thus inadvertently camouflaging themselves from these powerful brutes that, it was rumored, considered human flesh a delicacy.

Whether out of fear or curiosity, Jeda slowly raised her head to peer through a grassy veil of flower stems and low-lying leafy branches. Her first glimpse of these half-men astonished her. Their bodies were covered with coarse, burnt-orange hair; they had unusually long arms and squat legs, low-sloping foreheads and large teeth; they ascended trees with agility, and although somewhat stubby, they were, nonetheless, powerful, too much for any human to best, with the possible exception of dronnets. Fortunately, they were downwind and behind a wall of dense foliage.

In the back of her mind Jeda vaguely recalled someone telling her about these beasts that had cousins in other forests which were equally impressive but were vegetarian and fearful of man. But Ra-Amawl exerted a disruptive influence on almost every species under its bowers and these half-men, or gorrils as some called them, with physiques resembling humans, were undoubtedly at the top of Lurcan's mutation experiments.

Jeda watched in fascination as the gorrils stomped out a comfortable bedding arrangement, tearing additional limbs off trees for cushioning, heaping them in piles until all was satisfactory, only then settling down. The group seemed led by four large male gorrils who occasionally argued with grunts and bared teeth as they slapped their chests, but each confrontation ended non-violently. Their respective mates busied themselves with grooming their offspring; each female had one.

Jeda glanced over and saw Artil trembling, but Spoena remained calm, perhaps plotting a course of action should the situation turn dangerous. Jeda nervously fingered her Child of the Stars, wondering how effective it would be against those powerful arms and teeth. This small family group, however, appeared to have only their afternoon siesta on their collective mind and so, posed no immediate threat.

Spoena hand-signaled to Artil, then whispered in the softest of whispers to Jeda, "When they sleep we'll sneak away."

Jeda, not yet having mastered the silent tread so necessary to the brigade's secret existence, feared she might crinkle a leaf or snap a twig. A grimace informed Spoena of her doubts.

All the male gorrils quickly dropped off to sleep, having stuffed themselves so full of fruit that their bellies protruded like small, orange hills as they lay on their backs snoring. Their snorts and grumbles had a calming effect and soon the females drowsed, laying down after playfully cuffing their young or picking ticks and fleas off which they promptly popped into their mouths. Within half an hour all the gorrils succumbed to slumber except one, inquisitive youngster, the smallest and probably youngest, who didn't appear sleepy enough to join his snoozing troop.

Tiring of his nest, he cast his curious eyes outward and spied a small snake slithering through the broken twigs and bent fronds littering the ground. The youngster climbed out of the family nest and trailed the reptile for several feet, contenting itself to merely watch as the snake probed for crickets and worms. But when the baby gorril grabbed its tail, the snake, at last aware of being stalked, darted away—straight toward the three Ecclessite girls, with the young gorril romping behind in hot pursuit.

Artil and Spoena were still face down, eyes closed, though not asleep. Only Jeda was aware of their imminent peril. She gasped.

Spoena inadvertently jerked her head upright.

The young gorril, spying Spoena's movement amidst the veil of weeds, skidded to a halt with a huffy bark, his nostrils flared, his eyes wide, his fur bristled, and his teeth bared as he reached for a twig to slap the ground in a bluff of strength.

A mother raised her head in alarm, nostrils crinkling, eyes searching furtively for her youngster. She barked and rose defensively to all fours, ready to dash to her whelp's rescue. The other gorril mothers stirred. The males opened their eyes, but perceiving no immediate threat, resumed their nap, leaving the matriarchs to sort it out.

The adventurous little gorril, growling, backed away from them, eyes riveted on the spot where he'd detected motion. Had the situation not been so perilous, Jeda would have found the little gorril's actions adorable. But a gruesome fate would undoubtedly befall the three of them should the troop get aroused.

Artil, unable to bear the suspense any longer, raised her head. It was a serious blunder; the other adult females were instantly on their feet, hooting, growling, and shrieking an alarm, rousing the males. The youngsters swung expertly onto their mother's shoulders, including the little adventurer. At Artil's movement he'd abandoned all bravado and scurried to his mother's arms, climbing atop her powerful shoulder, clinging to the fur, shrieking his outrage and defiance from his safe roost.

But the males were formidable. They staunchly arose, dragging their knuckles through the dirt, tossing leafy debris overhead; growling, exposing their incisors, encouraging each other with threatening gestures, working up a proper rage to assault the bushes and flush any stalking foe.

The girls slowly wrapped fingers around their sword hilts but made no other move. Besides, where would they go? They couldn't outpace, out-climb, or outfight these creatures so magnificently designed for jungle life.

The males strutted back and forth, getting closer, sensing an intruder's presence, afraid to get too close until they knew what they were facing; it wouldn't do to find themselves confronted by Craniantium lions. In that event, even this fierce foursome would be outmatched. But a normal lion, or almost anything else, they could overcome.

One old fellow, indisputably the chieftain, hung back, directing the others. White hair mingled with orange down his spine, shoulders and about his head and chin, indicating great age. He sent two of the more ambitious gorrils forward to flush out the unknown creature stalking their bedding site. The two males approached the girls, snorting, growling, pounding the ground with their fists, then nervously kneeling to peer beneath fronds and stems. They came within a few feet, sticking their heads into the shrubbery. Then one of them locked eyes with Jeda.

He froze, gave a tentative, "Whuff," not backing away.

Jeda was unable to move, like a rabbit frozen by fear, hoping against hope to avoid the sniffing fox. Her spine tingled; messages from her brain were confused, all she could do was stare back at the feral eyes boring into hers.

Jeda felt Spoena tense.

A loud bark from the chieftain halted the gorrils; they suddenly stood upright. He craned his head backward checking over his shoulder, snuffling the air. The two probing gorrils obediently withdrew. The older gorril grunted twice and the whole band scurried into the undergrowth across the clearing. The chieftain was the last to go, casting a penetrating look toward the girls' hiding place, making sure all mothers and young were safely away before disappearing. Only broken tree limbs and trampled leaves on the ground remained as evidence they'd ever been there.

The three girls exhaled in unison, then looked wide-eyed at each other, then dissolved into laughter. Sensation returned to Jeda's hands and feet, allowing her to rise to her knees, joining Artil and Spoena. They laughed themselves breathless, inhaled and laughed again till the hysteria passed.

Spoena regained control first, saying, "Hush now! Whatever scared them off is possibly heading this way."

That thought sobered the trio.

"We're not out of danger yet. Things are wilder than I thought in this new region. We never worried about half-men in any of our old camp zones, only an occasional wolf pack, lion, or bear. And we weren't plagued with irks, either," she said as she pulled one off Artil's collar. "Keep your thoughts on Logon."

"Hadn't we better get back to camp as soon as possible. They'll be missing us," advised Jeda, wanting only to settle in at campfire and chat about the day's adventures in the safety of home and friends. "Which way is camp?"

Artil pointed. "The way the gorrils went, I'm afraid. There's too much danger of crossing their path if we head directly for home."

"She's right," said Spoena. "We'd best circle out wide in the opposite direction and eventually swing back in the hope of finding our way before dark."

"Before dark? Oh, you can't be serious?"

"I am, Jeda. In fact, I doubt we'll make it in by dark, and might have to bed down in the jungle. Who knows, if we hurry, we may make it if we display some of that raw courage you did facing down that gorril? Where you got the nerve, I'll never know. I was ready to bolt and take our chances but staring him down the way you did gave me courage."

"Me, too, Jeda," said Artil. "I was all set to run. But you were so calm, so sure of Logon's deliverance, I had to stay."

"Are you kidding? The only reason I didn't get up and run was that I couldn't get my feet to obey!"

The three stared at each other for a split second, then burst out laughing again.

"Well, what do we do now? "Jeda asked. "Do you think maybe we should stay here and not risk stumbling into any more creatures?"

Spoena picked up her basket. "No, something spooked those gorrils, remember, and more than likely it's headed this way. I think I can find the way; I have a pretty good sense of direction. Follow me." With that, she led off through a bush into the unknown forest.

They no sooner crested a small knoll when the scent of smoke caught their attention. "Campfire, out here?" questioned Jeda.

"No, I don't think so. Seems more like, yes, I'm sure of it, a forest fire. But the smell is faint. It's a good distance off. We're in no immediate danger."

"Probably got started by that thunder and lightning storm, don't you think?" asked Artil.

"I don't know. I'm not so sure there was any thunderstorm. There was just that one, loud thunderclap, that's all. But whatever caused it may have also started the fire. At any rate, let's head away from the fire."

"Do you think the smell of smoke alarmed the gorrils?" Jeda tugged her basket away from a bramble.

"Possibly, but there's danger on every side. I say we keep going." Spoena looked to the others for agreement.

They nodded.

"All right then, this way."

They traveled an hour when they encountered an ant mound as tall as Jeda. Fascinated, they watched an incessant parade of red ants arduously march in two columns, one going out into the jungle; the other returning with whatever fodder they chanced upon.

"I've heard about these ants," Spoena finally backed away. "Their bite can drive a seasoned warrior insane with pain. Their venom is so strong ten of them can kill a grown man. The elders have tales about coming to Ra-Amawl and encountering them. The stories they tell aren't pretty, nor is it a good idea to repeat them just now. Let's give them a wide berth so they aren't annoyed." Spoena backtracked a dozen paces to avoid contact with the feared blaze ants.

For the next hour they kept trying to turn toward camp, but their path was thwarted by a dismal, dark, and brooding swamp, replete with rotten trees, low-hanging vines draped in moss or cobwebs, brackish water that smelled of decayed matter, scurrying rodents, slithering reptiles, and clouds of famished mosquitos.

Jeda tugged Spoena's sleeve. "The smell of fire is stronger, Spoena. I think it's heading this way; either that or we've unwittingly headed toward it. We'd better soon turn toward camp."

"Don't you think I know that?" Spoena snapped, frustrated at yet again finding a quagmire as she parted a cluster of fern fronds. "Won't this swamp ever end? Reminds me stories of the Swamp Tophet, always spreading out, overflowing with evil beasts."

"Don't talk about such things out here," said Artil.

Spoena's usually tidy hair had come partially undone from snagging low branches and hung in tangles on her face; her jerkin, blouse, and skirt were smudged and torn in places; her shoes, though sturdy, were caked with mud. Worst of all were the bleeding scratches and unsightly insect bites on face, arms, and hands.

Artil fared no better.

Jeda surmised that she herself appeared in much the same state. It was Spoena's expression, however, that caused Jeda the most concern, for her brow was knitted with worry.

"I'm thirsty, Spoena. Can't we scout around for some clear water?" pleaded Artil. "We've been traipsing about all morning and half the afternoon with no refreshment except that little bit of manu, and I've had about all I can take."

Spoena ignored her sister's complaint. "Let's go a little further. If it doesn't pan out, we'll go back." She started off forward again expecting her companions to follow.

"I said let's look for water, Spoena. I can't go on without something to drink." Artil planted her feet and folded her arms across her chest defiantly.

"Artil's right, Spoena," said Jeda. "You need water as much as we do. What are you trying to prove? Let's find some water and rest a bit. That's all we want. Then we'll gladly follow."

"Yes, it's not as if we're going to make it to camp before nightfall anyway." Artil surveyed the surrounding jungle.

Spoena glared.

"Please, we're asking," said Jeda.

Spoena's shoulders slumped and her head drooped. "I guess you're right. I'm sorry for pushing so hard. It's just that I'm responsible for getting us into this mess. If only I had left when Gogar wanted to go. I keep hoping that the next break in the undergrowth will reveal the end of the swamp and we can turn toward home." She sank to her knees and sobbed. "I'm sorry, I'm so sorry. I should've listened."

Jeda knelt beside her and put an arm around her shoulders. "It'll be all right. Besides, it's not your fault alone; we boosted you up the tree. We didn't have to do that. We just need to trust that Logon knows our need and is already providing, either by giving us the fortitude to spend the night in these wilds, or, or, something else."

"Like what?" Artil asked.

Spoena's tears tracked down her smudged cheeks, completing the bizarre image of clownishness. Jeda and Artil couldn't help but laugh.

Spoena, realizing why they were laughing seemed at first insulted, but then joined in. All three laughed until tears washed pink trails down their begrimed faces.

"Drinkable water?" Artil reminded as their merriment subsided.

"Absolutely, water first." Spoena dabbed at her tears, smudging them more.

"Since we still have about an hour of daylight left," said Jeda, "I think we should press on to see where the swamp ends. Whether it does or doesn't, we'll know which direction to take first thing in the morning and can spend all day tomorrow traveling if need be. Agreed?"

"Agreed." Spoena turned a full circle.

Artil solemnly nodded. "I'm scared. I've never been outside camp at night my whole life."

"Well, we'll make nests from tree limbs, like the gorrils did. That way we'll be comfortable, after a fashion, and if anyone discovers our beds after we leave, they'll think they were made by half-men and not three foolish, lost girls."

"And if we hear noises at night, we can make noises like gorrils to scare away predators," ventured Spoena. "Unless, of course, those noises are other gorrils . . . "

"I'll gorril you." Jeda playfully punched Spoena's arm while mimicking, "Ooh, ooh, ooh."

Spoena threw her arm over Jeda's shoulders and wrestled with her. Then Artil joined the tussle, grappling with both of them until all three fell to the ground laughing.

A sudden rustle in the bushes and stomping feet instantly caused the threesome to quit their horseplay and reach for their swords. A doe stood twenty feet away across the clearing as if trying to identify these strange, new creatures in her domain. She stomped a foot again and waited. The bright blue lights they bore piqued her curiosity.

"She's beautiful," whispered Jeda, "and unafraid."

Artil extended her hand as if offering something to eat. At that, the doe bounded into the thickets snorting loudly and crashing through undergrowth.

"Oh, well."

"You offered pretend food? No wonder she bounded off," Spoena giggled. "But that's a good sign. If those gentle animals sleep safely out here, so can we."

"Absolutely!" agreed Jeda. "And, what's more, they have to eat and drink. We must be near a feeding place or watering hole, or both. Let's spread out and see if we can locate some fresh water."

Spoena took the middle position of their sweep, leading by ten steps so the other two on her flanks could keep her in sight. They set off following the deer, but the jungle closed in becoming impassable and they were forced to return. Then they investigated the side the doe entered the clearing and within ten minutes came upon a small, bubbling spring. They drank deeply and washed their faces, necks and arms. Finally, they drank again as a hedge against not finding any more water that night.

"I think, to save time, we shouldn't eat the rest of this manu until we settle in for the night." Spoena opened the lid on her basket. "And, since it'll only take a few minutes to make our beds, we should travel till it's almost too dark to see."

"Lead on," said Jeda.

They trekked another twenty minutes until Jeda tapped Spoena's shoulder. "Spoena, I smell smoke again, stronger. Don't you?"

"I do, but . . . " Spoena held her finger to the tip of her nose, "it isn't a forest fire; it's a cooking fire, clumsily made with smoke yielding wood. We have neighbors."

"Friend or foe?" Artil leaned forward to hear the answer.

"Can't say. It's not likely we'd find friends out here."

Spoena pushed through a clump of fern fronds and stumbled into a clearing littered with tree stumps.

Jeda and Artil pushed through the undergrowth and stood beside her gasping in delight. In the center of the clearing stood a log cabin with a porch. On either side of the doorway were two lighted windows.

~

Bonu rolled over and instantly became aware of every joint and muscle he had. Even his eyelids hurt. He forced his eyes open and noted the sky graying. "What time is it?"

"Gettin' on toward morning, I s'pect," returned the Eroton. Scung sat beneath the recently enlarged entrance holding his Child of the Stars across his lap. Early daylight spilled down on him illuminating just his outline, giving the Eroton a spectral appearance.

Bonu struggled to sit up. Scung came to his newfound friend's assistance, helping him lean gently against the wall. "Uhh, thanks. Is there any water? I'm thirsty. Must be from all the swelling."

"Gots some ready fer yer." Scung handed his water skin to Bonu. "Jest filled it from the waterfall a bit ago, so it be's fresh. How be's yer feelin'?"

"In a word, sore."

Scung's eyes revealed that he caught the hint of humor in Bonu's reply. "Aye, sore. I used ter wake up feelin' thet way all o' the time, whenever I was on leave, or arter a battle. Got so, thet I didn't feel right if summat warn't ahurtin'."

Bonu lowered the water skin from his lips. "Ahh, that's better. Thanks. I'm stiff and sore, but as soon as I can, we should head for camp."

"Yer trusts me enuf ter take me ter yer camp? How does yer ken I hain't jest foolin' yer ter learn where yer camp be's hid?"

"You're a new man, Scung, a brand-new creation. You're one of us now. Of course, I trust you."

Tears welled in the Eroton's eyes. "All me life folks would rather trust a p'isonous snake 'stead o' me. Me only brother died cause he'd rather a trusted me worst enemy than me." He dabbed at his cheeks and turned his head away.

"Don't be ashamed of those tears, Scung. Men were made to cry when emotionally touched, or in pain, just as women and children."

"But I hain't cried since I be's two years old. Thot I'd fergot how."

"That's evidence that you truly are a different man, completely made over by Logon Xychirion."

"Naw, I still be's me. I still feel the same ol' desires fer bad things; an' whut's more, I cain't make nuthin' shine on this here sword." It dropped to the floor. "If'n I was truly Ecclessite now, I'd be able ter sharpen summat o' this blade, doncha think? I been sittin' here fer an hour an all I gots done was wreck two perfectly good files. I don't think this bein' rescued took wi' me. Logon wasted his time, I guesses."

"Impossible. Logon never makes mistakes. We just fail to understand his plan." Bonu slowly rose to his feet, cautiously stretching his limbs and back. His sigh ended in a groan. He leaned over, hands on knees for support. "If you're still your old self, why haven't you killed me while I slept?"

"Huh! I hain't thot o' thet. Why hain't I kilt yer?"

"Because a work has begun in you, my friend. There's more to do, mind you, and the Advisor works from the inside out, so it may be a while before you or I, or others, see much of a difference. But that doesn't mean there's nothing going on. If you don't mind my saying so, you've led a pretty raunchy life up till now, indulging in things that would disgust most Carnalians, let alone Ecclessites; there's so much you need to be taught."

"Logon said thet me sword would help me ter learn, so, if'n I be's a kingsman now, why cain't I git the sword ter teach me?"

"Well, for one thing, didn't Logon tell you to only use the special file called a toller on that sword?"

"Yer means this?" Scung produced the file for inspection. "I done tried an' tried, but it takes so long ter git anything sharp. I decided ter use me regular files an' git the work done quicker."

"And that's why you've gotten nowhere. Your sword is made of a very rare metal, in fact, both, the toller and the sword, are of the meteors that Logon fetched from deep heaven, hence the name Child of the Stars. These metals interact only with each other and will destroy any other tool or weapon they come in contact with. Logon is never in a hurry. He takes his time and does things thoroughly, so that they're perfect in the end, like you will be."

"Me? I doubts thet. Summat the likes o' me kin never git perfect. They's too much evil. Someone like yer now, yer could make it, someday."

"You don't yet understand Logon. He doesn't waste time on merely difficult things; he delights in accomplishing the impossible. I myself wouldn't believe he'd have picked you, but here you are. You're his new creation. I see him in your eyes, Scung. Look, I trusted you; now you trust me. I'll show you how to toll your sword, but you must be patient; rune-work doesn't come swiftly, but, with persistence, it does come."

"Well, I be's willin' ter try, as long as yer be's willin' ter take a chance on me. Will yer brigade accept me?"

"Hmmm, most will. Some have suffered loss in clashes with Erotons. It may be prickly, but Logon has rules governing such situations, so I believe everything will work out." Bonu stiffly crossed his legs and reached around for his sword. "Hey! Where's my—oh, yeah! The dread. Let me see yours for a minute to show how it's done?"

The Eroton yielded his weapon haft first and stared in wonder as more of the blade lit up.

Bonu laid the sword across his lap. After demonstrating proper posture, he handed the sword back.

Scung's lips parted slightly and his brow wrinkled as at his touch the glow vanished from all but the very tip.

"Here, now, hold your sword and poise your toller like this, no, no, the other way around, that's it. Now, let your leg support the weight of the blade and stroke the toller at the point. That's fine, slowly, that's fine."

"But it hain't lit up."

"Do it again, and this time, instead of worrying about whether it's lit up or not, think about Logon."

"Yer means I'm s'posed ter think 'bout Logon? The whole time I tried usin' the toller afore, distractin' thoughts about Logon kept runnin' thru me mind."

Bonu laughed. "Yes, you crazy Eroton, you're supposed to think about Logon. That's the whole idea of lighting up the blade. His power is inherent in the swords to pierce a man's heart without harm and teach him to serve the king. This isn't a weapon for killing humans but rescuing them. As such, they can't harm except whatever opposes King Elyon and Logon. Here, strike me with your sword."

"Be's yer daft? I could break yer bones."

"Try."

Scung stretched forth his sword and touched Bonu's chest. "See, it wouldda cut yer open."

"No, I mean really try to strike me, hard."

Scung playfully jabbed at Bonu's shoulder with more force, but still holding back. Just before it would have touched, the blade veered away, skimming Bonu's sleeve. "Hey! Whuzzat?"

"I told you, Logon's power is in it. It can't harm his loyal followers, except of course, in a disciplinary way; but that would be well deserved and usually delivered by an officer."

"Bonu, look, I gots a rune glowin' on me blade."

"Let me see, well, well. Go ahead, stroke your toller on the edge beside that rune and see what happens. Mind, you should usually start tolling where you last left off, to get an orderly understanding of Logon's ways; but occasionally Logon sends a special, urgent message off what you've been learning."

Scung tentatively filed by the rune. He suddenly looked up wide eyed and exclaimed "Words be's in me mind!"

"Yes, Scung, the Advisor is interpreting the rune to you. You can say them aloud, if you don't mind. I'd like to hear."

CHAPTER THIRTY-ONE

THE SWORD IN SCUNG'S HAND vibrated a short tone as he slid his file across the blade. A look of astonishment crossed the Eroton's grim visage. "Whuzzat?"

Bonu sat straighter. "This is most unexpected. I've heard of this, but . . . Do that again."

Scung complied.

Once again, a vibrant, bittersweet tone filled the chamber.

Then for reasons he didn't fully comprehend Scung began singing to the sword's melody in perfect diction:

> *"Truth spoke Elyon, and true spoke his son,*
> *And true the Advisor, the three who are one.*
> *Then light from darkness burst forth at a word,*
> *Vast spectrum of truth was sighted and heard.*
>
> *Children of Mada rejoiced in that light,*
> *Safe and sound from harm's dark night,*
> *Truth was the source, the life in the garden,*
> *And trust was common, no need for a warden.*
>
> *Subtle and shrewd, with slick tongue of lies,*
> *The spoiler trespassed in creature disguise,*
> *Entered mischief, a vision corrupted,*
> *Distortion, rebellion, serenity disrupted,*
> *Opened a rip, a tear in the fabric,*
> *A portal of falsehood, deadly and sick.*

Mada and Ivi, so innocent, trusting,
Rejected the truth for false, evil lusting.

Somem, the wanderer, the bringer of law,
Foreshadowed Xychirion, restorer of all,
Yet Somem's hard rules could not restore life,
But quickened the lies, and death became rife.

All Mada's children fell through the rent,
Enslaved by death, Lurcan's ploy was well spent."

Scung stopped, his brow furrowed. "Is there no hope for Mada's children?"

"Do you know who Mada's children are, Scung?"

"All people on earth, I reckons, right?"

"Correct. But there is hope. Continue."

"The hope be's Logon, right?"

"Yes, you're about to come to that. Keep filing."

The Eroton bent to his task; as soon as the toller touched the blade, the sweet, sorrowful melody again filled the cave. Scung sang along:

"Till days were complete and Logon was sent,
To undo the lies and sew up the rent,
Proclaiming his mission, exposing lie's hate,
Then yielded himself to his painful fate.

His broken body made whole the gap,
The portal reopened to those in the trap,
And Mada's lost children find their way home,
To Elyon's Splendora, ne'er more to roam."

Scung scraped a few more times but the song was ended. He glanced at Bonu, who nodded. "But, whuzzit mean?"

"It's about Mada, the first created man and first ruler of Psychanan, turning away from King Elyon to obey Lurcan, plunging all Carnalia into the web of Lurcan's lies."

"Ah, so Mada be's why usn's gots born slaves ter Lurcan? Thet degenerate!"

"Think not harshly of your manifold-great grandfather, Scung. Remember, as his descendant, you're guilty of the same things. King Elyon created Mada and Ivi innocent, telling them to report any meteors that fell from the sky. But they chose to trust Lurcan instead of obey Elyon."

"I still doesn't see how this rune about a hole in some fabric connects."

"Elyon created the perfect environment, sort of like a garment, for Mada and his children, everything they experienced proclaimed King Elyon's goodness: everything filling their eyes was beautiful, everything filling their ears was harmonious, everything touching their palates was delicious, everything crossing their nostrils was aromatic, everything that met their senses soothed. In all the realm of Psychanan, as Carnalia was known before Lurcan's invasion, there was no such thing as sickness, crime, pain, strife, wearying labor, or death! Instead, everything proclaimed Elyon's love for his creation and provided abundantly for mankind's nurture and comfort."

"Musta been summat ter behold."

"It was, Scung, it was."

"Yer talks as if'n yer seen it."

"Not with my actual eyes, but it's scribed in the sword runes. As you learn more runes, you'll discover it, too. And you'll understand better what it cost Logon to come into this world corrupted by Lurcan to rescue us."

"Yer keeps sayin' we been tricked ter foller Lurcan, but thet we be's responsible, too. Which is it?"

"Both, actually. True, mankind was deceived, but only because they wanted the valueless baubles deception offered more than Elyon's genuine goodness. No one gets deceived except they willingly compromise what they know to be truth."

"Ridiculous. No one wants ter be deceived."

"Why did you follow Psa? Why were you in Mileer's regiment, under the rule of the notorious Hod-ya? Why had you given yourself to debauchery and mayhem? Because you thought such ways were truth and goodness?"

"Of course not! I didn't ken there was real truth and goodness. I been deceived."

"Yet you participated in violence against innocent victims, against harmless people who never did you any wrong, did you not? Didn't you stop to think that your victims didn't deserve their fate, that you chose to victimize them because you had no options? It was kill or be killed, right?"

"More or less, I reckons. So?"

"So, you prove yourself to be Mada's heir, who victimized his descendants for the sake of temporarily deluding himself with Lurcan's lie. But the great difference is that Mada did it despite having suckled Elyon's goodness. Mada chose to believe Lurcan when it was hinted that Elyon was holding back something wonderful.

"Thus, Lurcan tore a hole, as it were, in the fabric of the perfect environment by deceiving Mada, Ivi, and thereby, their descendants, drawing all humanity through that hole to an inside-out, topsy-turvy world where, instead of goodness, evil was unleashed. Now much of what fills our eyes is harsh and ugly, our ears hear dissonance, all that touches our skin freezes or burns, foods have lost much of their taste and many smells are noisome. Of course, some of the original character of goodness remains in nature, subtly proclaiming Elyon's love and provision, for Lurcan can't corrupt all Elyon's benefits. But mankind has become dull, unable, or unwilling, to recognize evidence of Elyon's influence. Mankind has been seduced into thinking that we are the sum of existence; that there's no accountability except to please ourselves."

"But hardly nobody kens there even be's a good king. Lurcan told us'ns thet the king be's evil. He told usn's thet pleasure be's not allowed in Ecclessa. How are we supposed ter ken different?"

"But you found out, didn't you?"

"Well, yeah, but I warn't lookin' fer no rescuin'! It jest happened."

"Logon sees to it that those who hunger after truth, even if they don't know they're hungering for it, receive an opportunity to be pierced. Fact is, I thought I killed you. That can happen when Logon's sword pierces a man, but he refuses to accept Logon's amnesty."

"So, back ter the rune. Whut's thet part about:
> His broken body made whole the gap,
> The portal reopened to those in the trap?"

"Ah, the crux of the matter. Mada's disobedience created a doorway whereby Lurcan snared the whole human race, dragging us through a portal to a corrupted world, holding us prisoner to suffer with him when Elyon comes to judge the rebellious of both man and kyllorn, or phantom beings."

"I kens thet."

"But Logon allowed himself to die on a stake. His obedience to do his father's will even unto death reopened the portal so Mada's children could escape by refusing the lies of Lurcan and coming back to trust in Elyon's promises. You see, Logon wasn't held in Lurcan's trap, for he never believed or obeyed the lie. He was and is Elyon's statement of truth to Mada's lost race, reversing the effects of the lie. Simply believing in Logon—that he himself became the portal in the fabric leading back to fellowship with his father the king, thus we find our way out of Lurcan's lies."

"Seems too easy. Yer mean, he gives it fer simply believin' him? Doesn't we have ter do summat special, or make some sacrifice?"

"Logon paid it all. When you met Logon on his rock, his blood healed your wound, remember? What could you possibly contribute that comes close to that? To even try is an insult. There's a rune where Logon said, *'I am the portal, the truth, the life, no man comes to my father except through me.'*"

"What about Somem? Why be's he mentioned in the rune?"

"Somem awakened mankind's conscience by showing Elyon's laws; but trying to keep the laws without the power to obey resulted in failure. Human nature is weak, always sliding back to its evil nature no matter how hard one tries to obey. That's why Logon put you to death when you touched his rock and removed your corrupted Mada-nature. Then he gave you life again by putting his own *true* nature in place of your old nature. By believing Logon, you escape final death, which is separation from King Elyon forever, by coming through the portal. And that's why it must be by trusting what Logon did on your behalf and not in any special or valiant thing you've done."

"Amazin'! But, they's summat I still doesn't understand. Why did he even make rules fer Somem ter write if'n he kenned people wouldn't be able ter obey 'em? Givin' usns's a conscience when we couldn't obey seems mighty cruel."

"Scung, you've grasped the essentials of being an Ecclessite. There are brigade leaders who don't have as good a grasp on these truths. Elyon gave Somem some basic laws to reveal to people how fallen they were. When they tried to obey, they couldn't, and that should have led them to seek Elyon's mercy. Instead, Lurcan spawned clever lies denying Elyon's laws, so people regarded themselves as not so bad. Pretty soon they replaced Elyon's laws with rules they could keep after a fashion.

"But Elyon's wrath against those who change his edicts will wait only so long. Someday soon Logon Xychirion will ride forth with a vast army of roamers in judgment. When he does, Lurcan and his dreads, firedrakes, tophets, cusps, and people that follow him will all be condemned to eternal torment."

"I don't ken all o' thet. My head be's full, now as it is. Makes me dizzy. But I sure am glad thet rune sung ter me. Now I kens I belongs ter Logon, an' not cause o' summat I done but simply 'cause he loves me."

Bonu smiled and leaned back against the wall. "Yes, Scung, you belong. And what's more, you've chosen to follow Logon at a most significant time."

"Eh?"

Bonu unconsciously fondled the dagger salvaged from Scung's discarded arsenal, eyeing it, enjoying the unique swirls and sparkling refraction off the highly polished steel. "The first of the dreads has been undone. That's significant. And to think I had a part in that venture, as did you, of course. Quite significant."

~

"It's morning, Jeda." Artil stood over her.

Jeda's eyes opened. She peered at the graying sky out the window. "So, it is, Artil, so it is. No sign of the owners yet?"

"None." Spoena had taken the last three-hour watch. Food was spread on the table: muffins, pastries, eggs, dried meat, butter, nuts, and fruit. Though famished, the girls decided to wait before eating, helping themselves only to water. The previous evening, they scrubbed mud and grime off their faces and washed their scratches, uncovering multiple insect bites in the process. Their garments worn outside their Logon dress, though torn and tattered, were sufficient for modesty and could wait until they returned to camp for repair.

"I could get used to living in a permanent house," Artil stared at the beamed ceiling, "rather than a tent that shudders every time the wind blows."

"I wonder who lives here?" said Spoena. "I mean, who would put all this food on the table and then leave?"

"Maybe they were scared away by the forest fire," suggested Artil.

"I don't think so. The fireplace was lit, too, remember? Nobody lights a fire and leaves for the night."

"Well, how do you explain it?" challenged Jeda.

"I think we frightened them away." Spoena turned away.

"Us?"

"Well, think about it. Suppose you lived in Ra-Amawl on the fringe of a swamp, and one night as you set your table and banked your fire for the night you heard noises from the swamp heading for your cabin. What would you do?"

"But we meant no harm," said Jeda.

"They didn't know that. I think they went for help."

"To Carnalian brigades?"

"Where would you go?"

"We don't know they were Carnalian," interjected Artil. "After all, living in Ra-Amawl doesn't make one Carnalian."

"Good point, but we must assume the worst. I say we help ourselves to some food and be on our way." Following her own suggestion, Spoena opened her basket.

"Ecclessites wouldn't have fled at mere noises, nor would Carnalian soldiers," mused Jeda. "So, who could our unwitting hosts be?"

"Who cares?" Spoena started stuffing food into her foraging basket. "Logon has provided, I think we should make the most of the opportunity and skedaddle."

"It may be too late for that." Artil stared out the window.

Jeda and Spoena joined her. Through the soft gray light of dawn, they saw four people emerging from the woods headed for the cabin.

Spoena hurriedly unpacked her sack while Jeda and Artil backed away to the fireplace. Spoena joined them, tying the thongs of her basket shut.

The door opened. "True, true, Balatz, but I maintain there was something bigger than we know going on." A large, bearded man dressed in fur down to his ankles looked up at the girls and stopped short. "Hullo, what have we here?"

Those behind bumped into him.

"Thoru, why the blastation did you stop?"

"We have guests, Balatz."

The three girls leveled their swords at the newcomers.

"Well, well, so we have," said Balatz, stepping around Thoru. "Thorma, Bletza, take a look." The four spread out into the room shutting the door behind. All were clothed in fur coats with fur leggings down to their ankles and fur-lined boots. Both men, Balatz and Thoru, were bearded with thick bushy eyebrows and magnificent mustaches that covered their upper lips. All four wore fur hats. The women, Thorma, and Bletza, were fair-skinned and dark-haired, their cheeks rosy from the chilly outside air.

"I believe they challenge us to a duel, Thoru. Shall we oblige?"

"By all means." At that, the two men parted their coats revealing grayed tunics of an unusual design as they withdrew swords that had shiny blue spots along one edge.

The girls let out a sigh of relief. "You're, you're kingsmen!" said Jeda.

"Close enough." Thoru smiled. "Please, be at ease. Have you eaten? How long have you been here?" Both men chuckled as they sheathed their swords.

"We came last night, just as darkness fell. We, we haven't eaten from your stores, though we helped ourselves to water. I hope you don't mind." Jeda secured her own sword.

"Mind? Splendora no. Would that you'd have helped yourselves to our sweetmeats as well. Indeed, fall to now," invited Balatz, striding forward. "Oh, I'm forgetting myself. Introductions are in order, are they not? I am Balatz, and this fair young lass is my wife, Bletza. I know, I seem old for such a young maid, but she makes me feel young. This is my brother Thoru, and his wife, Thorma. And you might be?"

"I'm Jeda, of the house of Kway. And these two are sisters, Spoena is the elder, and Artil. We're from a Runer brigade living in the heart of Ra-Amawl."

"A Runer brigade dwells in Ra-Amawl? We weren't aware there were any er, kingsmen, about these parts. How long have you been in the forest?"

"My father came as a young man, even before he was married." Artil helped herself to a muffin. "The whole brigade came into being at Logon's bidding."

"Indeed?" Thorma hung the coats of the four on hooks beside the doorway. "Logon sent you? Way back then? How is it we've never contacted your brigade?"

"We never moved this close to the swamp before," said Spoena. "What brigade are you with?"

"Well, we're not quite with a brigade, exactly. We are what you see. But we follow the rites of the Nutherway brigades." Balatz sat at the table.

"Nutherway brigades? I don't believe I've heard of—"

"No, Miss Jeda, I don't suppose you have." Balatz selected an apple and began coring it. "I see by the light on your sword that you're fairly new to Elyon's ways, and as such, probably only know about the brigades of the sword. There are well-meaning captains in those brigades, but sadly they've never found the deeper truths that the Nutherway brigades have discovered. It's our assignment to understand the mysteries of the runes that declare the end of Carnalia and to call people to follow King Elyon. Are you aware that soon he'll destroy this evil land and all its inhabitants?"

"Yes, we believe that, too. We believe Logon has placed our brigade in Ra-Amawl for some purpose related to that time," answered Spoena.

"Yes, well, for now, help yourselves to breakfast." Thorma glanced at her husband. "We can talk of brigades later."

The three girls didn't need to be asked again. All seven sat at table and helped themselves to a hearty breakfast.

"We were curious," Jeda took another handful of nuts and berries, "as to why this cabin was abandoned, with the fireplace lit and food spread on the table."

"That's not such a mystery," said Thorma. "Bletza and I were waiting our husband's return from hunting last night, having put fresh logs on the fire and supper on the table, when Balatz runs to the door out of breath. He'd seen a battle—"

"Not exactly a battle, Thorma, a rout of some sort that caused men to run panicked through the woods," corrected Balatz.

"Okay, something like a battle, but not a battle. Anyway, we went to gather whatever spoils might have been left lying around. Some things are hard to come by in the wilderness, as I'm sure you know. So, we went off with Balatz. By the time we stashed the loot from the battlefield in a safe place, night creatures were prowling, so we holed up in a cave till dawn. That's about all there is to the mystery, I'm afraid."

Jeda nodded. "Don't be disappointed. We're glad there's no sinister reason behind the empty cabin." She studied the eyes of the women, girls really. Bletza wasn't much older than she, and Thorma but a few years older. "Why don't you leave here and join our brigade? I'm sure Captain Varter wouldn't mind, in fact, he'd be glad to welcome you to our fellowship."

"Uh, that would be impossible," said Thoru. "That's like asking us to forsake steak for stale bread."

"Excuse me?" Spoena stared unblinking at her host.

"Now you've done it, Thoru. You must excuse my brother; he's somewhat zealous, and not very tactful. He didn't mean that like it sounds.

It's just that we have our assignment, you have yours, and we'll only be content doing ours."

"Oh, I see."

"Perhaps," suggested Thorma, "we should share what we believe, and invite them to join us."

"Do you think?" Thoru stroked his beard.

"What can it hurt? Besides, we could always use extra help bringing booty from the battlefield, if you girls wouldn't mind lending us a hand?"

"It wasn't a battlefield."

"Then what was it, when men fight each other, and bodies are strewn everywhere?" There was an edge in Thorma's voice that surprised the three girls; no woman in their brigade would dare snap in such a manner at their husband. Not that the men of the Runer brigade were fierce; in fact, they were quite gentle with their women and children, nevertheless, it would dishonor Logon's name to so disrespect any authority.

Thoru condescendingly answered his wife, "Well, it looked like a battlefield, but there was no sign of an enemy."

"Please excuse this little quarrel. We regard accuracy highly," Balatz spread his hands wide, "which is one reason why we've separated from other brigades."

"How so?" Spoena looked from Thorma to her husband.

"If you must know, we'll be glad to tell you. Of course, not right this minute. Later, after we bring some of the booty, er, if you would be kind enough to assist bringing some things in from the field in question? Later, this afternoon at our leisure we can pursue that discussion. I believe you'll find it most informative, even instructive."

"I don't know." Jeda glanced across the room at the door. "Of course, we'll help bring booty in from the field, as is only decent considering we've feasted at your groaning-board. But as far as staying longer I'm afraid our brigade will be searching for us, so we really should get back as soon as possible."

"Naturally, I understand. But should you change your mind, the invitation remains open."

Bletza added, "Nor should you feel under any obligation. Please accept our hospitality as a gift. If you feel such urgency, you should leave for your own brigade right after breakfast."

Balatz scowled at his wife.

"No, no, we'd like to help," said Jeda. "We should at least do that much."

"Well said, Jeda. I like a girl who recognizes her responsibilities." Balatz wiped his mouth with a napkin.

Bletza cast a curious glance at her husband but said nothing more.

After finishing breakfast all five women made short work of the dishes and stored the leftover food in cupboards. Artil was enthralled with cabinets, the pantry, walls with real doors and the fact that this brigade didn't have to vacate on a minute's notice. The men stacked firewood outside on the porch and drew more water from the well in the yard before getting their plunder sacks.

"Are you ready?" Balatz called from the open doorway.

"Just finishing," responded Thorma. "Is the weather warming up yet?"

"Yes. The sun is shining on the canopy to bring warmth this early. Let's get started."

Each girl was handed a bag large enough to crawl inside. The party set off into the woods following a well-worn trail.

They traveled quietly nearly an hour before Balatz broke the silence, "Here we are."

They stood on a small ridge overlooking a hillside with a pool at the bottom end. A small rivulet tumbled from a cliff. They would normally not have been able to see that far in this thick jungle, but a fire had recently obliterated much of the foliage; there was ample light shining through from above. Trees were strangely bent away from the pool or else lay on the ground, leafless, scarred with burns. A few deceased soldiers lay scattered about amidst vast quantities of weapons, armor, assorted clothing, and mess kits with food.

Jeda started to gag but controlled the impulse; the stench of burned and now bloated bodies wafting over the hillside made her eyes water, so she covered her nose to reduce the foul odor. Spoena and Artil did likewise. The Nutherway brigaders seemed impervious to the redolence.

"What happened here?" Artil stared downhill holding a handkerchief to her nose.

"This must be the fire we smelled yesterday." Spoena slung the empty booty bag over her shoulder.

"Indeed?" Thoru took a step down the hill. "I wonder why more scavengers haven't come."

"When do we bury the bodies?" Jeda stood still, gazing in horror at the carnage.

"We don't, dear," said Bletza. "That's why Elyon made scavenging animals."

Jeda's breakfast rose to her throat; this time she needed to step behind a tree. Afterward, she was better able to bear the bloody scene stretching before them.

"Delicate, eh?" Thoru's voice had a hint of disdain.

"Let's get busy," said Balatz. "Look for rings, jewelry, metal objects, coins, cutlery, tools, clothing, food—anything we can't get from the woods. Scrip money, however, is useless. Leave it. You can't just waltz into an inn or store and spend it, you know. But coins however, can be smelted."

Jeda and the two sisters worked their way downhill into the charred area where there weren't as many corpses. She overheard Thorma say, "Tophets have been busy. There were three times this many bodies yesterday."

Spoena motioned with her head for Jeda and Artil to swing more to the right side of the hill out of earshot. "Something's not right about our hosts."

"I know," Jeda drew alongside Spoena, "but they follow Logon, else their swords wouldn't shine."

"Did you notice that they speak only of the king but seldom his son, if ever. Have either of you heard them mention Logon?" asked Spoena.

"Maybe once or twice," Artil trudged behind, "but not as much as they mention King Elyon."

"King Elyon, Logon, what difference does that make?" asked Jeda. "It's the light of their swords that show their love, not whom they mention most."

"True. I guess we're jumpy because of this macabre chore," Spoena spied a tin cup and stooped to pick it up. "Still, things do seem peculiar: They use a well-worn trail, let alone choosing to live by scavenging. And the way wives brashly rebuke their husbands . . . "

"It seems odd to us, but living out here has its deprivations, as we well know." Artil kicked a stone out of her way. "An event such as this would be a great find for hard-to-get materials. And after all, Logon led us here, too."

"My stubbornness led us here." Spoena brushed a mosquito away. "Let's hope there's not a serious consequence to pay."

"Logon wouldn't do that if we're truly sorry, would he?" Artil asked, her eyes wide.

Neither Jeda nor Spoena answered as they wandered down to the pool at the bottom of the paddock well away from the other four busily plundering the dead. Jeda observed the surrounding devastation.

"Look at this!" she exclaimed. "Have you ever seen such destruction? It puts me in mind of the field of skulls Glend and I saw on the way to Suffer's Tree Inn. That battle must have been similar."

"Remember that thunderous boom we heard yesterday?" asked Spoena. "I'll bet it wasn't thunder at all but an explosion that originated here. Look at the way the trees are bent away from this spot. This pool seems to be the center of the blast. Hello! What's this?" She bent over and picked something up from under foot that was mostly covered by ashes. "A Child of the Stars!"

She pulled it from the dirt and cinders. Light instantly sprang down the blade from its tip to exactly match her own sword's illumination.

"Look at the handle," said Jeda. "It's cracked. And the blade is bent. I thought these were indestructible."

Even as they spoke, the light filling the blade caused the sword to vibrate, straightening the blade. The handle was another matter. It remained cracked, the two birds, a dove, and an eagle, remained split apart.

Artil grabbed Spoena's arm and shushed her sister and Jeda as she pointed to the cliff face looming before them and whispered, "There's someone up there watching us!"

CHAPTER THIRTY-TWO

TINGLES TRICKLED DOWN JEDA'S SPINE. Sure enough, someone large, garbed in Eroton gear and needing a bigger, denser bush was trying to hide.

"Artil, point in a sweeping motion as if at a bird, then return to searching the ground," said Jeda. "Maybe he doesn't know we've seen him."

Artil's arm swept broadly across the cliff and away from the not-so-hidden observer, then she fell to inspecting the ground with Spoena and Jeda.

"Now, turn and slowly make our way uphill towards Balatz. I said slowly, Artil. I know you're frightened, we all are, but we must act as if we don't know he's there."

"Jeda, what are we going to do!" Spoena whispered.

This confession surprised Jeda; Spoena was the adventurous one, most knowledgeable and bravest of the three. Yet, Jeda was the one who felt calm; intimidated, yes; but calm, certain Logon was in control and wouldn't let anything disastrous happen.

"It's all right, Spoena, Artil. Logon provided safe-keeping for us in the wildest place on earth, not to mention supplying lodging and food. Keep trusting."

They reached the uphill edge of the burned area. Jeda finally dared to glance over her shoulder. The Eroton was still huddled behind the shrub. But lo, another man joined him, also crouching low.

"Run, there are more!" Jeda held a sword out in front, hoisting her skirts as she fairly skimmed the ground, jumping deadfalls. Even so she was hard pressed to stay astride of the sisters flying over the broken terrain. Within minutes they stood panting beside Balatz and Thoru, describing the men on the cliff.

Balatz studied the distant cliff-face. "Well, I don't see them, but I believe you. We're finished anyway. Come, each of you lug a bag or two," he indicated several bulging, burlap sacks strewn around his feet. "I trust they're not too heavy. We'll be well on our way back to the cabin before whoever you saw can descend that cliff. Bletza and Thorma have already left with their loot and will have a meal ready by the time we return. I must say, you're not too experienced at looting. Your bags are nearly empty. Never mind, we have more than enough to keep you huffing and puffing all the way to the lodge."

Jeda grunted as she tugged her sack along. "Is it safe to use the trail? I mean, who knows how many Carnalians and Erotons might be back there?"

"Nah, don't bother about them. I counted enough Eroton corpses to comprise a company. The two you saw are probably terrified survivors. After what happened here they won't likely have enough gumption to follow us. Besides, why should they? They have no way of knowing we're not Carnalian."

"They saw Spoena pick up this sword, and it lit up. Then when I handled it, it glowed even more. They must have seen that. They must know we're Ecclessites."

"What? You found an Ecclessite sword?"

"Yes." Spoena paused to regain her breath. "I stubbed my toe on it. See how the handle is split. In fact, before I picked it up the blade was bent, too."

"Come now, Miss, this blade straightened by itself?"

"It's true," affirmed Jeda. "As soon as it lit up the bent metal straightened of its own accord."

"But the handle stayed cracked?" Balatz squinted at the sword.

"But it's obviously an Ecclessite sword" Thoru passed them by, dragging three sacks. "Where did you find it?"

"Down in that burnt area, close by the pool," Spoena pointed.

"So, it was a battle then," Thoru mused. "But who won, Ecclessite or Carnalian? There's an abundance of Carnalian loot lying around, but nothing Ecclessite."

"It's curious," agreed Balatz, "unless the Carnalians fell upon a very small hunting party from your Runer brigade; they're the only Ecclessites likely to be out here."

"Bonu!" Jeda muttered and looked toward the cliff. Had he fallen prey? "Bonu was out scouting alone."

"I doubt a one-man reconnaissance mission caused all this damage. No, this was two equally matched forces. How well did you know this Bonu?"

"She's sweet on him," said Spoena.

"Well, it's not likely it was him. Still, I wonder why there isn't more Ecclessite evidence scattered about."

Jeda said, "This might have been Bonu's sword." Her vision blurred. "There was only this one sword. There's nothing else Ecclessite on this battlefield. It must have been his."

"You're torturing yourself needlessly, Miss," said Balatz. "There's no way one man, no matter how valiant, could effect this havoc on what must have been three companies—nearly half a regiment."

"I . . . I hope you're right." Jeda swiped at her tears. "Hadn't we better get moving?"

"Yes. I'm sure you'll realize your Bonu couldn't have been involved in this fray. Here, heft this load on your back; it'll take your mind off your worries." He hoisted a bag of loot to her shoulders. "There's one for each of you, and two for me. Arrgh!" he grunted under the weight. "Lead on, Thoru, I'll bring up the rear."

The bags were heavy but not as heavy as the men's, so the girls were able to keep pace. They traveled over the same well-worn trail winding through the jungle. An hour later back at the lodge, perspiring and mussed, they deposited all but one of their sacks in an outbuilding.

Thoru kicked a bucket out of the way. "The wives can sort through these another day."

Upon entering the cabin all three girls sniffed a tantalizing aroma of cooking and beheld the groaning board laden with various food-stuffs. They washed up, and, at Bletza's invitation, sat down to enjoy the meal. A few minutes later Thoru and Balatz entered, finished with tidying up the shed.

"Where's Thorma?" Artil asked, glancing around the room.

Jeda caught the wary glance between Thoru and Bletza before Balatz answered, "She, uh, had some outside duties to attend."

"Right." The young wife kept her eyes on her plate.

"She'll be back soon," said Balatz. "In the meantime, after we dine, let us entertain ourselves with a little rune study,"

"We really must head back to our own brigade," said Jeda trying to sound non-confrontational yet conveying that they had other priorities. "They'll be worried about us as it is."

"Yes, yes, of course. But, I'm sure Thorma's errand won't detain her long. She'd hate to miss bidding you good-bye. Your being here has meant so much to her."

"It has?" Spoena looked up suddenly. "We hardly spent any time with her, with any of you, in fact."

"My, but you speak your mind, don't you?" Balatz shot a quick glance toward Thoru. "Truth is, it's been so long since we've had any visitors, believe me, it will mean a lot to her if you wait. Besides, the trek to your own brigade should be started earlier in the day. If you leave now, you'll likely have to spend the night in the forest."

"He's got a point there, Jeda," said Artil.

"Well . . . "

"It's up to you, Miss. Whatever you think best. We don't mind putting you up another night. And that would afford us all an opportunity to get to know each other better."

"I want to leave, Jeda." Spoena stood up. "Who knows but that we'll run into Bonu or a patrol searching for us. As nice as it's been visiting here," she forced a smile, "we need to consider our loved ones, too."

Balatz grinned back through clenched teeth and narrowed eyes. He finally said, "Of course, whatever you think is best."

Jeda was in a quandary. There were good points on each side of the argument and being the eldest if only by a year or two, felt the decision was on her shoulders.

Bletza still didn't look in their eyes for longer than a few seconds. What was she hiding? Jeda's discomfort deepened. "I think we'll take our chances in the forest. But, we'll wait until we can bid farewell to Thorma if she doesn't tarry too long. I haven't had time to attend to my sword today, so I welcome a rune study. When that's done, whether Thorma is back or not, we'll leave."

"Fine, fine," agreed Balatz. "We're merely trying to be good hosts."

"We'll help clean up these dishes." Jeda collected plates and utensils from the table.

Spoena joined her and motioned for her sister to do likewise.

"I think you have enough help," wheedled Artil. "I'll do something else until—"

"Oh, no you won't, lazy hands!" Spoena playfully tugged her sister's ear. Then she winked and mouthed, "Jeda has a plan; play along."

Artil looked up questioningly, but said, "Oh, all right! If you insist."

"Remember what father said he'd do if you slacked on chores."

"Apparently, a severe reprisal," teased Thoru. "My sisters always got out of chores, no matter the consequences." The men laughed and settled by the hearth to investigate the sack they'd brought inside as the women washed, dried, and stashed the dishes away.

As Bletza stacked dishes by the wooden sink, Jeda whispered, "Spoena, do something to distract the men."

Without a moment's hesitation Spoena gabbed the sides of the sink and leaned forward and pointed out the window. "Oh, is that a wolf?"

Jeda, Artil, and Bletza whirled around to stare out the window; the men lounging by the fireplace jumped to their feet.

"Where?" Bletza asked in alarm.

"Oh, it's gone now, if I even saw anything." Spoena winked at Jeda. Till that wink, Jeda herself had been taken in.

"We'd better go out, check the livestock, and have a look-around," said Balatz. "Come on, Thoru, if it's a pack I don't want to be out there alone." They each grabbed a crossbow and went out, shutting the door firmly behind.

As soon as the door was shut Jeda urged, "Bletza, what's going on? You can tell us. They won't know you told."

Bletza's eyes widened and her lips parted. "You . . . there's no wolf."

"Now you can speak freely. Where is Thorma? Has something happened to her?"

"Oh, no, I can't. I'd never, no. Nothing's wrong. Your suspicions are unfounded." She bent to furiously scrubbing a dish, biting her lip and staring out the window. The men carefully, methodically searched the yard for canine tracks, making several passes until Balatz straightened up, turned around looked in the window. His lips became a thin line and his brow furrowed.

"Uh," Bletza said with a start, "he knows! Your diversion is discovered! I won't say aught but you'd better not try anything like that again."

"We haven't much time then. Quick, tell us, are we in danger? You're kingsmen like us, so what harm can come of friend warning friend?"

"Nothing. You have absolutely nothing to worry about. They're coming in now. Act like we've been talking about your brigade."

The door opened and Balatz stood in the doorframe for a full minute observing the women as they talked of how the brigade washed dishes for so many people at once. He said, "We found no tracks, Spoena, perhaps you'd like to show us where you saw this wolf?"

"Well, I wasn't really sure, I thought maybe I saw something big and gray running past quick like a shadow."

"Come out and show us where," the larger, bearded man insisted.

"If the girl wasn't sure she saw anything, maybe it was just a passing shadow. Uh, we're done with the dishes now, dear." Bletza folded a dishtowel and hung it to dry. "Perhaps this would be a good time for that rune study."

Thoru came up behind Balatz and said, "No tracks of wolf, dog, or fox; nothing was out there. The girl's cusp-touched."

"I wasn't really sure," apologized Spoena. "Have predators been a problem?"

"Not until now." Balatz entered the large end of the room with his brother close behind.

"Could we do that rune study now?" Jeda held her sword in hand. "It's getting late and we should soon be on our way. I do hope Thorma gets back. Getting to know Bletza a little more made me think I'd like to know Thorma better, too."

Balatz studied the trio another few seconds. "Sure. It'd be good to start your journey with fresh insights to think about." He sat on a bench and withdrew his sword, as did Thoru. The girls joined him at table but Bletza busied herself at the far end of the room sorting items from one of the loot sacks.

Jeda scraped her toller across her blade.

"What are you doing?" demanded Balatz. "You're not to treat swords like that!"

"Wh-what do you mean?" Jeda looked up. "How else do you sharpen swords?"

"You study the runes, not erase them. Don't you know the damage those things do to a blade?" Balatz placed his sword across his lap and ran a finger down the flat of the blade to a large, raised rune. "Put those awful files away before you dull your blade. Now, look at this rune, the one that reads 'Laws to Scrupulously Keep'."

"You, you don't use tollers?" Jeda held her toller in her hand. "When Logon gave me this sword, he instructed me to use this toller to sharpen it."

"My dear," returned Balatz, "we don't even have tollers. You Brigades of the Sword have so many misleading ideas."

"Such as?"

"Well, since you ask, your most glaring mis-interpretation is the insistence that Logon isn't the chief of the roamers, but you seem to believe that he is actually the same essence as the king himself. Then, there's the belief that the advisor is a person. Our runes clearly show us that it's an impersonal force. Then, you also believe that Logon literally raised his pierced body from the dead—"

Jeda was on her feet. "Who are you?"

Balatz gazed calmly back. "As I told you, we are of the Nutherway Brigades, guardians of the Laws of Somem, and keepers of the Escha Mysteries. I'm afraid it would be a great disservice to let you return to your brigade knowing the untruths they're teaching you."

Artil gasped and said, "Jeda, what's he talking about. We love King Elyon, like we love and are loyal to Logon Xychirion. Why won't they let us go home?"

Spoena was on her feet beside Jeda, hoisting Artil up by an arm. "We're leaving, now."

Thoru lunged across the intervening space and grabbed Artil's sword out of her hand. Instantly the light receded, even the tip was extinguished.

"You, you're not even kingsmen!" said Jeda, her pulse pounding and a crimson flush overspreading her cheeks. "Who are you? What are you?"

Balatz pointed his sword at them as he moved to block the doorway.

Bletza came from the other end of the room with her own sword pointed downward. "I know how you must feel. Believe me, I once was Ecclessite like you, pretending to myself that I'd met Logon; I even tried to use a toller." Her sword had blue on the edges the same as Thoru's and Balatz's. "Then I met Balatz who showed me how to put a lasting edge on my sword."

"Jeda," Spoena spoke in a low tone, "look closely at their swords, look real close."

Jeda scrutinized the weapon. "The blue isn't a real glow like on ours."

"See, they don't shine." Spoena twirled her sword in a circle. "They've laminated metal edges on them that they appear to be aglow, deceiving themselves as much as others. I sensed something strange from the first. You're imitating Logon's glow!" Spoena suddenly lunged, sword straight out at Thoru, though he was twice her size.

Caught off guard, Thoru backed away and snagged his foot in the braided rug, sprawling to the floor. Artil's sword clattered free from his grip. Spoena scooped it up and tossed it to its rightful owner. She then advanced and landed a flat-sided blow to Thoru's stomach. A whoosh of air escaped his throat and he rolled over hugging his belly, gasping.

Jeda took the cue from her companion and lunged at Balatz who was blocking the doorway.

Balatz, however, was prepared and met her sword with his own. The jolt stung Jeda's hand. She dodged at him again, and again, but his sword always parried hers, clanging loudly, sending a tingle from wrist to shoulder each time.

"I've defeated brigade captains. You're not even warriors, but girls. Surrender; let me teach you what the runes really mean? We'll edge your swords, too, so they'll be protected."

"It's true, you can't beat him," said Bletza. "He's one of the best swordsmen in Carnalia. You'll only end up injuring yourself. Trust me. I wouldn't advise you wrong."

Thoru sat up, tears in his eyes, breathing easier, but still incapacitated.

Jeda backed off and stood between the sisters facing the Nutherway captain.

Spoena sidled to one side, keeping her sword aimed at Balatz. "If we all attack at once, one of us is bound to pierce him."

Balatz grinned. "Why don't you just try that?"

"Go," Spoena shouted and leapt forward. Balatz turned her jab away with a powerful thrust. Jeda and Artil followed a split second later but were likewise rebuffed. Artil fell to the floor holding her wrist.

"I told you," pleaded Bletza. "He has the truth; you can't defeat him. He's too powerful. Give up before you get hurt."

Spoena lunged again, but Balatz's sword turned the thrust away from his chest.

"Oww," cried Spoena. "My hand won't hold my sword. I think my wrist is broken! Jeda, could we be wrong?"

Artil looked to Jeda who alone still possessed a Child of the Stars in hand. Doubt clawed at Jeda's mind, but she cried out, "Logon, deliver us. I know that you have not misinformed me, nor has the Advisor. Come defend us."

"I've told you the truth, dear girl, but you refuse it," smirked Balatz. "I'll give you to the count of ten, then I'll disarm you. Your friends are beginning to see the light. It would be so much easier if you just quit all this fuss. One . . . "

Jeda tightened her grip. The runes she'd diligently worked on flashed brightly; she recalled the joy of lighting each one.

"Two . . . Three . . . Four . . . "

"Jeda, could Captain Varter be wrong?" wondered Spoena. Her wrist was discolored and beginning to swell.

"Five . . . Six . . . "

"If we had the truth, wouldn't we win?" asked Artil.

"Seven . . . Eight . . . "

Suddenly Logon's warning from meeting with her at the streamside flashed across Jeda's memory:

> From darkness and night,
> Comes freedom and light,
> 'Neath ocean deeps,
> O'er mountainous steeps,
> Rose up the one,
> Rose up the son,
> Claiming his throne,
> Redeeming his own,
> Reaping the sown,
> Re-gathering the thrown,
> Bestowing fair gifts,
> With zephyrous uplift,
> Thus weak becomes strong,
> And meek endures long,
> As small becomes great,
> Let love dominate.

"Nine . . . "

She'd promised to remember, but she hadn't. She'd forgotten to test friendships. She'd accepted imposters as friends because it appeared they had light on their swords.

"Ten! Well, you can't say I didn't give you a chance. I'll try not to harm you."

Encouragement poured into Jeda's mind: "Don't try to fight him, let your Child of the Stars absorb the blows. Don't use your own strength, allow the sword freedom to respond. Remember to love and forgive, even him. Your strength is Logon, and he won't move through you unless you choose to love."

"Logon, help me," was all Jeda had time to utter.

Balatz assailed with a furious rain of blows intending to end the matter quickly. But Jeda's sword rose of its own accord and met each strike. She was staggered as her hand received the jolt of his hammering blows, but the shock wore off rapidly. Balatz's brute strength forced her backward across the room, but in the drubbing, she found the ability to forgive, not because she wanted to, but because it was Logon's will. With her back against the wall, it was all she could do to handle her sword.

Balatz pressed the attack, confident of victory, but during the next barrage of blows a strange sound rattled whenever their swords met: *clang-slap, clang-slap.*

Beads of perspiration broke out on Balatz's brow. "You've got grit, girl, I'll give you that. Scrawny as you are, you deliver quite a blow." His brow furrowed in deep, angry lines as he renewed his efforts. So intense was his onslaught upon her that he didn't notice the *clang-slap-ap* accompanying each swing of his sword. Determined to end this frustrating duel, he lifted his sword high overhead in both hands. "If you get harmed girl, well it's your own fault for resisting."

Looking at the threatening weapon hovering over her, Jeda softly started singing:

> *"From darkness and night come freedom and light,*
> *'Neath oceans deeps, o'er mountainous steeps,*
> *Rose up the one, rose up the son,*
> *Claiming his throne, redeeming his own,*
> *Reaping the sown, gathering the thrown,*
> *Bestowing fair gifts with zephyrous uplift,*
> *So weak becomes strong and yet remains meek,*
> *And small becomes great as love dominates."*

Balatz's face turned crimson; fury trembled in his shoulders.

Seeing the rage about to descend on her, Jeda thought surely this blow would, at the least, shatter her arm.

He bore down, his sword descended.

Her arm didn't even quiver as it met his blow! *Clang-slap-ap.*

"Oww!" He stepped back to reassess his opponent. As he did, he looked as if for the first time at his disintegrating sword, noting the lamination coming loose from the edge. Jeda instantly saw that underneath the lamination it wasn't even an Ecclessite sword, but a black-iron imitation.

"There is only one sword that Logon gives which no other weapon can stand against!" Jeda lunged forward and engaged Balatz's sword. It felt like she was slicing through a stream of water; there was no impact. The lamination skittered to the floor as Balatz's sword fell into shards.

"Oww!" Balatz dropped the handle of his shattered blade and fell to his knees gripping his wrist.

Jeda leveled her weapon at Balatz's heart. But another thought welled up in her mind: "His heart is too hard. Flee immediately!" Jeda hesitated. Why would the Advisor tell her to let the villain off?

"Go on, finish it, Jeda," Spoena rose to her feet rubbing her wrist. "Pierce his heart. Teach him a lesson."

"Uh, I'm not sure. I . . . "

"What are you waiting for? Pierce his heart."

"I'm not sure it's Logon's will."

"What? It's always Logon's will when you win a battle to bring them into the king's realm."

"I suppose you're right." Jeda gritted her teeth, wrapped both hands tightly on the haft and thrust.

A look of horror crossed Balatz's face as the sword penetrated. He collapsed with a groan.

Bletza screamed hysterically and ran to her husband's aid. "What have you done? Witch! Get out of here. Get out! They're coming for you! Get out!"

Jeda looked around the room in confusion. "Maybe you should come with us."

Balatz, though in distress, was able to sit up. "No, just get out of here, leave us."

Jeda sought for words of apology. "I only meant it for his good, for all your good. You need Logon, come with us, please. I can't leave you in this condition. Bletza, surely you understand. You followed Logon once, convince your husband."

Bletza slapped Jeda. "Get out! Don't you understand, you've done enough. Get out before they come to get you."

Jeda stepped back stunned. She'd expected rejection when she pierced Tressa's heart, but this was different. Was it because the Advisor hadn't sanctioned this? She'd presumed to act on her own. She looked helplessly to Artil and Spoena. "What do we do?"

"Grab some supplies and git." Heeding her own advice Spoena headed for the cupboards. "Artil, get a water skin and fill it. There are some hanging outside by the shed. Jeda, help me gather food in our baskets. I figure they owe us that much for the way they lied about being kingsmen, tried to kidnap us, and used us like pack-mules to haul their loot."

"I suppose that's all right. But, we'd better hurry; it seems someone is coming for us."

Artil scampered outside, closing the door behind. A second later the door was flung open. Artil stood on the threshold empty-handed.

"Artil, quit playing around," snapped Spoena. "Get a water—"

Behind Artil was Thorma, pinioning the young girl's arms behind her back. Behind Thorma stood the black-clad form of Hod-ya, flanked by seven dronnets.

CHAPTER THIRTY-THREE

"Does yer hear summat?"

Bonu looked up at his oversized friend. "No, not really. What's it sound like?"

"Voices."

"Really?" Bonu rose stiffly, stood beside his benefactor and cocked his ear. "I don't hear anything."

"Hain't makin' noise now. I'm goin' up ter have a look-see." The giant Eroton hoisted himself over the lip of the adit. His visage appeared in the hole looking down. "Yer waits down there 'til I sees whut be's afoot."

"Glad to oblige," said Bonu. And he was, for just rising to his feet awakened bruises and aching muscles. "This is the price of falling in love."

"Yer say summat?"

"Just reminding myself to never fall in love again."

"Yer sure picked a peculiar time ter be thinkin' 'bout romance. Hold on, summat be's movin' down below. Two, no, three, no, there be's more up the hill, too. Looks like six or seven o' em altogether. Scavengers! Pickin' off'n the dead. Bad as tophets, 'cept human scavengers smells worse, in a manner o' speakin'. I thot it mighta been Hod-ya an' her lackeys."

"Oh, did they survive the conflagration?"

"I seen 'em climbin' the cliff when Psa blowed. They was knocked off'n the cliff, but I don't see 'em lyin' around. What happened to 'em

440

arter that I cain't say fer sure. If'n I moves careful-like, I kin probly git ter thet bush an' git a clearer view."

Silent as a shadow Scung moved away from the entrance allowing light to fall full on Bonu's face. He was glad for the sunlight, and glad that he was still alive after his foolhardy exploit.

"Thank you, Logon." He settled back down to the cave floor and took a swig of water. Out of habit he reached for his sword and was struck afresh by its absence. He searched the cave for Scung's, but the giant Eroton had it with him. "Well, we'll just have to go down the cliff and find mine. I'm not about to wander about Ra-Amawl without my Child of the Stars."

He busied himself with an inventory of his arsenal: his cross-bow and darts were lost when he leapt into the pool; he still had a hunting knife in his boot; a sling with a few stones in a pouch which he'd left by the bush. He also had his blow-tube with four darts—highly effective at close range—for edible animals only, and of course, the dagger from Scung's discarded arsenal. But that wasn't to be used as a weapon . . . unless . . . he needed to defend himself until he got his sword back. The brigade was too far away to obtain a new sword, and Ra-Amawl far too dangerous to travel without weaponry.

He rose to his feet again, went to the opening and called softly, "Scung?"

"I hears yer, laddie, but heshup! I doesn't want them scavengers ter ken we be's up here in case they be's friends o' Mileer."

"Mileer is still alive?"

"Hesh!"

"What's happening?"

"They found yer sword."

"What? My sword!"

"Heshup! They'll hear if'n yer don't qwitcher squawkin'."

"I'm coming up."

"Sssss! They's pointin' right at me. Stay still."

Bonu paused. "What's going on? How many? Are they armed?"

"Worse, they be's women-folk. Three o' 'em."

"Three women? What are they doing out in the jungle?"

"Summat people lives hereabouts close ter the road whut makes their livin' off o' whutever they kin find. A battlefield be's a boon. I cain't tell if'n they seen me or not. Now it looks like the one whut was pointin' at me was jest pointin' at a bird."

"What are they doing with my sword?"

"Funny, it looked like it glowed when they picked it up. Nah! I guesses not. Musta been sunlight hittin' it."

"Help me up." Bonu seized the lip of the entry and tried to haul himself up, but only got half way out of the adit before his arms and shoulders rebelled. He dropped back to the cave floor, groaning.

"Now yer done it. They musta heard yer carryin' on. They's leavin'."

"Owww, oohh, what about my sword?"

"Took it along. The oldest one took it in her hands; the sun glinted off it real purty when she did."

"What does she look like?"

"Hard ter say. She gots yeller hair, an' is a mite scrawny, if'n yer asks me. She might even be purty, too, but I cain't tell from up here."

Bonu shook his head. "No, no! It can't be. She's leagues away. Still, Scung, lift me up. I can't make it on my own. It's important that I see for myself. I'll know if it's who I think it is."

"But they'll see, an' if'n it ain't who yer s'pects . . . we could be in a vat o' hot oil afore long."

"Got to take that chance, Scung. Here, take my arms, and no matter how much I yell, pull me up."

"Well, seein' as they's movin' away anyhow, and ain't callin' fer troops, I guess it be's okay." Scung stepped over to the hole and dipped his brawny hand down to grip Bonu by the collar, extricating him with a minimum of effort.

Bonu gritted his teeth but made no outcry. Being lifted up and out provided just what he needed, a good stretch. The discomfort quickly passed, and some flexibility returned.

Scung set him down gently, asking, "Be's yer awright?"

"Omph, aw, yes, just, let me get my breath. Ooooh, that hurt. But, I needed that. Thanks, Scung. Now, where are those women?" Bonu shook his limbs and arched his back as his eyes followed Scung's point.

"Way up yonder, by the edge o' the burn. See 'em? Does yer ken 'em?"

Even as Scung pointed, the blonde carrying Bonu's sword turned and looked back.

Bonu and Scung ducked behind the small bush. "I can't quite, maybe, I don't know. It's too far. If I could see her closer . . . " He then glimpsed the sword in her hand, which shone bright blue several inches from the tip. "Jeda!"

The three girls were at the shady ridge where the leaf canopy was unharmed. Some men close by were gathering objects off the ground.

"Well, if'n they kenned who yer be's, I'd say yer ain't too popular."

"They'd have no way of knowing it's me, especially with a huge Eroton, er, sorry, I didn't mean—"

"Belay thet thought, laddie, I takes naught offense. Be's yer sure the lass is who yer kens?"

"As sure as I can be without getting closer. She moves like her, has her shape and hair, and brightness on her sword. Oh, Logon, if that's Jeda, please watch over her. Scung, we need to catch up to them."

"Be's yer daft? Yer ain't fit enuf ter climb neither up nor down."

"How did you get me up here?"

Scung stared at his mentor for a moment, then grinned and said, "Oh awright, I kin do it again, I guesses. But yer gots ter walk fer yerself oncet we gits down."

"Agreed."

"Lemme gather the rest o' our stuff then we'll be on our way." Scung dropped into the hole of the cavern and, ignoring his discarded arsenal, collected their gear, including a leather bag of dried food and a precious water skin Bonu had stashed there previously. He tossed them up to Bonu, then hoisted himself out. "Thet be's thet! Be's yer ready?"

"Ready as I'll ever be, I guess." Bonu strapped the gear to himself and climbed aboard the broad back of the rescued Eroton.

Scung turned his face to the cliff and dangled a leg over the precipice groping for a foothold. It seemed to Bonu that going down with a load on his back would be more difficult for Scung than climbing up, for toeholds couldn't be spotted from above but had to be felt; nonetheless, many good chinks availed themselves to Scung's probing hands and feet. Beads of sweat broke out on the giant's forehead but he didn't complain.

Twice bushes pulled loose from the rock under the combined weight of the descending kingsmen, threatening to plunge them both to the rocks below. The water in the pool that had cushioned Bonu's

leap would provide no such buffer now for it no longer was the collected waters of a sparkling stream plunging merrily off the plateau
to form a reservoir. Now it was little more than a shallow puddle, dark
and foreboding, befouled by burned and decomposing corpses.

"Scung, don't fall into the pool, whatever you do."

"I be's tryin' me best not to, laddie. Did yer think I be's needin' a
bath?"

Bonu chuckled. "No, of course not. I'm just a little nervous not
being able to help."

"Yer didn't help none when I brung yer up, but yer sure was a whole
lot quieter then."

"Sorry. I won't say any more." And he didn't, even when the ledge
under Scung gave way without warning, crashing to the rocks thirty
feet below. Fortunately, Scung had been testing a vine when the ledge
gave out. The two dangled precariously for several moments with Bonu
hugging the Eroton's shoulders and neck, sending urgent thoughts to
Logon. When the vine supported their weight and reached nearly to
the ground, Scung forsook feeling for crevices and descended hand
over hand to the forest floor.

Once down Bonu released his hold. His feet landed on ashes sending little gray ash-puffs into the air. "Well done, Scung. For a moment
there I thought, well never mind."

"Yer be's worried? I thot we be's gonna see Splendora."

"Now, show me where those girls went. I'm a pretty good tracker
if I say so myself; we'll follow their spoor and find out just who they
are and what they're doing in the wilds."

"I, uh, I wants ter ask yer summat, Bonu. Please don't be takin' it
wrong, but does yer want me sword? I mean, jest 'til we gits yers back?

I doesn't ken how ter use it yet, and yer hain't got no weapons 'cept a knife an' blow gun which ain't gonna be much use."

"Thanks, Scung, but no, at least for the moment. You keep it. Should the situation arise, I'll let you know. Meanwhile, you should think of it as your only weapon. You're now a soldier of life, bringing life, not death. Remember that. Now, about those tracks?"

"Right. Over yonder, look, those thet be's slightly larger must belong ter yer lady, eh? Course, things in Ra-Amawl ain't always whut they seems."

Bonu knelt and gently touched the separate sets of tracks. "Yep, they're from my brigade all right. See these two hashes on the heel? Everyone in our brigade wears them so our scouts can distinguish our tracks from others."

"I sees 'em. I'd a never seen them slashes if'n yer hadn't pointed 'em out. I don't see them marks in these prints though. Mebbe she hain't who yer thought arter all, eh?"

"No, Scung, that makes it more likely to be Jeda. She just recently joined our brigade and hasn't marked her heels yet. This one's probably Spoena, she's been hanging out with Jeda recently. I don't know who the other is."

Without further conversation the two kingsmen followed the tracks up over the hill and across a small ravine to the ridge where the girls had broken into a run. "Ahh, Jeda, if only you'd known I was—but then, maybe you'd have run faster."

"I thot she be's yer beloved? Why would she run from yer?"

"It's a long story, Scung, and a painful one. But, to make it short, the reason I came out here on my own was because she turned away my intentions. I was so broken-hearted, I needed time to be alone. In fact, the whole raid on your dread—"

"He ain't my dread!"

"Oh, right, sorry, the whole raid on *the* dread came about because of my depression over her. Dumb, huh?"

"If'n yer says. I don't ken how kingsmen does things, includin' fall in love and such, so whatever yer says goes. Look here," the Eroton pointed at the ground, "two sets o' man prints, and without them slash marks. Whut makes yer o' thet?"

"I don't know. The girls fled to their protection, that's hopeful. Perhaps another brigade arrived, and the camp is on the move again."

"Yer quite sure yer brigade will accept thet I been ter Logon's Rock an' all?"

"Just show them your sword. Every true kingsman has at least the tip of his sword aglow."

Scung withdrew his sword and examined it. "So, it be's. An' summat o' whut I tolled afore yer gots awake up be's still a glowin'. I truly be's a kingsman!" His happiness was spread ear to ear. "It be's a joy ter ken Logon, don't it? I never kenned happiness the likes o' this afore."

"Uh-huh. Back to the business at hand. Do you have any idea where these tracks are leading?"

"Nope. I been jest a soldier marchin' wi' the regiment. This section o' forest is new ter me, though I ken summat o' the lands south o' here, tother side o' the road."

Bonu pored intently over the ground. "Odd, they make no attempt to conceal their tracks. One man leads off, the three girls in the middle, and the other man follows, no false trails, no wipe-outs, nothing. Wouldn't you think someone spotted by enemy troops would be more discreet. Look! I don't believe it, they use a trail, an actual trail, well-worn and much traveled."

"Mebbe this be's the false trail?"

"Mmm, I doubt it. There's too much evidence this trail is used regularly. They're unconcerned about being discovered in such wild environs. Something is amiss."

"Hey, Bonu. I found summat." Scung, having ranged out further, pointed at the ground. "More tracks o' women, I'd wager."

Ignoring his aches and pains, Bonu joined him. "Let me see, yes, yes, two other women, dragging heavy burdens, going the same direction." He straightened up and studied the lay of the land. "Now why would they travel, heavily burdened, along a well-worn path making no attempt to cover their trail, unless . . . Scung, we've got to hurry."

"Whassa matter?"

"The only reason someone out here doesn't hide their trail is if they aren't in enemy territory. Whoever these girls are following is on friendly terms with Carnalia. And the girls, for whatever reason, don't seem to be aware. I fear treachery."

"Does yer want me sword now?"

"I'll let you know."

Bonu bent once more to studying the imprints, then rose and started off at a slow jog, maintaining full concentration on the tracks. The two trails merged. "These two women left first. Their tracks are nearly obliterated by the others? I wonder how much earlier they left? Did you see other women?"

"I seen three, mebbe four people at most up on the ridge, but couldn't tell if'n they was male or female." Scung trotted alongside Bonu who mostly kept his eyes to the ground while Scung scanned their surroundings for foes.

Despite dangers and toils ahead, Scung evidenced being filled with joy. He acted like a new man, as if, deep inside he no longer needed to justify his past cruelties. His face gleamed with the knowledge that he was forgiven for each and every Ecclessite or Carnalian he'd victimized!

"Quick Scung, hand me your sword." Bonu had stopped abruptly and was nearly trampled by the close-following giant. They were atop a slight descent with a small creek dribbling over mossy rocks at the bottom.

"Whut?" Scung whispered, handing his sword to his lieutenant.

"Shhh! Do you smell anything?"

Scung sniffed. "Swamp?"

"Maybe. Maybe something else, like a tophet. Are there any swamps around here?"

"I dunno." Then, seeing what his sword had become in the lieutenant's hand, he gasped, "Whut be's yer done ter me sword?"

Bonu glanced at the sword, which was glowing far more than when in Scung's possession. "Oh, that? That's not unusual. The light of Logon goes into the man, or woman, commiserate with the time spent tolling. No matter whose sword he touches, the light in him glows on the sword to the same amount. Here," he said, handing the weapon back.

Scung retrieved his Child of the Stars and instantly the blue light receded to the tip and a fraction of an inch on either side.

"You've added a nice little bit, Scung. But, let me have it back for now, just till we know whether we face a tophet or merely approach a swamp."

Scung handed the sword back to Bonu. "Funny, I thot I had more lit than this."

Bonu led down the incline, the sword held tentatively out.

"Be's yer daft? Yer gonna fight a tophet?"

"The smell is so faint that if it is a tophet, it's only one, and a small one at that. And probably not near. Come, stay behind me. I've fought off lots of tophets. It's dreads I'm not too familiar battling yet."

"I never kenned kingsmen be's so fierce. We always thought yers be's sissies."

Bonu balanced precariously on stones that protruded out of the stream. Scung, whose longer legs easily carried him across the creek in one stride, waited on the bank.

Bonu tested the air, sniffing deeply. "Well, if it's a tophet, it's a long way off. But it's probably swamp gas. This creek must flow to it. And the trail we've been following veers in the same direction. Why would they head for a swamp? There's so much contrary to common sense. What do you make of it?"

"Like I said afore, there's folk hereabouts, livin' off'n the land. Some be's pretty well set, livin' in cabins, some lives in caves an' holes, more like varmints than humans. Does yer think yer ladyfriends took up wi' swamp dwellers?"

"Not likely, unless they were lost. And our brigade did just move to this part of the forest, so that's a distinct possibility. None of them would be familiar with the lay of the land yet. Well, if Jeda is one of those you spied, she'll try to pierce the hearts of any that don't know Logon."

"Aye, she seems ter have pierced yers."

Bonu flashed a quick smile. "Wait till you meet her. She'll capture your heart, too. Here, you might as well have your sword back, we'll not encounter any tophets." He crossed the creek and climbed the far bank.

Scung took one last look around and when satisfied all was safe, followed.

"I'm feeling much better. My muscles are loosening, though the bruises still hurt."

"Glad ter hear thet. I got yer outta the beating as quick as I could, but not afore yer got pummeled senseless. No real harm done."

"Uh-oh." Bonu bent to the ground. Scung paused, looking over Bonu's shoulder. After a long minute, Bonu glanced in every direction before saying, "Craniantium lion. It's trailing them, looking for an easy meal. I hope those men know their business."

Scung checked over his shoulder. "Does yer reckon they be's more?"

"Can't say, but they usually run in prides. Not too long ago I led a patrol that fought off half a dozen cats, killing at least one and wounding others. I wonder if this fella's part of that pride? I read no sign of injury, but that may not mean anything. Wish I had my cross-bow."

"I wish I still had some o' me weapons. I'd be willin' ter face anything o' flesh an blood wi' me mace or battle axe, even a Craniantium lion. I dunno," he said doubtfully, "if'n I kens enuf ter use this sword yet; it gots hardly any light and be's powerful hard ter manage."

"Your old weapons were used against Logon, Scung, and would be harmful for you to keep. Anything that was in Lurcan's service must be destroyed or gotten rid of, else using it could potentially draw you back to Lurcan."

"I reckons yer kens best. But I kenned how ter use them weapons. This one . . . "

"Logon won't put you in any battle too great for your skills. But you must fight each fight he brings your way as preparation for the more severe battles to come. I've seen unprepared warriors harmed. But as you've demonstrated, you're making the most of your opportunities to sharpen your blade. You'll be ready for whatever Logon allows, including a Craniantium lion."

Scung said nothing as they continued tracking the people, going slowly, keeping a special watch out for any more lion imprints; but the cat seemed more curious than hungry and wasn't pressing his hunt.

"I be's not afeered ter die, leastways, not like I used ter be. I give me life ter Logon; anything happenin' ter me be's his concern. If'n he wants me ter die by a Craniantium lion, then thet's whut this worthless life he purchased is gonna do. An' if he continues ter spare me, then I be's gonna live ter serve him."

Bonu turned and faced the giant squarely. "Where did you hear that?"

"I hain't heered it nowheres. I thunk it out, jest now as we was walkin'. I ken whut I was afore Logon healed me, an' it ain't worth bein' thet no more. Thet was decided afore I even touched Logon's Rock. Ter spare this miserable flesh when Logon calls me out would be ter lose whut Logon promised."

Bonu shook his head and grinned. "You'll make a proper kingsman, Scung, if you keep that attitude, and you'll do much service for the king." Bonu peered through the surrounding undergrowth. "There's a clearing not far ahead. It may be their camp; I don't want to blunder into their midst. What say we split up? I'll circle around to the north while you sneak over to the western side and lie up in those conifers. When I give a hawk's scree, rush the campsite. If that looks unwise, I'll hoot like an owl, and we'll meet back here to reassess. If there's nothing there, we'll meet on the far side. Agreed?"

"Agreed."

Each went his way, maneuvering cautiously through the under-brush. Bonu kept an eye peeled, not wanting to accidentally barge in upon the lion. The smell of swamp grew stronger; but wasn't as putrid as a tophet. He did wish he had his sword, however. He crept to the fringe of the clearing where the bushes thinned.

A cabin was situated in the middle; stumps cluttered the ground, but no garden had been planted. This wasn't how Ecclessites lived in Ra-Amawl. Jeda and her friends hadn't fallen in with kingsmen, of that he was now certain. He melded into the shrubbery and waited, watching both the cabin and the western fringe of the clearing for Scung's arrival to his post. Someone that large would be hard to miss even under Ra-Amawl's gloomy flora. He shifted to get a better look and saw a dark form stealthily creeping beneath the drooping conifer limbs accompanied by a very small, but bright blue dot.

He smiled and switched his gaze to the cabin. Smoke poured from the chimney. Bonu prepared to scree like a hawk but stopped when his eyes detected something on the turf just before him. A lion's paw print, round as a kettle, was embedded in the ground. He studied the track, not wanting to broach the clearing until he interpreted the lion's intentions. Fifteen feet away was another indentation, another lion track. This lion had been running. Was it in attack or flight? Seeing that it was headed away from the cabin, Bonu assumed the latter.

What would cause one of those giant cats to flee? A troop of half-men, perhaps, but the cat wouldn't run, he'd merely avoid them, casu-ally walking around them. No, something else chased this cat away.

He studied the cabin's windows where silhouettes of people walked back and forth inside, but, as the windows were covered with gauze, he couldn't even tell if they were male or female. A tophet might cause a lion to flee, but wouldn't be welcomed into a human abode, nor would a dread. A column of Carnalian regulars, or a couple of dronnets might cause a lion to flee.

Bonu longed for his sword. Was Jeda a captive? He and Scung might pull off a rescue if that were the case, if he had his sword.

The cabin door opened, and a girl toted a basin of water out and dumped it on a flower bed.

The open door presented a chance to charge and catch any unwary soldiers by surprise. He might even, if Logon willed, find his sword before those in the cabin knew they were under attack.

Bonu *screed* like a hawk.

Bonu saw the large man twitch then break cover, his long strides crossing the yard swiftly, his sword with its tiny blue dot valiantly pointed at the doorway ready to rescue lives for the king. Bonu burst from cover and dashed as fast as his aches and pains allowed, trying to not startle the girl who had stooped to pull some weeds from her flowerbed.

In another moment the two kingsmen would invade the lodge and see what was what.

CHAPTER THIRTY-FOUR

BONU ARRIVED IN A RUSH terrifying the girl who recoiled with a squeal and fell into her flowers. Scung paused and bent over her, finger to his lips. The kingsmen nodded at each other, lowered their heads and jumped through the doorway.

The other girl spun around and dropped her cooking-pot at the sight of a huge Eroton and an Ecclessite bursting through the doorway. Scung waved his sword about menacingly as if to make up for it having the barest pinpoint of blue; while Bonu feverishly searched the room, moving various items, overturning baskets and chairs.

Bonu made his way to the kitchen where he stopped and apprised the young woman. "Where are they?" he demanded as he strode back to the center of the room.

Scung took one last look around and stepped back outside. A moment later he returned dragging the girl in from outside by the arm.

"I said, where are they?" Bonu demanded of the girl still at the sink who hadn't recovered from her shock. "And where is my sword?"

The one held by Scung looked up at the giant and replied, "You, you're from their brigade? I knew no good would come of this. I told Balatz to let them go, let them return."

Bonu approached the girl dangling by an arm in Scung's grip. "Where did they take them?"

"Hod-ya, she—"

"Hod-ya? Be merciful, Logon! Hod-ya took Jeda and the others? Where?"

"I, I don't know. Balatz, my husband, tried to persuade the girls to join our brigade, but they refused. If only they'd have joined our brigade, we wouldn't have turned them over, would we, Thorma?"

"Your brigade? What brigade is that?"

"Nutherway Brigade."

"Nutherway! If they had joined there'd be no need to turn them over to Hod-ya. Where did that evil woman take them? Quickly girl, tell me; we haven't all day."

Thorma muttered, "Are you going to stab Bletza and me, too?"

Bonu cocked his head. Restraining his anxiety, he asked, "Just what went on here? Tell me. We won't hurt you. As soon as you tell us what we need to know, we'll leave. I promise."

Thorma raised her eyes. "You'll leave if I tell you where they went?"

"That's all we want to know, where are the girls from our brigade, and my sword. Then we'll leave." He peered into her eyes. "What went on here."

"You won't stab us?"

"It wouldn't do any good unless you're willing. Piercing your heart without the Advisor's direction would only make needless suffering, and that I'm loath to do."

"She, Jeda, near to killed Bletza's husband."

"That doesn't sound like Jeda. Are you sure?"

"She attacked Balatz without warning. Now he's crippled with pain. He was our captain. What are we supposed to do without him? He had a treaty with the Carnalians so that they left us alone, but now he's incapacitated."

Bonu eyed Bletza, still held in Scung's brawny hand.

"Where's your husband?"

"Abed," she pointed to a curtained-off room. "He sleeps now. Don't disturb him."

"He's been wounded by a Child of the Stars?"

"Yes, but please don't disturb him. Whenever he's wakes, he's in great pain. I'll tell you what you want to know, just don't disturb him."

"My sword, where's my sword?"

"Hod-ya did it, along with the other Ecclessite swords—broke them in pieces. Over by the fireplace, in the basket, see the pieces?"

Bonu saw a tall basket by the fireplace containing jagged shards of gray metal.

"Balatz thought he could smelt them down and create a better sword out of the pieces for our brigade, but the pain in his heart was too great. Since you need a weapon, and yours is obviously ruined, feel free to take any you see here," she said, indicating a laminated sword. "It's almost as good."

"You don't understand. Your swords are cheap imitations, lacking Logon's power. It's Logon's power that I need, not just a weapon." He went to the fireplace and peered into the basket examining the fragments.

Scung closed the outer door firmly, then, after directing Bletza to sit beside Thorma, joined Bonu. "What're yer gonna do?"

Bonu sighed and said, "I don't know. I can't rescue Jeda without a sword, but I can't bear not to try." He idly picked up the handle with the two birds split apart. As soon as his fingers enclosed around the haft the dove and the eagle melded back together in one solid piece again as certain runes lit up on that portion of the blade.

The women now seated at the table gasped.

Scung's eyes widened.

Bonu's lips parted in a smile. Then he touched the jagged end to a piece in the basket. With a loud snap the pieces joined.

Bonu stepped back, surprised, waving his partially re-assembled sword. "Look at this! Would you look at this! Not even a seam! Logon said that his word could never be broken, that Carnalia, and even Ecclessa would someday be broken, but never would his word be broken. Not even Hod-ya and her witchy powers, nor the dreads she communes with can destroy Logon's word."

"Look, Bonu, another piece down in the basket be's glowin'."

Bonu lowered his incomplete sword into the basket. *Snap!* The glowing piece leapt like an iron filing to a magnet and joined itself to the blade. Even as Bonu watched the final piece of his sword, the tip still in the basket, began glowing. Bonu touched the end of his sword to it, and with a final *crack* the sword in his hand was whole and sound.

Bonu exultantly faced the astounded women. "Almost as good as a Child of the Stars? I think not!"

At that moment the curtain at the far end of the room parted and Balatz stepped from an antechamber into the main room. His eyes were bloodshot and his face ashen. Sweat soaked his shirt, his collar was open to the wound in his chest, which festered. He leaned heavily on a nearby chair.

"Who are you?" he gasped. In his hand he dragged a laminated sword behind with its tip scraping the floor.

Bonu sized the man up. "You're in dire need. Unless you immediately go to Logon's Rock, you'll likely die a gruesome death. And after that, worse."

"A curse upon your Logon and his rock," retorted Balatz.

Scung stepped forward, opening his shirt at the chest revealing his own freshly-healed scar. "Lookee here," he urged, "see, I got wounded dreadful jest yesterday. Logon healed me, jest by touchin' me wi' his blood. I hurt like thet, too, but no more. I be's free o' pain, an' guilt. Lissen ter Bonu, he kens ter help yer."

Balatz considered Scung's scar as he sank into a chair. "How long ago did you say?"

"Yesterday. Lookit me today."

"Can I get touched like that?" A spasm of pain crossed his face.

"No question about it. But you'll have to give up all you think you know and are," Bonu answered.

"Forget it then, ahhh!"

Bletza rose, intending to go to his aid, but a stern glance from Bonu stayed her.

"It's your choice, man. Logon won't be toyed with. Either you follow him or stay in your present condition till death takes you. Either way, I don't have time to trifle; I have to take up Jeda's trail before it gets cold."

The dagger in Bonu's jacket pressed uncomfortably against his ribcage for a moment.

Balatz considered, and as he did, his face softened and deep lines around his eyes and on his forehead revealed that his pain was lessened. "Would you guide me?"

"To Logon's Rock? Do you have any idea how far away that is? I can't possibly. I have to rescue Jeda and undo the damage you've done. Hod-ya is taking her for Scrarth and Avangar."

Bonu's sword dimmed slightly, and the lump in his inside jacket pocket pressed his ribs again.

"Please, I don't know the way. The journey is too dangerous for me, for us. I want us all to go. Pierce their hearts as well," he pointed at Bletza and Thorma.

"What!" Thorma jumped to her feet and backed away.

Bletza paled.

"Out of the question. I must get on with Jeda's rescue. What you ask would take a week or more. I don't have that kind of time."

"Excuse me, Bonu, but I doesn't understand summat."

"Well?" Bonu turned and snapped at his new comrade.

"It's not thet I disagrees wi' yer or anythin'. I jest cain't figure out why I met Logon as soon as yer sword pierced me heart, but these has gots ter travel ter Logon's Rock?"

"It's the way Logon does things. He knows each individual and requires them to come to him one way or another. He knew you'd serve him without making a long trek; others, like these, evidently need to firm up their commitment by persistently seeking an encounter with him."

"Cain't they git ter Logon's Rock alone?"

"Some do."

"I could lead 'em."

Bonu regarded Scung.

"Wait just a minute. Nobody asked me if I even want to go," challenged Thorma. "You promised you'd not pierce our hearts if we gave you the information you wanted. Hod-ya and seven dronnets, and Captain Mileer took Jeda, Spoena, and Artil to the old trail leading out of Ra-Amawl. If you hurry, you can catch them. The girls are blindfolded, bound, and so won't likely be able to travel fast. Now, keep your word and leave. We want no part of your Logon."

"And yer? Speaks she fer yer, too?" Scung asked Bletza. "Yer husband wants ter go ter Logon's Rock. Yer could come along."

"I was to Logon's Rock, once. But then I fell in love with and married Balatz. I swore an allegiance." Sobbing, she sat down. "I wish I'd never quit following Logon. Do you think he'll take me back? Won't you lead us to Logon?"

"I doesn't ken the way, ma'am, but since Bonu has gots ter pursue his mission, I reckons I be's the only one left whut kin take yers there."

Bonu slammed his fist on the table. "You can't take them, Scung. You know nothing of life in Logon yet. You don't know how to fight off tophets or cusps, or what to do for irk-bite. You don't even know the way."

"Yer be's right, Bonu, right as rain be's wet. I kens none o' thet. But somebody gots ter take 'em. Looks like thet somebody be's me."

Bonu angrily paced to the door. "Look, here's what we'll do. You wait here while Scung and I go after the girls. After we rescue them we'll come back to collect you. All of us then, all that want to, that is," he said noting Thorma's raised eyebrows, "will go to our brigade. Scung, you can stay there for training, and I'll lead an expedition to Logon's Rock."

"They be's seven dronnets wi' Hod-ya, Bonu. Not ter mention Captain Mileer. Yer really thinks the two o' usn's kin liberate Jeda from eight mighty warriors?"

"Your recruit is right, lieutenant," said Balatz. "What's to become of us if you don't return?" His color was slowly returning, and the profuse sweating had stopped; his breathing was easier, too. "Since choosing to go to Logon's Rock, I'm feeling much better. But if I don't go soon, I fear the pain will return."

"Then you'd better hope we return speedily. Ready Scung?"

Scung shrugged. "I s'pose so."

Bonu opened the door, looked back, and said, "I hope you understand. But I must do what I must do."

Balatz looked up from the table, making no comment.

Scung and Bonu exited.

"Do you know where this trail she spoke of might be?" asked Bonu, jogging alongside the footprints of five people and faint impressions of dronnets.

"I think it be's the trail we used wi' the patrol. Leastways it was a trail o' sorts, big enough fer a company ter travel. It lies west 'bout two hours march."

"Then we'll leave off following their tracks; take me straight to the trail. I'll follow. Hopefully, we'll come out on the trail somewhere ahead of them."

Scung's long legs churned unimpeded through small bushes and over logs which Bonu had trouble with. Nonetheless, Bonu did his best to keep pace. On through the dense undergrowth they pushed, alert for fresh sign of their quarry but finding nothing definitive.

Scung discovered obscure tracks here and there, but not being a tracker, wasn't sure if they were animal or human. Bonu, rushing to keep pace with Scung, didn't take time to discern the trail; their objective wasn't footprints, but the old road. At times the underbrush thinned and Bonu caught sight of the giant several paces ahead. At other times the undergrowth became so heavy that Bonu just blindly followed the crashing noise and broken branches left in Scung's wake. After an hour the pair slowed; they didn't want to accidentally overtake their quarry.

The topography of the land rose; Bonu tried recalling Captain Varter's map which showed a plateau rising gradually on one side while the three other approaches ended at sheer cliffs a hundred feet in height. They'd entered the thick of Ra-Amawl's jungle from the backside of the plateau. Bonu had never scouted here. This was wilderness of the wilderness, the untrammeled, unknown, secretive depths of Ra-Amawl.

They passed ancient trees with buttressed roots blocking their way, other trees were three, four, and even five feet thick, reaching so high that their topmost branches were obscured. Ferns, fungi, epiphytes, saprophytes, dangling vines, and multi-colored orchids littered the ground, branches hung down from overhead, making a virtual cavern of flora which they had to force their way through.

Bonu was driven to overtake Hod-ya's party before nightfall, for dronnets could travel in the dark, whereas Scung and Bonu would be forced to make camp, allowing even more precious distance between the parties.

Had they not been in such a rush, Bonu would like to have studied the abundant flora to see what was edible as well as check what manner of edible and predatory beasts inhabited these precincts. He also would have sketched a map in case the brigade ever needed to shelter or forage here, but such pursuits were for more leisurely times.

Bonu pushed through a dense thicket and stopped to get a fix on Scung's thrashing. Silence. He'd been out of contact with Scung for several minutes. Bonu stood still, turned his head this way and that but heard nothing. Bonu closed his eyes as he strained his ears, even holding his breath, but to no avail. Either Scung had come to a complete stop or more unlikely, had traveled beyond Bonu's hearing range.

Tossing caution to the breeze he called, "Scung. Scung?"

There was no reply. Which way to turn? He called louder, "Scung . . . "

Still no answer. He bulled his way through a thicket then pushed aside a fern that was tall as a man. It's stem suddenly gave way and he stumbled forward into a ten-foot, circular clearing.

Lying face down and unconscious on the edge of the clearing was Scung. Bonu whipped his sword out instantly as his eyes darted around the surrounding thicket for some deadfall. Nothing threatening appeared in the greenery, nevertheless he kept watch all around as he knelt to check on Scung.

He was rewarded by detecting a healthy throb from the Eroton's throat against his fingertips.

Bonu turned his companion over and spotted a knot on the back of Scung's head. "Well, that explains the sudden lack of noise."

"But it doesn't explain why you are here," came a voice.

Bonu stood up eyeing every break in the leaves, every branch, brush, fern or tree bole enclosing the clearing, his sword menacingly out before him. He turned round and round, waiting for the owner of the voice to reveal himself.

From behind came, "Ah, do you want to fight?"

Bonu spun around, slicing the air with his sword, challenging, "Show yourself and you'll find out."

"So many say that, so many," came the voice, again from behind.

Bonu whirled around to face nothing but shrubbery.

"Not there either?" teased the voice from behind yet again. "My, but your sword is pretty. What makes it glow?"

Something tapped the back of Bonu's head, unnerving the experienced warrior.

Bonu spun a complete circle with sword extended. Nothing was there. He reversed direction and spun three more revolutions the other way, then realized he'd get dizzy and lose his balance if he kept spinning. He slowed but kept swinging his sword about, trying to be unpredictable.

Scung groaned and rolled over. Bonu knelt to assist him. "Scung, are you—"

Bonu's head was knocked again, harder.

"Ow, now cut that out.' Bonu jumped up and snapped.

Scung groaned and sat up. "Ooooh! If'n yer wanted me ter wait, all yer had ter do was ask."

The mysterious assailant smacked the back of Bonu's head again in the same place; he could feel a lump rising.

"I said cut it out! If you want to fight, reveal yourself and fight man to man."

"I doesn't want ter fight yer, Bonu."

"Not you, Scung, but whoever struck us."

"It warn't yer?"

"It warn't yer?" mocked the voice, sounding alarmingly like Scung.

"Hey! Who said thet?" challenged Scung, rising to his feet, rubbing the back of his head.

"I did," replied the voice. "What are you going to do about it?"

Scung's sword swung about wildly as he furtively searched the clearing. "Whut goes on here, Bonu?"

"Stand back to back; it prefers attacking our blind side. I have no idea what it is, but it knocked you cold a few minutes before I found you."

"Be's it man or beastie?"

"I wish I knew. It speaks like a man, but the way it imitated you suggests it might be *kyllorn*."

"Oh, you join forces? You fear Voronon."

"Voronon? What are you, Voronon?"

"I stand in front of you, yet you cannot see me? How unskilled you are. Many fierce warriors enter my lair, many more than two, many more than four-fold two, at one time. None leave. Voronon prefers two-legged blood above four-legged. It's been long time since Voronon absorb humans."

"Well, come on and try." Bonu attempted to project more confidence than he felt. "Scung, let your sword, unsharp as it is, fight for you. Logon's light will defend you if you stay alert—"

A sudden rustling in the bushes drew both men's attention toward the disturbance. As soon as they looked to the side both were rapped resoundingly on the back of their heads.

Scung howled and staggered, nearly falling.

Dots of light flitted before Bonu's eyes, but he kept his footing.

"Seedling's play. Voronon thought you were fighters, worthy opponents. You are not much sport. Voronon enjoy playing with black lions more. They put up mighty struggle."

"Stand back to back again Scung, and this time, let's not get distracted if something shakes. Somehow it managed to shake branches over there and strike us from the opposite side."

"Right." The giant shook his head to clear his vision as he again stood back to back with Bonu.

"Ahh, you get smarter. Maybe you provide entertainment after all."

"Uh, Bonu?"

"What Scung?"

"Does yer think mebbe we ought ter jest leave this here clearing? It did say summat 'bout us bein' in its lair. Mebbe if'n we jest leave . . . "

The branches, vines and leaves all around the circular clearing bristled, compacting tightly together, becoming impenetrable. "Just you try escape; see what happens."

"It's bluffing, Scung. I think you're right."

Laughter surrounded them, light, almost musical, but definitely inhuman. "Yes, yes, you two brave men call Voronon's bluff. Try escape. This my lair, and you have come for dinner."

"Come my direction; my sword has more light. Whatever this Voronon is, he'll soon feel the bite of a Child of the Stars. Ready? One step at a time. Hold your sword upright from your waist and let it maneuver whichever way it tends. Logon's light on the tip will defend you."

"If'n yer says so, Bonu. But, lookit them leafs? They's formin' summat kinda wall."

"I noticed. I don't know what powers this Voronon has, but I know Logon's weapon will overcome whatever opposes us. Ready, your left foot, my right, and step. Good, now the other. Step. All right. Couple more paces and we'll—"

The bushes off Bonu's right shook violently.

"Don't look!" Bonu shouted. "It's a diversion." Bonu's peripheral vision detected a quick motion. He swiveled his head a fraction of an inch to see. Whatever had caused the commotion was gone.

Again, musical laughter filled the clearing.

"Go ahead and laugh, Voronon. We're wise to you."

"Yes, yes, you are so very wise, you two-leggers. When I devour you, wisdom will vanish from mankind."

"Ignore it, Scung. Ready, and step."

"Right."

"And step, good. One more step ought to bring us—hold up."

"Whussa matter?"

"I, I don't know. I've never seen the like."

The entire wall of greenery in front of Bonu had become like tightly entwined threads in a fabric even as he watched. In fact, all the branches, twigs, stems and leaves surrounding them did the same. What had been a thick but passable jungle, was now a sinister, impenetrable hedge. They were imprisoned. In addition, every tendril, twig, leaf, stem, and branch of the hedge seemed to reach out as if straining at the men.

"Go back, Scung. I want to think about this."

"Aw, two wisest humans afraid?"

"Whut yer thinkin', Bonu? I hain't never heered o' nothin' like this."

"Me either. I'm going to toll my sword and see if Logon will reveal a plan. Keep your eyes peeled."

"Right. Does yer want me ter toll, too?"

"No, one of us has to stay alert for that head-knocking thing. Besides, I have more experience at tolling and hearing the Advisor."

"Right, but, hurry, the wall be's closin' in."

Sure enough, inch by inch, the surrounding wall of tendrils, leaves, stems, twigs and branches was incrementally shrinking inward.

Bonu tolled his sword fervently, but to no effect. He looked up, anxiously gauging how much closer the wall had come, then energetically bent back to plying his toller again. He filed feverishly as he occasionally glanced up at the advancing, green menace. Still nothing. "Logon, where are you? Why have you abandoned us?" In frustration he lowered his toller and wiped beads of sweat off his forehead.

The interwoven wall of vegetation squeezed closer to the center of the clearing. "What? Wise humans not fight? Give up so easily? Come now, Voronon expect more from men with pretty swords."

There existed about three feet between the kingsmen and the encroaching wall. "Shall Voronon reveal what Voronon is? Yes, Voronon teach wise humans, make them wiser before they die."

The ground beneath their feet shifted and sank. A red and white gullet, like a cavernous maw, was revealed as the ground peeled away. Surrounding the opening and extending down into the mouth were thousands of prickly, glistening spines trembling as if in anticipation. Musical laughter filled the air again coming from the open maw at their feet as well as the encroaching wall of shrubbery.

"Come, dine with Voronon." The voice deepened; had it been louder, it could have been mistaken for thunder.

"Bonu, this all be's Voronon—the wall, the mouth gapin' at usn's, the clearin'—it all be's Voronon."

"What do you mean?"

"It be's a fiendish, man-eatin' plant whut kin talk."

Laughter filled the air. "Ah, big, stupid-looking man solve riddle. Voronon dissolve him last, preserve wisdom a little longer."

Bonu swung his sword at the tangled wall of vegetation. The glowing parts of his blade made a cut.

A shudder ran through the wall of greenery and a blast of air erupted from the yawning maw. The hedge halted and the spiny lips around the mouth quivered.

Bonu hacked again sending some branches, twigs and leaves to the floor of the clearing. It seemed for a moment as if the giant, man-eating plant was about to retreat.

"Scung, poke it with your sword."

Scung prodded his tip at the nearest branch. A deep slice appeared on the branch and a squeal erupted from the gaping mouth at their feet. Bonu hacked and hewed with both hands on his haft, sending plant fragments into the air and littering the floor.

Scung, emboldened by his first stab, jabbed again and again.

Sap ran from every branch he nicked. "Hey Bonu, this be's fun. Say, they be's a rune glowin' in the middle o' me sword."

Bonu was too occupied to pay much attention; he lifted his sword overhead and made for the yawning maw, intending to slice into it. His sword found its mark, but he discovered that the interior of the mouth wasn't as soft and yielding as it looked but rather, fibrous, and as such, resisted his blow. His sword only nicked a shallow slice; making matters worse, his hand was numbed from the force of his blow. Bonu pulled back.

Scung delightedly cut every branch and twig within reach, oblivious of Bonu.

Feeling returned and Bonu raised his sword again. "How'd you like that, Voronon? Ready for more?"

The mouth closed, returning to the deception of a mossy bed. The wall of vegetation retreated a couple of feet, leaving the kingsmen space to maneuver, but the density of the wall remained as thick as ever. Here and there pinkish sap dribbled down stems and dripped off leaves, creating puddles on the ground.

"So," resumed Voronon, sounding angrier, "humans show Voronon new weapons, cause Voronon small hurt. Entertaining, yes, but stinging. Voronon get angry. Voronon seldom angry, but anger useful, for Voronon no seedling, Voronon knows how to use anger."

The brush and vines receded another pace, almost returning to the clearing's original boundaries.

"How are you, Scung?"

"Fine, fine. But I be's doubtful this battle be's won yet."

"Won?" boomed the deep voice. "Voronon not eat you up at first bite, and you think you win? Voronon have many, many bites to take. Then see if battle won by wise humans."

Leaves rustled.

Both kingsmen lifted their swords in anticipation.

Instantly the hedge parted on all sides and branches thick as a man's wrist darted inward with lightning-quick speed, striking at them then retreating before they could retaliate. As soon as one set of attack-branches returned to position another set broke cover from another side, then darted back. This went on for several minutes.

Their swords met and scored several of the incoming branches, barely turning them in time. Bonu's sword, with its greater light hewed several inches off one branch and mangled many more. Scung's sword did little more than defend him from the onslaught. Whenever there was a pause both men's arms drooped from exhaustion.

Voronon seemed to grow weary as well; for several minutes there were no new attacks and the taunting voice was stilled.

As they took advantage of the breather Bonu noticed the glowing rune on Scung's sword. "How long has that been aglow?"

CHAPTER THIRTY-FIVE

"WELL . . ." Bonu waited for an answer.

"Eh? Oh, this?" Scung looked at the temporarily forgotten rune. "'Bout as long as we kenned this be's a man-eatin' plant. Why?"

"Quick, before Voronon resumes attacking, ply your toller by that rune and see what message Logon is giving us."

"I thot yer already done thet?"

"I did, but it seems Logon wants to reveal his plan to you."

"Wise humans ready for more? That was entertaining, but now Voronon tired of entertainment. Already cause much sap-shed. More than any lion. Voronon learn much from you. Tougher than Voronon thought. Taste all the more succulent when battle done. All this play makes Voronon hungry."

"Quickly Scung, he may be bluffing, or he may mean it."

The encircling hedge drew back as branches, now the size of a man's leg, were thrust through the openings. These limbs were fewer and moved slower, nevertheless, due to their greater mass they were more destructive and difficult to turn aside from their course. In addition to the deadly hazard coming through the hedge wall, the maw at their feet opened again and shot thorns up and outward at them. Most of these missed but a few struck outer garments. Bonu brushed one away with the heel of his hand and instantly felt a burning sensation.

Both kingsmen dodged the first volley of logs, but in deflecting the projectiles were caught off balance and leaning directly in the line of fire for the second barrage that wasted no time hurtling through the foliage.

Bonu noted when a large branch brushed Scung's chest, but he was unharmed.

He, however, was struck square on the shoulder, spun around and knocked face down and staring straight into Voronon's yawning maw.

"I gots ter get me toller out," said Scung as he fumbled beneath his leather breastplate and dodged another branch. "Got it."

Even lying face down Bonu saw the blinding flash of light erupting from Scung's sword.

Instantaneously every green leaf of the imprisoning wall was scorched to smoking ashes; smaller twigs shriveled, forcing the wall to unwind its tight weave. The hurtling logs ceased.

Scung yanked Bonu back from the pitfall by his collar, keeping him from sliding further into the maw just as Voronon's lips were about to engulf him.

"He's stopped again, perhaps to assess our strategy, or perhaps his own injuries." Bonu sat gasping for breath. "He'll resume his attack any moment maybe by hurling hundreds of poison darts or distracting us some other way while his roots entwine our feet and drag us . . . down there."

~

Only then did Scung notice that the wall was no longer densely packed, and he could see through to the forest beyond. A tall man in a gray, hooded cloak beckoned. Without a moment's hesitation Scung broke through the smoldering wall dragging Bonu by the collar.

"Ow, Scung, enough already!"

"Sorry, Bonu, I jest wants ter git yer away from thet nasty beastie."

"Actually Scung, it's not a beast, but conscious vegetation," said the stranger.

Scung released Bonu as he arrived beside the man. "Does I ken yer?"

Bonu rubbed the back of his neck. "Look at your sword, Scung. That ought to tell you something."

Both kingsman swords were completely alight with brightly glowing runes, even where they'd not been tolled.

Scung looked up at the stranger and gasped. "Logon?"

Bonu smiled and struggled to his feet. "Yes, Logon. Welcome, m'leige."

Logon threw back his cowl and cast only a somber glance at Bonu, then turned to Scung with a beaming smile. "Well done, recruit. Again, your consistent faithfulness has rescued your fellow soldier. Keep on in this way and you'll rescue many to my ways." At that Logon started to fade.

Bonu's mouth fell open and he blinked rapidly as if expecting a word from his beloved ruler. "Logon, wait."

Logon's visage returned, his face somber.

"Don't you have any word for me? Why did you not answer when I called?"

Logon started to fade again.

"Logon, wait, I, what's the matter? Have I offended in some way?"

Logon, still partially visible, said, "Search your heart for that answer, lieutenant." His gaze was heartbreaking, not judgmental.

"I, I don't know what to say. I was going to study it, expose its errors."

"Your heart lusted for its glitter, though you know it displeases me."

"Whut be's goin' on here, Bonu?"

"Show him, Bonu. He's proven true. Let him learn from your error."

Bonu lowered his eyes as his hand crept into his tunic.

Scung saw the dagger he'd rejected. "Thet be's a source o' offense ter yer? Then I be's in deeper need o' forgiveness, fer I carried it fer years, master."

"Not so, Scung. The minute you knew what I wanted, you forsook it. Whereas Bonu, knowing it to be false, allowed it to entice him by its sparkle, to his detriment. And make no mistake, if you hadn't been there, Bonu would have died in Voronon's maw."

"But he called ter yer, filin' away on his sword like he were gonna wear it through?"

"Sit down, Scung, Bonu." Logon's full form materialized again sitting cross-legged on the ground. "From the moment you picked up that abomination, Bonu, did you not feel a lack of the Advisor's joy and guidance?"

Bonu hung his head.

"Learn, Scung. Bonu deliberately ignored the Advisor, thinking it a small thing. When the Advisor is joyful and freely speaks to you of me, all is well. When he's silent, search your heart; he'll show you your offense as soon as you seek. Bonu knew that I was offended, but kept the defiling thing anyway, so the Advisor's voice became silent, his joy turned to grief. Did you not see Bonu's personality change?"

"I seen him lose his temper, back at the cabin."

"You also saw but didn't recognize the subtle effects of being out of my will, out of contact with me."

"Logon, I—" Bonu lifted his head.

"Bonu, you were distressed by your affection for Jeda, but only became deceived when you chose the banned object. When you ignored the Advisor's warning you purposely stopped your ears to the Advisor.

Bereft of my guidance through him, you made decisions on your own. As you see, those decisions would have proven disastrous. Know this, I allow the consequences of wrong choices—even consequences of the severest outcome.

"Even now, Bonu, the struggle within you is great. And you wonder that I have no commendation for you? As long as you hold any thing above my presence, how can I bless you?"

"M'lord." Tears dropped one after another to the ground. "I did make a mess of things, didn't I?" He couldn't meet Logon's eyes. "I'll throw it away. I'll rid myself of it." He raised his arm to hurl the bejeweled dagger deep into the undergrowth.

"Not there, but over there," Logon instructed, pointing at Voronon. "Throw it in there, where you'll never be tempted to seek it again. Throw it into that devouring maw that almost became your grave."

"There?" Bonu asked. "Are you sure just throwing it into the jungle wouldn't suffice. After all, I'd never be able to find it again in all this—"

Logon started to fade.

"Bonu, whut ails yer man? Do whut he says!"

Bonu slowly rose to his knees and flung the dagger where the ravenous maw waited its next victim. The tendrils and vines not burnt greedily seized the object hurtling into the small clearing.

Logon's manifestation was again full, seated in front of them as before. "Now the mending can come. You've exercised your will to rule your emotions in obedience to me."

"Yeah, Bonu. I mean, how could yer, arter all, right, Logon?"

"It's not for you to criticize, Scung. You've done well; be thankful the Advisor protected you. But don't judge Bonu. He's come through tests you haven't felt the weight of yet. I made sure you were along, so he'd survive.

Don't think you're special because I used your obedience to rebuke another. Don't despise Bonu. He's still a lieutenant, again in good standing."

"Logon," Bonu touched the hem of Logon's cloak, "forgive me. I desired the beauty of that thing and didn't care that I offended you. Thank you for your mercy, for confronting me, and for forgiving me."

Logon smiled. "I forgive. Now, return to Balatz and Bletza."

"But, but what about Jeda?"

"From the moment you took up that dagger you made bad decisions that only served yourself. Now, return to the duty I placed before you. You thought your decisions were wise but think back."

"I doesn't mean this personal, Bonu," said Scung.

"Go ahead, Scung," Logon encouraged.

"Yer took credit fer the fall o' the dread, as if'n yer done it all by yerself."

"What?" Bonu exclaimed.

"Listen to your brother," said Logon.

Scung watched as Bonu studied the ground at his feet, then slowly raised his eyes to Logon's.

"I see, m'lord." Bonu then turned and nodded at Scung.

"Logon, yer called me Bonu's brother. Is he the brother yer tole me 'bout when I was on yer rock?"

Logon's eyes sparkled. "You'll understand, in time."

~

Bonu pounded his knees with his fists. "Oh, Logon, I've been so blind, so arrogant! How could I fall into that trap after your great victory?"

"Indeed, Bonu. As you proceeded, your decisions became more self-centered. I led you to a freshly pierced heart, one that's been led astray, to try to help him. But you only considered rescuing Jeda."

"But she's in great danger!"

"Think Bonu; is it for her sake or your own that you follow this course of action? Is Jeda not in my keeping? You've neglected ones that are hurting in order to follow your own desires. Had I not allowed Voronon to intercept you, you'd have led this brave recruit to certain death, not to mention your own. I didn't commission that action, so I wouldn't support it. You were on your own, your mission would have failed."

"All that came out of one little act of disobedience?" Bonu asked.

"All that. A small seed grows into a plant with many seeds."

"I gonna be keerful whut kinda knives I picks up."

Scung's attempt at levity brought the slightest of smiles to Logon's lips. "Rather, guard your heart by dwelling in the joy of the Advisor. When the joy stops, investigate why and immediately make amends. And Scung, don't make light of serious lessons."

Scung's cheeks tinged red.

"Bonu, you know your duty. What I'm about to show you is for your comfort. You're to go back to the cabin and do as much as you can for Balatz and Bletza. You're to do nothing concerning what I'm about to show you until you've helped Bletza and Balatz as much as they'll allow, understand?"

"Yes Logon, but—"

Logon touched his finger to Bonu's lips, then rose to his feet, beckoning Scung and Bonu to follow. They followed Logon to a hedge. With his hand he drew back a veil of leaves and vines. They were on an embankment overlooking a woodland trail.

Some two hundred paces away a small campfire burned, surrounded by nine, black-clad figures, three dun-colored figures reclined nearby on a hillock. A tall black-draped figure carrying a dish went to the three reclining ones. That tall person knelt and spoon-fed the three one at a time.

Bonu's heart thumped. From the way the captive tossed her head he knew it was Jeda.

Logon lowered the curtain of vegetation cutting off their glimpse of Hod-ya's makeshift camp. "She's in my keeping, as are Spoena and Artil. They'll serve me as I've decided is best for them. You're to do likewise, even to yielding up certain rights that others take for granted. That's Jeda's heart, Bonu, to serve me no matter the personal cost. Is it yours also?"

Bonu and Scung were suddenly alone facing each other. Bonu reached up to peer through the curtain of greenery again but Scung's brawny hand gripped his wrist, staying him. "Bad idee, Bonu."

"Yes, of course, you're right Scung. Thank you. Anytime you feel I'm out of Logon's will, feel free to challenge me."

"Does yer think we oughtta try ter find our way back ter the cabin or make camp here? It be's gettin' darker. I sure doesn't want ter stumble inter no more plants the likes o' Voronon."

"We ought to leave while we still have some natural light to travel by. It's too difficult for me to remain this close to them all night."

Scung nodded as he checked his gear.

Bonu, reminded by Scung's example, re-examined his own gear. Most everything was in order; their food supplies were low, but they had enough water for overnight if they rationed carefully.

Bonu stood. "Ready?"

Scung slung his pack over his shoulder. "Ready."

"You want to lead?"

"Nhuh-uh! Remember where usn's ended up the last time I took the lead?"

Bonu smiled. "I think you learned your lesson."

"Lesson? They be's a lesson?" the Eroton grinned, his teeth shining in the darkening night.

Bonu felt joy from the Advisor as he again sensed inner guidance. "Yes, Scung, there was a message in what happened for you, too."

"Whut?" The Eroton looked skeptical. "Arter all, yer hain't 'xactly been over-useful as a guide."

"I know, and you're right. I was so caught up in my own desires that I neglected you. I ask your forgiveness. I know it's harder for you to trust me now, but you must. I'm in good standing again with Logon, and all he's taught me hasn't been wasted. When one disobeys Logon, he doesn't have to relearn old lessons over again."

"So, whut be's my lesson?"

"Do you remember that rune on your sword, the one that burst forth with light and scorched Voronon?"

"Remember it? How could I fergit?"

"What did it say?"

"Say? I doesn't remember it sayin' ought, jest that it got usn's outta a tight spot when the light burst forth."

"Well, you should always remember the runes Logon uses to help you, even after the danger is past. Learning the rune lesson can help you avoid similar problems, or at least give you knowledge of what to do if you encounter the same or a similar problem. Look, it still glows. Let's take a moment to consider the message."

"Does yer think we gots time?"

"We don't have time not to examine it."

Scung shrugged and promptly sat, extracting his toller. "Awright, let's git started."

Bonu squatted beside him. "This won't take long. It's an important, but uncomplicated rune."

Scung glanced at Bonu, then at his sword's glowing rune and pressed the file to the blade. The light intensified, but without searing heat. The surrounding foliage lit up creating a cheery atmosphere. "Words be's comin' ter mind."

"Say them aloud."

Scung self-consciously recited:

> *"Shun the wide, clear, and easy trail,*
> *'Midst peril, heartache, war and strife,*
> *For Logon gives a harder road, a deeper, higher gain.*
>
> *Stray-ers from the light know not until they fail,*
> *Seeking the quiet, carefree, happy life,*
> *Leads to the realm of those slain.*
>
> *Seek the dense, the fiercest fight, the upward-spiraled grail,*
> *Tho on the meanest path, problems arise rife,*
> *Deliverance is revealed through trust in Logon's reign."*

"Do you understand?"

Scung sighed, "I kens."

"Good, then let's be on our way. We can maybe travel another mile or two before we stop."

Scung was again on his feet, toller tucked away but sword held out ready for action. "Jest stay away from them clearin's."

Bonu laughed. "Yes, I'll keep away from them."

The two friends pushed through the surrounding fronds, hacking vines and small branches, forcing their way through clumps of vegetation, chopping greenery when necessary. As the last hint of daylight dimmed, the gleam from Bonu's sword provided enough illumination without revealing their presence through the jungle's density.

"Bonu," whispered Scung during a brief break. "Does yer think usn's could settle fer the night yet?"

"Yeah, I think it's time. Are you still thinking about the rune?"

"Uh-huh."

"Good. By the way, I don't believe I thanked you for dragging me out of Voronon's lair."

"Tain't necessary. Besides, whut would I a done out here on me own?"

"Scung, you only saved me for selfish reasons?" Bonu teased.

"Aw, cut it out, Bonu. Yer kens I only wanted ter protect yer. Yer be's me only friend. I hain't never had no friend 'cept me brother. Not even when I got surrounded by other soldiers cheerin' me on. I were their champion, but they used me fer their sport an' gamblin'. None o' 'em ever keered much 'bout me. So, I growed bitter, an' more savage, an' kept ter meself, mostly."

"When we get back to brigade, you'll have so many friends you won't know what to do."

"I hopes so."

"Well, as to the matter at hand, does this place suit to spend the night?"

"Good as any, I s'poses. There be's some large leaves we kin pull off'n thet there plant fer beddin'."

"I hate to leave any sign of our passing, but I guess the trail behind is rather obvious anyway, eh?"

Scung merely grunted, engrossed in harvesting leaves for bedding. Soon he had a massive armful and distributed them into two piles. "How far does yer think we be's from the cabin?"

"Hard to say." Bonu stretched out on a pile of leaves. "It seems like we're cutting an entirely new trail. I haven't seen any trace of our trail entering in. I can only hope we're headed the right direction."

"It feels awright, an' I gots a pretty good nose fer direction. Anyways, I was 'bout ter ask if'n I kin take the first watch."

"Sounds good to me. Voronon wore me out, and then hacking our way here I feel plumb tuckered. I don't really think we need a watch but wake me when you want to sleep." Bonu covered his sword and rolled onto his side. Within seconds he breathed deeply.

~

Scung took out his toller and softly filed by the glowing point, adding another small section of blue as thoughts of Logon flooded his mind. Drowsiness settled over him, his eyelids drooped . . . he caught himself and roused up to look around and listen and smell.

The forest all around was silent. Not that there weren't dangerous creatures on the prowl, for predators must have scented human blood in their vicinity, but Scung fancied he saw columns of twinkling lights surrounding them and had a peaceful, easy feeling that no threat would come near.

EPILOGUE

BONU AND SCUNG, LOVINGLY CHASTENED by their lord, gave up seeking their own paths, trusting their Prince to know best and lead them. Jeda, Spoena, and Artil also, were in their master's good keeping, though all outward evidences belied the confidence they felt in their hearts. They would all be tested to the limits of their ability in days ahead in loyalty to Logon, each other and to the benighted residents of the Carnalian Empire.

Lurcan, upon learning of Psa's demise, grew fearful that his reign of havoc in the world of men was coming to an end. With that fear came a fierce rage; he was intent upon wreaking as much destruction upon humanity as possible. Lurcan stepped up his campaign to remove Ecclessites from within the borders of his domain as well as increase the assault on the King's Gate Fortress and Logon's Bridge, planning to forever destroy the way into Ecclessa, thus stopping the flow of deserters from his authority.

Logon sent messengers throughout his brigades, both in Ecclessa as well as the empire, warning that the Tremendum—the most colossal of events that would herald the removal of all evil things—was nigh. Sadly, many of his brigades had been infiltrated by cusps and other Lurcanish *kyllorn* that the message had little effect to some. But those with ears keen to hear the Advisor confirmed Logon's message and guided faithful warriors to prepare for the greatest conflict Carnalia had ever known.

Jeda was led step by step closer to Pitland to take part in the savage Scrarth and Avangar contest. Little did Hod-ya realize that by taking Jeda into Pitland she was turning the key that would unlock the empire's destruction.

THE END

THE *SAGA OF THE SINGING SWORD BRIGADE* SERIES:

Book One: Inception of a Brigade

Book Two: Into the Gloom

AND COMING SOON:

Book Three: The Trumpets of Doom

Book Four: The Siege of Logon's Bridge

Book Five: Turit's Rise

Book Six: Tremendum

For more information about
J.M. MacLeod
&
Into the Gloom
please visit:

www.facebook.com/john.macleod.188
Lordswordwords.blogspot.com

For more information about
AMBASSADOR INTERNATIONAL
please visit:

www.ambassador-international.com
@AmbassadorIntl
www.facebook.com/AmbassadorIntl

*If you enjoyed this book, please consider leaving us a review on
Amazon, Goodreads, or our website.*